Mike Hodges was born in Bristol, UK. As a television producer in the 1960s, he was invited to join the investigative programme *World in Action*. This took him to the US, covering the 1964 presidential election, and that same year to the war in Vietnam. He produced and sometimes directed the arts programmes *Tempo* and *New Tempo*. He is perhaps best known for his work in cinema and television, including: *Get Carter, Suspect, Rumour, The Manipulators, Pulp, The Terminal Man, Flash Gordon, A Prayer for the Dying, Morons from Outer Space, Florida Straits, Black Rainbow, Croupier* and *I'll Sleep When I'm Dead*.

Unbound
6th Floor Mutual House, 70 Conduit Street, London W1S 2GF
www.unbound.com

Text design by PDQ

A CIP record for this book is available from the British Library

ISBN 978-1-78352-656-7 (trade hbk)
ISBN 978-1-78352-658-1 (ebook)
ISBN 978-1-78352-657-4 (limited edition)

Printed in Great Britain by CPI Group (UK)

MIKE HODGES

BAIT, GRIST & SECURITY

Unbound

**WITH SPECIAL THANKS TO
CLIVE OWEN FOR HIS SUPPORT
OF THIS BOOK**

**FOR
ALL
THOSE
OUT OF STEP**

If the young dace be bait for the old pike,
I see no reason, in the Law of Nature,
but I may snap at him.

Falstaff, *Henry the Fourth, Part II*

ONE

Summer is hell here.

Winter is the only time to be in this place.

On a wet night preferably.

Like tonight.

The dark sea, flattened by rain, laps against the long curving beach. White-painted iron railings and ill-lit weather shelters recede into the mist. An amusement arcade, boarded up, sits like a blind man watching nothing. The Grand Atlantic Hotel, a vast, corroding edifice, looms over the deserted esplanade. A torn canvas banner flaps over its darkened entrance, announcing the presence of the Brotherhood of Magicians Conference. Bedroom windows stacked up to the murky sky are black patches. The magicians are long in bed.

They'll need steady hands in the morning.

The clock tower strikes on the hour.

Twice.

An approaching motorbike cuts through the sound of rainwater smacking the tarmac. The red Yamaha rounds a corner slowly, ominously, powerful as a shark. A metallic titanium flip-front helmet glints under the street lamps. Moulded gloves with visor wipes, grinder boots, cowhide jeans and a leather jacket embossed with a bloody knife embedded in the rider's back. The rider steers his machine along the esplanade before circling a traffic island housing the public urinals, all the while scanning the empty street.

A municipal shelter with a noticeboard advertising local events for wet winter nights stands beside the amusement arcade. It's here the bike comes to rest. The rider leaves the engine running as he nervously pulls posters from a saddlebag.

He works fast, skilfully.

Soon the forthcoming amateur operatic production of *Annie Get Your Gun* is no longer forthcoming. But 'The Personal Improvement Institute: A Course in Leadership Dynamics' is. The etched face of a wild-eyed mountaineer intending to give a slide lecture the very next evening is replaced by the well-fed features of Dr Hermann P. Temple, who will show you the QUICK way to the TOP! during his impending weekend course on SUCCESS-POWER GETTING!

A similar fate is accorded 'Pinkie and Barrie, the Comedy Duo'; 'Diana Barnham playing Bach on the Clavichord'; and the providers of 'Merrie England Banquets. Book now to avoid disappointment.' All disappear within seconds to be replaced by five identical images of Dr Temple. A quintet of pointing forefingers, quiffs and eyes that would make a cobra back off.

*

A solitary light snaps on.

It's on the third floor of an office block five minutes from the esplanade. The bare bulb backlights the gold lettering on the window: 'Mark Miles Intercontinental'. Below that: 'Creative Publicity and Personal Management'. On the bottom line: 'MAKE your MARK with MILES. He's WAY ahead.'

The block housing Mark Miles' office is just that: a block. It has all the charm of a coal bunker. Built in the sixties, it's an early example of how easily even smart people can be conned. Concrete is beautiful. Or so the architects decreed at the time.

Providence House, for that's the block's portentous name, takes on a gloomy appearance in the torrential rain. Mark Miles appears at the window, taking off his helmet, while simultaneously dropping the slatted blind. One side falls faster than the other, which doesn't happen in movies, but almost always does in real life. Cursing, he tries to level it off, one-handed. Instead it becomes uncoupled and collapses on top of

6

him. Mark Miles and his blind have one quality in common. Both spend their lives dangling.

Mark is sick of being a small fish in a small pond. His only remaining heroes are the sharks in the local aquarium. These massive glistening predators eye the awed visitors on the other side of the glass with contempt as they sweep majestically past in their eternal search for a way out. Like them, Mark wants to command respect. To this end, his pinball mind has been hyperactive since being approached by Dr Temple's people to promote his weekend course. Leadership dynamics might just be the metamorphosis needed to take him to the top.

And quickly.

He switches on a battered desk lamp, puts it on the floor and kills the overhead. Mark has to be careful. The landlord suspects that, contrary to the terms of his lease, the office also doubles as his living quarters.

The landlord is right.

That's why the chipped commode with 'Hospital Property' boldly stencilled on its lid, and smuggled in under cover of darkness from his late grandma's council flat, is disguised with a potted palm. He lifts the palm and urinates into the china basin.

Slopping out has always been a complicated ritual. When he first moved into the building, the landlord – Fred Snipe, thin as a drainpipe – was wont to ambush him on his early-morning run along the corridor to the communal lavatory. After several narrow escapes, Mark devised a strategy whereby he transferred the contents of the commode into a plastic first-aid box before embarking upon this essential mission.

Now, on their occasional encounters, Snipe's nose twitches like a gerbil's at the odour. His mouth opens but words refuse to emerge. He just can't bring himself to ask what the container contains. Mark relishes these precious moments, smiling and patting the Red Cross on the box. 'Preparation H, Fred. Works wonders.' He sometimes varies the exchange: 'Glycerine suppositories, Fred. Never fails to get you moving.' Or, if he wants to make the landlord really blush, he adds, 'Clinically proven to be effective against irritation and itching piles.'

These words always play on Snipe's retreating figure.

Mark now eases out a crumpled futon and sleeping bag from under the defeated sofa, carefully avoiding any tangling with its bare springs. Rolling back and forth on the floor, he sheds his clothes and slips into the kapok envelope.

Light out.

*

In the street below Mark's office, a black umbrella is opened from the shelter of a shop door. A man, short and paunchy, steps out, his suet-pudding face glistening in the rain. His name is William Snazell and he's a private detective, a gumshoe. Dressed in a faded raincoat and shapeless trilby, he takes a final look at the darkened window before crossing the road. His shiny rubber galoshes shuffle through the sheet of rainwater.

TWO

Early that same night, the last train had arrived on time. At exactly 21.36. The two carriages, all that remained of the express from London, are shunted backwards to the deserted platform.

Ayling-on-Sea is at the end of the line.

Water gushes through a hole in the station roof. A solitary passenger alights, slamming the door shut. He notes the rain splattering the platform, puts down his tattered suitcase, and slips a finger into the galosh that's become dislodged. Opening a black umbrella, he proceeds to the unmanned ticket barrier.

Outside, a sign indicates a vacant taxi rank. The passenger moves to the courtesy phone housed under a plastic hood and picks up the receiver.

The line is dead.

Cussing, he starts his walk into town.

*

The Journey's End boarding house is at the unfashionable end of the esplanade. A 'Vacancies' placard dangles seductively between the frilly curtains of the front room. The passenger lowers his umbrella to study a scrap of paper before pressing the bell. The red and yellow sunrise pattern of the glass front door is abruptly illuminated as a figure comes to open it.

The passenger steps back to fully appreciate the woman standing before him. 'Mrs Westby?'

'Mr Snazell?

'That's me.'

'En suite for one night?'

'Correct,' he looks her over. Enough curves to drive a man crazy.

'Although the view's so good I may stay longer.'

Snazell eases himself past Mrs Westby's buffer breasts into the small hallway, his eyes fixed on her white silk blouse and the black ruched brassiere peeping out from behind a wayward button. Lewdness is an essential ingredient in Sandra Westby's life. She enjoys being an object of male desire. Her glistening blood-red lips shape themselves around each word before finally setting it free.

'You're my only guest tonight.'

'One-on-one. Great.'

'Choose a room between 1 and 15.'

'69.'

'Don't be saucy now. I'll put you in 13.'

'13 – that's my lucky number.'

'I'll put you in 7 then.'

She plucks a key off a board behind the small counter and starts up the stairs. Snazell follows, his attention alternating between her arse rotating inside a tight silk skirt and the immaculately straight seams of her black stockings. Reaching the second landing, she opens Room 7 and switches on the light. Snazell steps inside the small room. He immediately pumps the mattress, appreciatively.

'Very nice. Nice and hard. The way I like it.' He sits on it and bounces a couple of times. 'Bet this bed could tell a few stories.'

'Only cries and groans,' replies Mrs Westby.

'Of eternal love?'

'I wouldn't go that far, Mr Snazell.'

'Hanky-panky?'

'That's more like it.'

She sighs as she shuts the door then opens it again.

'The bar will be open for aperitifs in half an hour.'

Left alone Snazell snaps open his suitcase. Lifting out several pairs of thermal underwear and woollen pyjamas, he reveals the tools of his trade: binoculars, bugging equipment, and a Smith & Wesson .32 automatic with silencer.

THREE

Morning.

Grey sky indivisible from grey sea.

A deep swell drives long rollers gently across the bay.

On the horizon a tramp steamer rises out of a trough. The SS *Promised Land*, close to the end of her seagoing life, is a significant rust colour, bow to stern. From the esplanade onlookers can just make out a group of people huddled on the steamer's deck, at the base of a diagonal loading jib.

A small aircraft towing a sky banner suddenly appears.

It's a speck at the far end of the beach. The speck, along with the noise of its single engine, grows steadily larger and louder as it flies along the skyline, eventually passing low over the tramp steamer. Only then can the town's residents read its message: *Mark Miles Presents Reg Turpin, the New Houdini.*

Reg Turpin's voice drifts across the water from the boat.

'A bit tighter, Bela.'

The metallic clank of chain links being manoeuvred is followed by a painful yelp. 'That's my penis, not a fucking salami, you dumb wop.'

The chain, already wrapped like a boa constrictor around Turpin's torso, is being delicately adjusted between his legs by Bela Lugosi, his swarthy assistant. When his hands reach behind to take up the slack, Reg feigns being goosed, pursing his lips and fluttering his eyelids.

'Whoops! That's enough of that, sailor!'

It's all part of the act.

Reg keeps promising his assistant to leave it out, but he never does. There's a lot of coarse laughter. Lugosi blushes and seethes. His eyes blaze, his mouth and nostrils steam in the cold air. His machismo is like a fighting bull brought to its knees. Mark, quick to register Lugosi's fury, chips in, 'This is just a dry run, guys. OK? Give the media a taste of what's to come.'

Wearing a New York Yankee baseball cap, and clutching a wad of publicity handouts, Mark faces a pack of media hacks. The sea's swell is beginning to tell and most of them look distinctly green. Bile, normally reserved for their tabloid copy, is taking on a physical manifestation as it moves ever closer to their epiglottis. One hack with an especially bilious face volunteers a question.

'It says in the handout you're intending to take the act to America?'

'Correct, sir. New York Harbor. Frisco's Golden Gate. Miami…'

Turpin interrupts, his voice billowing in the wind, 'America! God's own country. Land of the Free.'

The irony of a proclamation vainly echoing the likes of Abraham Lincoln and Thomas Paine, but coming from someone encased in chains, is not lost on the smirking hacks. A large wave passes underneath and Reg lurches awkwardly, arms pinned to his sides, helpless as a baby. Lugosi, still hopping mad, steadies him and takes obvious pleasure in snapping shut a large padlock, locking the chain into place. Some would say that Bela has just executed a neat encapsulation of the human condition more vividly than many a philosopher.

Jack Dickenson, a seasoned tabloid reporter now freelance, tops up his plastic cup with more sweet wine. 'America? That'll cost a pretty packet.' He pulls his camel-hair coat closer, addresses his pencil to a dog-eared horserace programme, and impales Mark with ice-cold eyes. 'So who's financing all this?'

'Reg is! Not only is his life on the line, but his life's savings as well. Our American agent is even now negotiating the television and film rights. Not since Harry Houdini has any escapologist attempted such a feat. And Harry didn't even have the advantages of modern technology to heighten audience participation.' He takes from his pocket a small case, which he opens to reveal a minute clip-on microphone. 'With this little beauty we'll be able to hear exactly what's happening to Reg inside the trunk.'

He hands it to Lugosi.

'This'll provide cutting-edge coverage. State-of-the-art reality reporting.'

Lugosi finds a place between the circles of chain and pins the microphone to Turpin's tracksuit.

'What made you take up escapology, Mr Turpin?'

The question comes from Ralph Wilder, an aged lush desperately clinging to his job as a local stringer.

'Got sick of being a nobody, sir. Just another face in the crowd.'

Mark is like an echo.

'Just another face in the crowd? Did you ever hear such modesty? Sick of being a nobody? Not after today, Reg, baby. Let's have it, Bela, the final impediment for Reg to extricate himself from. The hood!'

Lugosi holds up a hessian bag, showing both sides to the hacks. On one side there's the Stars and Stripes stencilled in colour, on the other is the Union Jack.

'This hood,' intones Mark, 'is symbolic of that special relationship existing between our two great nations. Thank you, Bela.'

Mark applauds Bela but nobody joins in.

So he presses on, 'Let's now wind the clock back to when Reg was, indeed, just a face in the crowd. A nobody. To when Reg was a steward in the merchant navy. Twenty years serving the rich and famous on luxury liners. Twenty years on the high seas. Only signed off when he ran out of available flesh to tattoo.'

Nobody laughs.

Reg quickly picks up the theme.

'Dead-end job. No prospects. Escape seemed impossible until...'

He doesn't get to finish. Lugosi chooses to emphasise this low point in Reg's life by pulling the hood over his head. He grins vindictively as he secures it with a rope around the escapologist's neck.

Mark spiels on, 'As we wait for Mr Turpin to enter his metal prison, let me tell you about another of my distinguished clients: Dr Hermann P. Temple.'

He moves among the hacks dispensing flyers.

'Dr Temple will be here next week, residing at the Grand Atlantic Hotel, holding one of his famous courses in Leadership Dynamics.'

He reaches Dickenson, pencil still poised for a quote. 'Are you American?'

'No sir.'

'So what's with the accent?'

'What accent?'

Mark is genuinely puzzled.

He'd adopted his mid-Atlantic accent when he was a kid.

It came with American movies and American gum.

And stuck.

He turns away but Dickenson pulls him back. 'Ever been to the States?'

'Not had that pleasure, sir.'

Mark is grateful when Ralph Wilder, studying the flyer, interrupts with a question. 'Wasn't there an attempted exposé of this Dr Temple?'

'Where did you hear that, sir?'

'Two reporters infiltrated his course in London. That's what I heard. Temple's people got wind of them and the story was spiked.'

Mark rudely interrupts.

'Sorry, buddy, but you're on the wrong course. This is Dr Temple's first trip to the UK.'

He moves quickly away as the metal trunk is shut and locked. Sunlight plays on the letters *RT* stencilled in gold on the lid like royal insignia. Two seamen attach the trunk to a cable hanging from the jib.

The wretched Wilder, still desperate for a story, catches up with Mark. 'Didn't Houdini meet his end doing the same stunt in New York Harbor?'

'Nope.'

'I thought he did.'

'Facts don't seem to be your strong point. He died from peritonitis.'

The ship's winch moans as it takes the strain. Under stress the cable tightens and turns. A photographer, catnapping until this moment, suddenly becomes active, jumping, running, clicking.

Mark unties a microphone from the ship's rail and tests it. 'One… two… three. Can you hear me, Reg?'

'Like you were here beside me, Mark.'

Reg's voice is relayed over the ship's tannoy.

Mark turns to the hacks.

'Any further questions, gentlemen?'

Dickenson leans close to the mike, letting his question slip in smoothly like mercury. 'How about some famous last words for my readers, Reg?'

'Beware the computer, sir. The computer has more tentacles than an octopus. Once in its grip the victim is unable to act without it.' As the trunk lurches over the water, swinging about wildly, strands of rusted cable begin to twist and snap, unnoticed by the crew, while the sounds of Reg's titanic struggle compliment his octopod imagery. Grunts, groans, curses spill out of the tannoy until the escapologist finally raises his voice to ride the sound of his efforts. 'The computer turns its victim inside out, sir, exposing its soul for all to see. A sight to shock even the whore of Babylon.'

Mark tries to look happy. Not for the time does he marvel at Reg's apocalyptic rhetoric. The fire-snorting dragons and diabolical serpents tattooed across his entire torso seem to possess him. Reg is on a roll.

'Better I sink to the ocean's seabed, sir, than sink into the bottomless black hole of the computer.'

As if on cue, in a cloud of rust, the last strand of the cable snaps.

For a split second the trunk, silhouetted against the horizon, seems to defy gravity before plunging towards the ocean, hitting it with a mighty splash. The hacks rush to the ship's rail as Turpin calls pathetically over the tannoy, 'What the hell was that?'

'Holy shit,' moans Mark.

The trunk settles momentarily on the surface.

Then the ocean opens up, swallows the unexpected visitor, and closes again. Huge bubbles belch from the deep, seeming to transport Turpin's panicky voice to the surface.

'Careful boys! You're going too fast for me.'

'Get out, Reg. Get out,' screams Mark.

Reg screams back, 'Jesus! What's that gurgling sound.'

Turpin's pleas, growing fainter and fainter, and more and more distorted, start to sound like a wind-up gramophone winding down.

'Whasssss gooooing onnnnn?' screams Reg.

'Get the fuck out, you prick!' screams Mark.

'Pwwwiiiccck? Noooobeehoddy cawwws mhheee a pwwwwickkkk.'

Prick? Nobody calls me a prick! These were to be the last words of Reg Turpin. The hacks scribble them down with new-found professional zeal. It has to be admitted that other unfathomable, but definitely angry, noises did emerge from the deep. Although nobody could decipher them, it was generally agreed they concerned the retribution Reg intended to exact on Mark when he returned to the surface. Two seamen throw a red buoy overboard to identify the spot where the trunk was last seen.

Mark looks helplessly at the approaching rollers as they swell up like a huge sea serpent, and somehow finds it in himself to talk positive.

'Reg can escape in two minutes flat.'

Dickenson can't resist a quip. 'Come in Reg, your time is up.'

Nobody laughs.

In a futile attempt at intimacy with his client, Mark moves away from the group, whispering into the microphone, 'Reg? Reg, I'm sorry.' The hacks close around him, listening to his whimpers. 'Please forgive me. I really didn't mean it, Reg. Let me make it quite clear: you are *not* a prick. Reg? Reg, for God's sake, speak to me.'

All faces turn like sunflowers to the tannoy, which remains stubbornly silent. The scene on deck could be a burial at sea. Crew and hacks alike silently contemplate eternity as represented by the vastness of the ocean and the red buoy marking the exit point of the recently departed.

A seagull lands on it and defecates.

Sudden activity breaks the spell as a crew member, clad in a wetsuit and diving paraphernalia, stumbles from the wheelhouse. Albert Dingle is a big man in every department except intelligence. Lugosi attends to him as he struggles to remove his rubber mouthpiece.

'What's up?'

'The key.'

'Key? What key?'

'To the trunk.'

'Jesus!'

Lugosi finds it and Dingle tucks it into his belt pocket. He looks apprehensively at the huge swell passing under the ship and crosses himself. The captain yells from the wheelhouse.

'What the fuck are you waiting for, Albert?'

Dingle scales the ship's rail. Unfortunately, as he's about to plunge in pursuit of Reg, one of his flippers gets tangled with a cable lying on the deck. As a consequence, his projection into the deep is not as intended. Instead, he finds himself upside down, dangling against the ship's rusty hull. The SS *Promised Land* sighs as another hefty wave gently lifts her skywards.

Dickenson smiles an unpleasant smile at Mark.

'You organise this junket?'

'Only the PR side of it. Just the PR.'

Dickenson licks his pencil and writes beside the 3.30 race at Lincoln. He shows it to Mark: PR...ICKED! 'That's tomorrow's banner headline. Splashed across a full front-page photo of the bubbles from Reg's trunk. Has a wonderful symmetry about it, don't you think?'

The two seamen now have hold of Dingle's free leg while Lugosi extricates the flipper, allowing the diver to slide with little dignity or elegance into the water. He executes a painfully inept jackknife dive, and vanishes.

Mark cheers up. 'Quite a character, Reg. Probably on his way up even now.' Dickenson won't let that pass. 'Fourth fathom: yellow submarines, diving bells, and mermaid's underwear.'

The hacks snigger yet again.

Mark, however, is a bubble refusing to be popped.

'Reg is like a cork. He always bobs up.'

FOUR

Night.

The Grand Atlantic is ablaze with lights. A howling wind rattles the windows and tears at the canvas banner over the entrance. Sixty plus magicians in white ties and tails have assembled in the Residents' Lounge.

Mark stands before them.

'He just didn't come up. The diver couldn't find him.' Mark's Adam's apple seems to be struggling with each emerging word. 'Or the trunk.'

'No Reg! No Reg!' Lugosi is a passionate man. People are surprised to learn that Bela is, in fact, his real first name. His Hungarian mother named him after the star of *Dracula*, insisting he was the result of an enforced coupling with a vampire back in the old country. The performance he gives this evening is certainly on a par with his namesake. His shoulders rise above his ears as he flings his arms up to illustrate his disbelief. Bela could be singing an aria, or describing the Virgin Mary ascending to heaven.

'Diver take key,' he continues. 'No trunk. Where trunk? Believe me, misters, Reg one great escapologist.'

His passion has no effect.

The sea of perma-tanned faces remains frozen hard.

Mark tries to reassure them. 'We have another diver going down at dawn.'

Eric Wand, receding hair flattened with mousse, bangs his hands on the armchair he occupies, stands, and begins to angrily pace up and down. Wand is president of the Brotherhood of Magicians.

He finally speaks. 'Disappearing acts we can do without. Turpin was a damned amateur. It's a pity you didn't heed our warning, Mr Miles. We deal in illusions, reality is not our bag. A publicity stunt of this nature, especially when it goes wrong...'

Mark interrupts. 'Wrong is too strong a word, Eric. I'll admit there was a glitch...'

'GLITCH?' Wand goes red in the face. 'A hooded man wrapped in chains, trapped in a locked trunk at the bottom of the Atlantic Ocean is not a glitch.'

'We still have key,' Lugosi interrupts, desperate to reassure.

'Shut up, Bela,' snaps Mark. 'Gentlemen, Reg Turpin is a great showman. Publicity is like oxygen to him. You can rest assured Reg is not fishmeal. Reg is not in the belly of a shark, or the arms of an octopus. He's probably giving his girlfriend one in a hotel up the esplanade.'

The ice is broken with a sprinkle of laughter.

Mark beams, hoping to see doves appear from pockets, rabbits from top hats, cigarettes transformed into glasses of water, and endless lines of flags pulled from sleeves.

No such luck.

Wand impales him with a knife-thrower's eyes. 'Let me remind you, Mr Miles, that Turpin is not a member of the Brotherhood. His mindless stunt was in no way part of our conference. As press officer, I insist you issue a statement to that effect. Right?'

'Right.'

*

Opposite the Grand Atlantic is a seafront shelter. From here William Snazell observes Mark and the magicians as their meeting comes to its untidy conclusion. Beside him sits a grim-faced man with a head that would excite even the most mundane anthropologist.

Snazell can hardly bear to look at him.

'Put the fear of God into him. OK?'

'You can't do better than that, Mr Snazell.'

He stands and William Snazell can't help but look up in awe. Hare – his surname alone serves for identification purposes – lopes across the esplanade, climbs the broad fan of steps, and spins through the revolving door.

The hotel foyer has an air of elegant mouldiness. As does Arthur Springer, the hotel's owner, nervously pacing the worn carpet. Springer, known to his friends as Ace, is reputed to be a much-decorated ex-fighter pilot. But nobody knows in which war, wars having merged over the decades into one continuous stream of conflict. Ace's fatal character flaw is revealed by his nose, which is a blistering red. By way of confirmation, he clutches a large glass of brandy.

Hare looms before his oyster eyes. Or, putting it more accurately, oysters delicately tinged with cayenne pepper. 'Where can I find a Mr Mark Miles?'

Springer points a shaky hand towards the Residents' Lounge. With uncanny synchronicity the door opens and a white rabbit hops out. Haunted as he is by a fear of delirium tremens, Ace's drinking arm begins to vibrate like a tuning fork whilst trying to guide the brandy into his expectant mouth. The arm misses, spilling some down his shirt front.

'Shit!'

His nerve steadies when a magician immediately pursues the rabbit, pounces on it, and pops the creature into a voluminous inside pocket much beloved by his profession. Phalanxes of his colleagues now roll through the double doors into the foyer.

Hare struggles against this tide towards his target, while Springer focuses with some difficulty on Eric Wand among the flock of penguin suits. 'One of your chaps gone missing, eh, Mr Wand?'

Initially Wand seems hypnotised by Springer's nose, a map of veins leading only to cirrhosis of the liver. The manager ploughs on, 'Bad show. Nil desperandum. Remember during the war...'

Wand has had enough.

'Turpin was *not* one of our chaps, Mr Springer.' He clicks his heels sharply, turns and makes for the stairs. Springer sways and regards the vanishing magician. 'Must be a bloody Kraut. Damned fellow should be sawn in half.'

His attention is taken by angry shouts.

At first he can't locate their source.

Then his bleary eyes settle on the Residents' Lounge.

Hare is bellowing with rage.

'You calling me a liar?'

His encounter with Mark had started pleasantly enough. The big man had introduced himself as Reg Turpin's brother-in-law. 'So?' was all Miles had replied, but it was enough. The eruption was sudden and volcanic. Hare's face and eyes turned into molten lava, his voice louder than Vesuvius.

'You fucking septic turd. Lola, my beloved wife and Reg's sister, is a very sick woman. And all you can give me is lip? She's already in the grip of terrible angina, and Reg's demise will, as sure as night follows day, finish her off. Listen closely, you pile of vomit. If she should cross over to the spirit world because of this incident, you too will soon be meeting the Grim Reaper. Get me? Now what's the update on Reg?'

'Update?'

Mark has retreated behind the grand piano in the corner. His eyes dance in their sockets as if trying to escape, only settling when his tongue comes to their rescue. 'Reg was merely following in the steps of the late great Harry Houdini. Harry performed the same act in New York Harbor.'

'With one big fucking difference. Harry escaped; Reg didn't. At least as far as we know. Did the diver find the trunk?'

'No. We have another one going down tomorrow. At first light.'

'He'd better find it. Or you'll be as dead as the late, and not-so-great, Reg Turpin. You know the cunt borrowed off his sister to finance this fiasco?'

'Really?'

'Yes, really. Ten thousand pounds to be precise.'

Mark is close to fainting. As he steadies himself on the piano, Hare bangs the support away from the lid. It crashes onto Mark's hands. His scream hits top C with ease and reaches even higher as the big man puts his full weight on it.

'You're in deep shit, sonny boy.'

He picks out a tune with his free hand. Mark is in no state to recognise 'My Way'. But that's what it is. Hare eases the lid up.

'Reg told me he handed it over to you.'

'That's not true.'

Mark is not a quick learner.

Hare bangs the lid down, and, while Mark howls, changes his one-finger exercise to Chopin's 'Funeral March'. Another tune he'd recently learnt from *It's Never Too Late to Play the Piano*, newly bought online.

'Well, I ain't allowing my wife's savings to be spent on having Reg buried at sea.'

Mark foolishly tries to reason with him.

'What about the cost of the trunk? It came from Harrods.'

Again the lid crashes down; again Mark gives a banshee cause to be envious.

Hare is relentless. 'You think I'm kidding, don't you, you cock-sucker? You have just three days to return Reg to his sister. And if not Reg, then her ten thousand pounds. Right?'

Mark manages to nod.

'Three days or you'll be as dead as Mozart.'

With that Hare runs a finger the size of a courgette up the keys, executing a farewell glissando before raising the lid.

Mark slides to the floor.

His tear-sodden eyes shift from his mangled fingers to Hare as he powers through the swing doors into the foyer.

Only then does Mark feel safe enough to lose consciousness.

*

Snazell waits contentedly in the weather shelter for Hare to return. He muses on the eventful night spent at the Journey's End boarding house. It had unexpectedly allowed him to indulge his twin obsessions: Monopoly and big tits. These two stimuli had become paraphiliacally entwined at a very early age, thanks to an aunt who introduced him to the board game while resting her pumpkin-sized breasts on the table as she pursued her imaginary property portfolio.

Imagine his delight when, after a few aperitifs, Mrs Westby produced a Monopoly board and suggested a game. He'd won, easily, and his prize, as became increasingly evident with each throw of the dice, was to be the landlady herself. What a shame he was staying there for only one night. His rumination is interrupted when he sees Hare.

The enormous man carries a hideous smile as he lopes towards him.

'Softened him up nicely, Mr Snazell. He's like putty now.'

'And the fear of God?'

'That as well. Left him vibrating like a Jewish harp.'

'We are talking Old Testament God?'

'Is there any other?'

Snazell stands up, satisfied.

He rubs his hands and makes to leave.

'Right, a cheque will be in the post to you by the end of the week.'

His departure, however, isn't as imminent as he had hoped. Hare lays a hand on his shoulder, making him keel to one side like a yacht in a heavy wind.

'You said cash.'

'Cash?'

'Yes, cash. Cash in the hand.'

'Did I?'

Snazell contemplates disputing the point with Hare, but, after a shifty assessment of the giant's demeanour, decides against it. 'In that case we'll have to find a cashpoint.'

This they do.

Snazell looks furtively about as he inserts his cash card into the machine, and again before punching in the pin number. 'Do you mind standing back a bit?'

'Why? It's not nicked, is it?'

Hare looms over the podgy gumshoe.

'Piss off. This is my own perfectly valid card. You want your fee, don't you?'

Hare grunts his agreement.

'Then step back three paces.'

Hare does as he's told.

Even then, Snazell shields the screen with his raincoat while performing the transaction.

His back suddenly tenses. 'Bugger.'

'What's up?'

'Wrong pin number.'

'That happened last time.'

'No, it didn't. That was the wrong card.'

'What number did you use?'

'I'm not telling you. Never, ever, divulge your pin number.'

'Try 4402.'

'4402? That's the number for my other card. How'd you know that?'

'I'm a mind reader.'

'Don't give me that shit. You couldn't read a fucking gas meter.'

Snazell simmers with indignation while he fumbles in his wallet and switches cards. Moments later he's counting notes into Hare's red-raw hand.

'Twenty, forty, sixty, eighty. All right?'

'That's fright money. Fear of God costs a ton.'

'A hundred!' Snazell reluctantly smacks another note into his palm.

'What about my train fare?'

'You said you were coming by coach.'

'I changed me mind.'

'What mind? Here's another twenty.'

Hare adds the notes to his enormously fat wad.

Snazell eyes it enviously. 'So size really does count?'

'Yes.' A simple answer to a profound question. 'Will you need me back for a follow-up? Fear of God soon evaporates.'

'We'll see.'

Snazell looks up into the giant's empty eyes and recognises irrefutable evidence for Charles Darwin's theory of natural selection, a theory often foolishly ignored by those who regard themselves as civilised.

FIVE

The swing doors of the Residents' Lounge part slowly.

Mark's smeared face peers into the deserted foyer. He slips silently across the moth-eaten carpet towards the front exit.

'Got a minute, have you?'

Mark freezes before slowly turning to find Springer swaying in the door of his office.

'Me?'

'Yes, you, dear fellow.'

'I'm rather pressed for time, Ace.'

Mark consults the replica Rolex, fat as a shackle on his wrist.

'Is it important?'

'The Grand Atlantic pays you a not inconsiderable retainer for your services, Mark. Is that important enough?'

*

Every inch of wall space in Springer's office is crammed with war photographs, framed medals, ribbons and battle maps. Every conflict is represented: World War II, Malaya, Korea, even Vietnam. On closer inspection the observer will notice that Ace is featured in not one, although his image is sprinkled among them in the form of snaps taken at his numerous weddings, holidays abroad, staff outings, or posing with the glazed stars of summer shows and Christmas pantomimes. In each he is holding a drink; in none is he wearing a uniform. The source of his nickname, Ace, remains a mystery.

'Bad show, dear fellow. Losing a client like that.'

He's already fixing himself another large brandy when Mark enters, closing the door behind him.

'Born in a trunk is one thing; dying in one is another. Hope you haven't devised any publicity stunts for those peculiar American people arriving tomorrow.'

'No.'

'What do they do exactly?'

Springer eyes him suspiciously.

'Management training. High-powered stuff. Lots of charts. Graphs. Objectives. Forecasting. Marketing. Feasibility studies. Investment planning.'

'What's it called again?'

'The PII. The Personal Improvement Institute.'

'Jesus! Who'd believe it? An institute for personal improvement?'

Springer shakes his head incredulously.

'So what do they teach? Rampant greed? Greed, it seems, is now considered an improvement. And who better to teach us than our American cousins. You're too young to remember the GIs in the war: overpaid, oversexed and over here. That's what we used to say about them and now it seems the same can be said about you.'

Springer sinks his brandy, then lurches for a refill. 'Aside from that ridiculous Yank accent you put on, it turns out you have something else in common with the GIs. Like them you're cunt-struck. That's if Harvey's not given to exaggeration.'

'Harvey?'

Mark knows what's coming. He turns away as casually as he can, suddenly finding a new interest in the photos on the wall. Winston Churchill, phallic cigar clamped in his mouth, gives him the 'V' for Victory sign.

'Yes, Harvey. That leprous night porter of mine was shooting his mouth off in the staff latrine this morning, not knowing I was squatting in a stall trying to bring a spell of constipation to a happy conclusion. He went on at length about your nocturnal exploits in the empty bedrooms of my humble hostelry, old chap.'

The phone on the desk starts to ring.

Springer eyes it malevolently until it stops.

'It seems your carnal activities have even extended on several occasions to our communal rooms, including the Hertz office. I'm surprised the name of that particular location didn't frighten the young lady off.'

Again the phone rings.

Springer lifts the receiver an inch, then lets it drop back into its cradle. Silence.

Mark leans closer to the photograph as if he'd found some deep significance in Churchill's two raised fingers, muttering, 'Harvey has a twisted imagination. Every night, alone at his desk, listening to the groans of the central heating, with Atlantic storms howling like banshees trying to break in; it's not surprising he's mentally sick. You should have got rid of him years ago.'

Springer shivers.

His head shudders violently as if trying to shake thoughts of the deformed night porter from his mind. 'I have enough staff problems without trying to find another night porter. Harvey does a good job.'

'He frightens the guests.'

'That can be an advantage. It encourages them to be in bed before he comes on duty.'

'Then the bar receipts dip.'

'Nonsense.'

'No room service happens at night. Why? Because the guests can't face opening the door to Harvey. Some ask him to leave the tray outside the room, but he insists on having the bill signed. Then they complain of having nightmares. I've heard them talking about it over breakfast.'

Springer looks puzzled.

'Breakfast? When were you ever here for breakfast?'

Mark bites his lip.

'Ah, so you've been fortifying yourself after fornicating on the premises?'

Mark doesn't reply. He calmly moves to another photograph, sees his reflection in the glass and bares his teeth, relishing their gleaming whiteness.

Springer snaps in response, raising his voice, 'Don't want to sack you, old fellow. You do a good enough job publicising this place. Even so, I won't have you copulating...'

27

It could have been a stage cue.

The door flies open to reveal the voluptuous Avril Springer. Her green silk dress transforms her bodily undulations into rolling hills of lush pasture, with a soft valley starting at her pelvis and running down to meet the darkness of her black stockings. Avril had been the hotel's barmaid until she landed Ace some five years ago.

'Why aren't you answering the bloody phone? Temple's assistant turned up. Out the bloody blue. No bloody warning. Her name's Alice Honey but sweet she is not. She's up in the Empire Suite bitching about everything. You can bloody deal with her.'

'Course I will, my precious.'

Springer sinks his brandy and pats his pockets to locate a choice of mouth sprays. Avril's blue-rinsed miniature poodle, Sylvester, who follows her everywhere, jumps onto the swing chair behind Ace's desk and surveys the scene like he is the boss.

Which he is.

Avril pins Mark with her eyes. 'And a lot of stuff was delivered this morning for this course of yours. What's a wire cage got to do with personal improvement?'

'A wire cage?'

'A bloody big one at that. And a crucifix.'

Springer, busy spraying his mouth with a peppermint odour, nearly chokes. 'A crucifix?'

'High enough for Jesus Christ himself. She's had it all parked in the conference centre. And you know what? She wants the phone number of a local funeral director. What's that about, Mark?'

'How'd I know?'

A glint enters Springer's oyster eyes. 'Sounds damned kinky to me.' He sighs in memory of some past act of deviancy. 'Kinky, very kinky. Never been the same since Vietnam, the Yanks.'

Mark tickles the poodle's ears while panning up Avril's body until he reaches her eyes.

She feeds him a fleeting smile and a nod. 'He likes his chest being rubbed.'

Mark shifts his hand. 'Like this?'

'It makes him wag his tail.'

They watch and wait, but his tail remains stubbornly stationary.

'Try lower down.'

Mark slides his hand closer to Sylvester's back legs. Sure enough his tail starts to move vigorously. But so does his penis, which shoots into a long, lean erection. Avril glows with spite. 'Envious, Ace?'

'Good God!'

Springer looks away, blushing.

'I'm off to my life class. Feed Sylvester, will you? There's turkey left over from lunch, but don't give him any of the stuffing.' Leaning on that word, she shoots Mark a last lewd look and leaves. Her entrance and exit are a passing tornado, albeit a brief one.

The two men regard Sylvester in silence.

Mark lifts a paw to study the green nail varnish.

'He's going mouldy.'

'Look at him,' says Ace. There are tears in his eyes. 'The last of the Springer line.'

'You should worry. Some people have children.'

Sadness is the human equivalent of damp rot.

It almost has a smell.

Springer sniffs and smiles bleakly at the ridiculous blue-rinsed creature occupying his chair. 'They used to be hunting dogs.' He laughs. 'But then, we used to be hunters.'

His shaking hand manages to grip the doorknob.

'I'm to the Empire Suite, dear boy. Meant to change the name years ago. What an irony we have an American staying in it.'

He pauses in the doorway.

'Mark, leave room service to us, there's a good fellow.'

The door closes quietly behind him.

SIX

Snazell waits in the seafront shelter.

His beady eyes flicker as the match ignites and meets his pipe. Swearing, he snuffs the flame when Mark dances down the steps of the Grand Atlantic and sets a brisk pace along the esplanade.

Snazell follows, smoke rising in rings as he puffs in pursuit. His quarry, after turning several corners, reaches a Victorian school building. Evenings see it used for adult education. Light spills into the night from its high classroom windows.

Mark vanishes inside.

Snazell slides into a shop entrance to watch and wait. Behind him, on metal stands of varying heights, is a bizarre display of women's hats: boater and bonnet, cloche and pillbox, veils and paper flowers, all in salmon pink. His battered trilby, faded and stained, sits among them like a fly on a blancmange.

*

Mark runs up the stairs to the second floor and along a labyrinth of corridors. Sounds emanate from language lessons, media studies, classes on embroidery, philosophy, cookery, every conceivable form of human improvement.

He stops by a glass door, surreptitiously peering into the classroom. A cadaverous old wino models naked on a plinth, hands on his hairy legs, cock dangling unconcerned between them. Six budding Rembrandts attend to their easels. One of them is Avril. Miles catches her attention and moves on. Minutes later she excuses herself from the class.

*

Dark.

Deserted.

Mark unlocks the door to the science laboratory. Light falls from the corridor across the work benches littered with test tubes and Bunsen burners.

He waits inside.

Avril enters.

It's a well-oiled routine, Mark having duplicated the key some years earlier. They cross in silence to the storeroom. Its shelves are lined with biological specimens: locusts, frogs, snails, snakes, worms. Jars of chemicals. Containers of acid.

A street lamp shines into the storeroom, allowing them to examine the lust in each other's eyes before their mouths clamp in the moist fusion of a succubus. Mark's hands run from the contours of her arse, up her back, around her shoulders, to her breasts. Avril's unzips his fly, fondles in his underpants until she finds his penis.

He groans.

She, too, groans as his hand lifts her dress on its way past her suspenders to her knickers. A minimum of foreplay is needed for a successful, if brief, coupling.

As it is with most animals.

Avril bites his ear then whispers, 'That's my problem done.' Taking his head in hands as strong as a vice, she locks her gaze onto his eyes. 'Now what's yours?'

'I haven't got a problem.'

'Liar. There's no such thing as a free fuck. Especially not with you.'

Mark raises his voice. 'How can you say that?'

'Easily. Is it money again?'

'Money? That's all you ever think about.'

'If you want me to keep you as my toy boy, you'll have to up your workload.'

She takes his balls in her hand. 'Come on Fido, stand up and beg.'

Mark groans again, but his cock refuses to respond.

'Our relationship is dead.'

'Not again.'

'It's based on lust, not love.'

She kisses him violently, plunging her tongue into his gasping mouth. Unaware that his head is rammed against a grass snake embalmed in a jar, Mark manages to free his mouth in order to expand his theory on the male's baser instincts. 'Don't you understand? Lust is transitory. When I come, I am already gone. Now that's not fair on you. That's exploiting you as a sex object. Avril, you must learn to understand men.'

And so the ante is raised.

Her painted nails flick his testicles, firing up his penis and quickly demolishing his theory of sexual exploitation. Ironically, by a substantial erection.

'Oh my God,' he pants.

'God has got nothing to do with it.'

The jar with the preserved snake rattles seismically as he pulls her onto him. Hands locked onto her thighs, he thrusts back and forth with the precision of a piston engine. Then, a mega-second before the moment of sexual detonation, he murmurs in her ear.

'Ten thousand pounds. That's my problem.'

Avril shudders with the force of an earthquake; spasms ripple across the landscape of her body, her eyes shoot open with the ecstasy of someone lost eternally in the jungle of the senses, hopefully. Her mouth, however, remains rooted in the ugly compost of reality, screaming loud enough for all the adult education courses, including life drawing, to hear.

'Ten fucking thou!'

*

The battered alarm clock goes off, rattling against his callused feet. Time to capture the wino's life in charcoal, pencil or pastel is on hold for ten minutes. The old man breaks his pose, flips his testicles to one side, crosses his legs and lights a fag.

It's all very bohemian.

Avril's flushed face appears from behind the door. The surface of her dress, green and silk, now crinkled and stained, has more originality and spontaneity than any of the works sitting on the easels in that classroom.

She returns to her seat and studies her own effort. The fact that it bears no relation whatsoever to what's before her puzzles her. She can see clearly the old man, every wart and busted vein, but can't comprehend the skill needed to capture it on paper.

He drops his fag end into a cup of cold tea and resets the alarm clock for another half hour. Moving his frail frame into a new position, he eventually settles with his bony arse directed into their faces.

Undaunted, Avril confronts a fresh white sheet in her drawing pad and picks up a stick of charcoal. She stands, studies the stark bones in the old man's anus, then applies her first bold but inaccurate line.

Sex for Avril had started standing up, against an alley wall. She has liked it that way ever since. For her, unadulterated lust has such purity. No tentacles of attachment. It amuses her when men think they're using her, when all the time she's using them.

Mark's periodic attempts to exchange sperm for money gives their couplings an added piquancy. But this evening it was of an unusually high intensity. He had pleaded, saying his life was at risk. She had looked into his dancing eyes, as weak and spent as his dick, and smiled.

She studies the charcoal blackening the fingers that so recently played with Mark's pudendum, then looks at the old model and sees the future.

It looks eternally sexy.

She knew she knew all there was to know about men.

*

Snazell trails Mark back to Providence House and slips into the same shop entrance as if it was an old jacket. He lights his pipe while watching Mark's office on the third floor.

His quarry soon appears in silhouette to drop the blind.

It falls on his head.

33

SEVEN

The answering machine unwinds its snake of words as Mark moves into a corner cupboard to unhook a shabby dinner suit from behind the door.

A silky female voice insinuates itself into his office. 'Hi Mark. Broadway Entertainment Agency here. We have a client who wants to challenge the *Guinness Book of Records* for the longest time lying on a Bed of Nails. The record stands at seventy days, five hours, forty-three minutes. Do you have a suitable location for such an event? Obviously it has to be available for longer than the current record.' The voice becomes even more seductive when it moves on to the subject of money. 'Mark, this'll be a nice little earner. We had an extremely successful long-running event with a Buried Alive contestant on Brighton Pier. In the first week fifty thousand punters paid a fiver each to look at him in his glass coffin. And the outlay was minimal. Sand from the beach, with one plastic tube for an air hole. He was in there for nearly six months. Apparently he never once went to the toilet.'

She laughs.

'Unless he did it between our party tours, nod, nod, wink, wink.' She laughs again. 'Punters like to contemplate the little mysteries of life, don't they? Think about it, Mark. Bed of Nails could be even bigger than Buried Alive. If you're interested, give us a bell.'

Mark has donned his dinner suit before the next message starts. 'Mum here. Are you there?' She waits, breathing asthmatically. 'Sorry to hear about your escape person escaping like that. Someone said they

34

saw a man come out the sea further down the coast. Covered in tattoos he was. It was on the local news. People will try anything to get on telly.' More painful breathing, then, 'Will you be over tomorrow? It's toad-in-the-hole. Your shirts are done.'

She wheezes noisily before hanging up.

The machine clunks to a halt but is immediately activated by a live call. Mark clips on his bow tie as he listens to the voice booming from the speaker: 'Out of millions of numbers, you, Mark Miles, have been selected to take part in the lottery of a lifetime. You are the lucky winner of five thousand pounds. All you have to do is pick up the phone and answer one simple question.'

William Snazell chuckles into the machine, 'I know you're there, Mr Miles. I'm on a cell phone. If you look out the window, I'll wave to you.' And he does just that when Mark surreptitiously parts the newly restored blind. He then pulls from an inside pocket a wad of money, which he also waves. 'Pick up the phone, Mr Miles, and all this could be yours.'

Mark lets the blind flick back into place and steps away from the window. The answering machine purrs harmlessly while he circles it as if it's a cobra about to strike. Snazell appears to know exactly what's happening in the office above him. 'Pick it up. It won't bite you. Remember your logo? Make your Mark with Miles. It's up there in gold.' He roars with laughter. 'Go for gold, Mr Miles. Answer one simple question correctly and...'

Mark snatches the receiver from its cradle. 'What's the question?'

'That's more like, Mr Miles. I like a good sport. In our security-conscious age, we have, first of all, to ascertain we're dealing with the right person. Right?'

'Right.'

'You are Mark Miles?'

'I am.'

'Well done.'

Mark waits. He can hear Snazell breathing.

'Was that the question?'

'Indeed it was. And you passed with flying colours. You want another one? What's your mother's maiden name?'

'Maguffin.'

35

'Correct. Now I know you're the real McCoy and not the possessor of a stolen identity. So let's get down to business. Let me in, Mr Miles.'

Again Snazell anticipates Mark's reluctance. 'We could talk down here in the street but it looks like it's about to rain.'

Mark presses the door release.

'Push.'

*

The dumpy shape behind the frosted-glass office door resembles Alfred Hitchcock. Or so Mark thinks. When he opens it Snazell is ready with a business card, while his beady eyes play over Mark's face. It reads, *William Snazell. Private Detective. Licensed.*

Mark, assuming the man's come on behalf of a disgruntled creditor, curses himself for letting him in. He snatches the card impatiently. 'Let's make this fast. I have to be somewhere in thirty minutes.'

Snazell pushes past him into the room, scanning it as he moves. He picks Mark's baseball cap off the desk, examines it and tosses it disdainfully onto the anglepoise lamp. A headed notepad catches his eye. He picks it up and reads, 'From the desk of Mark Miles.' He chuckles. 'I must say you've picked up some very nasty transatlantic habits. Including that ridiculous accent. Do you chew gum as well?'

'What the fuck has…?'

As Mark's words dry up, so the blood drains from his face. Snazell is holding a gun in one hand while screwing a silencer into place with the other. He smiles at Mark. 'Talking of nasty transatlantic habits…'

Mark nearly chokes. 'Is that for real?'

The detective takes a bead on the dartboard hanging above the sofa and presses the trigger. He's a surprisingly good shot: double top splinters before the board crashes to the floor.

'Does that answer your question?'

The card in Mark's hand is shaking. 'It says you're licensed. Is that to carry a gun?'

'What gun?'

Mark looks up, but it's vanished. Snazell's eyes are like ball bearings. 'A little joke, Mark. My way of letting off steam.'

There's a neat hole in the wall where the bullet is lodged. Mark stares at it in bewilderment, then at the twisted dartboard. He attempts to speak, but only gurgles.

Snazell moves to a peg board covered with examples of Mark's work: a maze of tacky adverts and newspaper cuttings featuring pneumatic women, tired slogans and ludicrous claims. Disgust clouds Snazell's face as he mutters to himself, 'Lust! Avarice! Envy! All nurtured like monstrous babies, breastfed with lies and filth until they can crawl, walk and, worst of all, breed.'

His eyes finally settle on what he's looking for. 'What have we here?' He unpins a flyer for Hermann Temple's course. 'What do you know about these people?'

'Not much.'

'But you got them into the Grand Atlantic Hotel?'

'I negotiated a package at off-season rates. That's all.'

'Why did they come to you?'

'A friend had been on the course. They were looking for a hotel to locate in. So he put the two of us together, business-wise.'

'What about Dr Hermann P. Temple? Is he coming?'

'Course he is. Temple is the PII.'

'You ever met him?'

'No.'

'You wouldn't be lying, would you?'

'Why should I lie?'

'Because telling porkies is the publicity man's stock-in-trade. I was told you were PII's agent in the UK.'

'Speaking of liars, who told you that?'

'Never reveal a source, Mr Miles,' he laughs. 'Not even at gunpoint.'

He pegs the flyer back on the board, turns and fixes Mark with his piggy eyes. The idea that eyes are the windows of the soul is bullshit and Snazell knows it. Even so, when Mark doesn't bat either lid, the detective appears satisfied. 'It seems I made a mistake. Sorry to have bothered you.'

With that he speeds for the door.

Mark explodes, 'Who the fuck do you think you are? You barge into my office, give a lethal demonstration of ballistic darts...' He races after the detective into the corridor. '… insult me, dish up a sermon, then fuck off…'

Mark turns the colour of chalk when Snazell abruptly stops at the head of the stairs, spins around with the gun back in his hand. He strokes his bulbous nose with its barrel. 'Carbolic soap, Mr Miles. I recommend it for your mouth. Lest we ever meet again I'll have you know that I'm a practising member of the Church of Jesus Christ of Latter-day Saints. We Mormons don't like profane language.'

He continues down the stairs.

'Snazell,' Mark yells after him. 'I'm not fucking interested in your religion, place of birth, or inside-leg measurement. What was that guff about a prize? Five thousand pounds, wasn't it?'

The detective stops in his tracks, then retraces them.

'I wondered when you'd get around to that. It's a reward for information which I now know you haven't got.'

'What information?'

Snazell smirks with the satisfaction of a fisherman about to land a big fish. 'A client of mine, a rich and – how can I put it? – mature lady had her husband attend one of Temple's courses last month. He, the husband, is somewhat younger than my client and not too successful at running her numerous businesses. Even so, I'm told he came top of the class. Temple awarded him a prize – an onyx marble mantel clock with a battery-operated pendulum. Next morning, I'm told, he checked out of the hotel along with the other students. Trouble is that neither he, nor the onyx marble mantel clock, have been seen since. They never arrived back at Nirvana Nous, my client's home on the grassy outskirts of Guildford.'

He stops as if that was the end of his tale.

'So?' Mark is irritated.

'So my client's offering ten thousand pounds for any information as to his whereabouts.'

The synapses in Mark's brain are abruptly fired up. Fearful images of his fate at the hands of Turpin's giant brother-in-law bang about with the velocity of a squash ball. Now a possible escape route has suddenly opened for him. He can hardly believe his ears.

'Ten thousand pounds?'

'You heard me right.'

'Ten big ones. Is the husband worth it?'

'He's a Capricorn and very good in bed, so I'm told. It appears the two facts are unrelated, for which I'm grateful, being a Pisces myself.'

Ground bait successfully dropped, Snazell spins around and starts down the stairs. 'Walk in. Dance out.'

For such a podgy man, he's amazingly light on his feet.

*

Mark is on the phone.

'Rodney, I got to see you. Tonight! Can you come to the Starlight?'

His facial muscles begin to twitch as Rodney, obviously reluctant to meet up, drones on till Mark interrupts him. 'Rodney, I can't explain on the phone. I think it's tapped.'

Nothing deters Rodney. His voice has the relentless monotone of a lawnmower. Mark looks at the ceiling in frustration. He's close to screaming, his neck bulging with suppressed fury, causing his bow tie to pop into a congealed cup of coffee sitting on his desk.

'Fuck!'

He fishes it out while listening to Rodney, before again interrupting. 'Trust me, Rod, there's a lot of dosh at stake.'

Rodney starts up again with another boring excuse.

Furious swivelling of the eyes heralds a final explosion from Mark. 'Susan? That fucking dreary cow! You should never have married her. Tell her it's Scottish dancing night, all knobbly knees and limp dicks. That should put her off.'

Rodney Cole and Mark, close friends at school, had drifted apart when Rodney married money in the shape of one Susan Green. Mark rolls an ink blotter over the bow tie and lowers his voice to a whisper. 'Listen, Rod, lots of sexy bimbos get there on Saturday nights. I'll fix you up. Get you laid on the Crazy Golf course. Nothing quite like fucking on top of Buckingham Palace.'

Mark smiles, clipping the bow tie into place.

'Great. I'll leave a pass for you at the stage door.'

EIGHT

The cast-iron pier creaks with age. Its rusted joints shift painfully from the swell of an incoming tide. A gloomy, domed building squats above the waves at the far end.

The Starlight Ballroom.

Even the flickering neon sign above the entrance is dim. Music, filtered by the walls, is reduced to the ubiquitous drum machine – the true heartbeat of our civilisation – seeping out to the rain-saturated deck.

Inside is far from gloomy.

The corroding structure has been covered in a multitude of garish paints and twinkling coloured lights. Buzzing like a beehive, the place is already packed. Here the young can collectively escape their lifeless lives via booze and drugs.

Oblivion beckons.

On stage are the Solomon Brothers, five glistening, young white boys trying to be black. Dressed in lurid pink suits, green top-pocket handkerchiefs and powder-blue shoes, they move in unison.

One step forward.

One step back.

Turn.

Soft young faces with frozen smiles. Mechanical toys with shrill voices. Even the lyrics of Stevie Wonder's 'Signed, Sealed, Delivered' carry a certain ironic twist to this musical package.

Draped across the proscenium arch hangs a painted banner: *The Mark Miles Talent Contest*. The impresario himself hovers nervously in the wings. Beside him is the boys' mother, Mrs Solomon, a fleshy lady of major proportions.

Mark whispers into her large red ear, 'Train them yourself?'

'With their father.'

She points at the small, bespectacled man with a pencil moustache standing in the wings opposite. Mr Solomon is engrossed in simulating the routine being performed on stage. Mark watches, wide-eyed, bottling up his laughter. He can't resist popping one more question.

'Is he a choreographer?'

'No,' she shakes her head emphatically. 'A behavioural psychologist.'

'Are you serious?'

'Of course I am.'

On stage the boys are winding up with their final chorus. Mark wonders if he, too, hadn't just been wound up. Solomon looks more like a dodgy car dealer, or, in fact, a dodgy anything. A loud burst of applause breaks the spell. The act dances off as Mark dances on.

'That was the sensational Solomon Brothers.'

A rowdy gang of tattooed bikers drown him out, chanting for an encore. Mark unhooks the microphone in a futile attempt to ride the swell of drunken shouts. 'Once again, we at the Starlight...'

But the chant grows as others join in.

In desperation Mark looks into the wings where Solomon is handing out candy bars to his boys. 'Boys, have you got an encore for us? Or is that it?' Solomon and his five boys shake their heads in unison. Mark turns to the chanting crowd. 'Sorry, folks. The boys have to go. It's way past their bedtime. Say nighty-night, everybody!'

Everybody obliges.

Although it comes with a roar of booing.

The diminutive Mr Solomon makes a gesture not usually expected from a behavioural psychologist, before leading his troop to the stage door. Mrs Solomon, blood-red with fury, repeats the gesture but with two fingers instead of one. Not to be outdone, Mark gives her the full fist three times. This, in full view of the audience, detonates an explosion of raucous approval, thereby disturbing the dust in every corner and crevice of the building. The audience, already morphed into a rabble, is close to becoming a mob.

Mark cracks the microphone's cable like a lion tamer, yelling, 'Once again the Starlight is proud to present this month's Mark Miles Speciality Act.'

Cheering breaks out as two plump girls, bursting from fishnet stockings and sparkling tutus, wheel trolleys, each carrying a barrel of lager, on to the stage. A third follows with a trolley of rattling pint mugs. Waiting for the cheers to subside, Mark scans the audience, only to be taken aback when he sees Snazell sliding into a seat in the circle. The detective gives him a cheery wave before spotting, several rows away, a woman so buxom she could have stepped from a saucy seaside postcard. He rapidly changes direction, anxious to grab the vacant seat beside her.

Mark quickly recovers his composure, bringing the microphone close to his mouth like it is an ice-cream cornet. 'So yobs and yobettes, please give a big hand to Cyril Hammond, this month's Speciality Act.' A sallow man, gangly as a giraffe, dressed in an ill-fitting tuxedo, appears from the wings.

'Tonight, right now, Cyril will try for a place in the *Guinness Book of Records*. Tell us about it, Cyril.'

'This is a record listed in Chapter Eleven: Human Achievements.'

'That's very commendable, Cyril; which human achievement in particular?'

Mark tries not to look at Snazell, now seated next to the pneumatic lady, but can't help himself. The detective blows him a kiss.

'I will attempt to drink more than twenty point seventy-nine litres of lager in sixty minutes.'

'Wow! Twenty point seventy-nine litres in just sixty minutes? So, Cyril, you have this fantastic ability for swallowing things?'

'I do, Mark.' Cyril modestly studies his dazzling patent leather shoes. 'In fact, I think millions of people have but simply don't realise it.'

'Even me?'

'Even you, Mark, will certainly have a talent for swallowing things.'

Snazell likes that. He smiles and points an accusing finger at him. Mark drags his eyes back to Cyril. 'Let me just repeat the current record. Lads and lassies, the current record stands at twenty point seventy-nine litres in sixty minutes. Am I right, Cyril?'

'You are, Mark.'

'Held by?'

'Wolfgang Pretorius. Since June 1968.'

'Wolfgang, eh? A German?'

No sooner has he said it than the pus of nationalism boils up from a bundle of shaved heads with faces as blotchy and purple as turnips. They start to scream, '*Sieg Heil*,' stamp their boots and shoot their arms out in the Nazi salute. A regimented chant reminiscent of Nuremberg sweeps across the hall.

Mark catches Cyril's arm to stop him doing a runner, whilst barking into the microphone, 'Who said it couldn't happen here?' His eyes blaze with memories of orgiastic SS officers overacting in war movies on late-night television. He grabs one of the pints lined up for Cyril and shouts, '*Ja, ja, mein Kinder!* If you swallow Nazism, you'll swallow anything.' He raises the mug in a toast: 'To Adolf.'

The hall falls silent as the golden liquid slips smoothly down his gullet. With a flourish he tosses the empty mug to an assistant while cheers replace the jeers. A fickle creature is the crowd, rabble, mob. Mark bows most graciously before turning to Cyril.

'Good luck, Cyril. Girls, please.'

One of the assistants holds out a full mug to the quaking contender. The blitzkrieg has had an adverse effect on Cyril's nerves. With a supreme effort he steadies his hand and takes the lager.

Mark is in overdrive. 'Stand by the clock, girls.'

Cyril rests the glass on his bottom lip.

'A ready and a steady and a GO!'

The tacky chronometer, previously lowered from the flies, shudders into action. Within seconds the mug of lager is empty. An assistant takes it, while another stands by with a replacement. Mark shows his middle finger to the audience. 'One!'

And walks into the wings.

'Two!'

'Three!'

He can hear the chant all the way to the stage door.

Cyril is off to a cracking start.

*

'My guest arrived, Charlie?'

Mark has to repeat the question three times. Charlie's faculties had bottomed out years ago. In situ at the stage door since the theatre first opened seven decades before, no one can recollect ever seeing Charlie arrive or leave: he was just there. A permanent fixture. A much-loved but useless pet no one has the heart to put down.

When Mark finally catches his wavering attention, the old man says, 'Okey-dokey, Mark?'

That's all Charlie ever says.

Mark sees that he's clutching a pass in his shaking hands. Through the window he points at it. 'When my guest gets here, give that to him, Charlie. And tell him I'm in the Manhattan Bar.'

'Okey-dokey.'

*

Mark had recently persuaded the owners of the theatre to allow students from the local art school to carry out, under his personal supervision, a makeover of the extensive bar. His chosen theme had been the Manhattan skyline. Unfortunately, it quickly became apparent that painting and draughtsmanship were not the school's strong points, so the end result was a mixture of installation art and an excruciating mural.

Any vestige of talent is not in evidence.

But Mark was happy.

'Meet me in the Manhattan' sounded cool.

Alone, in a long black dress, on a long black bar stool, sits Ursula Letts. Ursula is a primary school teacher. She also has the dubious honour of being Mark's childhood sweetheart and very first lover. Sadly for her, the affair won't quite lie down and die.

'How are you, sugar?'

Mark kisses her on the back of the neck. No sexual shiver there.

She icily sips her cocktail and casts a jaundiced eye over the mural. 'That your idea?'

'Isn't it great?'

'Where's it meant to be?'

'New York.'

44

'New York, America?'

'It's Manhattan, sugar.'

'Don't call me sugar. I'm not feeling sweet tonight.'

She sinks her drink and drums the bar top with black lacquered nails. 'Art is whatever shit you can get away with. That's the motto for art schools now. Fuck skills. You didn't pay the useless pricks, did you?'

'Beer money.'

'Beer money? Oblivion as a currency. I like that.'

Her bleak humour always cheers him up.

'Same again?'

'Why not?'

Mark signals the barman, who deliberately turns the other way.

'Shit! Did you see that?'

'Maybe the décor's struck him blind.'

She sticks two fingers in her mouth, letting rip a whistle worthy of any doorman in New York. The barman swings around.

'Blind but not deaf, it seems.'

Ursula smiles sweetly when he arrives, and watches while he wipes the bar top with a sodden tea towel before emptying the ashtray full of butt ends with lipstick traces. She waits for him to look her in the eye before speaking. 'Same again.' The barman stares at her. His pupils are smaller than sheep shit. This guy has seen a lot of spaghetti westerns. But so has Ursula. She plucks a cigarette from the pack, fires up her lighter, inhales, blows a smoke ring, and only then says, 'Please.'

A sneer plays on the barman's mouth. He smacks the wet towel over his shoulder with a loud crack and turns slowly to face Mark. But Mark is in a different movie. His order comes fast, too fast, and worse, it's soft: 'Orange juice.' The barman tries to retrieve the scene. His long arms drop to imaginary holsters. He doesn't move. Or speak. He lets his black sheep-shit pupils bore into Mark. Mark returns the stare. One, two, three and Mark blinks, then capitulates: 'Please.' The barman shakes his head sadly and shuffles off. He gathers his long greasy black hair into a ponytail, slipping a rubber band over it.

Mark watches him uneasily until he's out of earshot.

'Where the fuck does he think he is? Tombstone City? The cunt hasn't noticed he's in Manhattan. Can you believe it?'

'Easily.'

Mark, troubled, ponders some more. 'Did he seem psychotic to you?'

'No way. Somebody pulled his ponytail and flushed his brains through his arse.'

Mark keeps shaking his head, looking nervously at the barman. 'Jesus, crazy people everywhere. Did you hear what happened to Reg Turpin?'

'Course I did. It didn't surprise me. Reg had the IQ of a haddock. Anyway, he's ended up on all the front pages, which is what he wanted.'

'Trouble is he's not around to read them. I wish I could say the same about his nearest and dearest. One of them, a fucking giant one at that, has even threatened to kill me.'

'Good. I love funerals.'

'Only because you look sexy in black.'

'Do I?'

'You were in black when I first fell for you.'

'Was it the school uniform that attracted you? Or what was in it?'

'You haven't still got that uniform, have you?'

'I'll wear it to your funeral.'

'Not before?'

'Not before.'

'An erection isn't much use when you're dead.'

'God'll take care of it. After all, he's been jerking us off since we invented him.'

Mark has stopped listening. His mind is on other matters than God or even gods. Hare's threat is still banging around his brain. 'You're good at pub quizzes. How old was Mozart when he died?'

'Thirty-five.'

'You're kidding?'

'Your age exactly.'

Mark is visibly shaken. He peers anxiously over her shoulder. She turns to look. 'Are you expecting somebody?'

'Rodney Cole.'

'That drip. I thought you couldn't stand him.'

'I can't. Unfortunately I need his help.'

'How?'

Mark tenses, seeing his quarry entering the auditorium behind her. 'I'll tell you later.'

Rodney Cole has the charisma of a tailor's dummy. He even looks like one in his immaculate blue pinstripe suit, pink shirt and matching tie. He stops to watch Cyril on the stage, disposing of another pint of lager. Most of it runs down his shirt as his long legs buckle like an aircraft's landing gear.

The mob roars, willing him on.

Distaste features on Rodney Cole's face as he surveys the bar. When he sees Mark approaching, he signals to somebody unseen in the hall. 'Tried to escape, dear boy. Afraid Susan has the genes of a limpet.' Mark groans when he observes Susan Cole struggling through the crowd to reach them. Bobbing up and down in her red jacket, she could be riding to hounds. Word has it that half the county's gentry had ridden her before Rodney got his hands on the reins. Her father was happy to give her away, along with a heathy slice of his property portfolio. After pecking her on both cheeks, Mark leads them, like the host of a television talk show, to a table in the bar.

*

Rodney stretches his long, sharply creased trouser legs under the table. 'The London venue proved to be unsuitable. That's when I thought of you. The PII are very grateful for the deal you did at the Grand Atlantic.' He sips his wine. 'Why the sudden interest in Hermann Temple, Mark?' As he speaks, he glances nervously at his wife.

Mark misses nothing, his eyes as alert as a ferret's.

'I'm thinking that maybe I should enrol on the course.'

Susan Cole chimes in, 'It'll change your life forever, Mark.'

She says with the fervour of an evangelist, 'It's like shampooing your soul. Hermann forces you to face your destiny, give up being a has-been or never-was. He will turn you into a leader. Frankly, if you'd done the course earlier, the trouble you're in with that Reg what's-his-name, the supposed escapologist, would never have occurred.'

Mark can't hide his astonishment. 'You've done the course, Susan? Where?'

'In London. Same time as Rodney. They run a parallel course for women.'

Mark turns to Rodney. 'What happens on it?'

Rodney's expression, at first unsettled by his wife's intervention, now sets like cement. 'Usual stuff. Modules. Lectures. Logos. Games. Graphs. And lots and lots of bullets.' He laughs, nervously. 'Bullets, as I'm sure you're aware, are thoughts fired into your head. All very boring.'

'That's not true, Rodney.'

Susan is adamant. 'Hermann thinks the world is suffering a famine of leaders. People who can inspire, guide, rule. PII is dedicated to finding those special persons, Mark.'

Rodney can't bear it. 'Susan, it's simply not Mark's style.'

His raised voice causes her to turn red. It's very unusual for him to be this dominant. Mark waits before applying the scalpel. 'Did anything go wrong on your course in London, Rodney?'

Rodney's whole body goes rigid. 'What do you mean?'

'Anyone freak out? Break down? Collapse? Die? Disappear? After all, it's not every day one becomes a leader.'

'Of course not.'

Rodney's fist, the one holding his red wine, tightens into a white knot. 'Why do you ask?'

Susan bites her lip.

'Loosen up, Rodney. Becoming a leader seems to have made you tense. The reason I asked is that a source of mine tells me that...'

Mark's question remains unanswered.

A huge roar of disgust erupts in the auditorium, followed by a loud crash, shouts, and the unmistakable noise of a brawl igniting. Then, capping even that explosive sound mix, fire alarms go off like the bells of hell.

Mark jumps up. 'What the fuck's happened?'

The blood has already deserted his face.

Rodney leans back to fully enjoy the moment. 'Loosen up, Mark.'

But Mark is already sprinting for the entrance, shouting, 'Don't go. I'll be back.' When he does get back some ten minutes later, they've gone. Their unfinished drinks are still on the table. The next day he rings them several times. Each time an answering machine kicks in.

They don't return his calls.

*

Ursula, sitting at the bar, witnessed the chain of events in the ballroom.

Once Mark left her to join the Coles, the barman made sure her glass was always charged. She never asked, he never spoke. As she slid slowly into inebriation, the antics of Cyril and his audience made for perfect entertainment.

The ruction happened very suddenly.

Cyril, despite the increasing elasticity in his legs, was on course to break the record, when he abruptly lurched backwards, then forwards, and threw up over the baying crowd. Unfortunately, most of it splattered the neo-Nazis. That done, he reversed into the trolley of glasses, which smashed to smithereens. The three assistants panicked, started screaming, and one of them, while running from the stage, tripped and knocked over one of the barrels. This barrel, in turn, hit the other one and together they rolled in every direction, spewing lager as they went.

Meanwhile Cyril had staggered to the footlights, where he teetered momentarily on the edge. One of the barrels took him from behind, catapulting him into the audience. Boozed to the gills, they were waiting for any excuse to move rapidly from audience to rabble to mob. Now they had it. Battle lines formed with surprising speed between those with shaved heads and those with hair – any hair. It was like a rerun of the English Civil War. Tattooed arms and fists hammered away like steam pistons – one of which hit a fire alarm.

Ursula switched her gaze to Mark as he left the Coles and ran into the ballroom. There, a scene evoking Hieronymus Bosch awaited him. He steadied himself before making a dash for the stage. Turning back to the bar for her cocktail, Ursula saw Rodney and Susan fleeing through the fire exit doors.

Now something magical happened, or so it seemed in her alcoholic haze. It started to rain. She held out her hand to see if it was real. It was. She looked up, almost expecting to find the roof sliding back, revealing billowing clouds and perhaps even a rainbow.

But life isn't like that for Ursula.

Ugly reality haunts her every moment.

The sprinklers had been activated.

*

Tempers instantly cooled in the downpour.

Neo-Nazis and bikers are no different to the rest of us when it comes to sartorial matters. They, too, like to look smart in their butch uniforms. Who knows what the chemical spray will do to their leathers and chains?

The hall empties in no time.

From the stage, Mark thanks everyone for coming, announcing that he's hoping to bring a Bed of Nails attraction to this venue soon.

He finds Ursula in the now deserted bar. The sprinklers continue to play over her but she makes no attempt to move. Her wet black dress glistens like jet.

She appears to be weeping.

But it's difficult to tell.

NINE

Waves crash over the sea wall onto the esplanade.

Two small figures, huddled in winter coats, make their way on the leeward side. Mark has his arm around Ursula. She sings to herself while Mark talks to himself. 'Rodney was lying. The shit was hiding something. I know it. I had him right in my sights when that arsehole Cyril chose to fuck everything up.' Ursula's rendering of 'Signed, Sealed, Delivered' is barely audible now.

Mark raises his voice in an effort to convince himself. 'My gut tells me something went seriously wrong on that course.'

Ursula quits singing. 'So what?'

Mark stops, turns her towards him and looks angrily into her bleary eyes. 'So what? So a reward of ten thousand pounds, that's what.' He shivers, and not just from the cold wind. 'Enough to get Reg's ugly relative off my back.'

'Just tell him to piss off.'

'And risk meeting Wolfgang Amadeus next Tuesday? You're not taking me seriously, sugar. This dude is big like King Kong, but not as loveable.'

They reach the Grand Atlantic. Mark rests her against the balustrade and gently pats her face. 'You up for this?'

'Why not.'

'Count to twenty, OK?

'OK.'

He dances up the steps and peers inside. Behind the reception desk, at the end of the dimly lit foyer, he sees Harvey, the night porter and Ace's nemesis. Mark quietly revolves the revolving door and moves in like a cat burglar.

Ursula turns to face the wind, letting it sober her up. She'd agreed to sleep with him, and now tried to remember why. Her lips move as she starts to count.

Much of her life is led by rote.

The only sound is the tick of the wall clock above Harvey's head. His disfigured face of warts and weeping pustules wouldn't be out of place in the horror comic that engrosses him.

Nor would his hunched back.

Nature has not been kind to Harvey.

Mark skirts the edge of the foyer, unnoticed. He ducks below the reception desk and waits. Harvey turns a page of the comic to find that the vampire with the blood of his latest victim still dripping from his white dress shirt has reached the graveyard as dawn breaks. Mark's timing couldn't have been better. As the vampire sinks into his coffin so Mark rises slowly into Harvey's vision with a low moan. The night porter lifts off with a gasp as Mark bangs the desk bell with his fist.

'Dr Death checking in.'

Before Harvey's heart is back on the beat, Mark grabs the comic from his trembling hands, riffling through the pages with evident disgust. 'Studying for a Bachelor of Satanic Arts, Harvey?'

Harvey is visibly shaking, barely able to get the words out.

'You can't stay here no more, Mr Mark. Sorry, but I got my orders.'

'You snitched on me, didn't you? What's even more disgusting is that you did it in the staff latrine.'

Mark spins the hotel register to read the latest entry for that day: 'Alice Honey, Miami, USA, Room 13'.

Harvey's interrupted blood flow is now back on course, along with his usual cringing manner. 'How was I to know Mr Springer was in there?

'Because latrines are Springer's natural habitat.'

He looks back in time to see Ursula slip from the revolving door into the dining room. Harvey, unaware of the pincer movement, is working himself into a lather, sweating and dribbling. 'Every morning the chambermaids come to me complaining about the Phantom Fornicator haunting our unoccupied bedrooms. It got to prey on my mind, Mr Mark. I had to talk to somebody.'

'I know what's preying on your mind, Harvey.'

Mark leans over to a shelf under the desk, lifting out a pile of soft-porn magazines. 'There's the cause of your troubled mind, Harvey. These sperm-speckled pages have overstimulated your imagination.' He dumps them disdainfully on the desk. 'A mind marinated in sex. As dark and dirty as a porno flick house.'

Mark sweeps flamboyantly towards the entrance.

'Adieu, Harvey. The Phantom Fornicator will never again grace the beds of this hotel. Good night to you, sir.'

He pauses at the door to the dining room, where Ursula waits in the darkness. He whispers, 'Room 13.'

She nods and goes to the wall phone.

Mark spins himself out into the night.

*

Harvey has abandoned his horror comic to ponder instead the intricacies of an orgiastic scene in one of the porn mags when the internal phone tinkles.

'Reception.' He listens. 'I'm afraid the kitchen's closed, madam. May I suggest a hot dog? Most guests compliment me on my hot dog.' He casts his eyes lustfully over the glossy pages clutched in his hand. 'Good choice, madam. Mustard or ketchup? Mustard it is. Room 13. One very hot hot dog coming up, madam.'

Replacing the receiver, he punches the air with his fist. 'Right up, madam!'

And hastens to the kitchen.

As the night porter is swallowed by the swing doors, so the revolving one is activated. Mark and Ursula reappear in the foyer simultaneously. She takes his proffered arm and together they move regally towards the sweeping staircase, pausing only for Mark to pluck a key from the unmanned desk.

He chooses Room 12.

Outside Room 13, a pair of woman's patent leather boots await the attention of the hotel bootblack. Tall and black, they are erotic even when unoccupied. Mark's eyes flicker with suppressed excitement as he unlocks the door opposite.

The décor in Room 12 embraces the colour range of an old potato, matching perfectly the dark mood of its occupants. Ursula lies on the bed, listless, still in her winter coat, angry with herself for being there.

Mark furiously goes through his pockets.

'Shit! I could have sworn I had one in this jacket.'

'So forget coitus interruptus. Let's settle for coitus non-startibus.'

Mark stamps into the bathroom. 'It's always been the same with you.' In his top pocket he finds a small toothbrush, which he waters and rubs vigorously into the soap. He contemplates himself in the mirror and calls to her, 'I have a question.'

'So?'

'Why wouldn't you go on the pill?'

'Why wouldn't you have a vasectomy?'

Mark starts to brush his teeth and instantly foams at the mouth. He pauses to wonder if this is the outer representation of the inner madman. Ursula calls from the bedroom, 'Are you going to answer me?'

He wipes the foam away with a towel. 'I might want kids one day.'

'But not by me?'

'I don't know yet.'

'After ten years you don't know yet?'

Mark doesn't reply.

The sound of knocking comes from the corridor. He darts to the door, putting his eye to the security spyhole. Harvey waits outside Room 13 with a hot dog on a silver salver. The night porter blinks in astonishment, as does Mark, when the door flies open to reveal Alice Honey in shimmering white satin. She is tall and slim, perfect in every feature, her nightdress swirling lovingly about the soft curves of her body. The only blemish is the wrinkle of fear playing on her face when she sees Harvey.

'Yes?'

She manages to drag her eyes off his deformed face to the hot dog he holds out to her. The sausage is peeking rudely from inside the bun.

'What the hell is this?'

'My hot dog special, madam.'

Alice laughs nervously. 'Is this some kind of sick joke, or what?'

As she says this, her eyes are back on Harvey's face.

'No, madam. What you see before you is resultant from shell-shock acquired during the Second World War. I answered the call from Sir Winston Churchill to take up arms and defend the world against the Nazi aggressor. And this physiognomy is what I got for my trouble.'

Harvey often spiels this schmaltz in the hope of a gratuity, especially to Americans unfortunate to end up in the Grand Atlantic Hotel. He pushes past her into the room. 'Will madam be taking it in bed?'

Alice, alarmed, doesn't follow him into the room, preferring the safety of the corridor.

'Listen. I didn't order...'

She stops when he reappears, wheezing.

'Also got mustard gas in the lungs, madam.'

'The Germans used mustard gas?'

'No, madam. I was in the Catering Corps.'

He lewdly gyrates his pelvis. 'Is there any other service I can offer you?'

Alice opens her mouth to reply but can only shake her head.

'No words are necessary, Madam. Self-restraint is a virtue I much admire. Goodnight to you.'

Harvey shuffles off, then stops to wag his finger at his crotch. 'Down boy!'

Alice waits for him to round the corner before gratefully closing her door.

*

Ursula and Mark are sitting back-to-back either side of the bed.

No clean break here.

Instead a multiple fracture of pain, misery and anger.

Ursula breaks the silence. 'You got an erection.'

55

'I didn't.'

'I saw it with my own eyes, bulging in your trousers.'

'It was my handkerchief.'

He pulls it out of his pocket.

'That's not what I saw. It was a hard-on. And it didn't have me in mind. We didn't come here to fuck. We came so you could ogle Temple's assistant. You bastard, you wanted to humiliate me.'

'Don't talk bilge, Ursula.'

'Why, of all the rooms in this dump, did you choose the one opposite hers?'

'For Christ's sake, all I want from her is information on the guy who disappeared on the course. Don't you understand? I need that reward.'

Ursula stands.

'Where are you going?'

'Out of range.'

She goes to the bathroom and shuts the door. He stretches out on the bed, closing his eyes. As sleep overtakes him, he hears the muffled sound of Ursula urinating.

*

A shaft of dawn sunlight, harsh as a laser, hits his eyes. They open in confusion. He feels the empty space beside him, then remembers what happened.

Ursula has made sure of that.

She's used a blood-red lipstick to sign off. An erect penis, beautifully drawn, runs the length of the dressing-table mirror. Mark sits up sharply, only to find his reflected image has the penis going in one ear and out the other. On his forehead Ursula has placed numerous lipstick kisses.

'Bitch!'

He rolls off the bed and opens the curtains. A man's dinner suit, so elegant and sexy at night, in daylight always looks tired and tatty. It matches Mark's mood. He tries ineffectively to brush out the creases with his hand. Only then does he see that Ursula had left the room door wide open, leaving a clear view of Alice Honey's boots.

The corridor is deserted.

He crosses to Room 13 and listens.

Silence.

'Alice, baby, only you can get me off the hook.' Picking up a boot, he rubs it against his cheek, whispering, 'Then you can ride me bareback into the sunset.'

He sighs as he returns to his room and shuts the door.

TEN

Sunday morning.

Cold and cloudless.

The SS *Promised Land* wallows gently on the horizon. Several tugs are already alongside and others are making their way towards it. Small figures move about the deck. Two divers roll off a rubber dinghy with a splash into the water.

Snazell lowers his binoculars.

He continues his walk along the esplanade, passing a class of obese men and women struggling with some simple exercises on the beach. Their sweat rains onto the sand. Dogs taking their owners for a walk are in abundance, running, barking, sniffing, hoovering the beach for smells.

The weather shelters are occupied, mostly by the aged staring vacantly into the void. Others avidly absorb the sensational and the sordid from the tabloid newspapers.

All human life is here.

By way of a purgative, a Salvation Army band thumps out hymns in front of the boarded-up amusement arcade. Snazell stops to watch as the major brings 'How Sweet the Name of Jesus Sounds' to a rousing conclusion. He's immediately entranced by a pretty young soldier who looks particularly enticing in her bonnet and pristine uniform, even when blowing spittle from her horn. The other band members lay down their instruments in preparation for the sermon. Waving his Bible angrily at the empty sky, the major raises his voice above the breaking waves.

'Wake, Lord! Why are you asleep?'

Snazell idly wonders whether the Lord takes sedatives. If the litany of horrendous events happening every day is anything to go by, it would seem he's asleep most of the time, if not all of it. He crosses himself and shuffles on to the weather shelter opposite the Grand Atlantic Hotel.

Through the picture windows he can see the waiters laying the tables for lunch. A bin full of breakfast leftovers, crested by congealed fried eggs and undercooked bacon, is wheeled out of sight. Upstairs, along the dark corridors, chambermaids push loaded cleaning trolleys, slowly, like beasts of burden, from bedroom to bedroom. Each room is treated like the scene of a crime, all evidence of the departed occupant is meticulously traced and removed.

Back on the ground floor, the magicians file into the conference centre for their final bonding session. A notice posted on a blackboard announces its theme: 'The Philosophy of Conjuring: Illusion as Reality'. No longer in their penguin suits, they look as lost as fleeced sheep. The magic has vanished – just like Reg Turpin. Reg's sensational disappearance has made it to the front page of every tabloid, and there's much talk among the Brotherhood about firing Mark – preferably from a cannon.

In the lounge, those armchairs in prime positions – meaning those with a view of the sea – are already occupied by the older residents. Among them is the blind and nearly deaf Humphrey Cox. Every morning without fail his wife reads aloud to him, usually from his favourite book, *Alice's Adventures in Wonderland*. Her voice booms across the room and into the foyer, '"In another moment down went Alice after it, never once considering how in the world she was to get out again."'

*

The door to Room 12 eases open.

Mark's head slowly emerges.

He notes that Alice Honey's boots have gone. Cursing himself for having fallen asleep again, he scampers for the fire exit stairs. At the bottom, he moves cautiously through the kitchens into the dining room.

59

A shimmering surface of flat white tablecloths and pirouetting napkins, sparkling glass and silverware, lies between him and the front entrance. Alice Honey suddenly appears from the foyer. They look at each other across the room.

'Breakfast?' she says.

Mark blinks as if checking out a mirage. His mouth opens and shuts like a goldfish before he manages to speak. 'Mark Miles of Mark Miles Intercontinental. You must be Alice Honey. We spoke on the phone. Several times.'

'Well I never. I thought you were a waiter.'

Mark looks sheepishly at his tuxedo. 'On my way to a wedding. A Jewish wedding. My accountant's.'

'A white one, I hope. I love white weddings. Do you have time to join me?'

'I think they may have stopped serving. Let me see what I can do.'

Mark retreats into the kitchen.

Alice sits at a table. She's wearing a sailor suit with pleated white skirt and white stockings. Alice likes crisp uniforms. Before joining the Personal Improvement Institute, she worked as an air hostess, masseuse and dental hygienist. Each of these occupations found her in tight, shapely uniforms that framed her perfectly. The effect this had on men was difficult to ignore, and profoundly influenced her approach to them.

*

Mark has managed to find a breakfast menu as well as a selection of breads in a basket. He now sits with her, seemingly spellbound by the Cupid lips currently engulfing the crescent of a croissant. She studies the menu.

'Are you going to have something?'

'A coffee will do me.' He changes his mind. 'No, a tea.'

'Nothing else?'

'Nothing. Just a coffee.'

'A tea, you mean?'

'Sorry, a tea.'

'Not even a fruit juice?'

'No thanks.'

Lust has invaded his faculties. His cock is running the show.

'No... I'll have a grapefruit juice. And that's it.'

She looks at him, dewy eyed. 'All we need is a waiter.'

'Yes.'

Unable to drag his eyes off her, it takes time for him to realise she's waiting for him to act. Alice expects men to summon waiters. He calls out loudly, 'Service.' And somewhat to his surprise a waitress appears immediately.

'Did you call?'

'Yes, I did.'

'You're too early for lunch, and too late for breakfast.'

Taken aback by her bluntness, Mark reddens. He feels Alice's eyes on him. 'We'll see about that. Get me the manager.'

The waitress retreats into the kitchen.

Alice continues to study him closely. 'Tell me, Mark, do you see yourself as successful?'

'Moderately.'

Alice shakes her head, sadly. 'Moderately? A word we never use.'

'We don't?'

'When I first saw you standing over there...' – she points towards the swings door into the kitchen – '... I saw a follower, not a leader.'

'You did?'

'You should enrol immediately with the PII.'

'I should?'

'Dr Temple can teach you scientifically how to invite and delegate responsibility. How to get people to carry out your orders and instructions willingly. How to handle men and women who make mistakes, who stall, who alibi.'

Mark shows willing, nodding thoughtfully, stroking a brow furrowed in concentration, forcing his eyes to blaze with fervour at each revelation. He desperately tries not to look at her sumptuous blood-red lips, fearing he might be engulfed in a ferment of erotic thoughts about what they could do to him.

Alice is as relentless as a dentist's drill. 'Dr Temple can explain what you must do to deserve confidence, obedience, cooperation, respect.'

Seeming to reach a state of almost unbearable ecstasy, she stops. Mark mumbles pathetically, 'He really is somebody.'

'Somebody?'

'Somebody special.'

'Extra-special.'

'Extra-extra-special. When does he get here?'

'Tomorrow night.'

'So you travel ahead of him and prepare the way? Like John the Baptist.'

That pleases Alice. She looks over his shoulder, prompting him to turn. The waitress is back. 'Harvey wants a word with you, Mr Miles.'

'Tell him to come to my office later.'

'He says it's either a word with you now...' Adding ominously, 'Or he'll have a word with Mr Springer.'

Miles stands and stutters, 'Oh, I see. In that case I had...'

The waitress interrupts, 'He said you'd know what he meant.'

Her eyes suddenly drop to his crotch and widen in astonishment. The crotch of his trousers resembles a bell tent. He drops sharply back into his seat, checking if Alice has noticed. She has, but he needn't have worried. Alice likes to arouse men. Before her, Mark is as helpless as an animal in rut.

'Boy, do you need Hermann.'

Her cute smile is suddenly switched off as she looks past him and gasps. Like a silent movie star, her hands shoot to her face in horror.

Mark turns to find Harvey peering through one of the waiter's windows. He looks even more grotesque than usual. His head, framed in an oval of green-tinted glass, takes on the appearance of a particularly unpleasant toad.

*

Alice hurries from the dining room, followed by Mark.

'I don't want to sound ungrateful but I'm not at all convinced this place is a suitable venue for the Institute.'

She stops in her tracks to let Mark catch up. 'It's full of weirdos. You sure it's not being used as a funny farm.'

'No way.' Mark tries to make light of it. 'The handbooks give it three stars, two crossed forks, a bidet – but no padded cells.'

Alice doesn't laugh.

She moves off at speed for the elevator. Mark joins her, determined to gain entry to her room, and maybe even the lady herself. He'd been encouraged by her reaction to his hard-on.

'Alice, has Dr Temple written any textbooks on how to scientifically influence...?'

She cuts him off. 'Hermann's seminal work is *Power over People: Secret Techniques Revealed*. You wanna buy a copy?'

'Could I?'

'Follow me.'

*

A chambermaid parks her trolley outside Room 13.

According to her clipboard it's occupied.

She notices the door to Room 12, supposedly unoccupied, is wide open, and enters. A howl of delight emerges ahead of the maid herself, calling to her colleague further along the corridor, 'Mildred! He's been at it again.' Further along the corridor the ancient elevator comes to a bumpy halt. Alice exits with Mark tagging behind.

She's humming like a dynamo. 'Say, for example, you went to the same university as a business colleague, and your degree was better than his. Yet when it comes to promotion he gets it, and you don't.'

Mark nods his head and mutters, 'That's too bad.'

'Too right, it's too bad. And when the company president throws a party, who heads the invitation list?'

Mark doesn't reply.

A commotion outside Room 12 has caught his attention. He curses himself for not removing the graffiti from the mirror. No wonder the chambermaids are rolling from wall to wall, holding their sides, screaming with laughter. When they see Alice and Mark approaching, they go quiet and disappear into the room. Alice ignores their stifled laughter as she unlocks her door.

'Did you hear me, Mark? Who heads the president's invitation list?'

'He does,' says Mark.

'Right. He tops the list. Not you. That's when you ask yourself what's he got that you haven't?'

'Bollocks,' whispers one of the maids.

An explosion of bawdy guffaws reaches Mark as he gratefully escapes into Alice's room.

*

It's filled with files, charts, posters, books, all carrying the image of Hermann Temple. As Alice bends to pick up a copy of the great man's seminal book, Mark catches a glimpse of naked thigh above a white stocking.

He visibly starts to shake.

'This book will make even your wildest dreams come true,' says Alice, unaware of the effect she is having on the mad-eyed Mark.

'Oh good,' he mumbles.

She holds the book with a reverence usually accorded the Holy Bible and fixes him with eyes full of spiritual promise. Not surprisingly he interprets this look as more secular than spiritual. Even the book's title – *Power over People* – seems to endorse this impression. She riffles through the opening pages. 'There's a chapter on "How to Unleash a Fantastic Reservoir of Mental Force".'

Mark moves beside her, ostensibly to share in Dr Temple's wisdom. In reality it allows his right hand to hover close to what she would call her butt. He had been driven crazy watching her from behind, moving along the corridor. Each part of her seemed to obsess him – separately. It was time he brought them all together in one glorious coupling.

'The next reveals how to turn that incredible force into action.'

Every chapter seems to Mark like a green light to seduction. His eager hand moves ever closer to her arse. Alice turns more pages. 'Here's another chapter: "Special Techniques on How to get Started".'

His hand lands gently on its destination.

'How to…' She looks sharply at Mark, snapping, 'Take your hand off my derrière right now.' The hand abruptly lifts off and she continues, 'There's a chapter on "Survivalism, Dr Temple's Unique Instant Self-defence System".'

By now Mark is too aroused to realise the significance of this chapter heading. Instead, he foolishly attempts a full-frontal kiss. As he wraps her in his arms, he finds himself unwrapped by an expertly executed throw. She swivels him over her hip and dumps him in a pile of books and photographs.

She towers over him.

'Hermann teaches us body language, Mark. Mine was saying, Don't Touch! Like in museums, right?'

Mark, stunned by his misreading of red for green, peers up at her from among the multiple images of Hermann. His confusion is compounded when she lifts her skirt to reveal a broken suspender. 'Just look what you made me do.'

Mark is only too happy to look. He feasts his eyes on her soft golden thigh, wondering what kind of body language Hermann taught.

Alice starts to rummage in the wardrobe, humming happily as she selects a fresh set of clothes.

Mark gets to his feet. 'Gee, I'm so sorry, Alice. The thermostat on my libido must have malfunctioned.'

'Forget it.'

She disappears into the bathroom, leaving the door ajar.

'I seem to affect some men that way. I don't know why.'

Mark creeps across to the small filing cabinet sitting on the hotel desk. Keeping a sharp eye on the bathroom door, he carries on talking while he begins searching through the folders.

'Could be you're sending out the wrong signals?'

'You think so? I must talk to Hermann about that. He reads me like a book.'

Mark runs a finger down lists of names while she prattles on, 'Hermann calls me Barbie cos I change my clothes a lot.' She laughs. 'My record is twelve times in one day. Do you find that peculiar?'

Mark pauses to contemplate this revelation, and finds it very peculiar. 'Peculiar? Not at all.'

His finger stops at the only name with a gold star beside it, then runs sideways across the adjacent columns. This student came top of the class and was, indeed, awarded an onyx marble mantel clock. His name is Claudio Cross. Mark finds a ballpoint pen to copy his address onto the back of his hand. It tallies with Snazell's account: Nirvana Nous. That done, he treads softly to the door and lets himself out.

Alice comes out of the bathroom in a new costume. Absorbed by her image in the full-length mirror, she doesn't notice that Mark is no longer in the room.

'Hermann likes me to look fresh. He says appearance is everything. Say, aren't you going to be late for that wedding?'

Even the ensuing silence cannot break the one-on-one she is enjoying with herself reflected in the mirror.

ELEVEN

Mark tilts his gleaming Yamaha into a bend: an apocalyptic apparition in his titanium helmet and leathers. The bloody knife embedded in his back flaps ominously as it zooms along the country roads. Bare hedgerows and trees, haystacks, gates, docile cows, farmyards fly by.

He slows at the entrance to an estate. The name of the house is woven into the wrought-iron arch curving above the open gates. Nirvana Nous, on the outskirts of Guildford, is a gloomy, gothic pile at the end of a long drive lined with yew trees. Tennis courts and stables are reflected in his visor as he approaches. Croquet hoops circle the huge lawn island facing the frontage. Fifty or more expensive cars with nail varnish veneers are parked higgledy-piggledy.

*

A liveried butler answers when Mark raps the heavy, sculpted knocker against the iron-studded wooden door. He holds out a hand, assuming it's a delivery, and looks surprised when Mark speaks. 'I've come to see Mrs Cross.'

The butler moves solemnly aside to let him enter, closing the door after him. Without a word he leads him across the marble hallway, pausing only to ring a hand bell. A uniformed maid materialises from behind a portable clothes rail laden with coats, many of them fur.

Mark pats his sweaty hair into place after parting with his helmet.

The girl gives him a cheeky look when he holds out his jacket. She can't resist touching the bloody knife before placing it on a hanger.

The butler speaks for the first time. 'This way.'

Mark follows him past the colossal chimneypiece, through a Norman arch, and along a half-timbered corridor until they reach a door. A Gaelic cross sits in an alcove beside it. The butler steps aside to let Mark enter.

Inside it's as dark and silent as a mausoleum.

Mark freezes as the door closes silently behind him. He panics, wants out; his clammy hands move around the door with all the delicacy of a safe-cracker, but can't find the handle. Deep breaths help to slow his pumping heart before he turns to face the scene before him. The only light comes from the flickering candles posted around a coffin. As his eyes adjust he can see rows of faces, old faces, gargoyles, staring at him.

He's in a small private chapel.

Feeling his way like a blind man, he finds an empty pew, kneels, crosses himself, and respectfully bows his head. No sooner has he settled than a long bony finger reaches from behind to tap his shoulder. Mark is reluctant to face its owner.

When he finally turns, he's confronted by an emaciated skull-face. The bony finger now beckons him back to the door and has no trouble finding the handle. They step out into the corridor.

Until now Mark thought he was dealing with an old man. The short, immaculately parted hair, white shirt and tweed tie had misled him. In the light of the corridor he realises his mistake. The bony finger is attached to an old woman. 'Can I help?'

'I'm sorry to intrude... eh... Mrs Cross.'

'I'm not Mrs Cross.'

'I do apologise. It's just that I have a very delicate errand to...'

He stops when the mourners begin to emerge, having dutifully followed them out of the chapel. Emily Block, the owner of the skull-face, now suddenly engulfed by commiserative embraces, abandons him before leading the way to a sumptuous drawing room. Giant potted palms reach up to a magnificent coffered ceiling. Ancestral portraits line the walls. Leather sofas and armchairs, tables crowded with silver-framed photographs, sideboards and numerous artefacts, fill the space.

Among all these treasures, uniformed waitresses circulate with fancy canapés and champagne.

Mark tags along, accepts a drink, helps himself to the elegant bites, studies the faces of the female mourners. Again, the bony finger finds his shoulder. 'You won't find Mrs Cross here.'

'It's important I speak to her. Maybe I could wait somewhere?'

'Try the cemetery. She'll be there tomorrow.'

Mark's smile dissolves into funereal obsequiousness. 'Oh. Oh, I see. She's dead?'

Block enjoys watching his discomfort. 'Who are you anyway?'

Mark fumbles in a trouser pocket, pulling out Snazell's card and presenting it: *William Snazell. Private Detective. Licensed.*

She studies it. 'I can see you're licensed. To do what? Gatecrash funerals?'

'I'm not William Snazell. I'm his assistant, Mark Miles.'

A waitress approaches with a tray of sushi. 'Can I tempt you, Miss Block?'

Block, intent on the card, waves her away. But not before Mark has grabbed a couple of tuna rolls and stuffed them in his mouth.

'So what brings you here? Apart from the food.'

Mark can't talk. He tries desperately to swallow the rolls while Block watches with obvious distaste. When he eventually speaks, a piece of raw tuna has attached itself to his upper front teeth.

'Mrs Cross employed our agency to...'

Block interrupts with a fury that fans his face. 'No, she didn't! I was her personal assistant for fifteen years. She told me everything.'

'This was rather a delicate matter.' He directs an equally delicate whisper into her ear: 'Concerning her missing husband.'

'Is that so?'

Her head swivels like a gun turret on a battleship until she has a group of mourners in her sights. 'You see that obese fellow over there? The one with a toupee that looks like a dead Pekinese?'

There's no mistaking it.

'That's Commander Jeremy Cross, Royal Navy retired. Her seventh and last husband.'

Mark can't help but be impressed.

'Seventh? I see. She never mentioned that to Mr Snazell.'

'Far from going missing, the commander never strayed far from his wife's booze cupboard and bank account.'

Mark remains optimistic. 'Maybe it was one of her other husbands?'

'Maybe we should sort this out in my office.'

He follows her through a small door set in a lancet arch, up some steps to a long fan-vaulted chamber. Crates of tinned foods are stacked to the ceiling on both sides. Mark takes in the stencilled markings as he passes – Peas, Asparagus, Carrots, Broad Beans, Sardines, Salmon. They draw alongside sacks of flour, sugar, dates and pause by huge bundles of toilet paper.

Block relishes his confusion.

'Mrs Cross was a Mormon. A young American sold it to her on the doorstep like it was a vacuum cleaner.'

She reaches another door and pauses. 'Mormons believe famines will sweep the world before Armageddon and the Second Coming. They stock up with enough canned food to keep the family going for a whole year.'

Block opens the door and resumes their walk. 'In the basement there's a swimming pool filled with Perrier water.'

'Mrs Cross certainly did things in style. May ask how she died?'

'Blew her brains out with an elephant rifle.'

Mark stops in his tracks. 'An elephant rifle? She must have been a big woman.'

'Not so. Just prone to overstatement.'

*

Not surprisingly for a blunt woman unconcerned with the social graces, Emily Block's office is a room dedicated to disorder and dust. Books, papers, hats, dried flowers spill over everything. She sweeps a pile of yellowing newspapers from a beaten-up sofa. 'Sit.'

Mark does as he's told.

'So what's your problem?'

'With Commander Cross, her current husband, not on any missing list, I am wondering who... Claudio Cross is.'

Block fires back without hesitation, 'A gigolo.'

'A gigolo?'

'That's what I said. You know what a gigolo is, don't you?'

'A gigolo using her married name?'

'Draw your own conclusions.'

'Have you any idea where he is?'

'Back in Italy.'

'Is that what the PII told her?'

'Correct. That's when she hit the roof. Literally. Brains all over the bedroom ceiling. The one thing she couldn't take was rejection.'

'What if the PII were lying? What if Claudio Cross didn't go back to Italy?'

'What are you getting at?'

'I think something went seriously wrong on that course. Something involving Claudio. They say he came top of the class and awarded him an onyx marble mantel clock. I don't believe them.'

'So?'

'So Mrs Cross offered us a reward if we could find him. You are obviously unaware of that.

'Did she really?'

'Ten thousand pounds!'

Block's eyes blaze as she reaches for the phone. 'I've seen too many young men like you in this house. Charlatans, snake-oil salesmen, blackmailers, grifters and now a bounty hunter.'

She finishes dialling.

'This call is to the police. I suggest you get the hell out of here before they answer.'

TWELVE

Snazell is back in the shop entrance opposite Mark's office. He's made himself comfortable on bags of garbage, carefully selected from the heap awaiting collection on the pavement. He was tempted to put his trilby on the step to test the charitable instincts of any passers-by, but decided against it.

Nobody passed by anyway.

It was Sunday, and the church further up the road had long since closed. During the holiday season, it's used as a disco. 'Hell' was painted in red above the dripstone, and again on the door. At least the owner had a sense of humour. He needed it. On summer nights the place lived up to its name.

The roar of Mark's Yamaha heralds his return. It turns into the street, coming to rest outside Providence House. Snazell watches as Mark unlocks the front door and waits for him to appear on the third floor.

*

Mark sometimes removes his helmet in front of the mirrored Victorian hatstand immediately inside the door of his office. He likes to observe the image change from hard metallic sheen to soft, vulnerable flesh.

This morning the flesh looks close to death, and for a good reason. The reward he'd banked on has turned out to be a dead end. He has only two days left to get the ten grand. A vision of Wolfgang Amadeus

Mozart beckoning from among billowing clouds keeps emerging from some dark cell in his brain, taking him unawares.

The phone cracks the dream, making him jump. He lets the ancient machine take the strain. It clunks loudly as the greeting cassette stops, and the one for messages starts. Snazell's nasal tones are now being recorded. 'I know you're there, Mr Miles.'

Mark angrily snatches up the receiver.

'Piss off!'

'Don't be like that. I've some good news for you.'

'Not again.'

'Just take a look outside and you'll see what I mean.'

Mark fights to resist but can't help himself. He sidles furtively to the window. There's Snazell on the pavement opposite, holding his cell phone to his ear. He sees Mark and waves the same fat wad of money as before. 'Look! No strings attached. Promise. Two hundred of these is not to be sneezed at.'

He crosses the road in anticipation of the door being released. 'Let me in, there's a good fellow.'

Mark wonders what his game is this time.

*

Snazell bustles into the office. As they talk he noses compulsively into everywhere and everything, lifting, turning, examining like a truffle pig. 'Nice touch that. Paying your last respects to my client.' He hurriedly crosses himself. 'May she rest in peace.'

Mark explodes, 'Mrs Cross wasn't your client. There was no fucking reward, you bastard.'

Snazell winces. 'Language. Language. Remember I'm a practising Mormon. In every respect, except polygamy.'

'Oh yeah? Got a year's supply of canned food, have you? Is your bath full of Perrier water? Or is it Evian? And what about hay for the Four Horsemen of the Apocalypse?'

'Careful, Mr Miles.' Snazell crosses himself. '"Behold, a pale horse: and his name that sat on him was Death," Revelation 6:8. For us believers, death is merely the departure lounge to eternal happiness.'

'And life is the shit you go through to earn enough air miles for that exclusive flight to heaven?'

'In a nutshell.'

'Full of canned food?'

'We need to be plump and healthy, so we can smile while others weep and gnash their teeth.'

He sits at the desk, opens a drawer and sees a ring of keys with a label. 'Office (spare)' is scrawled on it.

Mark has had enough.

'No more games, Snazell. Just piss off.'

'Oh, this no game, Mr Miles.'

Snazell slams the drawer shut, minus the keys, now in the pocket of his raincoat. His sleight of hand would have impressed the magicians now checking out of the Grand Atlantic Hotel. He pulls out the wad of money and starts to count four crisp £50 notes.

'Collect two hundred pounds for entertaining expenses.'

'What entertaining expenses?'

'Cream teas in the English countryside.' Leaving the money on the desk, he crosses to the door. 'Take Miss Honey out for the afternoon. I need to look around her room. OK?'

He closes the door behind him.

Mark goes to the desk, picks up the money and counts it.

'That's a lot of cream teas.'

He shrugs and opens his wallet.

THIRTEEN

With Snazell gone, Mark collapses exhausted on his collapsed sofa.
The two seem made for each other. His efforts to get the reward
from Emily Block, and the late Mrs Cross, had taken it out of him.
Sleep arrives with a nightmare in its wake. In it Mark is a worm
moving among a mass of worms in a can. The can is opened and
a fisherman – looking uncommonly like Hare – peers in. His great
callused fingers reach inside. A fisheye lens distorts the fingers as
they feel around for one special worm. Ignoring all the others, they
finally select him. With great care, he's picked up and taken towards
a barbed fishhook. At this point, Mark rolls off the sofa, sobbing
and crying, as he wriggles to escape. For a while he sits on the floor,
rubbing his eyes like a little boy. This is a recurring nightmare and
Mark knows the source.

*

One night, a long time ago, while on a bad LSD trip, Mark had
found himself watching TV. He was channel-hopping and ended up
with a programme on human procreation. Sperm, tens of thousands
in one ejaculation, zoomed into a womb, squirming, dodging, diving,
determined to be the one that survived.

His craziness took a sudden nasty jump, and he became convinced
there was a sperm in his brain. Even while hallucinating he knew this
was unlikely. No, not a sperm, a worm. Yes, there was a worm in his

brain, all our brains. Unseen, it eats away at reality, keeping it at bay, making sure it never disturbs our cosmetic surface.

A huge, rosy apple ballooned into his imagination. Redness filled his mental screen, until a worm's head gnawed its way into sight. He started to cry. Why? Because now there were no longer any worms in apples. The rosy apple with a worm inside, once the perfect metaphor for human imperfection, was a thing of the past. Supermarkets had managed the final solution for worms. All this nonsense made sense when he was out of his skull and should have been forgotten by morning. But it wasn't. Deep down he knew the worm was still there.

Doing its job.

After all, it's well known we can't take too much reality.

No wonder it was an apple Eve got to bite in the Garden of Eden. That was the Original Sin. She had swallowed a worm; that's how it got into our brains.

Eureka!

*

'Eureka!' murmurs Mark to himself, having escaped the nightmare, and barks a bitter laugh. He wipes away the tears and crosses to the hatstand. In its faded mirror he reflects on his reflection, before shaking his head violently, trying to dislodge the flashback from his brain.

No such luck.

FOURTEEN

Mark passes Snazell as he reaches the Grand Atlantic. The detective is on the esplanade, feeding bread to some particularly vicious-looking seagulls. They exchange glances and Snazell smiles, knowing his strategy is being executed.

Outside Room 13, Mark wonders how to make his cosmetic surface appear perfect. He roughs up his gelled hair and removes a fleck from his trousers. As he knocks on the door he feels the worm move. Alice calls from inside.

'Who is it?'

'Mark.'

Alice flings the door open. 'Where the hell did you get to?'

'My accountant's wedding? Remember?'

She eyes him suspiciously, but Mark appears to be suitably repentant.

'Alice, I'm here to apologise. I'm sorry about your suspender.'

'No problem.' She lifts her skirt to show him the black lacy replacement. 'Look.'

Mark is only too happy to look, but yet again, lust renders him helpless. Confused, he can't suss whether she's a coquette playing sex games, or just plain dumb. He struggles to regain the initiative. 'Alice, I was wondering if we could try again.'

'Try what again?'

'To be friends. I'd like to show you our beautiful British countryside: green fields, duck ponds, thatched cottages, four-poster beds, cream teas.'

'I never touch cream.'

'Do green fields appeal? Duck ponds? Thatched cottages?'

'Four-poster beds?'

'We could end up in one if you so desire.'

'Forget it, Mark. Run along now, boy. Go take a cold shower. And if you should jerk off with me in mind, I'll sue you for breach of copyright.'

She laughs and slams the door in his face.

*

A bowl of voluptuous red apples stands on the sideboard of the hotel's dining room. Mark spots them as he's about to leave the hotel. They're uniformly perfect in shape. Their redness is evenly spread and unblemished. He selects one and rubs it against his thigh before taking a bite.

Tasteless and pappy.

Even so it opens his eyes to a fresh approach.

*

The door to Room 13 flies open to reveal a smiling Mark.

'Can I tempt you?'

Alice stares at the apple resting on his outstretched hand and is impressed. '"Now the serpent was more subtle than any beast of the field which the Lord God had made." Genesis 3:1. I was brought up on the Good Book. How about you, Mark?'

'"And when the woman saw that the tree was good for food, and that it was pleasant to the eyes, and a tree to be desired to make one wise, she took of the fruit thereof, and did eat." Genesis 3:6.'

The Bible had been drilled into Mark at school. Much to his surprise, it had proved extremely useful in his business dealings, especially when he wanted others to trust him.

'You can trust me, Alice. I've seen the light.'

She looks into his unblinking eyes as intently as a clairvoyant into a glass ball, then impulsively snatches the apple, wraps her red-lipsticked lips about its red skin and takes a large bite.

'Delicious.'

'Like you, Alice.'

He watches her devour the fruit. 'It's Sunday afternoon. Time to transport Hermann Temple's drum majorette away from this hermetically sealed, thermostatically controlled cell that passes for a hotel room. So pull on your star-spangled panties and synthetic jackboots, button back your eagle wings, and fly with me across the green pastures of England to a far-off pagan place.'

Alice holds out the apple core for him to dispose of.

'You have such a cute voice, Mark. It's so English.'

'Would that I were some English knight of old, who, by a daring deed, could win your fair hand.' Adding with a lewd smile, 'And all that comes with it.'

'Now stop that.'

She smiles, and he knows she isn't dumb.

Chivalric shit has done the trick.

The game is on.

*

The Yamaha penetrates the narrow country roads. It corners gracefully, sweeps up hills and under bridges, passes green fields, duck ponds and thatched cottages.

But it's four-poster beds that play on Mark's mind.

With Alice clinging to him like he's a horse on a carousel, he's frantically thinking how to capitalise on their unexpected intimacy. Where to take her? If he was a Bedouin, he could take her to his tent and feed her sweetmeats. A knight of old would ride her into his castle, and raise the drawbridge.

Then he remembers Old Nick.

*

Their leathers creak as they dismount.

Alice looks good in Ursula's gear. He'd retrieved it from his office where it had hung, unused, for years. Even the helmet fitted. They could have been sisters. She shakes her hair into shape and surveys the scene. They are parked at the foot of a hill, with a path winding steeply towards the sea fret that hugs its summit. Distant waves can be heard crashing against the rocks beyond.

'Where now?'

Mark pulls a white handkerchief from his pocket. 'It's a mystery tour. A magical mystery tour.'

'Cut it out, Mark.'

'Trust me.'

'Why should I?'

With a sweep of his arm, he encompasses the craggy peak ahead, and the mist swirling around it. 'Imagine this is Camelot, Alice. A sacred place where virtue and virginity remain forever untarnished.'

She stops him as he tries to blindfold her. 'What are you up to?'

'I'm taking you to see a giant.'

'A giant what?'

'That's the mystery.'

Alice giggles, and the handkerchief flutters like a flag of capitulation as he knots it about her uncertain eyes.

'You're crazy.'

'And single-minded.'

He spins her around as if they were playing blind man's bluff, before taking her hand and leading her up the path like an innocent in a nursery rhyme.

*

William Snazell stops outside Room 13. He checks the empty corridor before inserting a skeleton key into the lock, completing his illicit entry into Alice's boudoir with ease.

Mark should be so lucky.

*

Mark and Alice climb the hill like Jack and Jill. The fog, as damp and clingy as candyfloss, soon swallows them up. Silence envelops them;

even the sound of the waves is lost. Alice shivers and stops in her tracks. A distant, eerie sound penetrates their bubble of silence. It's not a human sound, yet it carries human pain and melancholy with it. Her blindfold swings about in alarm. 'What the hell was that?'

'A foghorn. There's a lighthouse just up the coast.'

She tries to take back her hand, but Mark won't let go.

'Wait. We're nearly there.'

'Nearly where?'

'The giant's lair. A penthouse cave with a pool. A pool the size of the Atlantic Ocean.'

Alice laughs and he leads her on.

'What was the giant's name?'

'Old Nick.'

'How old is Nick?'

'Very. But he'd have lived even longer if he hadn't upset the local goblins.'

'What happened?'

'As you might expect of a giant, Old Nick had an enormous penis, which he would use to taunt them. He was literally a cock swinger.' Mark is grateful she can't see his shifty eyes. 'He would terrorise them, using his meaty member as a pendulum, knocking them over like skittles. His laughter was thunder in their ears, rattling the windows of their little goblin houses. The little goblin men were helpless. Worse, their wives came to mock their little goblin dicks. There was unrest and dissatisfaction in the little goblin world.'

This nonsense delights Alice, now a little girl listening to a fairy tale. 'Something had to be done?'

'Too right. The little goblins had to come up with a big plan. They sent out messengers to all the goblin communities across the land, asking them to convene right here.' They've now reached the top of the hill and can feel the breeze coming off the sea. Mark continues, 'In the summer, Old Nick, after he'd serviced the mermaids in his cave, would come up here where it was cooler, to sleep.'

He hesitates, trying to find the right words.

'Go on,' says Alice impatiently.

'It was the night of the summer solstice, when the goblins, thousands of them, crept up on Old Nick as he slept. Each of them had brought

81

little bed sheets, which they tied together. They swarmed as lightly as ants over the giant, passing the improvised ropes across his chest, legs and hands.'

'Like the Lilliputians.'

'Exactly.'

She was more literate than he'd expected.

'You've read *Gulliver's Travels*?'

'No, silly. I saw the film.'

'Ah.' He remembered it. 'The cartoon film?'

'Animated feature. It was just great.'

It was tasteless and pappy, thought Mark. Much like the apple she'd recently devoured.

'So what happened after they tied him up?'

'They castrated him.'

'They WHAT?'

Mark savours the moment. He hasn't forgotten his own emasculation in her bedroom. 'They cut off his giant cock.'

'Oh my God.'

'And his big balls.'

'Stop it!'

'Old Nick rent the air with a volcanic bellow and died. The goblins, with the help of winches and cranes, stood his penis, still miraculously erect, on its severed end as a memorial to their great victory. Over hundreds of years it has calcified and stands erect to this day.'

With that he whips off her blindfold.

'Meet Old Nick!'

An ancient standing stone towers over Alice. Her jaw drops as her head tilts back to take in its size. She gasps then screams with primal joy.

'Oh my God! Phallic, so phallic.'

She embraces the stone, running her hands up and down the soft yellow lichen. It seems to grow more fulsome the further she looks up to its cap-shaped tip. With the clouds racing in the sky above, it even seems to be steaming.

Mark points her towards a pair of huge round stones on the horizon.

'And those are said to be Old Nick's testicles.'

He can hardly believe their tryst is progressing so smoothly, and so rapidly towards a conjunction he hadn't anticipated even in his most lustful dreams. Even so, he proceeds with caution. 'As might be expected, Old Nick is worshipped as a god of fertility. The fecundity of the local crops and animals is supposed to be dependent on the stone's preservation.'

He pauses, choosing his words with even greater care. 'Maidens still come here after dark, strip naked, and offer themselves to him. Several reliable sources have told me that, by dawn's rising, these maidens always feel replenished, both physically and spiritually. One source actually described the experience as virtual intercourse.'

Alice is so involved with hugging Old Nick's calcified cock, he fears she didn't hear him. He holds his breath and chews his lip, curious to know just how naive she can be.

The answer is very.

'Why don't we stay the night?'

Mark doesn't want to appear too enthusiastic. 'We don't want you catching cold, do we?'

'I never catch colds.'

Mark's smile is like the moon rising.

'So be it. Old Nick will be pleased.'

*

The tiny spot on Mother Earth, now occupied by Mark and Alice, spins into darkness, and a full moon appears to climb in the sky. Owls sound territorial hoots. Rabbits graze the grass, running in and out of their burrows. Determined badgers pass along well-defined tracks.

Alice sits with her back resting against the stone phallus. Mark has positioned himself some way off, anxious not to cause her fear or fright, or even the remotest suspicion of his hopes and desires.

'Mark.'

'Yes.'

'Nothing's happening.'

'You know why?'

'Why?'

'Old Nick won't approach until you strip naked.'

'Are you sure?'

'Absolutely sure. The maiden must be naked and stretched out in supplication.'

He sees Alice stand.

Unfortunately, a bank of cloud, until then scudding unnoticed across the sky, finally reaches the moon and plunges the scene into darkness. Mark muffles his curses. He can see nothing, but he can hear plenty. Alice is removing the leather jumpsuit.

Above him the infuriating cloud seems to be stuck, then suddenly the moon appears in a small gap. Now he can see her laid out on the ground, white as a lily flower on its pad. It's a magical moment but, sadly, a fleeting one. Another cloud quickly skids into place like a blackout curtain. And with it comes the eerie sound that followed them up the path. Now he realises it can't be a foghorn. It's up close, too close, and, while its primal nature is even more clearly evident, it stops before he can locate it.

Silence follows.

This quiet interlude is abruptly breached by Alice moaning, softly at first, but speedily gathering momentum in both volume and pace. Mark can see nothing but darkness. His confusion grows as quickly as Alice's apparent, and unexpected, ecstasy. The culminating mixture of alternating groans and screams sound to him very like she's having an orgasm.

At last the cloud moves away and the moonlight settles like a diaphanous sheet over the writhing Alice. Mark's attention is grabbed, not by this sensual sight, but by the dark shape hovering next to her. He can just make out four cloven hooves glinting in the harsh light. From the curvature of its head Mark deduces that the creature, whatever it is, is quietly grazing the grass. Only when he sees Alice stroke its bowed head is this illusion shattered.

It's not grass it's grazing.

He hears Alice whisper in its ear, 'Oh yes, Old Nick... that was something else.'

Mark leaps to his feet, stamping his grinder boots on the rocky surface like an angry bull, unsure what further action to take. His rage is a weird and incomprehensible combination of blind fury and perverse sexual jealousy. Being cuckolded by a fucking donkey is bad enough, but the idea of that stupid bitch thinking it was Old Nick going down on her is a near-mortal blow. It is he, Mark Miles, who is meant to be standing in for Old Nick. That dickhead giant is his invention and now she's stolen it for her own gratification.

Worse is soon to follow when she strokes its temple and murmurs, 'What beautiful eyebrows you have.'

Not surprisingly, the donkey, too, is now wantonly aroused. It lifts its great beastly head, emits a mournful bray that is a fair impersonation of a foghorn, before dropping onto its haunches and revealing an erection comparable to a roadworker's pneumatic drill. Mark's eyes bulge to the size of gobstoppers when Alice takes it into her hands and attempts a feat that can only be described as spatially impossible.

By now, it's not only the donkey with a pressing need for sexual satisfaction. Mark is also in a state of carnal excitement, and, when it comes to sex he's not a proud man. Taking off like a ballistic missile, he propels himself in the direction of the standing stone, at the base of which the action is happening. His grinder boots carry reflections of the moon in their steel caps as they pound across the rocky terrain.

When it hears Mark's approaching grunts and sees the flinty sparks from the impact of boots on stones, the donkey tries to raise itself. Unfortunately for him, Alice won't let go. This allows Mark time to take a flying leap, landing both boots on the poor creature's testicles.

A howling, hee-hawing bray of agony rends the heavens as the donkey tears itself away from Alice's grip. As her outstretched hands slide down his great penis, the hapless animal has no alternative but to ejaculate. Now the donkey literally doesn't know if it's coming or going. It is, in fact, doing both. Its cloven hooves kick up a cloud of dust as it races away.

If the donkey was confused, now it's Alice's turn. A shadow slides across her now glistening body. She looks up to find, standing over her, a great black blob of beastliness etched by an iridescent white light as it's silhouetted against the moon. She whimpers in bewilderment. If her previous debaucher was Old Nick, who the hell is this? Or was the first beast an impostor and the new arrival the real Old Nick? The sound of a heavy-duty zip fastener focuses her mind.

The blob hovers momentarily like a magic carpet before dropping clumsily upon her. Any planned strategy for a smooth and confident approach is abandoned for a crash landing. Mark pins her arms to the ground and tries to clamp his mouth about her Cupid lips. She wrenches them from his and plunges her gleaming white and perfectly ordered teeth into his nose, at the same time driving her delightful dimpled kneecap hard into his scrotum.

Mark yelps in a strangled falsetto, arms flailing aimlessly, not knowing which to attend to first, his cock or his nose. He staggers to his feet, whereupon Alice resolves his indecision. She punches him on the nose, turning on a gusher of blood. For Mark the moon is switched off, and the stars come out, dancing in his eyes. All he remembers is Alice screaming at him.

'You spoilt everything, you little shit.'

She spots the wilting erection protruding from his leather suit.

'Look at that pathetic thing, that little worm. If you think you can ever take the place of Old Nick, forget it.'

Mark falls to his haunches, groans and rolls over. The bloody knife embossed on his jacket shimmers in the milky light, yet again taking on a reality of its own. The knife appears to have been plunged straight into his back.

Alice is too crazed to notice this.

She, too, takes on another reality.

With donkey semen sliding down her torso, she appears to be melting. Just then another dark cloud, darker than the others, draws a curtain on this tragic final act. As Alice faints, she lands softly on Mark's motionless body, ironically forming a tableau worthy of Romeo and Juliet.

FIFTEEN

Mark's nose is still bleeding when he lets himself into his office. A short, rotund shape is silhouetted against the street lights. It's lying on top of his desk, like a body waiting for a post-mortem. Mark moves cautiously across the room to get a closer look.

It's Snazell.

He's sound asleep, his every contented breath accompanied by a light whistle. Mark barks into his ear, hoping to make him jump, 'How the fuck did you get in here?'

Snazell moves not a muscle; his breathing misses not a beat. He slowly opens one bleary eye. 'I'm a private eye, remember?' The eye focuses on Mark's bloody nose. 'And from the state of your hooter, I can deduce you didn't stick to cream teas.' He winces in fake sympathy. 'Teeth marks, oh dear. Looks like you bit off more than you could chew.' He sits up and swings his short legs off the desk. 'After dark it's a jungle out there.'

'That bitch is a cockteaser!' Mark whimpers, 'She gave me the come-on, so I came on and she got upset.'

'When it comes to reading people, you're obviously dyslexic.'

It is as if Snazell has lit his touchpaper. Mark explodes. He stomps to the door and nearly yanks it off its hinges. 'Fuck off, Snazell. Get the fuck out of my office and my life. You've brought me nothing but trouble.'

'Don't be like that, Mark,' says Snazell, soothingly. 'I bring you good news.' He produces a fat envelope from his raincoat pocket. 'You've won second prize in a tango contest.' The package flies across the room and Mark catches it. 'Collect ten thousand pounds and advance to Hermann Temple's Personal Improvement Institute.'

Money in the hand invariably acts as a calming agent. Mark opens the envelope, removing a stack of notes. 'It takes two to tango, Snazell.'

'You lead, I follow. I need to know exactly what happens on that course. Every detail.'

Mark ponders the stack of £50 notes as Snazell makes to leave. 'That's five thousand for the enrolment fee; the rest is yours. And there'll be another five grand when you're done. That's ten big ones.'

He pauses at the door.

'Plus a free course in "Leadership Dynamics". Come top of the class and you, too, could be the proud owner of an onyx marble mantel clock – with a battery-operated pendulum. Not bad, eh?'

And he's gone.

Mark hesitates.

His fingers dance a jig on the lucre.

But the temptation to keep it evaporates abruptly when the wounded membrane in his nose haemorrhages yet again. Great globules of blood land on the wad of money. This bad omen freaks him out. He rushes to the window, struggling to open it. By the time he prises it up, Snazell is emerging on to the street below.

'You forgot this, Snazell.'

The envelope floats down along with a galaxy of blood drops. It lands at Snazell's feet. He looks up as the blood peppers his face like measles spots.

Mark yells, 'I don't want your blood money.'

He notices a plastic red rose stuck in a dusty jar on the windowsill. It was a promotional gimmick for some long-forgotten, amateur production of Bizet's *Carmen*. He grabs it, reappearing through the window with it clamped in his teeth. Snazell watches in astonishment at this pseudo-flamenco-dancer madman glaring down at him. Wiping his blood-spotted face with a handkerchief, he backs nervously away.

'Go find yourself another tango partner, Snazell.'

The plastic rose flies into the night as he slams the window shut. Snazell and the money are already gone by the time it lands.

SIXTEEN

Next morning Mark sits for two hours in the doctor's reception, waiting for his name to be called. The remaining patients, snivelling and shivering from a flu epidemic that's gripped the town for over a month, are grateful to see him depart, along with the blood-saturated Kleenex protruding from both nostrils.

The doctor looks up impatiently when he enters, wasting not a moment on social niceties.

'You seem to have been bitten.'

'It was a dog.'

'A dog? In that case we'd better give you a rabies jab.'

Mark didn't like the sound of that. 'It was a toy dog.'

'A toy dog, poodle or otherwise, is still a dog.'

'No, I was playing with my nephew's toy. A dog. A toy dog. It barks as well.'

The doctor examines the wound and looks puzzled.

'A toy toy dog gave you these teeth marks?'

'Toys are very realistic nowadays. This one is called Bad Dog.'

'I'm not surprised.'

'It's made in China.'

'So? What's that got to do with it?'

'Nothing. It was just an observation. A lot of Chinese toys had to be recalled from the shops. I think Bad Dog was one of them, but my nephew wouldn't let his go. Can we get back to my nose? If I blow it, or just touch it, it bleeds. And then I can't stop it.'

'Do you pick it?'

'Certainly not.'

'I could cauterise it but that's a bit extreme.'

'Yes, well, we don't want to do anything extreme. After all it's only a nosebleed.'

Mark is beginning to regret coming here.

'I think we should wait. Meanwhile, don't pick it. Let it heal. If you get any more bleeding I suggest you lie down with an ice pack. Hold it against the upper bridge.'

Mark feels for the tip of his nose.

'Not there. The upper bridge. Here.'

The doctor jabs the spot. Blood immediately drips onto Mark's immaculate white shirt, recently hand-washed by his mother.

'Oh, shit!' says the doctor.

*

The Bengal Curry Palace is one of those Indian restaurants that seem to be always empty. Regular passers-by can't help but wonder how it survives, especially with the four motionless waiters permanently staring out the window. They conclude, rightly or wrongly, that it has a late-night clientele who are so drunk they no longer know nor care what they are eating.

This lunchtime, passing locals note with surprise and some sympathy that it has two customers. Snazell and Hare. Both have food-stained white napkins tied around their necks. Their table is covered with numerous different dishes that mysteriously all look the same, each brought by one of the four waiters in strict rotation. Hare shovels onion bhajis into his mouth like they were peas, before starting on a murderous looking extra-hot Madras curry.

'You paying for this?'

'Certainly not,' says Snazell. 'We'll go Dutch.'

'You said fee and fodder on the phone.'

'I was referring to breakfast.'

'You didn't phone until after breakfast.'

'Didn't I? I must have meant breakfast if you had to stay over. Although I hope that won't be necessary.'

Hare shakes his head, puzzled. 'I've never known fear of God needing a top-up so soon.'

'Well, it does. Mr Miles gave me a lot of lip last night. Very uppity he was. You obviously didn't do the job properly last time.' Adding as an aside, 'That's another reason for us going Dutch.'

Hare glares at Snazell, eyes and breath both blazing. It's rare for him to pause while eating, so it must be serious. 'Was that a complaint I heard?'

'Certainly not.'

Snazell finds it hard not to turn away in the face of such hellish fumes. 'God himself couldn't be more fearful than you.'

'It sounded like a complaint to me.'

'It wasn't meant to be.'

'So what was it then?'

'An observation, that's all.'

'But an observation that was a complaint?'

'Look, to show you it wasn't a complaint, I'll pay for this. OK?'

Hare carries on eating before Snazell's offer sinks in. When it does, he summons one of the waiters. 'Hey, Gandhi, I'll have another Madras. And a nan. Oh, and a couple of stuffed chapattis.'

'Would you like mine?' Snazell tries to stem the tide of dishes. 'I've had enough.'

'What is it?'

'Prawn biryani.'

'Don't like prawns, poor little blighters.'

'There were only two in it. I've had them both.'

'Yeah, but they was once in there, swimming around, and that's enough for me.'

He wipes the departing plate of Madras curry with the newly arrived naan. 'So what's this Mark fella been up to that you had to call upon my services again?'

*

Mark is lunching with his mother. Or, strictly speaking, without his mother, since she isn't eating. He tucks hungrily into her meal-on-wheels, which she pretended not to want.

Mrs Miles gave birth to Mark when she was forty. Only one other person knows who the father is and that's the rapist. She'd never seen him before or since, and he'd never been apprehended. Despite Mark's traumatic conception, she dotes on him.

'Is that a bite on your nose?'

'No. I caught it in a filing cabinet.'

'Never did. That's a bite.'

Mark gives up. 'Yes, it's a bite.'

'Was it a woman?'

'Yes.'

'Sometimes I wish you was gay.'

'But I am gay. That's why she bit me.'

She cackles with delight. 'You randy little bastard. You're lucky it was only your nose.' Their maternal relationship is profoundly unhealthy. She then remembers something: 'The hospital people came round last Thursday, looking for Mum's commode. They've only just found out she's dead.'

'After five years?'

'I palmed them off with her Zimmer instead. Just right for your office, wasn't it? That commode? You still pleased with it?'

'P for perfecto.'

*

When Mark returns to Providence House, Fred Snipe the landlord is lurking in the entrance hall. He looks unusually pale, and bites his nails.

'There was man here looking for you.'

'Did you get his name?'

'I did ask.' Snipe savours Mark's transparent anxiety.

'And?'

'He said it was King Kong. Although obviously false, it certainly didn't breach the Trade Descriptions Act.'

'Oh shit, he's big?'

'Very.'

'How was his disposition?'

'Ugly. Like his face.'

'Where is he now?'

'He ran upstairs. I haven't seen him since.'

Mark wants to leave there and then but fate plays yet another random card. His mother's meal-on-wheels begins careering around his intestines and is now threatening to go into reverse. He runs for the stairs and into the communal lavatory on the first floor. Too preoccupied with his own evacuation, he fails to notice the pervading odour of powerful curry and the awful noises coming from the next stall.

A peaceful silence finally descends.

The sound of a dripping cistern adds an almost Zen-like atmosphere to this unlikely location. The occupants of both stalls rest momentarily before drawing their trousers back into place, simultaneously flushing their respective toilets and opening the doors.

Mark glimpses Hare reflected in the mirrors above the washbasins and tries to slam the door shut. Instead an arm, not dissimilar to a hydraulically operated shovel, picks him up and dumps him head first into the very bowl that had only recently carried his waste product. For a moment he fears he's going to follow it.

'You got that ten grand yet?' Hare lifts his dripping head out by the hair.

Mark splutters, 'You said I had three days.'

'It is three days.'

'It's Monday today. The money's due on Thursday.'

'Thursday? Fuck that. We had our little chat on Saturday. That's Saturday, Sunday, Monday. Your three days is up.'

'But that's not three working days. We had our chat on Saturday like you said. So the first day is Monday. That's Monday, Tuesday, Wednesday – the money is due on Thursday.'

'I didn't say three working days. I said three days.' He slaps Mark on the face, punctuating each day with another blow: 'Saturday, Sunday, Monday – that's today. Where is it?'

Mark sits heavily on the toilet seat. 'I haven't got it.' He looks pathetically up at Hare. 'Under normal business practice, it would be three working days.'

'Normal business practice? What's that? Any more lip like that and you'll be round the S-bend into the sewer. Get me?' He bangs him on the head like it was a tent peg. 'OK, I'll give you until noon next Monday. That's a week's extension. But I want an advance right now to cover my expenses.'

'How much?'

'What you got?'

Mark frantically pulls out his wallet. He expects it to be empty as usual, but there are the notes Snazell had given him. He smiles as he hands them over to Hare. 'That's a lot of cream teas.' Then can't resist giving Hare a knowing wink.

'What was that? Cream teas?' Hare grabs him by the throat. 'You calling me a perve? A fucking fairy that hangs around public toilets? Well, think again, sunshine. I'm in here because my lunch took a turn for the worst.'

Mark cringes. 'I never thought you were a fairy. Honestly.'

Hare relaxes his grip, takes the money from his wallet and counts it: 'Two hundred on account.' He laughs. 'No, let's call it interest on the three-day extension I just gave you. Five thousand by noon on Monday, right?'

He strokes Mark's cheek, then gives it a gentle pat.

'A tip for you. Don't ever eat in that Indian on the High Street.

'The Bengal?'

'That's it, the Bengal.'

He then abruptly throws Mark out of the stall, and slams the door shut. 'No more fucking curries for me.' Awesome gurgles and eruptions rebound off the toilet walls. The occupant groans to himself, 'It should change its fucking name from Bengal to Bhopal.'

Mark flees.

*

Monday is not normally known as a day of rest.

But this Monday is an exception. On returning to his office, Mark locks the door, lowers the blinds and rolls out the futon. Before turning in, he shampoos his hair, rubs arnica into his head to ease the bruising, and sticks a plaster on his nose to hide the bite.

As he drifts off into a troubled sleep, he feels his worm move. He's only too happy to let it masticate the memory of his recent unsettling experiences. It feels like it's hard at work. In his dreams, he clings like King Kong, with one paw to the Empire State Building, while with the other paw he picks up Hare and drops him into a sewage plant somewhere in Manhattan. That done, he momentarily surfaces in a clammy sweat, fighting with the futon as if it were an octopus. Then, going under for the last time, instead of drowning in human waste, he is wafted into more sensual realms. He floats towards a huge four-poster bed, filled with silk pillows, on which the naked Alice waits for him. Her peachy legs and arms are bound with silk thongs to the four corners of the bed. Despite her bondage, she gives a welcoming smile. His landing is to be as soft as a dragonfly's.

An ear-shattering, juddering alarm bell goes off as he touches down. He didn't need a flight recorder to recognise the problem. His phone, which is close to his ear, has been activated. Six rings and the answering machine takes over. Mark sinks back into his dream. Soon submerged in the sublime, he is about to enter Alice's dark cave, when he hears Snazell's voice.

'Mr Miles, this is my final offer – ten thousand pounds in cash immediately, five thousand pounds of which is your enrolment for the PII course. With a further five thousand pounds on completion of said course. That means you'll have ten thousand pounds in your grubby hands by next Monday.'

His worm stops munching and listens.

Next Monday! £10,000!

Snazell's words slowly penetrate Mark's consciousness.

He leaps up and grabs the phone.

SEVENTEEN

Tuesday morning.

Rain and wind batter the esplanade. Staff at the Grand Atlantic Hotel struggle to hoist a banner for the Personal Improvement Institute above the entrance. With each gust, the canvas billows like a spinnaker, then dips with a loud crack in an attempt to escape from the hands grappling to hold it.

Mark, huddled under a raincoat and fedora, runs up the steps into the foyer. The plaster across his nose is the only sign of the horrors of yesterday. Refreshed, he knows he has the rather tricky business of placating Alice. He runs through his plan while hanging his wet clothes in the cloakroom.

One of the weekly classes Avril attends is Floral Arrangement. The result is there, for all to see, in the foyer. A huge display, fanned out like a peacock's feathers, sits on the sideboard, alongside piles of leaflets for the numerous local theme parks. Mark waits for the right moment before removing a handful of blooms and rearranging others to fill the gap.

So far so good.

His intention is to present his bouquet discreetly at her door, make abject apologies and suggest they breakfast together.

But fate intends otherwise.

He turns to find Alice descending the stairs, slowly, like a glacier. All hopes of a discreet reconciliation are dashed. It is to be a public performance. A ballet. He runs to her with the flowers held out before him.

'Alice, please forgive me.'

She sweeps around the final bend of the staircase, ignoring him and his bouquet. One delicate hand, with pillar-box-red fingernails, glides along the brass banister. One silver high-heeled slipper follows the other, across the worn carpet leading to the foyer. Mark, still proffering the flowers, follows her, pleading, 'Alice, I made a terrible mistake. It was far too dark to read your body language.'

The hotel porters, having abandoned their efforts to fly the banner, at this moment return to the foyer. Drenched, miserable, clutching the dripping canvas, they are to become the chorus in the drama unravelling before them. Mark has to raise his voice as Alice moves swiftly towards the dining room.

'I honestly thought you wanted me to...' He hesitates, trying to find the right word. He finds them: '... court you.' Desperately seeking some silver lining among the clouds, he continues, 'Thank God for Hermann's Unique Instant Self-Defence System. Without it there's no telling what might have happened. It'll haunt me for the rest of my life, just thinking what might have happened.'

The chorus applauds as Alice sails into the dining room. Mark pursues her. 'I don't want you thinking I'm some kind of flasher...' – he lowers his voice when he sees the room is full – '... going around jerking off in public places, coating the world in semen, abusing, molesting...' The guests, intent on gobbling up their breakfasts, pay little attention to his entrance. Most are hard of hearing, so he needn't have bothered. 'I'm just not like that.'

Alice reaches Table 13 and sits.

Mark hovers, then decides he has no choice but to join her. She acts as if he hasn't, picks up the menu and disappears behind it. The wind howls and the rain smacks against the large picture windows. Mark sees his face reflected in the one behind Alice. Drops of water running down the glass, superimposed on his cheeks, look like tears. It's an image that provides extra motivation for his performance. 'I want to prove myself to you, Alice. I'm going to take your advice. I'm going to enrol with the PII.'

Alice lowers the menu and studies him closely. His eyes are certainly shining with a new intensity. Little does she know that it's £10,000 worth. He takes out 5,000 of them and bangs the wad dramatically on the table.

'My life savings. I withdrew everything I have from the bank on my way here.'

Alice is suspicious. 'Yesterday you tried to rape me, Mark. Twice.'

'I tried to make you, Alice, not rape you. There is a difference.'

'Not in my book, there isn't. You must think we Americans are very gullible.'

'Never.'

'All that crap about Old Nick.'

'It's pagan, like you said. You seemed to relish that.'

Alice blushes. 'I'm not sure we at the PII can help you.'

'Sure you can. On your flyer it says the course turns men into gods.'

'Hang on there, boy. We're not talking pagan here. We're talking strictly Christian.'

'Give me a break, Alice. I'm a wild stallion that needs breaking in. Get Hermann to iron me out. Flatten my pagan tendencies. Make me unnatural.'

Alice wavers.

Mark's challenge is made even more tempting when he adds, '"Joy shall be in heaven over one sinner that repenteth." Luke 15:6.'

That clinches it.

Alice snaps up his enrolment fee.

'We start Friday evening. Dr Temple arrives at five o'clock. All students will form a welcoming committee on the steps of the hotel. I'll leave a registration form for you in reception.'

Mark pours a glass of water and stands his bouquet in it.

'You're as fragrant as any flower, Alice.'

And holds it up for her to smell.

*

Avril is waiting for him in the foyer. She's been watching him and Alice through the waiters' window in the kitchen door. Its bilious green-tinted glass captures her mood exactly.

'Trying to get your leg over that American filly?'

'How dare you suggest such a thing. My relationship with Miss Honey is purely professional. You may remember I'm acting on behalf of the Personal Improvement Institute. I was personally responsible for bringing their business to your hotel.'

Mark dances past her, making for the cloakroom. She follows. He grabs his hat and coat but she blocks his exit. 'You ponce! What's this then?' She handles his crotch. 'A stick of rock?'

'Avril, has anyone ever told you that you've got a one-track mind?'

'Often. Will I see you later at school?'

'Your lust for knowledge is insatiable. What's it tonight?'

'Art History.'

'And tomorrow?'

'Oral French.'

'Oral French? That sounds more promising. Tomorrow it is.'

She moves closer, whispering in his ear, 'What about now?'

Mark is horrified. 'Out of the question. I've got to be in court at ten.'

'A paternity suit?'

'That's not funny, Avril. It's Reg Turpin's inquest.'

Behind her he sees Ace sway from his office into the foyer, clutching his first brandy of the day.

'Cool it. Your beloved husband has just appeared on the horizon, giving another brilliant impersonation of W. C. Fields.' He calls out, 'Morning, Ace.' Then dances past Avril and the bemused hotelier. 'Must fly.'

*

On the esplanade, wind and rain crash and howl against the weather shelter like some demonic force trying to get at Mark. He has Ursula on his mobile. 'But it's urgent, sugar.'

He listens, impatiently tapping the window.

'You have to believe me. It's a matter of life... Ursula, let me finish...' – his voice turns tremulous – '... and death.'

She interrupts again.

'Whose do you think? My death.' He's having difficulty bottling up his frustration. 'What? I've never ever said that before. Please, Urse, you're the only person I can trust.'

Ursula still resists.

'I know… I know… only this time I really need help.'

He smiles into the mobile.

'Sure, baby. Bring the kids.'

EIGHTEEN

Twenty prim little girls in green school uniforms wait to cross the road. Ten pairs of clasped hands are checked by Ursula before she leads the way across to the Coroner's Court. Cars wait impatiently until the last pair of pink legs reaches the safety of the pavement opposite, before roaring on their way. Exhaust fumes belching over such young, unblemished flesh is even more nauseating than usual: a harbinger of the decay and pollution that awaits them in later life.

Ursula puts a finger to her lips and the girlish chatter dies as they file into the public gallery. Jack Dickenson, Ralph Wilder and some of the other hacks who witnessed Turpin's dramatic departure to Davy Jones' Locker are already present. Below, in the court itself, the inquest is under way.

The coroner is a mannish woman in her late fifties. Sporting severely cropped hair, and dressed in a heavy tweed suit and tie, she dominates the proceedings. Mark is surprised to see a wedding ring in place. In the duller moments of the bureaucratic procedure, he fantasises about her marital relationship. He can see her saddling her spouse, mounting him and spurring him on to a painfully pleasurable ejaculation.

Right now, things are far from dull.

Bela Lugosi, bound in a chain, stands in for the missing escapologist, while Mark illuminates the coroner on the events of that fateful morning. The coroner watches intently as Mark snaps a padlock into place.

'And the escapologist expands his torso as the chain is put on?'

'That's correct.' Mark isn't sure how to address her, adding, 'Madam.'

'He then relaxes it when attempting to escape?'

'Right. That way the chain is loosened, and the artist can wriggle out of it.'

'Hopefully.' The coroner's smile is thin.

'Hopefully,' groans Lugosi to himself.

'Mr Miles, this is not necessarily relevant, but is it a special kind of chain that escapologists use?'

Mark meets the steely glint of excitement in her eyes with a look as discreet as a Freemason's handshake. They understand each other. 'No, you can get it in any decent ironmongers. And you can choose any gauge you want, from heavy-duty links to small ones, depending on individual taste.'

'Thank you for that. Presumably the canvas hood you have there goes over his head?'

'It does, indeed. Incidentally, madam, the hood is just a vegetable sack, which you can get from any reputable greengrocer.'

'But not with the Stars and Stripes on one side and the Union Jack on the other?'

'No, that was my idea. We had hoped to take the act to America. The dual image represents the special relationship existing between our two countries.'

'Yes, I must say an escapologist is the perfect icon for that curious relationship. Especially when it's always us British wearing the hood. Would you oblige, Mr Miles?'

Mark pulls the sack over Lugosi's head.

'Thank you. Now, Mr Lugosi, please show us what happens next.'

Lugosi doesn't move.

Mark pats the hood, shouting, 'Off you go, Bela.'

Bela immediately shudders, then writhes, wriggles, tosses and turns, before he finally staggers. A table covered in court papers is sent flying. He drops to the floor and continues his contortions there. The coroner watches in horrified bemusement and intense agitation bordering on sexual arousal.

'It has no bearing on this particular case but are there any women escapologists, Mr Miles?'

'There was one in the north-east. Some years back. I believe she gave it up and became a belly dancer.'

'Really?'

The coroner can't take her eyes off the contortions being executed before her. Ursula and her girls stare, open-mouthed. The hacks snigger. Wilder takes a surreptitious slug from a hip flask before passing it back to Dickenson. Lugosi grunts and groans as he rolls from one end of the court to the other.

'Mr Miles, what drives a person to choose escapology as a career?'

'Reg... Mr Turpin always said it was his form of self-expression.'

'Self-expression?' She shakes her head, obviously nonplussed. 'I'm not sure Mr Lugosi would go along with that.'

She looks down as Lugosi tumbles past her again. Sweat exudes from his every pore. He flaps weakly, like a tired fish just landed. With one superhuman lurch he disappears under a substantial table stacked with files and finally comes to rest.

A court clerk stands to whisper in the coroner's ear. They both look at the clock. Its hands rests on one. The coroner picks up her gavel and brings it down with a bang.

'We'll break for lunch. Please be back in one hour.'

NINETEEN

The Corner Café may not seem an imaginative name, but it is an accurate one. Situated in the same block as the Coroner's Court, it has a sandwich board on the pavement, offering breakfast and lunch at prices so low they beggar belief. They must barely cover the cost of the ingredients. Any doubts as to their quality is confirmed by the burger placed in front of Mark. It looks regurgitated rather than cooked.

He sits at a table with Ursula. The gaggle of chattering girls surrounding them have chosen more wisely, sticking to biscuits rather than the cooked fare. Mark has to raise his voice above the din. 'Can you remember his name?'

'Claud something?' Ursula is more concerned with the chocolate stains appearing on some of the girls' uniforms. 'Charlotte, come here.'

'Not Claud! Claudio. Claudio Cross. Ursula, please pay attention.'

'Look what you've done, Charlotte.' She points at the dark brown stain. 'Go and ask the waitress for some water. And wipe your mouth.' Charlotte looks directly at Mark, pokes out her tiny pink tongue and runs it along her lips. The rim of chocolate is wiped clean. Mark watches, wide-eyed, alarmed at her precocity and his own reaction to it. Something was badly out of kilter today. He'd even started to fancy the coroner.

'Ursula, it's important. If I should disappear while on the course, you must go straight to the police.'

'Why?'

'Why? Claudio Cross went missing on the London one. And hasn't been seen since. That's why. And that's why you have to remember his name.'

'You said he disappeared after the course was over?'

'That's what the PII people say. But I think he died during it and they're covering up. Remember how Rodney and Susan clammed up as soon as I started asking awkward questions?'

'You're being paranoid. Even if Claud what's-his-name did die, why should they cover it up?'

'Because a student popping his clogs during a course is not a good selling point. Especially on a course for personal improvement. Being dead cannot, by any stretch of the imagination, be considered an improvement. And Claud what's-his-name is not Claud anything. He's Claudio Cross.'

He studies the burger in his hands.

'OK, smart-arse, so what have they done with his body?'

Mark takes a bite. His chewing immediately goes into slow motion, then stops. Disgust spreads across his face as he grabs a paper napkin into which he deposits the contents of his mouth.

'Maybe he's being served up somewhere as a beefburger.'

The girls hear this and make gagging noises. Ursula is furious. 'Don't be revolting.' She finishes her coffee. 'I don't want anything to do with this.'

'Ursula, I need you.'

'You don't need anybody, Mark.' She stands. 'I don't want to see you again. Ever.'

'Ursula, please.'

'No, I've had enough.' She looks away to hide the lie. 'Besides, I've met somebody else.'

Mark registers, in quick succession, surprise, uncertainty, distress and lastly, incredulity.

'A man?'

'Yes. I thought I'd try one for a change.'

Charlotte returns with a damp cloth.

'We'll do that back at school. We're going now. Girls!'

Surprised to see tears in Mark's eyes, she plants a condescending kiss on his forehead. 'It's none of my business but I'd stay well clear of that course.' She shoots him a smile for old times' sake. 'Despite your obvious need for personal improvement.'

'I need the money.' He pokes at the evil-looking burger. 'Jesus, it couldn't be any more dangerous than this.'

The waitress moves in to clear the table. 'Anything else?'

'Yes, penicillin.'

It was then that he remembered Lugosi.

TWENTY

Mark arrives back in court as the coroner takes her seat and bangs her gavel. 'The inquest into the disappearance of one Reginald Turpin, Part II.'

The ensuing silence is broken by muffled sobs surfacing from behind the witness stand, followed by the ominous clank of a chain. Lugosi, still in chains and hooded, rolls wearily into the centre of the court for all to see.

'It would seem Mr Lugosi hasn't had lunch.'

Somebody titters in the public gallery.

'Mr Miles, can you account for this oversight?'

Mark turns bright red, stands and stutters, 'I... I... I... forgot him.'

'You forgot him? Really, Mr Miles.'

Mark is tempted to air his theory about worms in the brain but wisely desists. The coroner is an unlikely customer for revelations engendered by the ingestion of hallucinogenic drugs. Instead he says, 'The tragic circumstances of Mr Turpin's departure have severely affected my health. It seems the flow of blood in this artery is intermittent.'

He points to the carotid artery on the left side of his neck.

'I am, in fact, due to have a brain scan to assess any damage.'

His eyes remain resolutely fixed on the coroner to see if she swallows his excuse.

She doesn't.

'Are you suggesting the fate of poor Mr Lugosi was located in those cells temporarily deprived of blood?'

'It's the only explanation I can come up with at the moment.'

Lugosi whimpers and Mark looks at him but does nothing.

'And the location of the key to Mr Lugosi's padlock? Is that in the same cells?'

Mark panics, searching all his pockets. No key. He looks up at the coroner, helpless and close to tears.

'I think you'll find it on the table. Exhibit D, next to where your left hand now rests. But before you use it, Mr Miles, let me say that any further cogitating on the reasons for Mr Turpin's disappearance is pointless. Mr Lugosi has given us a graphic demonstration as to why Mr Turpin is almost certainly still in his trunk at the bottom of the Atlantic Ocean.'

She bangs the gavel.

'Death by misadventure.'

The coroner rises, about to leave. On a sudden impulse she turns back, angrily silencing the court with the gavel. 'I must say the part played by Mr Miles in this sad story is less than pleasing. As my namesake, Cordelia in *King Lear* put it, "That glib and oily art / To speak and purpose not." One can only hope Mr Miles will in future direct his glib and oily art into a more fertile endeavour than providing worthless celebrities for the tabloid press to exploit.'

Mark looks up at the smirking hacks scribbling away in the public gallery. He knows he'll be tomorrow's tabloid fodder. As Cordelia retires to her chambers, Dickenson raises his flask in mock celebration. 'You're toast, Mark.'

Mark flees.

The worm has a lot more work to do.

*

The old adage that today's newspaper is tomorrow's lavatory paper, no longer holds good. Not just because it's now called toilet tissue but because a couple of cute puppy dogs, frolicking with rolls of the stuff on TV, have helped wean us away from the newspaper's traditional secondary function. As a result, they tend to hang around longer than is healthy for those they have traduced.

That's why Mark stayed off the streets for the next two days.

His mother slept on the sofa, leaving her double bed for him to rest up in. The day following the inquest she went out to buy all the papers, local and national. The nationals ignored the story and the tabloids were preoccupied by a millionaire footballer's diminutive penis, as reported by a lap dancer he'd consorted with.

Whilst the local rag did carry a report of Cordelia's hatchet job, it was abbreviated and buried on a back page. The front page, luckily for Mark, carried a story that broke the same day. A prominent town councillor had been arrested for indecent behaviour, ironically enough, in the esplanade's public lavatory.

On the Friday, rested and refreshed, Mark returned to his office and prepared himself for induction into the Personal Improvement Institute.

*

Earlier that Friday morning, Snazell had watched Alice Honey leave her room for breakfast. As before, he let himself in with ease, only this time he had to work fast in case Alice returned or one of the chambermaids arrived. He anticipated that the name tags for the students would be already prepared.

They were.

Displayed on the desk in alphabetical order, it took him no time at all to locate the one for Mark Miles. At the point where the cheap metal chain was attached to the tag itself, he clipped on a microphone no larger than a pinhead. The whole operation took less than a minute before he slipped back into the deserted corridor and returned whence he came.

TWENTY-ONE

A convoy of three liquorice-black Cadillacs with mirror windows glides through a storm that would have impressed even Richard Wagner. Nose to tail, each abnormally stretched, they take an eternity to pass.

Like a funeral cortège.

Pedestrians trapped in doorways, sheltering from the torrential rain, bow their heads out of respect for the dead. Forked lighting reflects in the waterfalls pouring off their roofs. Cannon balls of thunder roll in from the Atlantic.

Hermann Temple and his entourage have hit town.

For Hermann every second of every minute of every hour of every day of every week of every month of every year of his life is, in his own words, power productive. His mind is a thought-processing plant. Like any other commodity – cars, clothes or candy – thoughts equal dollars and dollars equal power.

Simple.

The first two limos carry Temple's assistants.

He sits alone in the third.

Inside, the storm can be seen but not heard, baffled as it is by the pea-green, tightly stuffed upholstery. Temple is talking into a recorder. He has the soft voice of someone who is hard. When he speaks, people listen. His life is a never-ending tapeworm of spiel. Seeking – and finding – inspiration from the deluge outside, he continues his dictation. 'And when they saw Jesus walking on the sea, they were terrified, thinking Him a spirit.'

Lightning briefly illuminates his face.

He nods his approval at the cosmic intervention. 'But He spoke to them straight away, saying, Be of good cheer. It is I. Be not afraid.' He presses pause on the machine, briefly, then releases it. 'And it is I, Hermann Temple who now speaks to you, students of the PII, saying, You, too, will soon be walking on water. Be not afraid. For I am here to take you into the land of milk and honey.'

Again, he pauses before adding, 'And money!'

*

The leading Cadillac carries Hermann Temple's three male assistants. A trio of crew cuts and chiselled heads top the hard, muscular bodies sprawled on the back seat. Rip Kubitschek, Randy McMingus and Biff Paretsky are all ex-US marines. Now they work for a private security company, constantly circling a planet wrapped in America's military might, happily doing the Pentagon's dirty work. It's more fun being freelancers. The bounty is bigger and there are no sheriffs in sight. Another bonus is the occasional cushy tour of duty with the Personal Improvement Institute.

Sucking a can of beer, intent on a porn video, Randy lives up to his name. On the small screen a team of pneumatic women set about each other with simulated enthusiasm that involves a lot of ululating tongues, and not much else. Randy's taste in porn extends only to coupling females. Men screwing discomfit him. Since he's unwilling, or unable, to articulate the reason for this, his buddies have concluded the size of the jocks' cocks undermine him.

For Randy, porn is an addiction. On a recent mission to the Horn of Africa, a drug dealer in the casbah sold him a hot video called *Virgins Only*. The cover showed women in burkas who, when up and running, so to speak, turned out to be rampant Arab faggots. Randy was so disgusted by the ensuing scenes of buggery, he sought out the dealer the very next night and broke his neck. He now deals exclusively with a website back home that barters porn for photos of torture and massacre. As he's taken plenty of those on American bases around the world, Randy now finds himself in porn heaven.

*

The limos float like black bubbles across the countryside, through the towns and villages. Their windows reflect but don't reveal. Their uniformed chauffeurs, dark figures in sealed cabins, are cut off from their human cargo as effectively as an undertaker driving a hearse from the occupant of the coffin behind him.

*

The scene in the second Cadillac would have been very much to Randy's taste. Marjorie Negroponte and Loreen Rutter, two female assistants from the same security company, are locked in a sexual configuration. End to end across the back seat, with Loreen on top. Their various limbs move slowly and in different directions, so they look at first glance like a large crustacean. For Marjorie, this is a first-time experience. After a couple of beers, Loreen had come on to her and young Marjorie was game for anything.

Besides, it was a way of passing the time.

It so happens Loreen and Alice Honey had worked together as cabin staff for American Airlines. When Alice left to become a dental hygienist, Loreen had found employment as a guard for a company running a chain of prisons for women. Only then did she recognise her true sexual orientation and shed the shackles that restrained her. Unfortunately, whilst doing duty on Death Row, the sheriff and his execution party arrived in the early morning to find her and the condemned woman engrossed in a sexual act that involved the electric chair.

One was fired, the other was fried.

Loreen, finding herself out of a job, was a natural for employment in the private-security sector now burgeoning in America. It was pure chance that she had been allocated to the PII contract.

Alice was in for a surprise.

When the muffled groans finally stop and their faces reappear, they smile at each other, knowingly. Marjorie blushes. 'Not a word to Biff?'

'No way, sweetheart.' She kisses her. 'Biff? How the hell did he get a name like that?'

'At high school his nickname was Beef Steak. It got shortened to Biff.'

'Has Biff boffed you yet?'

'No way,' says Marjorie, shocked. 'We're waiting till we get married.'

'Oh yeah? Wise up, sweetheart. Biff's a faggot. That's why he hasn't boffed you.'

'How could he be a fag? He's an ex-marine.'

'Shitloads of marines are fags. All those buddy-buddy macho guys are fags. Look at footballers. All that bending over with their butts stuck in the air like baboons in tight silk pants, right in your face. What do you think they're up to?'

'You're crazy, Loreen.'

'And you're dumb, Marjorie. Biff's a fag name like Tab or Rock.' Loreen can see doubt spreading across the girl's face like poison. 'Sweetheart, Rip told me he's only too happy to fuck Biff's butt when he can't get no woman.'

'Rip said that?'

Loreen nods and looks out of the window. They turn a corner and are suddenly on the edge of the world, tracking past white railings, weather shelters and an angry ocean crashing silently over an esplanade. Out of the other window, Marjorie sees the Grand Atlantic Hotel looming out of the storm, grim and gothic, and is suddenly afraid.

*

Alice Honey addresses the students now gathered in the hotel foyer.

'None of Dr Temple's thoughts go unrecorded.'

Marks chips in, 'You mean like Richard Nixon's?'

Alice ignores him. She's already beginning to regret allowing him on the course. She continues, 'There are microphones in all his cars, notebooks at strategic points in all seven of his residencies, with Formica boards and grease pencils in every shower.' Irritated when some students giggle. 'You'd all do well to emulate Dr Temple's discipline. Ideas are like butterflies. Pin them down immediately or they will flutter away.' She fixes them with a steely look. 'At the end of each day, all Dr Temple's recordings, notepads and Formica boards are collected by his assistants and word-processed throughout the night. For posterity.'

Her cell phone vibrates, then tinkles cheerily.

She connects. 'Thanks Biff. We'll be right out.'

Snapping her mobile shut, she holds up her hands to silence the chattering students. 'Dr Temple's cavalcade is approaching. We'll now congregate outside to form a welcoming committee.'

*

Alice and the students wait under the canopy at the top of the hotel steps. As the convoy draws up they start applauding. Biff is the first out, followed closely by Randy and Rip. It's a well-oiled routine. They're in place as Temple's car reaches poll position, right below the flapping PII canvas banner.

Biff opens the back door, while Randy and Rip both open umbrellas. The wind catches them, snaps their insides out and their well-oiled operation abruptly falters – as does the applause. The two ex-marines now have a fight on their hands. Watching anybody trying to tame an umbrella in a high wind always has comedic potential. Rip and Randy don't disappoint. Up and down, in and out, grunts and groans, spokes in eyes and ears, they battle on, bursting with curses they dare not let out.

Alice douses the laughter stuttering into life among the students with a look from hell, while Biff, rain pouring from his crew cut down to his trainers, watches in horror as his two drenched assistants finally capitulate. All three turn to look into the darkness of the limo's interior.

Temple does not physically emerge, only his voice. '"And Moses stretched out his hand over the sea; and the Lord caused the sea to go back and the waters were divided." Exodus 14:21.'

His soft voice rises in tone. 'Alice, are you there?'

Alice grabs Mark's raincoat from his hands and runs to the open door. A tubby little man emerges, ducks under the sheltering coat and climbs slowly up the steps.

Alice hisses at the stunned students. 'Applaud, you assholes.'

They respond but it's all a bit ragged.

Temple pauses on the top step, turning as if to bless them. 'It is I, Hermann Temple. Be not afraid.'

And disappears inside.

But Mark is afraid.

Randy caught him smiling during his bout with the umbrella and transfixed him with a venomous look.

The worm sat up, ready for action.

Pain was on the horizon.

TWENTY-TWO

When conferences began to replace communities, every seaside resort in the country built a centre for them. These centres, with the greedy fingerprints of local burghers all over them, were inevitably portentous, ugly and in a prime location where nobody could ignore them. Each centre contains as many bars as space will allow. These bars are clustered around halls the size of Valhalla. Here, in these centres, and in the surrounding hotels, politicians and business people get to fuck with each other, fiscally and physically. Conferences make the world go around or, more exactly, give the appearance of making it go around. Like carousels, they tend to end up pretty much where they started.

The conference centre at the Grand Atlantic Hotel had been built three decades earlier on land at the back of the hotel. In a vain attempt to compete with the big resorts, it has attracted only a trickle of conferences from the smaller trade associations. Its two halls have witnessed passionate discourse and extensive debates on, for example, fast-tanning sunbeds, thermoplastic housings, nail extensions, dry cleaning, wedding videos, drain clearance, corrective walking devices, automated garage doors: all manner of services designed to make human life bearable.

Both its halls open onto a communal area which houses a long bar, sofas and armchairs, toilets. Swing doors reveal a long, windowless corridor that links the centre with the hotel itself. Alice leads the party of students from the foyer into this corridor. They automatically form a line, moving two by two into the narrow space. She turns to face them, marching backwards like a drum majorette, chanting, 'I want to be a leader. I want to be a leader.'

The students join in enthusiastically, 'I want to be a leader. I want to be a leader. I want to be a leader.'

Mark is less enthusiastic.

'Come on, Mark, don't be a party pooper,' yells Alice. She's in her element, her face ecstatic, eyes glistening with excitement, the centre of everybody's attention.

'I want to be a leader.'

'I want to be a leader.'

Mark can't believe he's chanting with the rest. Joining in is the easy way out, easier than he expected. He's tempted to break into a goose-step and throw his right arm into a fascist salute, but restrains himself.

Alice's skirt swirls about her shapely legs as she pirouettes to face the swing doors, bursting through them into the communal area of the conference centre.

'I want to be a leader.'

'I want to be a leader.'

The chant swells as the students file past Alice, leaving her to close the doors and lock them. She has to yell for them to halt.

'OK, everybody! Gather round.'

She jumps onto the bar counter with the skill and agility of a professional dancer. Her mother encouraged her to learn tap dance and the bar's Formica surface is tempting. She can't resist. Her high heels click tentatively, sound crisp and she's off. This touching glimpse of a faded dream ends almost as soon as it begins. Twelve steps at most.

Alice kills the applause.

'This is where in the next two days your personalities will be taken apart and rebuilt. When you walk out of here on Sunday, you will be fully equipped to make your dreams come true.' She points to a portable clothes rack on which a line of plastic handbags dangles. 'Each of you take one of those bags and empty yourselves of all personal possessions – cell phones, watches, rings, lipsticks, cigarettes, lighters, everything. There's a pouch with a name card for you to fill in. Any questions?'

A man in his mid-sixties, with a defeated face and thinning hair, speaks up. 'What about cufflinks and collar studs?'

'What about cufflinks and collar studs?'

'Do we take them off or not?'

'Didn't I say all personal possessions? And where's your ID?'

The man takes a plastic name tag with a ribbon attached from his pocket, holding it up so she can read it. 'Wally Straw. Well, Wally, the reason you got an ID in your enrolment package was so the instructors can identify you. Now hang it round your neck like a good boy. And remove your cufflinks and collar stud. OK?' She extends her smile to the whole group. 'We at PII want you to start the course with nothing. Like when you were first born.'

'So we can be born again?'

The question is put by a young man shaped like a beach ball, short and obese, with a smooth ,innocent face.

Alice is pleased with both the question and the fact that his ID hangs from his neck. It shows he's been labelled for his life's journey as Roger Buckle.

'Right on, Roger.'

Buckle is pleased that she's pleased.

Alice claps her hands. 'Listen up, you all. From now on, you do only what you're told to do. Got that?'

The group mumbles as one.

'You won't speak, eat, drink, smoke or leave the classes without permission. If nature calls, hold your hand up. Nobody goes to the bathroom without an instructor, OK?'

Mark is impressed, even excited, by her authority. Her long, svelte legs stand firmly apart, up there on the bar, in a pose much favoured by magazines devoted to dominatrixes.

Alice continues the induction, 'And if any of you witness another student breaking any of these rules, you must instantly report that student to one of our instructors. Got that?'

The students look slyly at each other. Treachery, like joining in, is another easy option. But not for Wally Straw.

'So you want us to become quislings?'

Nobody recognises the word, including Alice, so she ignores him. 'Failure to do so will only bring retribution on you all. Just do what you're told and it'll be a breeze.' She snaps into a tap routine, singing out, 'So let's get this show on the road. The guys will be in the Nelson Hall. She points to the double doors on her right. 'And the girls will be in the Hamilton Hall over there.'

There's more excited applause as she jumps down from the bar.

'We'll get the guys underway first, girls, if that's OK by you?'

'Yes,' the female students reply with one voice.

The men wait sheepishly while Alice unlocks the door to their hall and moves into the dark space beyond. She stops inside, by a bank of light switches, allowing the students to pass. Mark takes up the rear.

'Close the door, please, Mark.'

He does just that, cutting off the shaft of light from the communal lounge. Letting the darkness sink in before she speaks, Alice says in a soft voice, 'Be not afraid.'

There's a loud click and a spotlight is switched on. A pool of light hits a rough wooden crucifix over seven feet high, resting against the stage at the far end of the hall. There's a collective gasp from the students.

Another loud click and a spotlight reveals a large wire cage. Then another finds a hangman's noose dangling from the ceiling. A long pause is followed by several lights coming simultaneously to life, highlighting a coffin placed in the middle of the hall.

But the climax is yet to come.

A strobe light backstage zaps a tacky gold-plated, bejewelled monstrance standing on a pedestal, giving off a spectacular display of shimmering colours. At its centre, in the transparent container which usually carries the consecrated host, is a ghastly painted portrait of Hermann Temple.

Alice's voice follows in the wake of some tentative handclaps. 'I repeat: be not afraid. The props you see before you are simply aids to help you on your journey to a new self.'

A gangly, young nerd with big, black-framed, yellow-tinted spectacles looks up at the crucifix. 'So just hang in there, guys.'

Nervous laughter ripples across a sea of uncertainty, only to be silenced by Alice. 'Cut that out. What's your name?'

The nerd looks at his ID, as if to reassure himself. 'Robin Moore.'

'OK, Robin, no more wisecracks, right?'

'Right.'

Moore bites a thumbnail and turns red.

'The course will start in fifteen minutes. Do any of you want to go to the little boys' room?'

Nobody does.

'Right. Just relax while I go look after the girls. They have a parallel course, which I myself conduct, so you won't be seeing me until it's all over. Good luck to you all.'

Again, the applause is less than enthusiastic.

Mark waits for Alice by the door. 'Will I be seeing you when it's all over?'

'Cut that out, Mark. Forget what happened between us, OK?'

'But nothing did happen.' He tries a small smile. 'Regrettably.'

Alice hisses, 'If you screw things up between me and Hermann...'

Mark is stunned.

'You and Hermann? He's a bit old...'

'Fifty-one is not old.' She's livid.

'Fifty-one?' laughs Mark. 'Are we talking age or waist measurement?'

Alice leans into his face. 'I'll never forgive you for that.'

She slams the door and locks it.

Mark turns to find his fellow students staring at him. The whispered exchange with Alice hadn't gone unnoticed.

Wally Straw speaks for them all. 'So we do have a quisling in our midst.'

Now they all know what that word means.

TWENTY-THREE

Snazell sits in a corner of the lounge bar. His eyes should be on the buxom woman sitting with him, but they aren't. Instead they're watching the three men at the bar, Biff, Rip and Randy. All three seem to have stepped from the pages of a Marvel comic: heads of weathered wood, tall as trees and just as thick. Their raucous laughter even silences the storm raging outside.

Sandra Westby, landlady of the Journey's End, is that buxom woman. Not surprisingly, she's miffed not to have Snazell's undivided attention.

'As you were saying?'

'Was I?'

'About being a Mormon.'

'Oh yes, sorry. Was I telling you about Brigham Young?'

'The one with thirty children and two hundred grandchildren?'

'That's him.' Snazell warms to his subject. 'He said that the only men who become gods, or even the sons of gods, are those who enter into polygamy.'

'Clever sod. What a ruse? Humping for Jesus?'

Another burst of coarse laughter forces her to look around at the men. Her distaste is evident as she quickly turns back.

'That's one place I have no desire to visit.'

'America?'

'How did you guess?'

'Not even Florida?'

'Especially Florida. Friends of mine left Miami airport in a rented car and have never been seen since. It was their first time in America.' She sighs and her wondrous bosom heaves as she adds, 'And their last. What a holiday they had, poor loves. Only been there an hour before they were being fed to the crocs in those Everglades swamps. Anyway, that's what I think happened to them.' Another sigh. 'Sad. They were vegetarians, both of them. Can you believe that? Well, I'll never be crock food, I can tell you.'

Snazell's attention wanders back to the bar.

Two women, Loreen and Marjorie, have joined the three instructors. Sandra Westby, really irritated now, turns to see what's taken precedence over her. The party at the bar raise their bottles of beer in a toast, irritating her even more.

'In my day only babies drank from bottles.'

Snazell doesn't react. He's too engrossed in the scene across the room to notice Sandra furiously gathering up her handbag and coat. 'Well, I'll be off. Next time you ask a lady to join you for a drink I suggest you improve your manners. I must say I'm glad you're no longer staying at my place.' She scans the dowdy lounge. 'This dump is far more suitable for someone as sleazy as you.'

Snazell watches as she sweeps out, her robust legs fighting to find space inside her tight skirt. He laments her departure, muttering, 'Brief but beautiful.'

Calling the waiter, he signs the bill and leaves. He crosses the foyer and wearily climbs the stairs. As he reaches the top, Alice emerges from the conference centre. Biff, his arm around Marjorie, spots Alice crossing the foyer towards the bar. 'Here comes Hermann's little prick-teaser.'

Rip turns to look. 'Shit! The gooks must be in there already.'

Randy, watching Alice, grunts, 'I'd sure like to get it up her.'

'And risk frostbite?' says Biff.

They're still laughing when she enters, unfazed and smiling. Alice likes nothing better than to feel the voltage rise as she enters a room of boys.

That is power.

Leadership dynamics in action.

She approaches the bar. Only then does Loreen recognise her. 'Alice? Alice Humperdinck, as I live and breathe. What the fuck are you doing here?'

Alice tries not to believe her eyes.

Her worm eliminated Loreen years ago, and for good reasons. She and Loreen had crewed many long-haul flights together, wheeled their wheelies across many a concourse and shared many a hotel suite. The freshly metamorphosed Alice Honey has no intention of winding back the clock.

'I'm sorry but I can't place you.'

Loreen sings to her, 'Hump-hump-hump-a-dick! You must remember that?'

'I've no idea what you're talking about.'

'Alice Hump-erdinck?' says Randy, savouring the name.

'Or Alice Honey? Who cares.' Rip bangs the bar. 'What'll you have, Alice?'

'I don't drink alcohol. As you well know, Rip.'

'Try a Virgin Mary? That'll hit the spot,' says Randy.

The instructors laugh uproariously. Alice's smile holds up as she waits for it to recede. 'You weren't called Randy for nothing, Randy. I've briefed both classes. They're all yours, guys.'

She faces Loreen. 'Are you Loreen or Marjorie?'

'I'm Marjorie,' says Marjorie.

'Then you must be Loreen, Loreen.'

She holds out her hand. 'I'm Alice Honey, Vice-President of the Personal Improvement Institute. Dr Temple's assistant. You'll be working with myself and Marjorie in the women's class. We'd better get started.'

'Whatever you say, Alice. You're the boss.'

As Alice leads the way, she can't help but be proud of Hermann's manual. 'Chapter 9: Power to Inspire and Motivate your Subordinates'.

It really works.

Best keep a tight rein on Loreen, though.

Keep the bit tight in her mouth.

TWENTY-FOUR

Students are disposed around the hall like statuary in a park. A blanket of boredom lies over them. Few talk, and then only in whispers. Miles, sitting close to Wally Straw, notices him surreptitiously popping some white pills.

Straw sees Mark watching him.

He whispers, 'I've got a serious heart condition.'

'Really. Why are you here then?'

'My boss suggested it. Reading between the lines, I felt I wouldn't get promotion if I didn't enrol.' He puts the pillbox away. 'Bet the whole thing's a pile of shit.' He looks at his watch, irritated. 'It's meant to start at six. You'd think they'd at least start on time. It costs enough.'

Mark stifles a yawn.

Robin Moore removes his spectacles and rubs his eyes.

Roger Buckle regards his coated tongue in a wall mirror. He nearly bites it off when Biff, Randy and Rip burst through the door assaulting their eardrums with bloodcurdling screams.

Moore drops his spectacles, breaking the left lens.

Biff, blood vessels in his neck near bursting point, yells at them in a frenzy, 'On your feet, motherfuckers.'

The students look at each other with startled eyes, frozen with fear. Mark is the only one to stand, in a slow, incredulous movement.

The three instructors dominate the centre of the hall, slavering like Rottweilers. Randy's eyes are red and bulging with hatred. 'That was fucking pathetic! Whenever we enter the room you jump to attention.'

124

'Erect! Like pricks in a brothel,' screeches Rip.

Biff hasn't stopped running on the spot. 'OK, cunts, arseholes, dickheads, cocksuckers! Is there anybody I've left out? We'll try that again! Only this time, you'd better sharpen up your act. Right?' The instructors jog off in step and in line, leaving the class bewildered and terrified.

Mark's mind-worm curls up, unable to cope.

The prospect is too repellent.

Moore's hands are shaking as he hitches his spectacles behind his ears. The retreating instructors are reflected in his broken lens.

Wally Straw alone is unshaken, thereby endorsing the effectiveness of his medication. 'Ill-mannered louts. Are we going to tolerate this kind of behaviour?'

His question is answered a few seconds later. For when the three instructors stamp back into the room, the whole class, including Straw, come to attention as one man. This time, however, the instructors return as mere outriders.

Hermann Temple follows them in.

Everybody moves aside for him, silently clearing a pathway to the stage. His rubber soles squeak as he mounts the steps to stand beside the monstrance.

'Gentlemen, welcome to the Personal Improvement Institute. I am Dr Hermann Temple. Our training methods are the result of forty years running courses across the Unites States of America. While other courses – let's call them fads – in psychological growth have come and gone, the PII is still at number one. And you know why? Because the foundations of my Institute are strong and resolute and deep, embedded as they are in Christian and military values of leadership. This weekend my senior instructor is ex-marine Biff Paretsky.'

Biff raises his arms like a politician on the stump.

'He will be assisted by Randy McMingus and Rip Kubitschek. Also ex marines. Give them a big hand.'

The class obediently applauds as the instructors swagger among them.

'Which of you is Mark Miles?' Temple's voice is so quiet Mark is uncertain if he heard correctly. And if he did hear correctly, he didn't want to. He's rooted to the spot while a small shudder passes through his body.

'Mark Miles, make yourself known.'

Mark looks to the doors, only to see Rip turn the key and pocket it. There's no escape and nowhere to hide. He tries to speak, but something worse than a frog prevents it. Fear freezes his oesophagus. Instead, he holds up his hand, pathetically, a little schoolboy again.

Temple, on the stage, looks down on him but says nothing. At floor level all three instructors move in on Mark. When Biff comes face to face with him, Mark, close to fainting, is revived by a wave of halitosis. He fights to hold back the bile gathering in his throat. Biff, hoping for some action, looks up at Temple, who shakes his head. 'Later, Biff.'

Frustrated, Biff jogs away while Temple picks up where he left off. 'Our task over the next two days is to rid you people of your hang-ups. Your minds are full to the brim with crap of a negative nature, crap that stops you seeing a clear path to the top.'

Looking across at the crucifix, images of the path to Calvary immediately crowd Mark's quaking mind. Confused, he can't understand why a faith discarded decades ago should suddenly return to haunt him. He can actually feel the crown of thorns pressing into his skull, the blood pouring down his face. He even feels it drip to the floor. He looks down. it's only sweat.

Temple smiles. 'Our course acts like a mental laxative. And like most laxatives, it can be both pleasurable and painful, depending on how constipated you are.'

The students laugh, nervously.

'Now the more observant of you will have noticed unusual props standing around the room.'

While the instructors guffaw, the students only manage a few bleak smiles between them.

'Biff, if you wouldn't mind.'

Biff jogs to the coffin in the centre of the hall, patting it like a friend. 'Take this little fella, for example.' Temple continues, 'There may well be someone in this class who is dead but doesn't know it. A lie-down in here will soon make him realise what it means to be alive. It will spur him on to join in the human race, and more importantly, compete in it. Rip, please.'

Rip crosses to the cage and, running on the spot, points as if it was first prize in a TV quiz show.

Mark reels from the nightmare scenario unfolding before him. Until now, he'd never thought of the human race as a race you actually compete in. No wonder he felt so fucking tired all the time. And now there was this cage. Temple fills them in on its significance. 'Another student may feel he's trapped, penned up, feel that something is stopping him from reaching the top of his game. A spell in there...' He pauses to allow their imaginations full rein.

'Do I have to go on?'

The class remains silent, still contemplating the cage, too stunned to reply. Temple casts his eyes across them, pausing on each face, cold as a camera. He suddenly screams, 'Well, do I? You dummies.'

'No,' the class stutters uncertainly and certainly not as one man.

Randy adds to the growing hysteria, yelling, 'No, SIR!'

'No, SIR,' they yell back.

Temple closes his eyes, bowing his head over hands flattened for prayer. His voice is barely audible. 'Forgive them, O Lord, for they know not...' He pauses to change tack. 'Let me hear that again.'

The class, pleased with itself for not missing his instruction, lifts off as one: 'No, SIR!' Only to be ambushed by the instructors: 'You dickheads!' they bellow in unison.

'No, SIR?' screams Biff.

'Not, no SIR!' screams Randy.

'Yes, SIR!' screams Rip.

'Yes, SIR!' screams the class.

'That's better,' says Temple. He steeples his hands and moves to the crucifix leaning against the stage. 'Then there are those of you who think they're martyrs, think that they're being persecuted, think they're...'

His words are cut off by someone shouting.

He jerks like he's being electrocuted. Nobody has ever before interrupted Temple. Spasms ripple through his body before reaching his eyes, which spin in their sockets, seemingly incapable of accepting the signal from his ears. They finally settle on Wally Straw, whose simmering anger has boiled over.

'This course is a pile of crap.'

Straw turns to Mark for support but Mark will have none of it. He looks at him like he's a leper and tries to escape. Straw catches his arm. 'I told you what it would be, didn't I? A pile of fucking crap.'

Mark shakes himself free as Straw swings around, making for the double doors but not reaching them. The instructors descend on Straw like starving wolves. Mark gets out of their way as they expertly belabour the old man with boots and fists. It's all over in seconds, leaving him groaning on the floor, bloodied and bemused. Such malevolence is beyond his comprehension. Nobody in the class moves. They seem to have stopped breathing. Their bloodless faces, white as snowmen, observe everything and do nothing.

Temple's soft voice insinuates itself into their frozen consciousness. 'Listen, everybody, there's an easy way to get through this course. All you have to do is tell the truth. You know what, though? You won't. You'll lie and take all kinds of punishment and pain before you'll face the truth. Yet that's the secret: telling the truth, the whole truth and nothing but the truth.'

Biff has positioned himself by the bank of light switches. On a cue from Temple he plunges the hall into darkness. Not a speck of light reaches the windowless room.

It's as silent as a tomb.

'Gentlemen, this is your goal.'

Temple's voice cues the strobe light to cut through the blackness. It hits the gaudy monstrance on its plinth, causing it to sparkle and shimmer, scattering iridescent shafts of light across the room, giving it an almost mystical aura. He raises it on high like a priest. 'As each of you reaches that moment of truth you will be allowed to take this ancient Holy Grail into your hands and pass from failure and despair to untold riches and success, to what we at the Institute call the Other Side.'

Rip has activated a CD player. Synthesised violins seep from wall speakers, melding with Temple's oratory into a sugar-sweet aural melange. 'Over there, on the Other Side, you'll be enveloped in a sublime feeling of achievement that'll stay with you for the rest of your life. Over there, all your latent talents will blossom like spring flowers. Over there, you'll have great wealth and good health.'

As Temple returns the monstrance to its pedestal, the strobe light and violins are rudely cut off and the harsh overhead lights snapped on, returning the class to a bleak reality. Wally Straw drags himself into a chair. Blood drips onto his suit.

'If you motherfucking dickheads think passing to the Other Side is easy,' Biff shouts, 'think again.' The marine staff sergeant that he once was still inhabits his body like a voodoo spirit. Nothing and nobody will ever exorcise it.

Temple smiles, glad Biff's on his side. 'Words of wisdom, gentlemen. But then Biff has a way with words. Gentlemen, during the next two days, we're going to turn you into leaders. To do that we first have to unscrew your heads and take a look at what's in there. Then we'll throw away the garbage and reload you with motivation of a more positive nature.' Another smile, even more sickly than the synthesised violins now finally silent, plays on his lips. 'More words, Biff. Please.'

'OK, guys, back this stuff against the walls. Move!'

Randy and Rip enjoy the ensuing bedlam, bellowing, 'Move motherfuckers! Move! Move!'

The class jumps into action, stacking the coffin, crucifix, cage and chairs against the walls. Of all the props only the hangman's rope remains, dangling ominously from the ceiling.

Biff circles the room, supervising the evacuation, while Temple descends from the stage into the space cleared. He moves from student to student, stopping to look at their faces and name tags. 'This space, gentlemen, is known as the Ring. From now on, when I say, "Into the Ring," I want you in here faster than…'

He's interrupted.

'Quicker than crapping in your pants.'

'Thank you, Randy.'

Temple can't hide his distaste for the instructor's simile as he addresses the whole class. 'Do I make myself clear?'

A 'yes' comes loud, clear and as one collective sound.

The meltdown into tyranny is complete.

Mark stands, rigid as a guardsman. Only the occasional shiver differentiates him from a figure in a waxworks. When Temple pauses in front of him, Randy's prediction nearly comes to pass. His bowels are

129

close to evacuation. Temple leans imperceptibly forward and whispers, 'Mr Miles, I'm saving you for later. Something to look forward to. Like after-dinner mints.'

Temple turns away as a distant and muffled sound filters into the hall from across the communal area. From the hall opposite a high-pitched and horribly distressing scream underscores the fear already gripping the class.

Temple smiles. 'It seems like there's some traction on the women's course.'

Nobody laughs.

TWENTY-FIVE

The Ring has already been cleared on the women's course.

Loreen and Marjorie watch as Alice circumambulates it, perusing each student in turn. 'Everything we are doing to you, we are really doing for you. Out of love. Love of freedom and democracy. Love of the individual.'

She pauses to stroke a student's cheek whilst glancing at her name tag. 'That may be hard to understand right now, Lizzy, but once you pass to the Other Side all will become clear.'

Loreen leans in to Marjorie's ear, reminding her of their sexual intimacy in the Cadillac, whispering, 'I'm on the other side already.' They smile conspiratorially as Alice continues, 'Once on the Other Side all the pain, sweat and tears will be forgotten.' She stops in front of a student with blood streaming from her nose.

'Do I make myself clear, Sylvia?'

Sylvia Merton is pitiful.

She no longer even bothers to staunch the blood.

'Did you hear me, Sylvia?'

'I still can't see what I did wrong.'

She bursts into tears.

Alice produces a paper handkerchief and gently wipes the blood and mucous from Sylvia's face. Loreen, watching intently, is incredulous. Her eyes sparkle with excitement as she again whispers to Marjorie, 'Who'd believe it? Alice is on my side, sure as shit.'

Sylvia snivels some more. 'I only asked about society as a whole.

131

Where does society fit into PII thinking? Vis-à-vis its emphasis on the primacy of the individual?' She blows her nose. 'I only asked.'

Alice steps aside, calling sharply to her assistant, 'Loreen!'

'Don't ask! OK?' screams Loreen.

Then smacks Sylvia hard across the face.

Alice winces at the ferocity of the blow.

TWENTY-SIX

Hermann Temple, with surprising agility, spins like a top. He stops abruptly, facing a short, fat man.

'Roger Buckle, into the Ring.'

Buckle hesitates, then jumps forward with alacrity. A puppy dog wagging his tail couldn't be more anxious to please. Mark notices how similar in size and stature the two men are. Maybe that's why Temple chose him. Is it possible this is a manifestation of self-loathing? The idea amuses him. He and the class watch with morbid fascination as Temple stalks around his victim.

'What do you do for a living, Buckle?'

'I'm an insurance agent.'

All three instructors scream in unison, 'SIR!'

'SIR!' screams Buckle.

'Selling insurance is a tough business,' says Temple. 'Competitive. A jungle. Eat or be eaten.'

'Right on,' says Buckle, recognising the scenario.

'SIR!' scream all three instructors.

'SIR!' screams Buckle. He has to swivel to keep his tormentor in sight. Temple's technique turns dangerously soft. 'Tell me, Roger, do you think you'll ever be a millionaire?'

'Doubt it... SIR,' Buckle laughs at the idea.

Temple shakes his head in mock disappointment as he solemnly addresses the class. 'Will you ever be millionaires?'

'Yes, SIR!' they trumpet in unison. Miles and the other students are quick learners when it comes to the truth.

'You know you're trouble, Buckle?'

Buckle doesn't.

'Rigor mortis set in the day you were born.'

Buckle's head is like a nodding dog in the back window of a car. Temple looks to Biff, who picks up his cue with an ear-splitting rant. 'Hey, you dickheads, why the heck are you letting Hermann do all the work around here?'

He pulls up a chair for Temple.

'I'm going to sit this one out,' says Temple, 'and let you guys find out what Buckle's problem is.' He plonks himself dramatically in the chair and crosses his little legs.

The students are confused, suddenly leaderless. They look at one other, not knowing what's expected of them. Randy helps solve their dilemma. 'Ask Buckle questions, you stupid shits. Grill him. Turn him on a spit, you dumb fuckers.'

Mark, seeing a possible way to salvation, is quick to please. 'Why are you so fat, Buckle?'

'It's glandular,' squeals Buckle before adding a tentative, 'sir!'

It's as if Mark has lit a fuse in a box of fireworks. The class explodes with questions. Besides vying for Temple's approval, they actually relish baiting the unfortunate Buckle. It takes them back to those glorious days in the school playground. The first to fire off is Jack Lovett, dowdy, middle-aged and mostly memorable for his cheap toupee. 'You'll never be a millionaire…'

'Like we will!' proclaims the chorus.

'… cos the competition's too tough, isn't it, Buckle?'

'And you're too fucking fat.'

'Isn't it, Buckle?' cry the chorus.

'Course it isn't,' sobs Buckle. He's confused, freaked out, unable to comprehend such ferocious cruelty. That's because his memory is short. Mark would put it down to the worm in his brain. For Buckle, it will have been working overtime all his life.

Robin Moore now closes on the unfortunate Buckle as he backs into a corner. 'Didn't they teach you to compete at school, Buckle? Or didn't they bother with useless fat slobs?'

'I'm not useless,' moans Buckle.

Moore, peering at him through his cracked left lens, is relentless. 'Yes, you are useless.'

'And you're a fat slob.'

The class has followed Moore, mobbing the weeping man on all sides. He cowers, slipping to the floor as Mark leans over him.

'You'll never find out if it's lonely at the top, will you, Buckle?'

He casts a look at Temple for any sign of humour. Not a flicker. His one-liner goes unacknowledged, but not by the class. They laugh.

Laughter is heady stuff.

The students add it to the hysteria that's gripping them.

'Why do you eat so much, Buckle?'

'I don't,' protests Buckle. 'It's glandular.'

The class jeers and mocks Buckle.

Having failed to impress Temple with humour, Mark gets serious. 'We want the facts about your business, Buckle. What about growth? Is your annual turnover up there with the national average, Buckle?'

'Gross, Buckle. Gross National Product,' chants the class.

'Not gross like you, Buckle.'

'Why aren't you lean and hungry, Buckle?'

'Hungry to sell insurance.'

'Everybody wants more and more insurance.'

'Insurance for their homes.'

'Fire insurance.'

'Flood insurance.'

'Personal accident insurance.'

'Insurance for their cars.'

'Their pets.'

'Their holidays.'

'Their pensions.'

'Their health.'

'Their lives.'

Riff gets the nod from Temple and the litany is brought to an abrupt close. 'Stop this crap, you dumb shits. You couldn't find the source of Buckle's problem if it jumped out and bit you in the balls, you stupid pricks.'

The class backs off Buckle in disarray, frustrated like bloodhounds losing the scent of a fox.

Temple jumps up energetically. 'Thank you, Biff.' He takes Buckle by the hand, gently bringing the sad, sniffling wretch to his feet. If Buckle thinks his torment is over, as he appears to, he is sadly mistaken.

Temple has other ideas. 'OK, let me show you how to go about exposing Buckle for what he really is.' He turns to his victim with almost a whisper. 'Roger, your obesity is not glandular.'

Buckle lets go an anguished cry. 'But it is... sir!'

Temple sighs with mock despair. 'OK, if that's how you want to play it, let's have a look at the real Buckle. Take your clothes off.'

Buckle stares at him, not quite believing what he's heard.

Randy confirms that what he thought he heard is actually what he heard. 'Strip, arsehole. Take your fucking clothes off. Now! And make it fast.' Buckle sways, about to faint, recovers and starts to pull his clothes off.

He's not a pretty sight.

But then not many of us are.

TWENTY-SEVEN

A dream we once shared of women making more humane leaders than men remains just that, a dream. And the course under way in the Hamilton Hall only confirms that it was all an illusion.

One chunky student of uncertain age, much made-up and with popping eyes, weeps pitifully. Mascara runs like tribal war paint down her face. Joan Lovett screams in defiance at Alice, who is circling her, a shark sensing blood.

'It's not true.'

'Don't be stubborn, Joan. Throw the reality switch. Let the truth shine out. Your husband's been fucking other women from the beginning. During your honeymoon he was already bed-hopping. His mistress was in the next chalet, remember? OK, so Jack's a respected Presbyterian lay preacher, right? So what? So he's taken the lay in his job description very seriously.'

Joan Lovett blocks her ears, still screaming, 'No. No. No!'

'Yes. Yes. Yes!'

Alice pulls Joan's hands away from her ears, forcing her to listen. 'We have witnesses, Joan. Witnesses who have seen him at it. Bonking on chapel pews across the country, on altars, on his office desk, even on the back seat of the family people carrier.'

She gently lifts Joan's head up, looking into her eyes, eager to find the truth. 'Face the facts, Joan. Jack's cock won't stay in the box. It's spring-loaded through all the seasons. Spring, summer, autumn, winter, suffer the little pussies to come unto me and forbid them not.

137

When it comes to adultery, Jack's an overachiever, Joan.'

She raises her voice to include the whole class.

'Like all men!' Hermann comes to mind. 'They need to be tamed, then kept on a tight leash.'

A good vibes player is Alice.

She has struck a chord that makes the class rise as one woman. Their collective consciousness has been expertly tapped, unleashing instincts as primal as those driving termites to build a hill. The students let go a cheer that would have pleased Nero.

TWENTY-EIGHT

Cheers and derisive laughter also occupy the airwaves in the Nelson Hall. The object of the students' derision is currently in the Ring, sitting on a gold chair. He's Jack Lovett, Joan's husband. Lay preacher and chief clerk in a chartered accountant's office, Jack's reputation as a philanderer, a dowdy Don Juan in crumpled pinstripe, is being parodied by the instructors.

Rip minces up to him. 'Show us your technique, lover boy.'

Lovett looks at him in helpless dismay.

Randy joins in. 'You need an object of desire, don't you, Jack?' His eyes alight on Mark. 'Mark Miles, into the Ring.'

Mark jumps up.

He alone remains spruce and manicured. It's way after midnight. The past six hours have seen all the other students blooded and roughed-up. He is, as Temple promised, clearly being saved for later. Was this the moment for the after-dinner mints? He flicks a glance at Temple sitting against the wall, eyes closed. It didn't look like it.

Randy yells at him, 'Sit on Jack's lap.'

Mark does as he's told, sitting like a ventriloquist's dummy.

'Now show us your technique, cock swinger.'

Lovett puts his arms around Mark; both struggle to hide their disgust. Mark can't take his eyes off the preacher's toupee, which now clings like a baby koala to his right ear. Lovett clumsily begins to unbutton Mark's shirt. The class crowds around the pair, jeering and making obscene gestures.

'Get on with it, darling.'

'Give him a kiss, Casanova.'

'Stick your tongue down his throat.'

A cheer goes up when Lovett adds to the grotesquery by nibbling Mark's ear.

Mark is rigid with revulsion.

His worm can't keep up.

Reality is all too horribly real.

And remorse hovers in the wings.

This pantomime is too close to his own life for comfort. He notices Temple signal Biff to his side and whisper in his ear, before sending him off at the double.

What the fuck are they planning to do now?

Rip interrupts his musing. 'Get on with it, Lovett. Wouldn't you be stroking her crotch by now?'

Lovett grunts in agreement. His right arm slides slowly from Mark's chest to his groin. The class, far from sharing Mark's obvious disgust, exhort the arm to go further.

A command cuts through the din: 'OK, let's stop it right there.'

Temple has cued Randy to bring the class to heel. Temple hates to raise his voice. The students back off, deflated, sheepish, but still sniggering. Smut is in their blood, our blood. Saucy seaside postcards, Christmas pantomimes and end-of-pier comedians made sure of that.

'We don't want to arouse Mr Miles more than we have to.' Temple allows himself a smile.

For once Mark is pleased to hear Hermann's hypnotic voice. He jumps from Lovett's lap. Some students, fickle as ever, congratulate him with pats on the back.

Temple gets Lovett to stand. 'Jack, have you learnt anything from the experience you've just shared with us?'

'Yes, I have, sir.'

'And what is it? What truth about yourself has been unveiled?'

The instructors silently corral the students into the Ring, so that they can symbolically share Jack Lovett's impending metamorphosis.

'Sir,' says Jack, 'just now I realised how Satan tricked me into treating my wife so badly. Sure, the other women were good…' He can't bring himself to say the word.

Randy obliges: 'Fucks!'

Lovett starts to blub and snivel. 'Joan was just as good. Honestly.' Embarrassed, he pulls a white handkerchief from a pocket, waving it loose in order to blow his nose. Temple winces at each rasping honk. Jack goes on. 'By doing this course, Hermann, sir, I've come to understand myself better. The other women meant nothing to me. Nothing.' Jack gives another emphatic honk as if to emphasise the point. 'Except a good fuck.' He looks wistfully at the ceiling, seeming to fondly recollect his numerous dalliances, and starts to blub again.

Mark is surprised to feel a lump in his throat and wonders if it's a cancer. Jack wipes the tears away. 'If only I had redirected my sexual drive into work, rampantly earning money, I wouldn't be the failure I am, bankrupt spiritually and financially. Instead of being a spent force, I'd be a happy, successful man, and my wife and children…' Overcome, he drops to his knees at Temple's feet. His performance banishes the lump in Mark's throat, replacing it with a fear of impending projectile vomiting.

'I'd be a success, Hermann,' says Jack. 'A leader. Like you.'

'Jack, do you really love Joan?'

'Oh yes. Yes!'

Temple brings him to his feet and tentatively binds him in his arms, making sure his mess of a face comes nowhere near his immaculate monogrammed shirt.

'And you'll never betray her again?'

'Never! Never!'

'Then why don't you tell her yourself.'

Temple turns Lovett to face the double doors now open behind him. There stands his devoted wife, her face a waterfall of tears. She's flanked by Alice and Biff.

Temple rests his hands on Jack's heaving shoulders. 'Did you hear what Jack just said, Joan?'

Joan nods.

'Do you believe him, Joan?'

'I do. I do.'

She runs to her husband, takes his head in hands raw red from endless washing-up, and kisses him lasciviously. Her eyes are closed, while Jack's swivel wildly about like a trapped animal, but no matter. The class bursts into spontaneous, respectful applause, emotionally awed by Temple's skill at divining the truth.

Temple, followed by Alice, leads Jack and Joan ceremoniously onto the stage. 'Take hold of this ancient Holy Grail, Jack and Joan, and prepare yourselves to cross to the Other Side.'

Each with a hand clutching the monstrance, they raise it above their heads. Blood, sweat and tears. they look like boxers at the end of a gruelling bout.

'What does it feel like over there?' says Hermann.

'Wondrous,' says Jack.

'Magic,' says Joan.

'Right on,' says Temple. 'Over there, that sublime feeling you now feel will stay with you for the rest of your lives.'

Jack starts to cry, almost certainly motivated by the thought of monogamy for the rest of his life. Joan cradles him in her arms, rocking him. 'There, there, don't cry, Daddy. It's all over. You're better now. We'll be together forever and ever.' At this prospect Jack's tears turn into convulsions. His whole body is racked with terrifying spasms and contractions.

Temple looks alarmed.

Mark can't help himself, calling out loudly in another pathetic attempt to ingratiate himself. '"And when the unclean spirit had torn him, and cried out with a loud voice, he came out of him." Mark 1:26.'

The class applauds.

Temple dislikes sharing the limelight. His eyes flash angrily at this affront to his authority. Especially when Lovett does indeed cry out, with a howl that would raise the dead.

The charismatic leader quickly recovers and goes into the attack. 'Saint Mark – not this heathen Mark, this viper in our midst – says in 1:27, "With authority he even commandeth the unclean spirits and they do obey him."'

Lovett's convulsions stop immediately.

Even Temple can't hide his surprise.

The stunned students, open-mouthed, applaud again, leaving Mark to shrivel before the wave of hate breaking over him, the viper in their midst. Mark wouldn't have dared bandy biblical quotes if he'd known Temple was a telly evangelist until caught on camera with twelve hookers in a Las Vegas hotel. Temple's excuse that they represented the Apostles hadn't washed with subscribers to his ministry.

'Thank you, Hermann,' says Joan.

'Thank you, Hermann,' says Jack. 'And thank you, Joan. Thank you for persuading me to come on this course.' He extricates himself from his wife to face the class. 'She had to force me, you know. I didn't want to come. Just think of that. Missing all this companionship, all this love.'

'Do you want to share that love with us, Jack?'

Randy beckons them both down from the stage. Mark watches, incredulous, as the couple mingle among the students. They appear to be so happy, smiling, embracing each student in turn. When Jack reaches Mark, he claps his head in his hands, eyeball to eyeball.

'Thank you, Mark. Thank you for your positive contribution.'

'My pleasure, Jack.'

Mark looks for a flicker of deceit in Jack's eyes, but there's no life let alone deceit. They're as dead as glass marbles. Jack escapes Mark's penetrating scrutiny by suddenly planting a mushy kiss on his lips.

Temple watches from the stage.

He turns to Alice, whispering, '"Whomsoever I shall kiss, that same is he: hold him fast." Matthew 26:48.'

'Hold him fast, Hermann,' whispers Alice back.

'Your attention please, class,' says Hermann. 'As you will have witnessed, extracting truth is an exhausting business. Like a coal miner working deep below the surface, and in the dark, I periodically have to surface for air and sustenance to refresh my body and mind. So, I am leaving you now for a short break, leaving you in the capable hands of Biff and his boys. Keep the truth coming, Biff.'

The class applauds as he takes Alice by the hand, helping her from the stage. Mark looks across at Jack, his latest date, then at the lovely Alice, and seethes. Life is a bitch.

The students step aside as Hermann and Alice move regally towards the doors. Once there, Temple suddenly stops, remembering something.

He crosses to the cage. Inside crouches Roger Buckle, naked. Temple bends to talk to him. 'How we doing in there, Buckle?'

'Very good, SIR!' Buckle barks back like a soldier on parade. Even more surprisingly, his face is beaming with rude health and happiness, seemingly pleased with its lot.

'Why are you fat, Buckle?'

'Because I eat too much, SIR!'

Biff raises his arms and the students immediately salute Hermann's exposure of the truth with a riotous cheer. They jump up and down like kangaroos, embracing each other, crying crocodile tears. Herd instinct and mass hysteria have finally fused into a deadly concoction.

They are zombies.

'That's more like it, Buckle,' says Temple. 'See how easy it is? Telling the truth?'

'Yes, SIR!'

'You'll eat anything, won't you?'

'Anything, SIR.'

Buckle, thinking his torment is over, prepares to exit the cage.

He's wrong for the second time.

Temple stands aside as Randy returns from the kitchen with a pail of slop. Temple smiles when he sees it. 'Feeding time at the zoo, gentlemen. So, which of you is going to be the keeper?' Temple's eyes pan slowly around the class, deliberately passing Mark, then sadistically whip-panning back to him. 'Into the Ring, Mark Miles.'

Mark reacts as if he's been tossed a hand grenade with the pin out. 'Me?'

Randy holds up the pail to him.

Temple moves closer to Mark. 'Yes, you. Feed him.'

'With that?'

Temple nods.

Mark gags, turning away in disgust. 'I can't do it. Sir.'

His response reverberates around the room, bringing the whole circus to a halt. It's as if a seal has refused to balance a ball on its nose. Temple's face drains white with anger, his mouth and eyes tighten into mean little slits. 'Well, here's an interesting case.' He starts to circle Mark like a lion tamer. 'Mr Miles is in marketing and publicity. He must dish out more lies and garbage than anyone else in this room. Now, he suddenly can't do it no more.'

Randy holds out the pail again.

All eyes are on Mark. He stares back at them in turn, but the students look away one after the other. One starts a slow handclap, others join in until the beat is deafening. Mark goes to take the pail, hesitates, looks into Randy's bleak eyes and capitulates. He holds the slop over Buckle's cage.

He can't bring himself to pour it.

'Are we putting you off, Mark?' says Temple. 'Hey guys, why don't we all shut our eyes so that sneaky Mark can dish it out without anyone seeing?'

The class obeys, giggling and peeking. Yet again they're back in the school playground. Mark checks that all eyelids are firmly shut before shutting down his own.

His worm is already bloated with too much reality.

He slowly pours the disgusting mess over the demented Buckle, who perversely starts to chant, 'I want to be a leader. I want to be a leader. I want to be a leader.'

Mark, hoping it's just a nightmare from which he's just woken, is almost too fearful to reopen his eyes. When he does, he finds Buckle smiling up at him from his cage. Strange how fear of freedom can drive us into the darkest corners. Mark is looking into one such corner.

'Thanks, Mark. That was cool, man,' says Buckle, wiping the slop from his face.

'They're all yours, Biff,' calls Temple from the door.

Alice smiles directly at Mark then closes it behind them.

TWENTY-NINE

The economic viability of the Bengal Curry Palace is still a matter for conjecture. The theory about it filling up with drunks late at night is plainly wrong. Despite being the only place in town serving food after midnight, there are still only two customers. That's two less than the four waiters standing in line by the entrance to the kitchen, watching Hermann and Alice picking suspiciously at their supposed vegetarian dishes.

Hermann was hungry when they left the conference centre, and when Hermann's hungry, Hermann has to eat there and then or Hermann turns even meaner than he normally is. With instant gratification being the rock on which his homeland's economy rests, Hermann feels patriotic each time he bangs his spoon and pusher to demand food.

Alice had warned him against ordering in the hotel, but he'd insisted on ringing for the night porter. The sight of Harvey's face emerging from the darkened Residents' Lounge, where he'd been sleeping, had immediately convinced Hermann they should look elsewhere. It turned out that elsewhere was limited to one restaurant and they were now in it.

Every so often Hermann shakes his puzzled head slowly, sadly trying to grapple with this simple fact. 'In Vegas I could choose from a thousand different restaurants. Italian, French, Spanish, Polish, Cuban, Thai, Chinese, Vietnamese, Japanese – every cuisine in the world is represented there. All open twenty-four hours a day. And that's in the middle of a goddamn desert. What's with this country?'

Alice lifts the silver-plated lid to a recently arrived dish, bending forward to examine it. What she sees doesn't please. 'Waiter.' The waiter at the head of the line peels off while the others move up one place, leaving room at the tail for when he returns. 'Yes, madam.'

'What's that? It looks like meat.'

She pokes her fork into a square object occupying the centre of the dish. A red liquid oozes out. The waiter studies it for some time before coming to a conclusion. 'No, madam. It's beetroot.'

'Beetroot?'

'Curried beetroot. It's a vegetable.'

'I know it's a vegetable.'

'That's right, madam. You ask for vegetable curry. Beetroot is a vegetable.'

'I've never had curried beetroot before.'

'It's a speciality of the house, madam.'

The waiter retreats, taking his place at the back of the line, leaving Alice spooning some of the murky mixture onto her plate.

'I didn't know you lived in Vegas, Hermann. What were you doing there?'

'Working in television.'

'That must have been great. What as?'

'A presenter. Daytime shows.'

'Wow. Why'd you give it up?'

He studies Alice's face before answering, hoping not to jog any unwelcome memories. The sting that caught him cavorting with twelve hookers had been headline news at the time.

'I found the lifestyle too shallow, Alice. I needed to do something deeper.' He fills his mouth with stuffed naan, chewing his way to the next exchange. 'I never thanked you properly for taking care of things in London.'

'That's OK.'

'It was best I didn't stick around.'

She covers his hand with hers. 'I understood. Anyway, it all went off as planned. It's official now: Claudio died in his bed in the hotel, not on the course. The police, the doctor, the relatives – they all bought it.'

'And they took the body back to Italy?'

'He was buried in Rome last week. Full requiem mass. His parents have an ice-cream parlour close to the Vatican. A lot of cardinals go there. They give the parents a blessing and get a free Cornetto. Isn't that cute?'

'Smart, those Catholics. Always have been. Jesus, I wouldn't mind a piece of their operation.' He sighs, then plunges his spoon into the fried rice, after pouring a liquid not unlike axle-fluid over it. Chomping hard, he shakes his head sadly, thinking not of Claudio Cross, but of Sunday collections in Catholic churches around the world. All that cash. He drags his mind back to more pressing matters.

'Alice, something's come up that you should know about.'

'Yes, Hermann?'

'A consortium of Vegas businessmen has approached me to run for political office.'

'But that's wonderful. What office exactly?'

Hermann takes a furtive look at the waiters before whispering, 'The highest.'

Alice catches her breath, and he points a fork at her. 'It's important you say not a word of this to anyone.'

'My lips are sealed.'

Her eyes betray the excitement bubbling inside. She looks deep into Hermann's drawn features and is suddenly concerned. 'You look tired, Hermann.'

'I'm not sleeping too well.'

'Would Valium help?'

'They're addictive.'

'Maybe you need more exercise? Try some press-ups before going to bed.'

Temple puts his hand over hers. 'Only if you agree to make them more interesting.'

Alice's blushes. 'You know I don't like that kind of talk, Hermann.'

'Alice, I'm aching all over for you.'

'And what's the cure for that?'

He mouths the words silently, pathetically.

'That's right. A wedding in white.'

He pleads, 'But you know that's not possible.'

'Get a divorce, Hermann. Until then, it's press-ups without me.'

Temple looks like a burst balloon.

His much-flaunted secret techniques have deserted him on the glacier face of life, leaving Alice unassailed.

THIRTY

Biff sits on the edge of the stage swinging his legs and waving a swagger stick to conduct the music coming over the speakers. A scratched version of 'Rule Britannia' comes to a rousing end. The final chorus amuses him enough to repeat it: '… never, never, shall be slaves.'

He laughs before jumping down. 'You Brits used to have an empire that covered the fucking world. That's when you were top dog, the turbo-arseholes who crapped on everybody.'

'So what the fuck happened?' Randy bellows.

'You blew it, didn't you?' Rip bellows.

Randy and Rip stride among the students, whacking their open palms with swagger sticks, screaming, 'We want fresh, dynamic ideas.'

Biff joins in, 'And fresh, dynamic leaders.'

The class look at each other in confusion. They're a sorry sight with torn clothes, black eyes and blood-spattered faces. Fresh and dynamic? Even their credulity is being stretched. Biff can't help but laugh. 'After we've finished with you guys, you'll be turbo-arseholes again, crapping over…'

A voice from among the students explodes, 'Bullshit! Don't insult us any more with this nonsense.'

The instructors freeze in utter astonishment. Biff is the first to come back to life. 'Who the fuck was that?'

It's Wally Shaw again.

He's had enough and is on his way to the door, yelling as he goes, 'You're right. It was us Brits who started this dumb rat race. And when we dropped the bloody baton, who picked up? You Yanks.' He stops to point at the open-mouthed instructors. 'And you've been running with it ever since. Now you're the turbo-arseholes shitting over everybody.'

All three instructors reach him at the same time.

They grab him as he nears the door, throwing him back into the room. He trips over the cage. Wally points at Buckle cowering inside. 'Look at him! Now tell me life isn't a rat race. This stupid course has confirmed what I've always thought. All our goals are shit, the stuff of madness. Wealth creation, growth rates...'

The instructors catch him again.

He struggles violently, twisting his head from side to side, foiling all attempts to clamp his mouth. 'Ludicrous goals set by power-crazy politicians, bankers, teachers, management consultants, advertising fucking agents...' Randy grabs his hair, pulling back his head sharply but still failing to stop the tirade. 'They've harnessed us like slaves. We're shackled with mortgages, overdrafts, debts as deep as the ocean. They've stolen our souls. That's why we all feel so hollow...'

While Biff and Rip hold him, Randy manages to stuff a handkerchief into his mouth, stemming the flow of unwanted words. Biff quickly addresses the class: 'Gentlemen, you don't know this, but Wally here is a chronic alcoholic. Our token lush.'

Straw grunts and shakes his gagged head.

'Wally knocks our goals because he can't achieve them. He sneers at our ambitions because he can't get it together any more. We've been here just twelve hours and already he's suffering withdrawal symptoms. Poor Wally is hallucinating. Right?'

The brutalised class is numb and struck dumb until Randy and Rip verbally whip them with another volley of abuse.

'Right, SIR!' is their ragged reaction.

'Right,' repeats Biff. 'But this is a good example of our methods working in top gear. What has emerged under stress is Wally's acute paranoia. Right?'

'Right, SIR!'

'He thinks he's been harnessed like a slave, trapped by everyone setting him the wrong goals. Right?'

'Right, SIR.'

'Right. Wally has a persecution complex. And for us that means only one thing!'

Biff enjoys waiting for the awful realisation to sink in.

Mark breaks the eerie silence. 'Not the crucifix, sir?'

'Yes, the crucifix!'

Mark looks around, expecting the class to finally revolt. Fat chance. Randy and Rip raise their swagger sticks and scream, 'The crucifix! Get the crucifix!'

The students obey, dragging the crucifix into the Ring, laying it on the floor. A way is cleared as the traumatised Straw is led meekly to it. The instructors jeer as they insert his arms and legs into the metal clamps.

'See how he likes it?'

'Wally's always wanted to be a martyr.'

'Well, today's his big day.'

Mark can bear it no longer. 'Biff, SIR! You must stop this. I happen to know Wally has a serious heart condition.'

Biff raises his swagger stick to hit him, then stops. Mark is Hermann's meat. Instead, he strikes with words so close to his face that Mark can feel his breath wafting the hairs in his nose. 'You turd. You fucking douchebag. You, Mark, are a two-bit publicist not a goddamn cardiologist. Right?'

'Right, SIR.'

'So shut the fuck up.'

Mark backs off, helping the other students hoist the crucifix. In a scene as bizarre and perverse as any Passion play, they struggle to lift the cross into its mount while Wally moans and shows excruciating pain, mingled with scorn for his tormentors.

Randy looks up at him. 'You asked for it, Wally, and you got what you wanted.' He laughs. 'That's how it works in a world driven by consumer choice. Isn't that right, Wally?' Straw closes his eyes but still manages to smile. This really pisses off Randy. 'You still think you're so fucking superior, don't you?' He plucks the gag from Straw's mouth. 'Well, let's hear from you. What car do you drive, Wally-boy?'

Straw, floating in a painful ecstasy, can only whisper, 'I don't have a car.' Randy turns in triumph to the class. 'Wally-boy doesn't have a car.

How about that? Jesus, Wally, I drive a customised Cadillac. Cost two hundred thousand dollars. Still think you're better than me, Mr Lush? Mr Drunk?'

Straw doesn't answer.

There's no need to.

Instead, he continues to smile in the certain knowledge that it's harder for a rich man to get into the Kingdom of Heaven than a camel to pass through the eye of a needle. Or so he was told at school.

'How much investment capital do you have, Wally?'

'None.'

Again, Randy is triumphant. 'Zilch! Wally has zilch. Well, I'm worth near on half a million dollars, dickhead. Still think you're better than me?' Straw patently does and is about to say so when Randy jams the gag back into his mouth.

'OK, Wally, you stay up there till you're more like the rest of us mortals.'

He goes right up close. 'Listen to me, arsehole. Your ambition has gone fucking AWOL. Absent without leave! Go find it. Find that get-up-and-go spirit you was born with, boy. Then come back down to earth, get your hands dirty, get your nose stuck in the trough.'

Mark thinks he's hallucinating. He shuts his eyes tightly, then opens them again, wide. Straw is still hanging from the cross. He hasn't ascended into heaven, yet.

The class sways with exhaustion.

Wally's crucifixion has taken them to a new level of madness which will, like all the previous levels reached, soon become the norm. The course has unscrewed their heads, just like Temple said.

There's a loud knock on the door.

Biff runs to unlock it, revealing Temple with Alice holding him steady. His complexion is a septic green, not unlike the curried pea puree he'd ordered just two hours ago. Specks of vomit sit on his silk tie.

'Jesus, Hermann, what happened?' asks Biff.

'An Indian meal detonated inside him,' says Alice.

'What you have, boss? Curried suicide bomber?'

Temple is not amused.

He's short on humour, period.

His shifty eyes shift beyond Biff to Buckle in the cage and the kitchen slop congealed on his bare back like a gangrenous tattoo. His green complexion turns greener, marbling with the straining red veins in his face as he fights to control the next rush of vomit.

Biff has a military past that includes incidents of friendly fire, especially against officers. It's a habit that dies hard. He beckons to the assembled class, goggle-eyed at seeing their leader's charisma so badly tarnished. 'See here, everybody, Dr Temple has the shits. Montezuma is having his revenge on Hermann for eating Indian instead of Mexican.'

He puts a buddy-buddy arm around his boss. 'The only thing poor Hermann will be embracing tonight is a shapely latrine bowl.' Alice reddens as the class titters. 'But before he leaves us, you can be sure he wants to say something. He always does. Let's have a big hand for Hermann.'

Rip and Randy leap into action, driving the weary students into a frenzy of applause. Mark notices Alice's eyes on him and joins in, if only to impress her. After all, she has Temple's ear and one day may even have the rest of him.

Temple takes one step into the room and sees Wally Straw hanging in there. A crucifixion is not what his bowels want right now. He staggers and Alice has to hold him up while he speaks. 'Everything we are doing to you, we are really doing for you. Out of love. Love of freedom. Love of democracy and the individual.' Again, he fights back the bile. 'It may not seem like that right now but it will when you pass to the Other Side. Then, and only then, will you fully understand the truth in what I'm saying.'

All three instructors shout in unison to ignite the students into fresh zealotry. Even Mark jumps in the air, shouting loudly, hoping Alice will notice. She smiles but not at him. Temple raises his hand and silence falls like a guillotine. The students fix him with the glazed eyes of the indoctrinated.

'God bless you. Good luck and good night. It's going to be a long one for all of you.'

'Good night, Hermann,' shouts the whole company.

Hermann and Alice dispense a few gracious waves, then exit.

As soon as the door clicks shut, Biff is there with the key, yelling, 'I want everybody into the Ring.'

The students jump to it, falling over themselves in their new-found enthusiasm. Some even seem to relish having the next deviant line of attack revealed, especially those who have already passed to the Other Side. Those who haven't, regard the empty hangman's rope and coffin with apprehension.

'You didn't mean a word of the shit you just gave Hermann, did you? You were just kissing arse, weren't you? You lying, hypocritical motherfuckers. So you want to kiss arse, right?'

Biff rarely smiles but he does now.

'Then kiss each other's. Drop your pants!'

And they do.

THIRTY-ONE

The sun rises above the flat mirror of water.

A crisp, clear dawn breaks over the deserted beach.

The banner for the Institute flaps gently above the hotel entrance. Below it, a cleaning lady sweeps the front steps. In the foyer, another vacuums the stair carpet while a third polishes the brass handrail.

Outside Room 13, Harvey squats on a stool as he polishes Alice's long black boots, quietly humming to himself. He finishes them off, moves to the Empire Suite and a pair of men's brown-and-white two-tone shoes. Picking them up, he holds them alongside Alice's boots, chuckling, 'Didn't know Fred and Ginger was in town.'

The door behind him bursts open.

Temple, dressed in a bathrobe, steps out and grabs his shoes.

'Thank you. They look just great.'

And disappears inside.

Harvey wearily gets to his feet and moves off. As he rounds the corner, Temple's head re-emerges, checks the empty corridor, crosses to the door opposite and knocks tentatively. A sleepy-sounding Alice eventually calls out, 'Who is it?'

'Hermann.'

Twitching and impatient, Temple paces about until Alice opens her door. She looks ravishing in her swirling silk nightdress. 'Hermann, sweetie, you look so much better. Did you have a good night?'

'I didn't sleep. Not a wink.'

'Did you do your press-ups like I said?

'Screw the press-ups, Alice. I couldn't close my eyes without you swimming into my mind.'

'Why, that's just beautiful, darling.'

Temple checks the empty corridor both ways, before whispering, 'I've decided to divorce Tammy.'

Alice leans out, allowing the curves of her body to be more evident as she pecks his cheek. She coos, 'You perfect sweetheart.'

He slides his arm around her waist, still whispering, 'Can I come in now?'

'Stop that, Hermann. We have to wait for you-know-what.' She slips away from his grasp like a bar of fragrant soap in the bath.

'Alice, I'm going to be senile by the time we...'

Alice interrupts, sharply, 'Not if you take cold showers, like I said.'

Another peck on the cheek and her door shuts in his face. Temple is a dog on heat, desperate. He knocks again, whispering loudly, 'If I promise to publicly announce our engagement, will you let me in? Please, Alice.'

The door stays closed.

THIRTY-TWO

The students have no idea a new day has dawned. Deprived of daylight and wristwatches, they have lost all sense of time.

Biff has them now doing press-ups, while Randy and Rip wander, swagger sticks twitching, among their heaving, exhausted bodies. Biff's voice is like the drum on a slave ship: 'Sixty-five, sixty-six, sixty-seven.'

There's a sharp rap on the door.

Biff crosses slowly, still counting as he unlocks it, 'Sixty-eight, sixty-nine.'

Temple is revealed, looking wretched and bad-tempered. He pushes Biff aside and storms into the room. The sight of the class doing press-ups does not improve his mood. He stops at the foot of the crucifix and looks up at the unfortunate Straw. 'Be grateful we forgot the nails, Wally.'

Straw, still with the handkerchief gagging him, groans.

'Only kidding, Wally.'

Temple moves among the students as they painfully struggle to lift their bodies off the floor on weedy white arms. He sneers, 'Up and down! Up and down! Maybe doing press-ups is a metaphor for the ups and downs of life itself? How about that for lateral thinking, everybody?'

The class uses Temple's intervention to collapse into a pulsating layer of flesh, spread across the room, whilst gasping as enthusiastically as possible, 'Too right, sir.'

'Right on, sir.'

'Magic, sir.'

Temple turns back to Straw. 'Up and down, Wally. Up and down.' Seeing the students so demeaned has cheered him up. He even laughs. 'From up there, Wally, you look down on us. And because you look down on us is the very reason why you're up there. It's a conundrum only the good Lord can answer.'

Turning to face the class and looking each in the eye, Temple connives to involve them in his taunting of Straw. 'Shall we see if some miracle has occurred during the night and changed Wally's mind?'

The students nod their approval.

Temple tries to reach the gag in Straw's mouth but finds that he can't reach it; he's too short. Randy obliges. Straw barely moves. His eyes, having retreated to the back of their sockets, are hardly visible.

'Anything to report, Wally?' shouts Randy.

'Anything new to tell us?' asks Temple.

Straw is hardly audible as he croaks through cracked lips, 'Our... goals... are...'

Randy cups an ear to catch every word. 'Our goals are...?'

Everybody waits, craning to hear his every word, as if he were an oracle.

'Are what, Wally?'

Summing all his resources, Straw finally spits out, 'Shit!'

Disappointed groans are hushed as his parched voice rises to a loud rasp. 'Bull... shit!'

Randy quickly stuffs the handkerchief back into Straw's mouth while Temple rounds on the class, fixing them with a look of fury wrapped in a smile. 'OK, not exactly from the Book of Revelations. But we can wait until Wally sees the light, can't we?'

'Yes, sir.'

'So Wally thinks it's bullshit that makes the world go round.' Temple's face pans across the whole pathetic, brutalised class and smiles again. 'Looking at you lot, I'm thinking Wally may be right.'

The students are too tired to laugh.

'Listen to me, all of you. Do you think we kept you up all night just for the fun of it? Or because we're insomniacs?'

Nobody volunteers an answer.

'Are you really too dumb to realise that the more exhausted we make you, the harder it is for you to lie? Easier for the truth to emerge. And that's what we're after. The truth!'

Mark looks around his fellow students and knows his time has come. Temple's ferret eyes settle on him. 'Isn't that right, Mark?'

'Yes, SIR. The truth and nothing but.'

'Get your brown nose out of my arse, Mark, and into the Ring.'

Mark lifts off like a jack-in-the-box. As Temple slowly circles him, he fights to control a twitch that's unexpectedly taken over his right eyelid.

'Marketing is Mark's game, gentlemen. He owns his own company: Mark Miles Intercontinental. With that fancy name, who'd ever believe it's a clapped-out, incompetent outfit that nobody wants anything to do with? But that's what it is. How come you screwed things up so badly, Mark?'

Mark desperately racks his brain for a reason.

Any reason.

'That's a tough one, SIR. Maybe it's because I've been preoccupied with a deep personal problem?'

'What problem?'

Mark's face remains blank as his thoughts scuttle in all directions. Even his overworked worm pauses to watch the mental helter-skelter. A straw drifts past and he clutches it. 'Strong homosexual tendencies, Hermann.'

The instructors correct his familiarity, yelling, 'Cut out that Hermann shit.'

'It's SIR. Remember?'

'SIR!'

'SIR!'

'SIR, asshole.'

Mark winces at the barrage. 'Powerful homosexual tendencies, SIR!'

'You mean you're a faggot?' Temple is taken aback.

'Not yet, sir. That's the problem.'

'You're a closet queen?'

'King, SIR. Closet king. I'm dominant by nature. If I ever did come out, I'd be on top, SIR.'

He knows immediately he's gone too far. Temple nods to Randy, who whacks him with his swagger stick across the face. Mark reels backwards through the ring of students onto the floor, where he is seized by Biff and Rip. They bring him back to face Temple.

'You deal in lies, Mark. That's your job. But in the Ring things are different. In here, we only deal in the truth.'

He addresses the whole class: 'I'll have you know this fake faggot tried to rape our own Alice Honey. And you know where this obscene act happened? On one of your ancient fertility sites.'

The class read Temple correctly, giving him what he wants – a collective gasp! For a moment Mark considers building his defence around the active participation of a donkey. But, after noting the messianic fervour in Temple's eyes, he wisely decides it might just cost him his life. Albeit the crucifix is currently occupied. Instead, he lets Temple do the talking.

'Just think. If Mark Miles had achieved his end and on that particular site, the odds are Miss Honey would have been impregnated. It was only my Unique Instant Self-Defence System that saved her.'

Mark hangs his head in an attempt to show remorse. It was now perfectly clear why Temple had saved him as his after-dinner mint. It was personal. Mark's fingerprints were all over Alice Honey.

'But what is it that makes Mark a rapist? A serial liar? There must be some reason hidden in his psyche. What is it you're hiding from us, Mark?'

Mark's brain is a pinball machine zapping his thoughts everywhere, except into the hole that's his mouth. He looks around, crazy-eyed, and settles for another old chestnut.

'I hate myself, sir.'

'That doesn't surprise me. What form does this hatred take?'

'I don't rightly know, sir. All I know is I hate being myself. So much so I'm always wanting to be somebody else.'

'Like who?'

'Anybody.'

'Just anybody?'

Desperate to ingratiate himself, Mark makes a fatal choice. 'Anybody American, sir.' This was, in fact, the truth. But Mark, as so often before, has to embellish it. 'That's why I'm here on the course, sir. Personal improvement can only mean becoming American.'

Temple steps closer and drills into his eyes.

Mark's sycophancy is so blatant, his unblinking gaze so sincere, Temple weighs his performance with some amusement. 'If that's really what you want, Mark, you'll have to be born again, won't you?'

'Yes, sir. I suppose I will.'

'And to be born again, you first have to die.'

Mark recognises the trap too late.

He looks across at the coffin and shudders.

THIRTY-THREE

A fly buzzes.

Mark first hears it when the instructors stop screwing down the lid. He'd seen flies buzzing around the slop on Roger Buckle. That was to be expected. But what had made this bug-eyed bastard desert the slop to come in here? He tried not to take it personally.

When they'd first manhandled him into the coffin he'd been surprised to find the inside both comfortable and decorative. No wonder Yanks call them caskets. It was lined with fancy white satin and the base mattress was soft and springy. Not that any cadaver would notice. Perversely, we want our deceased loved ones to travel first class, probably for the first time and certainly the last. Funeral directors are, of course, only too happy to wave them goodbye, fluttering extortionate invoices.

The fly lands on his face.

'Oh shit. Why me? Why?'

He weeps, desperately struggling to free his right hand. The satin feels so like a woman's skin that touching it generates an unexpected sensation. A corpse certainly wouldn't feel aroused, but Mark isn't a corpse. He slides his arm with difficulty in the cramped space towards the fly now patrolling his nose. As his hand passes over his erection, he groans, 'Oh God, am I now a necrophiliac?' He tries to discourage it with a whack but there's not enough room to inflict any punishment. Indeed, his pathetic attempt has the opposite effect. It causes it to grow some more.

'For fuck's sake, lie down! Pretend to be dead.'

His fingers finally reach the fly. It hops out of their way, landing on his lips. Mark freaks out in disgust, then whimpers, 'Jesus, what did I do to deserve this?'

The fly lifts off and settles on his eyebrow.

Earlier Mark had impressed the class with his composure while the lid was being closed. He lay still, shut his eyes and thought of Reg Turpin. Where the hell was he now? A conspiracy theory had grown around Reg like a fungus. The tabloids were soon hallucinating on it. Sightings of tattooed men walking out of the sea were being reported from all over the country. The theory espoused was that the stunt had been a ruse for Reg to disappear. Whilst we all want to disappear now and then, Reg, it seems, had more urgent reasons than most. His wife was after a divorce, citing bigamy, while the police were anxious to talk to him on a matter so serious that they, like Reg, were anxious not to talk about it. And, finally, he owed shitloads of money. Mark rues the day he met Reg, his loathsome family and especially that gorilla of a brother-in-law. Because of them he has been literally screwed, and into a coffin to boot. Fate was so goddamn twisted that he was now the escapologist. He recalled Reg's breathing technique and tried to apply it.

At first it worked well.

Then he heard the fly.

If Temple's course was meant to turn men into gods, why did he feel like a piece of shit every time that fucking fly landed? With that thought, his hard-on subsided. Some independent and mysterious law of nature had come into play. He always knew his cock had a life of his own; only now did he realise the truth. Their relationship was a *folie a deux*.

A muffled burst of applause and cheering percolates into the coffin. Mark strains to hear what's happening in the world outside in the hall. He catches the name Buckle shouted by the instructors and assumes Roger's been let out of the cage, naked, red-marked like a barbecued steak. This's a sight he's happy to miss. Another roar suggests Buckle has finally passed to the Other Side. How odd that Temple, when rewarding the truth, should chose a term normally associated with death.

'The ugly truth,' mutters Mark.

His worm nods its head.

Even the fly couldn't spoil the tranquillity that suddenly descends upon him. At least he hadn't paid good money for this bad karma. Now he can hear the class chanting, 'I want to be a leader. I want to be a leader. I want to be a leader.' Those arseholes must have invisible rings in their noses. They can be led anywhere, sink to any depravity and actually pay for the privilege. No wonder tabloid newspapers and reality television are the lifeblood of the nation.

The fly walks into his left nostril.

He snorts like a bull, blowing it out, past his own invisible ring. His face reddens when he remembers the depraved scene with Jack Lovett. Oh my God! He'd let him kiss his neck, caress his chest, stroke his leg. He, too, had cooperated in the depravity. No way had he refused to comply or told Temple and his apes to go fuck themselves. He'd even poured kitchen slop over Buckle. The horrors of the last twenty-four hours were suddenly being regurgitated. They stung like heartburn. But he had stood up for Wally Straw, even if his protest had collapsed as quickly as his recent erection.

How was Wally doing? Wally was the only one who hadn't been hoodwinked by Temple, and for that he was paying a painful price. How did it go? *'Suffered under Pontius Pilate, was crucified, dead, and buried.'* Things remembered by rote tend to come back when the mind is idling. He descended into hell… Why did Christ do that? When hell is right here on earth? But then, once upon a time, so was heaven, until Homo sapiens arrived.

The cheering and jeering coming from the class bring back memories of his last night at the Starlight. He can hear the Solomon Brothers singing 'Signed, Sealed, Delivered'. Those little shits! How their fucking father, the behavioural psychologist, would laugh if he could see him now. Signed, sealed and delivered! Mark smiles as Cyril Hammond drifts into his mind's eye, well pissed, legs like two wobbleboards, then nosediving into the bikers.

Remembering his interview with Cyril makes him laugh out loud. *'So you have this amazing ability for swallowing things? That's right, Mark. I think a lot of people have this ability to swallow things. Even me? Even you, Mark.'*

Cyril's answer brings William Snazell into sharp focus.

He'd swallowed everything that fat bastard had fed him. But why? In retrospect, it was so obviously bullshit. Didn't he, Mark Miles, have a mind of his own? Tears spring to his eyes as he realised that he didn't. His mask was always somebody else's. If, as he'd read somewhere, our minds are mirrors set up to reflect the mirrors that are other men's minds, then he was living proof.

Mark dozes.

Blankness and blackness merge.

The blackness is that of a cinema before the film starts. The curtain divides to reveal a coffin. The coffin divides to reveal his body, which divides to reveal his brain, which divides to reveal his mind, which divides to reveal... what?

Him?

A void?

A nobody?

The fly lands in his palm.

His hand snaps shut, crushing the fly to death.

THIRTY-FOUR

Mark sleeps and dreams.

Even the screws being eased out don't wake him. It's only when the lid's lifted, and the light pours in, that he knows he isn't dead. Or, if he is dead, it doesn't matter. He's in heaven. Then he hears Temple's quiet voice close to his ear and knows he's in hell.

'Mark?'

He lies still, eyes closed, breathless, composed like a cadaver ready for disposal. Hermann, Biff, Randy and Rip peer down at Mark. His face is a white mask. The blood of the dead fly on his hand could be a stigmata.

'Mark Miles, how you doing?'

Still no reply.

A glimmer of uncertainty plays on Temple's face as he gently shakes him. 'You've been away from us for many hours, Mark. What have you learnt on your journey?'

Mark lets them wait some more, enough for the grim possibility of his demise to take hold. Just when they start to panic he suddenly speaks. 'My journey has taken me into the black hole that was once the late Mark Miles, listening only to the tom-tom of his lonely heart. It told me you were right, Hermann. I have been dead all these years. Stillborn. Now I want to be reborn. Now I want to be alive. Now I want to be a leader like you. Now I want to get my nose back in the trough and take my rightful place in the pursuit of happiness. Meet the brand-new model, Hermann, the gleaming, razor-sharp, cut-throat, hard-edged Mark Miles.'

His steely eyes snap open.

Con man to con man.

Temple recoils as if he's seen a zombie. Mark follows up with a smile as thin as a fuse wire. Quickly reassured, Temple smiles back. The alchemist has turned base material into gold. So touched is he by the miracle of conversion, he lets the tears roll. It's curious how ruthlessness and sentimentality so often go hand in hand.

'You are one of us, Mark. Pass to the Other Side.'

Mark sits up like Lazarus.

'"Loose him, and let him go." John 11:44.'

THIRTY-FIVE

The women's course is winding down.

Every student has passed successfully to the Other Side. They now sit, relaxed and happy, in a circle with Alice, Loreen and Marjorie. Bruises, gashes and black eyes are their campaign medals and ribbons.

Amy Straw, unaware of husband Wally's crucifixion on the men's course, describes the effect the course has had on her.

'I feel resurrected, Alice.'

'That's a great quote. Have you got that, Loreen?'

Loreen is armed with a notepad and biro.

'Sure have.'

'Great, Amy.' She pans around the class. 'How many of you would recommend the course to your friends?'

The approval rating could not be higher. Every student holds up her hand.

'And you, Sylvia. How would you describe what happened here over the last two days?'

Sylvia, no longer voicing her concern for society as a whole, has a new fervour in her eyes. 'Fantastic. Life-enhancing. I feel self-confident. Confident of Self. An individual at last.'

Loreen yawns as she enters this original thought into the annals of the Institute.

'It makes you more aware,' says Amy.

'Right on, Amy. It does, doesn't it? It makes you more aware of what freedom and democracy – which we so easily take for granted –

actually mean for Mr and Mrs John Doe. And what about husband, Wally? Do you think he'll be as positive about the course?'

'Oh yes,' says Amy. 'Always looking for new experiences is Wally.'

The whole class applauds and cheers.

THIRTY-SIX

An end-of-term atmosphere pervades the men's class as the students congratulate Mark. He holds up the monstrance, kissing it like it is an Oscar. Television has taught the world one important lesson. Young or old, black or white, rich and pampered, or poor and deprived, all now know how to behave should we ever make it onto a talk show or award ceremony.

'Thank you,' says Mark. 'I want to thank my mother and all the students here for their support. I want to thank Jack Lovett for showing me what love and human warmth mean. Thank you Biff, Randy, Rip, and, most of all, Hermann. Without them, I wouldn't be where I am today. A leader of men. It's great to be on the Other Side.'

While the students holler, the instructors embrace Mark in turn.

'Hey, man, most students freak out in the coffin,' joshes Biff.

'Unless they're Count Dracula,' joshes Randy.

'Are you a vampire, Mark?' joshes Rip.

'If I am, you'll be the first to know, Rip,' joshes Mark.

The class laughs, albeit nervously. They didn't know who or what to believe any longer.

'Seriously, Mark, how'd you stay so cool in there?' says Randy.

'One of my clients was an escapologist. Great guy. Taught me all he knew. Never really took him seriously until I found myself in that there box.'

The class cheers with false enthusiasm.

'One of his favourite sayings was, "Chains are for slaves; wise men know how to shed them."'

171

Randy is impressed. 'Was he Chinese?'

He never gets an answer.

Wally Straw interrupts with a muffled gasp that could be his last. If not his last, then it's certainly the last but one or maybe two. Temple, students and instructors reluctantly look up at him. They'd forgotten about Wally. Limp and immobile on the crucifix, he looks ready to really cross to the Other Side. And never return.

Biff whispers anxiously to Randy, 'He's OK, isn't he?'

Temple, Biff, Randy and Rip exchange fast, furtive glances. They've been here before. Temple doesn't have to tell them what to do. They quickly unshackle Straw while Hermann takes care of the verbals. 'Gentlemen, I don't have to remind you that it was you who put Wally up there. It was you who tightened the straps. It was you who raised the crucifix. And you know what? You did it out of love. Isn't that right?'

The class is uncertain about this new tack until Temple screams, 'Isn't that right, motherfuckers? It was you who crucified Wally. And you enjoyed doing it. The poor sap is up there to atone for your sins, right?'

This is the first time Temple has raised his voice or used an expletive. And it works. The class obediently conforms, sheepishly nodding their heads, murmuring in the affirmative.

Temple smiles and drops his voice to a purr. 'I know you'll want to tell all your friends about the course. You'll want to share the experience with them. Isn't that right?'

Some students nod but not too enthusiastically.

'OK, so here's the game plan. Recommend it by all means. But under no circumstances must you reveal our secret methods. Outsiders simply won't understand? Right, Mark?'

The gleaming, cut-throat Mark Miles manages a frightened nod. What was new has already drained away. He, and the other students, find it difficult to drag their eyes away from Straw being lowered to the ground. Temple lifts his voice in a vain attempt to hold their attention. 'Outsiders will hear only what they want to hear. The bad parts. The conflict. The rough-and-tumble. And yes... the pain!'

The students nod more enthusiastically.

'But not the love and compassion I see in your eyes. The trust. The bonding. The deep inner experience and growth we've shared together. Only we know about that. It's something precious we can share with nobody outside this room.' He pauses to sear each student with a look of such intensity that some shiver with fear.

'So let us obey our pledge of secrecy at all times.'

Like all successful demagogues, Temple's tone is perfect, as is his timing. He waits before making the final pitch.

'Agreed?'

The class, intent only on getting out of there alive, agree with a resounding, 'Yes!' The incentive to agree is undoubtedly Straw's inert body being carried from the room by the instructors.

Biff stays inside and relocks the door.

Temple smiles reassuringly. 'Be not afraid. Wally is in good hands. He has but fainted.' He shrugs like a stale stand-up comedian. 'All he had to do was hang in there.' The joke falls flat and Temple doesn't even attempt to help it up. He quickly turns to schmaltz, which never falls flat. 'I remember my mama saying to me when my papa was lying in his open coffin, "Your daddy's not dead, little Hermann. He is but sleeping." I was but six years old. That was one lesson I never forgot.'

'Good one, Hermann,' sneers Biff from the door. 'I'll go make sure Wally is but sleeping.'

As the door closes Temple steps across, relocks it and faces the class alone. Without the imported muscles rippling around him, he suddenly shrinks to nothing. Mark beholds a little man strutting before him. podgy, balding, shabby, ridiculous, devoid of any charisma. How could he, Mark Miles, ever have seen him differently? Had he, like little Hermann's daddy, been but sleeping? He scans the other students. Had they, too, all been sleeping? If so, how, in hell's name, had they fallen under his spell?

Easily, came the undisputed answer.

It's one lesson Mark will never forget.

THIRTY-SEVEN

Hermann Temple unlocks the doors and stands aside as the class rush for the toilets.

The humiliations of the past two days are quickly forgotten as the students jostle for the urinals and washbasins. Worms have an enormous capacity for hard work. Blood, sweat and tears are soon wiped away, revealing excited, beaming faces in the mirrors. Not so with Mark. He stares at his image and sees only failure and resentment.

It doesn't need Temple and his assistants to regiment the students; they do it themselves. They file from the conference centre two by two, chanting like a slave gang, 'We are the leaders. We are the leaders. We are the new leaders.'

They move mechanically along the corridor towards the hotel foyer and the outside world.

Mark finds himself beside Roger Buckle, who confides in him, 'That was the greatest experience of my entire life, Mark. I want to thank you for pouring that slop over me.'

'My pleasure,' says Mark, without daring to look at him.

Buckle brings out his pocketbook. Tears well up as he extracts a business card, handing it to Mark. 'If you ever need life assurance or a pension, Mark, my old friend, just call me.'

Mark takes the card, reads it and, while Buckle dries his tears, lets it drop to the ground. Marching feet trample over it as they reach the double doors where Biff awaits them. He leads them across the hotel foyer towards the dining room, still repeating the mantra, 'We are the new leaders. We are the new leaders.'

Residents come to the lounge doorway to watch the phalanx pass. Harvey, having clocked in early for the night shift, sticks his gargoyle face out of the kitchen. Ace Springer, brandy in hand, watches, horrified, through the office window. 'My God, it's like the Nazis entering Paris.' Avril joins him at the window and sees Mark marching past; she mutters to herself, 'No wonder the little shit didn't turn up for Oral French.'

'Who didn't turn up?' burps Ace.

'Jean-Paul Sartre.'

'Oh, him!' He looks at her, confused. 'Didn't know he taught at the Poly.'

Avril, ever ready with the brandy bottle, charges his glass, thereby hastening his demise from sclerosis of the liver. This is a new strategy for attaining her freedom, via a sizeable life-insurance policy recently taken out in Ace's name.

In the foyer William Snazell appears at the top of the stairs. He's just in time to see the class enter the dining room. As the doors swing open, a great cheer rents the air. Alice and her students are waiting inside. From the foyer, they are briefly glimpsed, embracing the men like heroes returned from a war.

The doors swing shut.

THIRTY-EIGHT

The sideboard is littered with the remnants of a buffet lunch. Leftover cuts of chicken, turkey, ham and salami lie on silver salvers like carnage on a battlefield. Traces of demolished salads hide at the bottom of bowls. Severed cheeses, decimated breads, demolished cakes and broken biscuits, crushed fruits, melting ice creams and spilt juices stain the starched white tablecloth.

A long table runs the length of the dining room. Here, the ravenous students sit, stuffing themselves, their limpet-like eyes locked on to plates piled with food, their mouths opening, closing, grinding like sink disposal units. Mouth, gut and anus define the earliest form of life, and is still the chassis for all later forms.

Roger Buckle, having lost a few pounds during the course, is already restored to his former glory. Evidence for this lies with the buttons on his suit, as they take the strain again. Sitting next to him, Mark is as unaware of this pneumatic shift as he is of everything else going on around him. He's too withdrawn to eat, or even take in the speech coming from the head of the table.

Temple plants a beatific mask on his face as he looks from the bingeing students, lining both sides of the table, to the sublime Alice sitting at his right hand. 'Attaining perfection, like climbing a mountain, is a dangerous endeavour. Sometimes someone slips off. So it was with Wally Straw.'

Mention of Straw's name brings Mark crashing back to earth. He's no longer the ghost at the feast. The image of Wally, hanging on the cross, still haunts him. When they'd first entered the dining room, he'd witnessed Amy anxiously looking for her husband. Temple had taken her aside, counselled her, reassured her, before having Biff lead her away to the foyer. Now it wasn't just Amy that Temple wanted to reassure.

'Wally suffered a minor stroke this morning. A local doctor, who also happens to be a former student of ours, is attending him at his private nursing home. Only moments ago he phoned to say Wally is doing just fine.' The students stop gorging momentarily, contemplate applauding, then decide against it. It's heads down again as Temple continues.

'Amy will soon be at his bedside. She sends you all her best wishes and insists Wally would want this celebration of our achievements to go ahead.'

Alice applauds politely.

'Now, in Biff's absence, Randy would you like to say a few words. Randy!'

Randy stands.

A student farts, loud and rasping. Heads swivel accusingly in all directions, but the culprit, preferring anonymity, remains undetected. This, together with the sniggers that follow, completely undermine Randy. The swaggering bully, for the first time without his buddies, shrinks to a blushing, tongue-tied cretin. So startling is the metamorphosis that the students pause in their feeding to savour the moment.

'Er... er... er... er... thanks, you all.'

Randy sits abruptly then inexplicably jumps back to his feet. Something's bugging him. 'You know what? You guys can really take it. I just remembered it was in the *Reader's Digest* I read on the plane over. You took it in two fucking world wars, man. As if that wasn't enough, you took it in Israel, Malaya, Kenya, Egypt; you even fucking sailed around the world to take it in the Falklands. Jesus, you're a bunch of warmongering motherfuckers! But you know what? You're my kind of guys!'

The bloated students, struggling to keep lethargy at bay, are stirred to cheer. Randy grins, well pleased with his eloquence. 'And you'll take it again when the Apocalypse finally happens. According to this preacher I saw on TV, it ain't far off. If it's anything like the movie, I can hardly wait.'

More cheers, sprinkled with laughter.

Randy loves it. 'You guys can take punishment and come up smiling. You are born survivors!'

Temple waits for the tumultuous applause to die down before he stands to deliver the closing speech. 'Thank you, Randy.'

They trade looks and understand each other. Randy will be on the next course. And Biff certainly won't.

'Leaders, this is just the beginning,' spouts Hermann. 'Let your fellow countryman, the late Dr Charles Darwin, be your inspiration. He was wrong about evolution but right when he came up with that immortal slogan: "the survival of the fittest". This is no glib sound bite. This is the truth. This is the bottom line at the Institute. Personal Improvement is our name; personal improvement is our game. Have you any idea where the verb to improve comes from?'

Nobody does.

'I don't have much time for the French, but I do have time for that *petit* verb of theirs. It means to turn to profit. Isn't that neat? The very source of capitalism lies at the source of that French verb to improve.' Everybody cheers and some even start to sing the Marseillaise.

Temple holds his hands up for silence. 'OK, leaders, get up and go. Capital-ism is the answer man has been seeking ever since he first stood on two legs. Go out there and show those other fucking -isms the door! Get thee behind us, all -isms – except capital-ism!'

'Right on, Hermann,' shout Alice and Randy.

'Right on, Hermann,' comes back like an echo.

They turn to find Biff and Rip returned from their mission, with the doors still swinging behind them. Why the students are pleased to see these two thugs is beyond Mark, but they are. They erupt in ecstasy. Temple shows pique at having, yet again, to wait for hysteria not of his own making to evaporate.

'Some of you may have wondered why, apart from my temporary gastric indisposition, I didn't spend as much of last night with you as I would wish.'

Biff and Rip, busy picking at the pickings, chuckle and shoot lewd looks at Alice.

'Well, fellow leaders, I must level with you. I was preparing myself for a momentous decision. One that doesn't come easily. After due consideration, I've decided to run for the presidency of the United States of America.'

Fear for his sanity is the initial reaction.

That's before collective memory kicks in regarding recent incumbents of that office and quickly comes to the conclusion that the idea isn't that crazy.

'As you know, behind every great man stands a great lady. Last night, while you were hard at work, I asked Alice Honey to be that great lady. My First Lady!'

Alice dips her head like a swan.

Hermann, imagining himself as the most powerful man on earth, tiptoes further to the edge of madness. He needs only an enthusiastic mob to carry him deeper and deeper into delusion.

They always oblige.

'And she agreed.'

Mark can vaguely hear the students cheering. His eyes glaze over as the scene seems to slow down, then stop. It's all a dream. Everybody is on their feet except him. He seems paralysed by the news. Temple beams loving looks at Alice and wonders if the way to her bed has been made any easier.

It hasn't.

Whilst looking as radiant as a bride, she leans behind him and whispers to Randy, 'It's cold showers until the divorce comes through.' The whisper is loud enough for Hermann to hear. He sinks, dejected, into his chair.

As the tumult subsides, Mark slowly rises to his feet. He speaks quietly, like Temple. And like Temple, he immediately commands their hushed attention. Even the words are Temple's.

'Everything I'm about to do to you, Hermann, I am really doing for you. Out of love. Love of freedom. Love of the individual.' He pauses to sip a glass of water. 'Love of an individual like Wally Straw.'

All applaud, thinking Mark is simply expressing his well-intentioned zeal for the course. Temple, whilst suspicious of Mark's motives, is nevertheless transfixed as Mark continues, 'Wally Straw is not sleeping. He's dead. Now, Hermann, it's your turn to tell us the truth.'

Temple, Alice and Randy go white as milk. Their mouths open but no words emerge as Mark continues to carefully extract his pound of flesh. 'All you have to do, Hermann, is tell us the truth. But you know what, everybody? He won't. He'll lie.'

Temple's heard enough. He leaps to his feet, yelling angrily, 'Are you prepared to repeat that in a court of law?'

'We know Wally died on the cross, Hermann. But now tell us how Claudio Cross died.'

Alice jumps up, screaming at Mark, 'Claudio's not dead! He's back in Italy. Isn't that right, Hermann?' Her fiancé is so shaken, he feels for his chair and plops into it. Since announcing his intention to run for the highest office in the world, Hermann is not handling his first international incident with much aplomb.

His prospective First Lady, however, acts like she's already in the job. 'Claudio Cross was a pimp. He wasn't even married to Mrs Cross. He was her lover. A gigolo. A parasite.'

'Claudio Cross is dead, Alice.'

Mark, like Alice, has slipped comfortably into a new role, that of prosecuting council. 'I might draw your attention to the fact that his mistress, Petronella Cross, blew her brains out because she was told by a certain person that he, Claudio, had dumped her and made off to Italy. Having interviewed several crucial witnesses, I can now reveal the name of that certain person.' He points at the disconsolate figure sitting at the head of the table. 'It is Dr Hermann P. Temple.'

Nobody moves.

Everybody seems to have stopped breathing, less they should miss any of these soap-operatic revelations. Mark kicks his chair away and makes for the doors. There, he pauses to point at Alice.

'Alice, you are engaged to a murderer!'

With that he's gone.

The room is as silent as a mass grave and about as foetid. Only eyes dare move. Alice's frightened ones swivel to Temple's, who shifts his uneasily to Randy's, then to Biff's and on to Rip's.

Alice goes to speak but Hermann snaps at her, 'Not now, Alice.'

He stands and takes his instructors to a corner, where they go into a huddle. It could be time out in a football game.

Except the game is over.
Mark's blown the whistle on them.
There's only injury time left.

THIRTY-NINE

Miles, now on his way to Springer's office, stops when he hears his name called. He turns in a daze to see Harvey manning the reception desk.

'Not now, Harvey.'

'It's important. A message from a Mr Snazell.'

'That little shit!' Mark goes an angry red. 'Where is that fucking bastard?'

'Room 11. He says go on up.'

'Does he now?'

Mark takes the stairs three at a time.

*

A 'Do Not Disturb' sign dangles from the door handle of Room 11. Mark pauses to recover his breath before knocking.

'Snazell?'

There's no answer.

He knocks louder.

'Snazell, are you in there?'

Silence.

He tries the door and it opens. He enters cautiously, closing the door quietly behind him. The curtains are drawn. It takes him a moment to adjust to the darkness. A crack of light comes from under the bathroom door.

'Snazell? Are you in there?'

'Out in a jiffy, Mr Miles. Sorry about this, but nature must take its course.'

'If it's a laxative you need, I'm your man.'

'Even seeing you won't help. I've eaten nothing but sandwiches these past few days.'

Mark eases back the curtains. Light pours into the room. The dressing table and desk are stacked with recording equipment. It's sophisticated state-of-the-art stuff. There are radio receivers, back-up recorders, spare miniature microphones, a tangle of leads with each source identified on gaffer tape. Several pairs of headphones lie on the back of the chair facing the desk.

'Shit!'

Mark feels like he's sleepwalking. He sees a stack of used audio tapes, neatly numbered and packaged, lying on the bed. Beside them is Snazell's handgun with the silencer already fitted. Mark's hand hovers above it, fearful of touching it, yet, as the anger swells up inside him, sorely tempted to pick it up and use it.

'You bastard! You set me up, didn't you?'

'Afraid so,' says Snazell, breezily.

'Was Reg in on it?'

'Of course not. Don't be so paranoid.'

'Paranoid? Even Sigmund Freud would be paranoid if he'd been through what I've been through, you arsehole.'

'Language, Mark. Remember what I said about coarse language?'

'Fuck you!'

Mark's hand touches the gun, then pulls back sharply as if scalded.

'What about Reg's brother-in-law? He was certainly in on it. Presumably you paid that fucking gorilla to finger me?'

'Absolutely correct.'

Mark is almost crying as he trawls through the events that brought him to this room. He peers at the gun through welling tears, hardly believing that he'd ever thought of using it. Choking on his own embarrassing contribution to this farce, he keeps shaking his head in confusion.

'Why me?'

'Simple. You have the personality of a windsock.'

'Thank you.'

'And someone had to do it.'

'Do what?'

'Expose Hermann and his monstrous Institute.' Snazell chuckles. 'It certainly wasn't going to be me. If you check that ridiculous name-tag around your neck, you'll see there's a microphone attached to the chain.'

Mark does, and there it is, the size of a full stop.

'It amused me, using your tag to tag you.'

'You shit!'

'Don't be like that. Put it down to experience. After all, your name will be in all the papers. You'll be the man who uncovered two deaths, possibly murders, while on, of all things, a course for self-improvement. The media will love it. You'll be famous, which is what you've always wanted. The telly talk shows will be clamouring for you.'

Mark reels. He should have known the raison d'être was money. It always is.

'My God, you'll sell the story. You'll clean up.'

'Too right, I will.'

'What's in for me?'

'If you'd played your cards correctly, you be the proud possessor of an onyx marble mantel clock with a battery-operated pendulum.'

Snazell is laughing so much Mark doesn't register the first knock. The second he hears. And Biff's voice coming from the corridor: 'Mr Snazell?' Mark freezes, grabs the package of tapes, darts into the bathroom, slams and locks the door. Squatting on the lavatory is Snazell, content as a broody hen. He lets out a furious squawk when he sees Mark. 'You dirty pervert!'

Mark claps his hand over his mouth, whispering in his ear, 'Shut the fuck up. Biff and the others are out there.'

They hear Biff knock again.

'Mr Snazell? The hall porter says Mark Miles is with you.'

Biff tries the door and it opens. Snazell and Mark listen as the instructors case the room, uttering expletives.

'Hermann had better see this,' says Randy.

'I'll go get him,' says Rip.

The door onto the corridor opens and closes.

'Shit, man, see that .32 on the bed?'

The gun is cracked open and the cylinder spun.

'Loaded. What shit is this guy Snazell into?'

'There are no goddamn tapes here, Biff. He must have them with him,' says Randy.

Somebody tries the bathroom door. It won't open.

'OK, come right on out, Mr Snazell.'

Silence.

Then the pummelling begins.

The door groans and creaks but doesn't succumb. Snazell is beside himself with indignation, yelling with unexpected force, 'Is there no such thing as privacy any more?'

Mark throws open the frosted window by the bathtub. 'Let's go.'

Although alarmed, Snazell doesn't budge. 'I haven't finished yet. You know you should never force it.'

The ruckus suddenly ceases and an eerie calm follows.

They both look at the door.

Whoosh!

Whoosh!

Whoosh!

Three small holes appear around the lock. Water spurts from the cistern as Snazell slumps forward. Mark gasps, 'Oh shit!' which seems inappropriate under the circumstances. He watches, horrified, as Snazell topples from the toilet. The triple puncture in his torso is now clearly visible.

Biff uses his shoulder to sever the door from the lock, but Snazell's stocky body prevents the door from opening fully. Biff's face, purple with rage, glares at Mark through the gap as he climbs out of the window onto a narrow ledge and sidles away.

*

Celia Cox is brushing her blind husband's hair. She does it every night before dinner. Reflected in the dressing-table mirror, she's startled to see a man appear behind her. At first she thinks he's actually in the room. Only when she turns does she realise he's outside the window.

185

Mark, clutching the package of tapes, is balanced precariously on the sill. Years ago, he'd paid a hypnotist to cure his vertigo. It hadn't worked, although, curiously enough, he did stop smoking. With nothing to grip, Mark is petrified, barely able to tap on the windowpane and encourage Celia to open up. Sadly for him, Celia is a no-nonsense person, especially when dealing with tradespeople.

She steps over to the window.

'Not today, thank you.'

And closes the curtains.

*

Two chambermaids prepare a guest room for the night, drawing the curtains, folding away the coverlet, turning back the top sheet and placing a chocolate on the pillow.

Outside, Mark, clinging to the wall like a barnacle, finally reaches the darkened window. He manages to grip an adjacent downpipe. It creaks and a shower of rust breaks away as he slowly bends to stash the tapes on the sill before trying to lift the frame. It won't budge.

The chambermaids stop chattering and listen.

'What was that, Edina?'

Edina opens the curtains. Light floods on a blurred figure falling downwards. Fingers clutch momentarily at the sill before they, too, slip away in the direction of the esplanade below.

'Who was that?' says Edina.

'Don't know. He was off like sodding Batman.'

'You don't think it's…? Could it be…?' She pauses for them to say it in unison: '… the phantom fornicator?'

Both rush to the window and throw it open.

'I saw him first.'

Looking down, they can see a figure clinging to the banner stretched above the hotel entrance. They watch, open-mouthed, like kids at the circus. Edina notices the audio tapes on the sill, picks them up and examines them.

'Probably his memoirs.'

Mark looks over the top of the banner and realises he's dangling plum in the centre of the word **Personal**. Desperate to take the weight off his arms, he kicks his legs towards **Improvement** in an attempt to straddle it.

He fails.

An unpleasant growl adds to his misfortune. Randy waits below like an angry bulldog. 'Come on, sweetheart. Come to me, baby.' His tattooed arms are beckoning.

Mark again tries to propel himself up and over. This time the rope at one end parts company from the ring in the wall. Gravity now takes charge. Mark swings, pirate fashion, into Randy. The stunned instructor goes over like a skittle, rolling away onto the esplanade.

Touching down gracefully on the steps, Mark calculates that, even with Randy sprawled on the pavement, his escape route towards the town is cut off. Instead, he makes for the hotel foyer, only to find Hermann, Biff and Rip coming down the staircase. Veering away from them, he piles into the Residents' Lounge.

Afternoon tea is being served.

Every seat is taken.

Heads like old apples, shrivelled and lined, rest against every antimacassar in the room. These guests literally come out of the woodwork at teatime. Mark can see Temple and his instructors conferring in the foyer and realises that only a bold gesture will save him.

He moves to the centre of the lounge and screams, 'Murder!'

There's no reaction.

It's as if they're all hard of hearing and, indeed, most of them are. An agitated head waiter, new to the job and unaware the lunatic in their midst is, in fact, the hotel's marketing director, hurries across, but not before Mark bellows again, 'Wake up, for fuck's sake!'

That does it.

The F-word still registers with this generation. So he lets them have some more at the top of his voice: 'Fuck! Fuck! Fuck!'

It's like waking the dead.

Major Jellicoe's monocle falls with a loud plop into his cup of tea. Harvey, waiting on Madge Trafalgar, looks around at the commotion and inadvertently pours milk into her lap. She screams and jerks her mechanised wheelchair into reverse. It careers off at speed, sending tables flying and causing Freddie Mason, a retired judge, to have a heart attack. His face plummets into a plate of trifle and stays there. Jellicoe lets out a savage cry as the wheelchair careers over his desert boots, while the head waiter, now distracted from apprehending Mark, trips over Lucy Turret's stick and collides with the cakes and dessert trolley. This now takes off at speed. It heads straight for the swing doors just as a late arrival opens them, stands aside in astonishment, and watches it sail out into the foyer.

The jellies and blancmanges ripple as the trolley rolls past Temple, Biff, Randy and Rip standing in the foyer. The quartet are as still as a display in a waxworks. A porter, unaware of the approaching puddings, opens the door to welcome a guest. The accidental choreography is like that of a silent movie. The trolley passes neatly through the open door, bounces down the steps onto the esplanade, and comes to a rest in front of a weather shelter.

Inside sits a tramp with a white, shovel-shaped beard. He lowers his tattered newspaper and can't believe his eyes.

Nor can Ace, watching from his office. He begins to shake and not just his hands, but all over. When he sees the tramp stick a dirty finger into a towering gateau and lick it, Springer sinks his brandy and wonders if this heralds the onset of delirium tremens.

'Steady on, old boy.'

If he had any doubts, they're blown away when Avril bursts in, screaming, 'For Christ's sake, get the police. Number 11's been murdered.'

The tramp scoops a large piece of cake into his mouth and idly looks out to sea. Unnoticed by him, three liquorice-black Cadillacs with mirror windows, returning from London to collect Dr Temple and party, glide on to the esplanade and proceed towards the Grand Atlantic Hotel.

FORTY

The atmosphere in the dining room after Hermann and his platoon leave is one of desolation. The students look stunned. Some hold their heads in their hands. Others contemplate the vastness of the Atlantic Ocean and think they can see the Statue of Liberty on the horizon. Not all of it, just the tip of the torch.

It's a mirage and they know it.

Alice sits in a catatonic state, unchecked tears pouring down her carefully blushed cheeks, her dream of becoming the fourth Mrs Temple on hold while she considers her next move. Loreen and Marjorie watch her closely, trying to look concerned but unable to contain the delight bubbling in their eyes.

'Alice ain't in Wonderland no longer,' whispers Loreen.

'Shame. She'd be such a lovely First Lady,' whispers Marjorie.

Roger Buckle, unfazed by recent revelations, finishes off a third helping of trifle, wipes his mouth with his napkin, stands, lovingly rubs his belly and guffaws. 'Hey, everybody, I feel personally improved. And that's the truth.' His laugh, worthy of Falstaff, shatters the dam of built-up resentment and recrimination.

'Shut up, fatty.'

'You haven't fucking improved.'

'Have any of us?'

'Why did we come on this dumb course, anyway?'

'They told me I was like an oil field with vast hidden reserves of success-power lying untapped?'

Several students recognise the pitch. They nod their heads, muttering the mantra like pilgrims: 'Success-power!'

'They said you can't just stumble on these hidden reserves.' The same students collectively chime in with, 'You need expert guidance.'

Silence.

They look lost and confused.

'You don't think we've been indoctrinated, do you?'

'You mean like suicide bombers?'

'If we have, how would we know it?'

Paranoia takes them in its sweaty hands. Suspicious eyes dart about like fireflies, never stopping anywhere long, for fear of revealing they were, in fact, programmed to some alien channel.

Silence again.

Roger, back at the buffet, calls over his shoulder, 'What the hell got into us?' He piles some cake remnants onto his plate.

Alice explodes, banging the table with both fists.

'You wanna know what got into you, Buckle? Hermann P. Temple got into you.' She stands, roughly wipes the tears away and stares at Loreen and Marjorie. 'And I want you two bitches to know Hermann sure didn't get into me!'

Loreen and Marjorie, initially taken aback, explode with laughter. Alice ignores them as she strides towards the foyer. She's still convinced it's all a mistake.

It must be.

*

Hermann is briefing his men as Alice approaches.

'Hermann, we have to talk.'

'No, we don't,' snaps Hermann. 'Right now, I got more important things to do, sweetheart.'

Mark, watching every move from the Residents' Lounge, sees Hermann involved with Alice and decides to make his move. He runs past them to the revolving doors. They spin him out onto the esplanade. Biff and Randy start to give chase but Temple stops them. 'Forget him. Bring the cars to the back. Load our friend Snazell into

190

the casket. We'll dump him on the way to the airport.'

'Wally's already in the casket, boss,' says Biff.

'Then find a laundry basket.'

Biff, Randy and Rip make off, leaving Hermann and Alice alone. She's distressed and angry as the truth begins to bite. 'Hermann, I put myself on the line for you with Claudio. I lied to save you the embarrassment of having to explain his death. And you promised never to crucify another student. You promised me, Hermann. You promised that, from then on, the cross was only for display purposes.'

'Honey, it wasn't me. Biff and the boys did it while I was indisposed. Remember?'

Alice stamps her foot with rage. 'Why didn't you tell me Wally Straw had died? And who the hell is this Snazell? My God, it's like working in a mortuary.'

Uncontrollable tears start to run down the courses already cut into her make-up. Hermann's torn between soothing her and escaping. 'Not now, honey pie. We have to move on.'

She stares at him like a little girl who's just been touched up by Father Christmas.

'Hermann, I believed in you.'

'Of course you did, sugar. And rightly so. Don't you realise, it's Satan up to his old tricks. Satan is testing your belief. That's why it's imperative we get out of here. Other flocks are waiting for us, Alice.'

He takes her hand but she pulls it away. Her eyes are popping out with incredulity. 'You don't really think people are going to fall for that leadership crap again? Not when all those stiffs start to surface?'

Temple turns on her, outraged, indignant, hurt at her lack of faith. 'Are you kidding? Look at all those preachers on TV. They get caught fucking hookers, embezzling, using drugs, you name it. Right? Within days they're back on TV creaming contributions from their congregations. Right? Alice, sweetheart, people like what I have to say. They believe in me. We'll come up with a different name and start all over. Like the Nazis did.'

Her tears have dried up, along with her dreams.

'Not with me, you won't!'

She swings away, head held high like a drum majorette, sexed-up

191

and proud. OK, so she'll go back to being a dental assistant, or airline cabin staff, or maybe she'll become a lap dancer. Why not? She likes driving men crazy. Revenge is a dish to be eaten hot.

It's Temple's turn to weep as he watches her beautiful bouncy butt retreat. And his tears are genuine for once. He knows he'll never find another woman with such perfect physical specifications. Alice is no airbrush job. She's real and exactly what every American alpha male is conditioned to desire. He can't let her go that easily. 'Alice, they need us. Jesus Christ, we're the leaders, remember? Alice! Alice! You're walking out on the next President of the United States of America.'

'Up yours, Hermann.'

She doesn't even look back.

The last thing he remembers is her index finger.

*

Mark is still running.

The esplanade is crowded with people taking the air on this crisp, sunny Sunday evening. Dodging and weaving. he looks back several times but can't see his pursuers among the promenaders. Scared witless, and not taking any chances, he doesn't let up until he hears the approaching police cars. A slew of them, tyres squealing and sirens screaming, speed past him towards the Grand Atlantic Hotel.

Mark has reached the farthest point of the esplanade where there are no buildings and no people. His throat is burning, his lungs bursting, his heart pumping, his body sweating; he collapses onto a wrought iron bench. Looking up at the clear blue sky, he yells at the gods, 'Shit! I'm not even worth following.'

And he laughs like a madman.

*

Unaware of the drama being played out in the foyer, Celia Cox and her blind husband sit in their usual armchairs facing the sea. While waiting for the dinner gong she reads, as always, from his favourite book. '"And who are you?" asked the Caterpillar.'" A cacophony of police sirens draw closer but Celia never falters. '"Alice replied, I hardly know, sir, just at present – at least I know who I was this morning, but I think I must have changed several times since then."' Even Celia has to look up when the police cars slam on their brakes at the entrance to the hotel. Smoke and the smell of rubber waft towards the picture windows.

*

Mark walks determinedly back towards the Grand Atlantic. With the police now on the case, he feels safe, excited even. He's anxious to retrieve the audio tapes from the windowsill. Like Snazell said, they could be the key to a financial killing. He wonders if he should edit out the embarrassing scene between him and Jack Lovett, but decides against tampering with evidence.

His mind is dancing again.

It abruptly performs a *jeté* when he sees three Cadillacs proceeding at speed along the esplanade towards him. He flings himself over the railings onto the beach, head down, scared they've seen him, listening lest they stop.

They don't.

He hears the cars swish past in quick succession.

Sitting up, he brushes sand from his hands and face. Scanning the view, he notices the waves breaking over an object a stone's throw out at sea. He knows it isn't a rock, having played on this beach many times when he was a kid. Mark stands to get a better view but is again distracted. The sound of police sirens starts up at the farthest end of the esplanade. He watches the cars grow from small dots to large thundering projectiles, flashing blue streaks of light as they hurtle past in pursuit of the Cadillacs. The sight of the boys in blue moves him. For the first time since he was a boy, he feels proud to be British.

When he turns back to the object, his heart gives a leap. It looks like the top of a trunk, but he can't be certain. A small, dark cumulus cloud briefly obscures the sun. When it clears there's a sudden flash of gold. It's the embossed *RT* on the lid of a trunk.

The trunk.

Mark crashes into the water, ploughing his way towards it. The tide is coming in fast and he has to struggle. Reaching it, he closes his eyes, praying, before looking down. The lock lies open. Even so he feels sick. He shivers fearfully, muttering madly to himself, 'Dear God, may Reg not be in it.'

His hands shake as he rests them on the lid. Taking a deep breath, he flings it open and peers inside. His cry rents the heavens, soars above the sound of the waves, rings across the beach, time and time again. Gales of relieved laughter break like squalls among the seagulls circling above. Inside the trunk, there's just a canvas bag, a padlock and a length of chain.

Marks looks out across the ocean and hears Reg's voice carried in by the wind. It must have circled the planet many times since he'd tempted fate with his crazy act. '*Bind me in your strongest chains. Lock me in your strongest prison. Strip me naked. Search my body. I will escape. For no power on earth can hold me!*'

Reg had escaped.

But so had he, Mark Miles. He knew he'd just been blessed with the mysterious mark of celebrity. Like the famous finger on the ceiling of the Sistine Chapel, it had come to rest on him. Within hours he'd be on every television network, radio station, website, and in every newspaper and magazine, and every branch of social media.

He could market himself.

He could start again.

With a brand-new accent.

Walking back along the beach was, for Mark, like the last scene in a movie. The hero silhouetted against the skyline, footsteps in the sand, clouds scudding overhead. He could even hear the music, mawkish and treacly, composed with a sentimentality peculiar to the cinema and much treasured by box offices around the world.

As Mark approaches the Grand Atlantic Hotel he sees Alice Honey, hidden behind massive black shades and a cloche hat, hurrying to a taxi. He waits for his heart to miss a beat, but it doesn't. Even his cock shows no interest. The taxi pulls away. He's in such a daze he hasn't noticed how deserted the esplanade is. All the crowds previously there, when he'd panicked and run off, are now on the beach looking at something floating in the sea. Two people have waded out and are pulling it in, whatever it is. By the time he reaches the arc of onlookers, and eases himself close to the front, whatever it is has been dragged onto the shore. His first glimpse of whatever it is only happens when people at the front turn away in horror and a gap between them opens.

Mark sees a human arm, deathly white, bloated, with rich tattoos stretched obscenely out of shape. He thinks he recognises them. Somebody else up front moves. And he knows that he does. This fresh gap reveals Reg Turpin's disintegrating face. Through the eye sockets small crustaceans wave their limbs as if saying goodbye.

Mark slams his eyes shut, reeling away in disgust, fighting his way through the crowd, running across the beach. He starts to retch, seemingly forever. When the bile finally runs out and the pain subsides, he collapses onto the sand, sobbing. This, in itself, is not unusual for Mark. What is unusual is that he's not sobbing for himself. He's sobbing for Reg, his mother, for Ursula, Wally, Alice, even Snazell and Temple. He's sobbing for the whole human race.

Mark knows his worm is already at work. He also knows there is one reality even his worm cannot dissemble. He buries his head in the sand to stifle the scream that comes with this awful realisation. The sobbing slows, then stops.

He rolls onto his back and screams at the heavens for all to hear.

The crowd watch from a distance, motionless, grim faced.

Mark's scream hovers above them like a vulture, ugly and brutal, coming in to land. They, too, had to face the undeniable truth.

'Once you're born there's only one escape!'

The dead escapologist is living proof.

I draw from life but always pulp my acquaintances before
serving them up.
You would never recognise a pig in a sausage.

Fanny Trollope

Violence is one of the most fun things to watch.

Quentin Tarantino

ONE

His mouth is taped shut. White and tight. The shape of a letterbox. His nose above shimmers with running mucous. His eyes are so scared they spin like symbols in a fruit machine. A sudden flash of steel, sharp as a samurai's sword, and Marshall Grist's head is a millimetre above where it was a split second before.

The gap between skull and trunk widens.

Blood starts to spurt like a gusher.

It hits the big screen full on.

*

On a sizzling afternoon in East Harlem we are in a movie house packed with bodies kept cool by air conditioning.

Like meat in a deep freeze.

The audience, armed with buckets of popcorn, scream their approval. Some are horrified, not many. The rest stare impassively at the screen dripping with blood.

A munching Greek chorus.

Among them is Primo Vargas.

On screen the blood drains away as Grist's severed head lands on a wooden floor, bounces and rolls until it comes to rest by a pair of patent leather half-boots. Dead eyes face upwards until the lids close as slowly as a cinema's curtains.

The show is over for Marshall Grist.

How the fuck could this happen to one of the world's most successful crime writers? Well, it wouldn't have if Primo Vargas hadn't gone to the movies. The crazy thing is that Primo never normally went to the movies. On this particular afternoon it so happened he needed an alibi.

A watertight alibi.

Somebody close to him, a business partner, one Felix Rivera, is to be executed.

And *not* by the State.

When that happens, Primo will be top of the cop's list of suspects.

The cinema's ticket kiosk houses a battered old peroxide blonde. Primo prances up to the window and jig-a-jigs a lewd tongue at her. Her pancake mask sits like a sphinx while her watery eyes scan him good.

As good as any security camera.

Perfecto!

She'll remember him all right.

Primo takes his ticket and sashays into the foyer, craving attention. The cutie selling the popcorn is next in line for his alibi.

Again his tongue shoots out.

Only this time it means business.

Lively as a lizard catching flies, it curls lasciviously over his harelip.

'See that, honey? It make you juicy like melon.'

But the girl ain't no fly.

More of a wasp.

'Fuck you, you ugly creep. My turds look better than you.'

'May you stay *dry* for rest of your life, bitch.'

Primo laughs as he spins across the foyer and into the auditorium. He knows he's ugly and the ugly are harder to forget.

The movie's already running, so he's missed the opening titles.

Not that Primo cares.

He doesn't give a fuck who's starring in it or even what it's called. When he does finally pay attention to what's happening on the screen, he nearly dumps in his pants. Shit, he sees himself up there. What's more, he's sitting in a flick-house watching a movie.

Primo Vargas is up there, larger than life!

The harelip.

The cheap clothes.

The sniffling nose.

The toothpick twitching in the mouth.

Even the dialogue is his.

Only it *isn't* Him.

He sinks low in his seat. Man, although he knows it's some cocksucker actor, he starts feeling his body, checking it's still with him. He feels faint. It's like his soul has been stolen. His brain starts to steam. What he sees up there on the big screen he *doesn't* like.

Not one bit.

The guy is a larger-than-life scumbag.

At least his name hasn't been stolen.

The scumbag is called Ray.

Primo watches the action, mesmerised.

Ray, twitching and sweating in the movie *within* a movie, suddenly cracks when he sees himself in close-up. His yellow rotting teeth fill the screen, causing even the gore-addicted audience to gag with disgust.

That does it.

Ray freaks out, jumps from his seat, crashes wildly along the row, elbowing faces, stamping on feet, knocking aside buckets of popcorn, racing for the exit.

Primo – himself close to running from the auditorium – covers his eyes but can't resist peering between his fingers. On screen Ray crashes out of the cinema into a bar next door. He sinks four shots of tequila faster than the balls hit the pockets of the pool table behind him. Panic, now fortified by the liquor, turns to fury.

Who the fuck has voodoo-ed his spirit? Blown it up big like that?

Ray's belly and brain are on fire as he staggers back to the flick-house and tries to focus on the poster out front. Another close-up follows his forefinger as it runs slowly along the names at the bottom, working backwards from the director, past the seven producers, pausing at each of the ten scriptwriters.

None of them mean shit to Ray as he slowly mouths their names.

Back in the movie house Primo's hands drop from his face in seething horror at Ray's dirty, chewed fingernail now filling the screen.

Fuck this shit.

The one part of his twisted anatomy he took pride in was his hands. Didn't the shit filmmakers know that Romina, his older sister, was a nail technician and once a week applied her skills to his nails – in particular the one on the index finger of his right hand.

It was his Talisman.

An inch-long, pearly, polished scoop for sampling cocaine.

Like Ray in the film, Primo jumps up to leave – then remembers his alibi and slumps back into his seat just as the giant finger on the screen moves on from the tenth scriptwriter to stop like a divining rod at the guy who wrote the *novel* from which it was adapted.

Both Primo and Ray, his screen double, knew this was the Sorcerer.

The Vampire Bat.

The shitface Soul-Sucker.

Ray's lips, now in huge close-up, meticulously chisel the name into an imaginary gravestone.

𝔐𝔞𝔯𝔰𝔥𝔞𝔩𝔩 𝔊𝔯𝔦𝔰𝔱

*

Primo is close to collapsing by the time the film ends and the interminable credits begin to crawl relentlessly up the screen before the auditorium lights snap on. He rubs his bloodshot eyes and peers at the audience. A sea of bodies locked together as tightly as a printed circuit, frozen in an orgy of multiple *coitus interruptus*. Smeared faces emerge from the meltdown of flesh and clothes, slowly reforming into separate beings. Reluctantly they all file from the cool interior into the blazing sunshine and sweating city.

On the sidewalk outside, Primo, like Ray in the movie, looks around and sees a bar. The *same* bar – with the *same* pool table and the *same* players. As the balls hit the pockets so he, too, sinks shots of tequila.

Four.

Just like Ray.

And just like Ray, Primo is soon fired up. He storms back to the cinema and forces himself to focus on the poster. Like Ray he runs a finger across the names of the production team until he reaches the one name he remembers – Marshall Grist.

His brain is now like a whirling fan.

He stops breathing to see if he can hear the fan gyrating.

He can.

That's when the shit arrives.

It splatters crazy thoughts through every functioning synapse in his head until eventually it smacks against his cranium and sinks unconscious into his Unconscious.

Somehow, he's become trapped in a crap movie.

OK, so this was possible when he was *inside* the movie house – shit, we all get lost in movies – but now he's *outside* and he's still playing the star fucking role.

That was something else.

How the fuck could this be?

Primo – not surprisingly – knows zilch about quantum theory and the phenomenon of parallel worlds and entanglements. But he does know – and again not surprisingly – all about Padre Pio. His mother, a fervent Catholic, was a Padre Pio groupie. She'd told little Primo how the priest would appear in two, three, four, five different places at the *same* time and thousands of miles apart. All around the Planet. It seems the padre didn't mind being franchised like that and God made him a Saint for his trouble.

This got Primo thinking.

Maybe this movie entrapment – inside *and* outside the cinema – is a sign from God that he, Primo, is due for a dramatic change in his fortunes? Like being taken up into Heaven. Or better still, becoming rich like the rich man mentioned in the Bible.

His mother has also told him about the numerous apparitions of the Virgin Mary. She'd popped up in France, Portugal, Italy, Peru, Brazil, every place. Solo appearances in the clouds. In ships at sea. In grottoes. Although, as far as he remembered, *not* in any movie house.

At first this helped Primo batten down his brain.

Maybe Ray in the movie was also an apparition?

After all he, Primo, has spent much of his life hallucinating.

That made him smile and resolve to seek the Madonna's help.

Primo knew his case was shaky because as a teenager he'd confided in confession to having *touched* himself while contemplating the Virgin's image. The priest, recognising the code words for masturbation, asked if any sperm had been spilt. Primo quickly assured him that his cock had instantly wilted before the Virgin's purity and the priest deemed that only a light penance was necessary.

Three Hail Marys.

That was then.

Now was now.

Now Primo's guilt and paranoia begin to surface like sulphurous lava from a volcano. Christ's bloodied body hanging from the Cross looms large in his imagination. He had *lied* that day in the confessional and now becomes convinced his long-overdue penance is about to begin. Terror causes him to vibrate with the intensity of the hammer that nailed God's son to the wood.

TWO

Primo has never been in a bookstore before. He enters cautiously, stopping inside the entrance. Chamber music oozes its way over and under the tables piled with books and along the endless lines of loaded shelves. The hallowed ambience in there spooks him in the same way it does in church. He sniffs, expecting to smell incense, before slouching up to the main counter where a female assistant sits reading.

A smoker's cough, not often heard in today's bookshops, gets her startled attention. Her eyes immediately lock onto his vivid harelip. For a split second, Primo is tempted to give her the oscillating tongue treatment – but resists.

'Yes?'

'You have book by Marshall Grist?'

'Marshall Grist has written many books. Do you know the title?'

She removes her glasses and manages to refocus her eyes away from the hideous deformity. Unfortunately his eyes are waiting like highwaymen to capture hers. Primo has never had the privilege of seeing a doe in the wild. If he had, he'd recognise the fright in her eyes.

He's mesmerised.

His eyes try to penetrate hers.

He watches as fear is replaced by contempt. Primo is used to that. Mother Nature is merciless when it comes to selecting partners for sex and procreation.

The doe jumps up.

'Shall I show you our crime shelves?'

'There's a film of it.'

'Many of Grist's novels have been turned into films.'

'This is a new film.'

'Ah! *Vicious Circle*. I'll get it.'

The doe swiftly makes her getaway. It's not long before she returns, lolloping back with a paperback, which she lays on the counter. There, on the cover, is Primo's alter-image taken from the film poster.

Not that the doe notices.

Primo holds the book up beside his own face for her perusal and smiles hopefully. The assistant's eyes swivel from the cover to his face and back again.

She tries to hide the shudder but fails.

'That's seven dollars fifty.'

THREE

Primo has Maria read it out loud to him.

Maria is his youngest sister. Smart in every department. She works in a bank as a teller and can read real quick. As she's about to start the last chapter the cops crash through the front door and swarm over the apartment. Primo had been expecting them. Fuck the novel, he knows how the film ends and thinks it's shit anyway. The guy's head bouncing across the floor may have made the audience shit in their pants, but he'd just laughed.

And that's what he does now.

He laughs like a hyena as a sweaty cop snaps the cuffs onto his wrists. The elevator in Primo's block is busted and the officers have climbed eight piss-stained garbage-strewn flights to reach their suspect.

They are not in a good mood.

The sergeant, looking like he's about to expire, arrives last. He's the fattest in the squad with a belly hanging over his belt like a cow's udder. He gasps.

'Primo Vargas, you're on a homicide charge.'

'Hey man, you fat like pregnant woman or what? Someone fuck you up the ass?'

Primo's laugh is cut short by a swingeing blow crunching into his nose. Blood flushes from both nostrils as if from a faucet. He shakes his head, sprinkling their uniforms with red polka dots, and smiles.

Even the sergeant's fist couldn't dent his alibi.

Primo knows he'll be freed as soon as the company lawyer corroborates it. The blonde hag in the movie theatre will remember him all right.

So will the chick selling popcorn.

As he's led from the building, Primo waves his cuffed hands at the rubber-necking neighbours crowded around the patrol cars. Blue lights smear rapidly across the watching faces. Instead of a murderer under arrest, he's a victorious boxer leaving the ring.

*

Sitting alone in a cell, waiting for the lawyer to arrive, Primo gets to thinking about Marshall Grist. That mother has skinned him alive, then put his skin on some crap actor like it was a suit.

But how?

How the fuck had he done it?

He stops pacing about and lies on the cell bed while his thoughts bang around as if they were bumper cars.

Yeah!

Yeaah!

YEAAAH!

A neurotransmitter in his brain suddenly fires off – as haphazard as a sun storm – which in turn short-circuits another crack-defected cell and he *knows* the answer.

Some years back, this big lump with a bum's beard, a young guy already past his prime, had moved into this flophouse round the corner from the crack joint Primo was running at the time. After a couple of weeks, this hairy creep had slimed words out onto the street that he would pay (PAY!) people to talk about their dumb lives into his little fucking tape machine.

Lives the poor motherfuckers thought worthless.

Until this cash offer came along.

Primo knew drugs, guns, knives, cars, televisions, sofas were commodities – but not your story, man! Shit, even slabs of time (LIVES!) are now a commodity for some dealer out there.

Just like his packs of crack.

The lump said he worked for some university and what he recorded (BOUGHT!) would be research and used to make their shit lives better. He sounded like those jerks on television talking about saving some dumb animal from extinction.

Still, it was easy money.

Like selling your blood.

So Primo had talked.

Primo talked about Primo – his favourite subject – for hours and hours.

What had that big turd called himself?

Jay something?

With the company lawyer having finally sprung him, Primo asks around.

Nobody remembers this Jay man.

Nobody.

Most of the dudes who talked into that machine have either died, been killed or are in jail. The rest have memory meltdown. What Primo does hear on the street is that Marshall Grist's book has made millions. And the film zillions.

You see?

Money makes more money

Success fuels success.

The whole hyped-book-movie shit had lifted off like the Virgin Mary into heaven. *Dollar Heaven!* A place created to drive the poor crazy. A place they can see but not enter.

Back in his apartment Primo is still turning all this over in his head. Was this Jay really Marshall? He gets so crazed thinking about it that he binges on crack and gets more crazed, screaming at the ceiling, 'I no mind them words going to some shit university where they might do some good telling kids what life is like in the fucking gutter. But this not the fucking story now.'

His nose is like a vacuum cleaner. A week's supply, meant for the street, vanishes up his nose into his bloodstream. He's been fucking cheated. And he doesn't like that.

Nobody fucks with Primo.

This Jay-stroke-Marshall has taken his words (LIFE!) under false pretences. And cooked them into fiction. Its street value as book-stroke-movie has shot into some fiscal outer stratosphere.

A nirvana of greenbacks.

Primo sees it all.

His pupils are now red pinpricks from hell.

'I want my cut. My cut of my own shit life.'

So?

So where the fuck can he find Fat Jay?

FOUR

Next afternoon Primo wakes feeling like shit.

He fucks Carmen, who happens by the family apartment looking for his sister, then makes for the flophouse where Fat Jay had rented a room. He bangs on the door but the new tenants won't open up.

No problem.

The lock is pathetic.

He kicks it in and shows the cringing family eight inches of glinting steel.

No problem.

They let him search the place.

No complaints.

Seven pairs of terrified eyes as wide and round as black olives watch as he searches the cupboards and shelves, under the beds and mattresses, even in the solitary pisspot.

Nothing.

He sits down and allows his mind to go back to when he was last there, feeding his voice into Fat Jay's recorder. It was always on a table beside his pack of Marlboro Lights and Zippo. He scans the room until his eyes arrive at the only table.

That's it!

It used to be in the middle of the room but the family living in this tip have pushed it against the wall. Another flashback and Primo sees Fat Jay incessantly checking he had spare packs in its drawer. The guy was a crazy, twitching nicotine addict, as bad as any junkie he knew. He pulls the table from the wall, finds the drawer and eases it open.

Nothing.

Again nothing.

In a fury he yanks it out.

Right at the back, caught in the frame, is a used envelope.

It's addressed to a Jay Carrion.

Only *this* Jay ain't living in no flophouse in a stinking slum. This Jay lives in a fancy apartment in a fancy part of town.

*

Primo borrows Maria's shiny new Dodge Dart compact, finds Carrion's apartment, parks opposite – and waits. Not once do the cops move him on. He can't believe it. The dickheads living in this neighbourhood must think cops are bad for realty prices.

Good.

Day and night he watches his prey. Jay has got even fatter in the five years since they met. He lives alone. No women go there. Primo shakes his head when he thinks about that. No fucking? Jesus, how can a guy live not getting pussy every day?

Every evening Jay leaves with a sports bag and returns looking as rosy as a shiny apple in a supermarket. Primo knows the cause is some shit health club. He's seen them places downtown – through huge plate-glass windows – heaving with bodies, pumping and pedalling, sinews bulging and straining, sweat dripping and steaming. When he was a kid his parish priest, in a desperate throw of the salvational dice, had shown him a picture of Beelzebub's hang-out. Hell! Primo remembers every Soul in Hell looking red as fire – and in fucking agony. Trust me, man, these health clubs the same as that picture Father Carlos showed me.

One night when Fat Jay gets back from pedalling and pumping, Primo and his brother, Caesar, are waiting for him. It's as easy as stealing a tub of lard from a food store. The brothers already have a cellar in a condemned building close to the crack house they ran for Felix Rivera, the *late* Felix Rivera. They use the place when they need to get lost.

This is where Jay is destined to lose more pounds than he ever did working out. He squeals like a stuck pig even before their knives

214

touch him. Primo and Caesar, frazzled by crack, begin to score his flesh and giggle.

They're enjoying themselves.

In truth Jay doesn't need the knife-work. From the off he's blabbing everything they want to know. No, he is not (NOT!) Marshall Grist. He just works for him. The bestselling crime writer, famed for his stories of violent low life, is too shit-scared to leave his penthouse in a high-security apartment block. Jay uses a fancy word to describe Grist's condition – a word Primo doesn't understand.

Big mistake.

Primo is super-touchy about his limited vocabulary and tries to cut out Jay's tongue. Caesar, realising they need his tongue in place, manages to stop him. When Jay ceases screaming, he tries to explain *paranoia* in simple lingo. Marshall's books are so black, so scary, he's made himself sick in the head. He, Jay, has worked twenty years for him and seen the man deteriorate. Marshall has become a crazy sicko hermit, as crazy as Howard Hughes.

Now Primo understands.

But Caesar doesn't.

How can a crazy living in a luxury penthouse he never leaves write about shit life on the streets – and make zillions?

Fat Jay explains.

Whatever stinking location or flaky character Marshall wants to write about, he, Jay, goes out and brings back the goods on tape. Jay Carrion knows where to look. He has the skill of a truffle pig when it comes to seeking out the depraved and corrupt. He'd been a top crime reporter on a tabloid, the *New York Post*, when Grist offered to pay him twice his salary as a journalist.

And he's never regretted it.

Until now.

Primo keeps his red-rimmed, glazed eyes on Jay's punctured torso. It reminds him of a picture pinned above his mother's bed. A saint. But which fucking one? He jigs his knife once again into the enticing white flesh. As the blood emerges so the name comes to him.

Saint Sebastian!

He's pleased and grins with satisfaction. Primo forgets a lot these days. Remembering something – anything – gives him confidence. He's buzzing. Now he knows words will come easy.

'You fat cocksucker, you come down here, you pretend you care, you see the shit lives we live, you listen our histories, you fucking know it's not our fault, you know we no can escape, you land on us like a fly on dog shit. Why? So you can make movies for those dickheads and bitches who work in shit offices. Make them crap in their panties. Scare them shitless as they sit on their fat asses eating fucking popcorn!'

Primo is screaming now.

'They know shit about street life. And they no give a shit either. After movie they go home and take shower. Next morning they back in their offices, telling other dickheads like it's real. Real? This is what's real!' To make his point he scags Jay's testicles, yelling above his victim's howls, 'You think I wanna spend my life cutting people. For scum like me there's no way out. Cos of scum like you! I try get job in office. Bitches see me and shit their panties again. You try get job then? Me, I want big piece of my fucking cake. My life! My fucking cake!'

He pulls out Carrion's cell phone, ramming it into his fat hand.

'Get this Marshall Grist on the line. Now!'

*

Primo does the talking while Caesar produces background screams from their hostage. By the time Carrion gets to speak, Marshall is convulsed with laughter. The two brothers can hear him cracking up even as Carrion pleads with him.

'Marshall, for Christ's sake, they're for real. Get me out of this shit. They're going to fucking kill me.'

Grist is unmoved, treating it like it's a joke.

'You're unreal, man. Listen Jay, stop fucking winding me up. It's not funny.'

And to prove it's not funny he stops laughing.

'Get lost, you cunt.'

The phone goes dead.

Primo explodes.

He grabs Jay's hand, clamps it on the table before bringing his knife

216

down like a butcher's cleaver, severing one plump pinky finger, the one with a ring on it.

A chunky 'J' gold item.

Not that Jay notices.

He's fainted.

'Let's see if motherfucker writer laughs when he finds this in his mailbox.'

But next day, when they call him up, he *does* laugh.

FIVE

Fat Jay always knew his employer was a cold son-of-a-bitch, but it never occurred to him, until now, that he nurses a deep hatred of his own species. Alone at last, chained to a wall, it comes as a revelation how he, Jay Carrion, has been exploited by Marshall.

Just like Primo Vargas, his life has been stolen.

And for twenty goddamn years.

His blood boils as he remembers the great man laughing over the phone. 'That was a dirty, filthy gesture, Jay. Giving me the *finger* like that. After all these years. After all I've done for you. Treated you like my own son. Fuck you, man! How do I know it's your finger? That cheap ring always gave me the creeps. Was it your idea to stick it on that flabby bit of flesh? That's sick, man. And you expect me to pay off those scumbags you've fallen in with? Jay, you asshole, look what it says on the back of the first fucking page of every single one of my novels: "All characters in this publication are fictitious and any resemblance to real persons is purely coincidental." You and your buddies are trying to rip me off. Go fuck yourselves.'

He hangs up.

Revenge is the engine driving much of what we humans get up to. Sadly it's not something we like to contemplate, but it's true. Vengeance saturates the daily news of life on planet Earth. Jay's sudden need for retribution takes over his whole being. There's a particularly repellent parasite that takes possession of an ant's brain so completely that the insect will sacrifice itself to be eaten alive, thereby allowing the parasite to enter and procreate inside the creature that ate it.

So it is with Jay.

Revenge takes possession of his brain.

The instant Grist laughed and hung up, Jay became preoccupied by one overwhelming obsession – albeit one that may cost him his own life – to destroy him.

With the same deviousness common to all parasites, Jay Carrion comes up with a game plan that will appease his new obsession. It's grisly. Even Primo and Caesar pale when they hear it. But what makes it so appealing to Jay is that it comes from one of Marshall's early novels. The great man of letters thought it one of his classical best – still sadly unacknowledged.

The narrative begins when a headless corpse is found inside a rented room. The window is sealed and the door locked from the inside. There are no fingerprints. There are no witnesses. Nobody has been seen going in or out. How did the corpse get in there? It's a familiar conundrum crime writers love to set their fictional law-enforcement officers. Marshall Grist had solved it very elegantly. But that was a long time ago, long before he adopted both a *pseudonym* and a writing style that would earn him the megabucks.

Jay Carrion intends to give that original plot a *new* twist. For this he needs to extend his cast to include a corrupt accountant, an avaricious cosmetic surgeon, an ageing unemployed actress, an alcoholic impersonator, and a safe-cracker. Tall order? Shit, they're all characters he'd found for Marshall. Better still, with one exception, all are totally *unaware* they were featured in his novels.

Now they're about to find out.

Like being unexpectedly named in some wealthy, now dead friend's Last Will and Testament, it'll be to their considerable advantage. That's because Fat Jay's version of the plot ensures Grist's fortune will come to those who have earned it.

Literally gave up their lives for it.

Primo and Caesar like that twist.

So much so that in the early hours of Jay Carrion's fourth day in custody, they return with him under cover of darkness to his apartment. Within hours the walls of his office are covered with maps, book covers, text samples, photos of locations and faces, all produced from his labyrinthine filing system. It's like the hub of a murder inquiry – only the murder hasn't *yet* been committed.

First up is Gloria Minette.

SIX

Gloria Minette is a star that imploded.

Her equivalent in the cinematic cosmos – the bigger screen, so to speak – is the career black hole. For most of the 1950s and into the sixties, Gloria twinkled in movie houses around the world. She was as recognisable as the Milky Way or the Plough. In those days the Hollywood studios controlled the placement of stars in their galaxy. Many actresses were shooting stars, but Gloria was not one of them. She hung on up there for most of two decades, then abruptly suffered a total eclipse – not for giving a bad performance, but for not performing at all. She refused to go down on the new studio head.

Retribution was swift.

The gravitational forces inside the system tore her apart.

She would never work again.

Most people thought Gloria was dead, including Jay. About ten years ago he found out otherwise. His mother, who also lived in New York, Queens to be exact, had a cleaner come to her apartment twice a week. Over time they'd become friends and Emily – his mother never knew her surname – would bring news from the other side of the tracks.

In this case Brighton Beach.

Emily had a new client: an old-time movie star who'd fallen on hard times. Living in a one-room apartment that she rarely left, Gloria Minette's existence was frugal. Her time was spent reading, listening to the radio, watching television, but mostly dreaming of the past. Her mind was still lolling beside the pools of Beverly Hills.

Gloria desperately missed the warmth and the light, both of which were lacking in her apartment. She also missed the parties and the sex. The studio boss, knowing of her promiscuity, assumed she'd be acquiescent. Her refusal was not only sexually frustrating but also humiliating. Fellatio performed in the studio offices was, and probably still is, an important ritual in Hollywood's power games. For a start it usually requires the woman to kneel.

On hearing of her existence, Jay quickly recognised an interesting specimen for Marshall's delectation. The Master enjoyed making literary forays into the seedier side of Hollywood. Gloria Minette sounded like she was very much his meat. Jay sent a letter with Emily on her next visit to clean the old star's apartment. He used *New York Times* headed paper recently filched on a visit to a friend employed by that newspaper. In it he requested an interview, saying he was both an admirer of her films and a contributor to the paper's culture section. Her reply was immediate and handwritten, revealing a bold and expressive prose style: *'You're doing a terrible thing to me. I've been killing myself off for thirty years and now you're going to bring me back to life.'*

That was ten years ago when Jay was slim, big and strong, a country boy with a full head of hair. It's hard to believe he was handsome then, but he was. He pressed the bell outside her apartment and waited an age while the numerous locks and chains were loudly disengaged. The door grated as it swung open to reveal a small woman in a worn, almost threadbare, dark double-breasted pinstripe suit over a white shirt and red tie. Her jet-black hair was badly dyed and cut short.

Enveloped in a cloud of smoke emanating from the cheap cigar clamped in her mouth, her black eyes flashed mischievously as they settled on young Jay holding a bunch of flowers and a bottle of champagne.

'My God, you look like a stage-door Johnny. Wow! You come to interview or fuck me?'

A laugh as rough as a pneumatic drill blasted Jay's face with cigar smoke, causing him to cough. That first single emission gathered momentum and soon he was convulsed in a full-blown asthmatic attack. Barking and hawking and worried about dropping his gifts, he sank to one knee, laying them on the stained carpet close to her tiny bare feet.

In a terrible biopic – now gathering cobwebs in film vaults around the world – Gloria had played Queen Elizabeth of England. With Jay kneeling before her she immediately recognised the scene and *how* to play it. She touched her cigar lightly on his heaving shoulder and delivered the line that brought down many a movie house.

'Arise, Sir Walter. Thanks for the baccy. *And* the spuds.'

The guffaw that followed would have rent Sir Walter's breeches and blown away his ruff.

Only when the spasm receded and his eyes stopped watering did Jay take in that her left foot had three toenails freshly varnished *black* and that tufts of toilet tissue were stuffed between the rest. Jay's eyes widened with incredulity when the toes wiggled before lifting off to snuggle into his crotch and caress his suddenly expanding penis.

He still blushes when he remembers what happened next.

Once in her apartment Gloria bestowed on him the very gift she'd denied the film executive all those years earlier. And she hadn't lost her touch, teasing his cock with her lips and tongue, bringing him time and again to the very point of ejaculation. She had Jay the way she wanted every man: whinnying and begging for mercy. Then it was over and she was soon lighting up another cigar.

'Screw acting! We were blow-job artists.'

She pulled out a lipstick and applied it to her mouth. Like the nail varnish, it was black.

'Now that's a credit you *never* saw on any film. Blow-job artist! Louis B. Meyer never asked for it. Although, if he was honest, he should have. Sam Goldwyn was more likely to give credit where credit was due. He was wittier than Meyer.'

She waved her cigar about like Groucho Marx.

'Babe, you *don't* go down on me, you *blow* job.'

She blew smoke around the room as if fumigating the place. Each time she laughed he winced. It was as if the two hemispheres of his brain were being cleft apart by a hatchet.

Later, much later, having talked non-stop about her childhood in St Louis and the paedophiliac theatrical agent who started her off on the Yellow Brick Road, she finally got around to talking about the executive who aborted her career.

Jay asked why she refused to pleasure him.

'Cos his penis was smaller than a toothpick. OK, so the poor little shit had pulled the short straw. Mother Nature's cruel like that. That wasn't the problem. Trouble was – when I saw it – I couldn't stop laughing. You see, it would have been like trying to play a piccolo and that's a tricky instrument to play, believe you me. He took umbrage.'

Gloria, sipping champagne and stretched out on the single bed occupying one corner of her room, began to expand on penile deficiency in Hollywood. 'Irving Thalberg – head of production at Universal and MGM in the twenties and thirties – had a cock that even when engorged resembled a tadpole. Mind you, that didn't stop him marrying a movie goddess. Norma Shearer.'

Another laugh rent the air.

'But as Hollywood's the Mecca of make-believe, this was no problem for Norma. In bed with Irving she had to do just that. Make believe! Besides, out of bed, her husband was the most powerful man in the movie colony. That must have been some consolation.'

The little red light of Jay's tape recorder, standing on the bedside table, flickered as the machine captured the words flying from Gloria's mouth. When she painfully crossed to a wall cupboard and lifted out a pile of battered albums, Jay furtively produced a miniature camera and quickly covered every aspect of the room.

He didn't have to rush as the old star's batteries were running down. The unaccustomed booze was taking its toll and she was moving very slowly. His most prized shot – the one Marshall still has pinned to his office wall – is the one of her tiny feet with the nails varnished black. The toilet tissue still stuck between the toes.

'This'll show you what a whore I was.'

Dust rose from every page of the album as she turned it to reveal herself on the arm of man after man after man. At party after party. At premiere after premiere. At restaurant after restaurant, there she was with the same excited smile and eyes. Each man looked like he owned her, as if she was some exotic pet he'd just procured.

'Even when I was earning a big salary from the movies, I was always a *kept* woman.'

She paused to point at a grey-haired giant with a smile as wide as his Stetson, dwarfing her in the photograph.

'George was a darling man. Forty years older than me but virile as a stallion. Made all his money from carpets and that's where he liked to fuck me. Each time on a different pattern. I never knew if it was *me* or the *carpets* that aroused him most. The affair was terminated when his wife blew his balls off and then his head with a Smith & Wesson .32 automatic. Texans are like that.'

The album seemed to have charged her up with fresh energy.

'Now here's a story.'

She stopped at a photograph taken outside the Sands Hotel in Vegas sometime in the 1960s. It was a low-angle shot backed by the casino's marquee. Frank Sinatra was topping the bill. That night Gloria was under the arm of a swarthy guy with jet-black, greased-back hair, a black helmet glinting in the neon lighting as if a cockroach was sitting on his head. Clad in a dark suit and darker glasses, gold bracelet and rings adorning the carefully manicured hand resting on her slender shoulder, this was someone most of us would *not* want to spend time with.

Not so the plucky little star twinkling in the yellowing snapshot.

'Rocky was a darling man. A sweet man. Like a father to me.'

A single tear trickled down her cheek. Jay's investment in the bottle of champagne was beginning to pay off.

'Rocky Sorvino was obsessed by me. Ran my films every night in his own private screening room. I tell you I wanted to have kids by Rocky. Unfortunately in bed he fired *blanks*. Out of bed it was a different story.'

She belched, then farted, before continuing, 'Now this is the story. I won't mention names cos that wouldn't be ethical. There was this role, a big one – big like Scarlett in *Gone with the Wind* – that I was up for. A string of my recent roles had been shit so this one I badly needed. And Rocky knew it.

'Rumours suddenly began to emerge about this up-and-coming bitch starlet, under contract to the same studio, that had started fucking the movie's producer out of his brains. In the race for the role she was coming up fast on the outside and under the whip. That was the kind of sex he was into. It looked like the bitch was going to be first past the

225

post. Then shortly after these rumours began circulating she was found dead in a bungalow at the Chateau Marmont. A heroin overdose.'

Gloria sipped her champagne and belched again.

'That filly's career and reputation crashed simultaneously. Rocky smiled when he told me of her demise that morning at breakfast. You know what he did then? He called room service and ordered two Bloody Marys. Rocky had style.'

By now Jay's eyes were dancing in their sockets. He knew Marshall would go crazy when he heard this stuff and couldn't resist checking his tape recorder. Until then Gloria had forgotten about the little machine trapping her every word. Her beady eyes followed Jay's to the little red light still blinking reassuringly.

'Best not put that last story in the article, Jay.'

'Whatever you say, Gloria.'

He took her glass and carefully topped it up, watching the bubbles rise to the surface, hoping the same would happen with the old star's memories. But Gloria was now on her guard.

'When you running this piece?'

'That's up to the editor.'

'Soon as he's made his mind up, send word with Emily.'

'Emily?'

Jay had forgotten about the cleaner his mother shared with the actress. She'd carried his introductory letter to her. Gloria soon cleared that up.

'Emily's the only person I get to talk with nowadays. I trust Emily. Give me your phone number before you go.'

'Sure.'

He wrote a number down in his notepad and tore the page out.

'I didn't think you had a phone?'

'I don't. But I'd still like to have it.'

Jay handed her the piece of paper.

'I thought all you smart guys carried cards these days.'

'We do. It's just that I left in a rush and forgot mine.'

He switched off the recorder and put it in his bag.

Time to make an exit.

Gloria insisted on seeing him to the door.

When Emily next came to clean her apartment, she told Gloria it was for the last time. Her excuse was her mother's sudden illness. In reality Jay had paid her off to ensure there was no feedback. At the time he never thought he'd be back ringing her doorbell.

He was wrong.

*

A mole looks confused when it surfaces in daylight.

So it was with Gloria Minette when she emerged from her apartment late one morning shortly after Jay's visit. Previously she only went out after dark to shop in the all-night supermarket. Often in the early hours. Her neighbours in the block were surprised to see her. Many of them had never laid eyes on her and had no idea who she was.

Nor did they particularly care.

Every day for the next week she set off to the nearest drug store and every day returned with a copy of the *New York Times*. With each journey her demeanour grew more leaden, her shoulders more hunched, her eyes more dull, more despondent.

Then her appearances stopped as suddenly as they'd begun.

The previous day she'd rung from a public phone the number Jay had left her – a number he'd plucked out of thin air. Even he, with his intimate knowledge of plot lines and the role of coincidence, could not have anticipated the outcome of the call.

She got through to a funeral parlour.

Gloria knew then that she'd been duped.

But had no idea *why*.

Ten years later, aged eighty-five, she's about to find out.

*

A slim package is partly pushed into her mailbox.

It doesn't drop.

It protrudes into Gloria's room like a rude tongue. She's still in bed, although it's mid-afternoon and nearly dark. An eerie light comes from the muted television, dispensing a constant string of mindless images into the gloom. Grinning faces, sets of searing white teeth snapping endlessly at each other, a desperate succession of products intended to bring meaning and hope into our lives.

Her emaciated hands tear the envelope apart to reveal a paperback. *A Role to Kill For* by Marshall Grist. Gloria has to sit down while she searches the package for a letter, a note, anything to explain its mysterious arrival.

Is the novel going to be adapted for television?

Would she be interested in playing...?

She can even hear the producer's voice: *Who's your agent, Gloria?*

But there's no letter, not even a compliments slip.

Only the book.

She starts to read it, not putting it down until she's finished.

It doesn't take long because she already knows the story.

It's *her* story.

*

Hours later the doorbell sounds.

Confused and angry, she struggles with the locks and bars, finally leaving the door on a chain to peer outside.

Fat Jay is standing there.

At first she doesn't recognise him.

Then she hears a familiar voice.

'Time for revenge, Gloria. One more great role beckons.'

Unfortunately, Primo, having chosen *not* to let Fat Jay out of his sight, appears beside him, smiling, trying to look warm and friendly. The old actress takes one look, gasps, slams the door and secures the locks with surprising speed.

Jay rounds on him furiously.

'I thought we agreed you'd stay out of sight.'

'Hey, man, it *you* who scare her.'

'Me?'

'Yes, you ugly fat shit! All old lady love Primo all time.'

'Is that so?'

Jay instinctively sticks a finger in his ear and waggles it about as if checking that it's functioning properly. Satisfied that it is, he shakes his head and continues, 'Well, you just met *one* old lady who no love Primo. Primo make her shit herself.'

As it happens, this is not strictly true.

Although shaken, Gloria is also wondering if she'd heard correctly. Had the fat guy offered her a role? Not just a role but a *great* role? Making sure the safety chain is still on, she releases all the locks before slowly prising the door open until she meets Jay's beaming face.

'Jesus, Gloria, I'm sorry about the piece in the *Times*. The goddamn editor spiked it. Forgive me for...'

'Fuck the article, what's the role, Fatso? I only play leads.'

'You'll be the sole woman in the cast.'

'What is it? A film, a play? What medium are we talking here?'

'It's reality television *without* the cameras.'

'No cameras? What's the money like?'

'Ten percent of the gross.'

'Nothing up front?'

'How about a new face? A younger one?'

Gloria's current one lights up.

SEVEN

Unlike Gloria, whom Jay happened upon accidentally, Marty Graf was uncovered at the special request of Marshall. 'I want to write a story about a cosmetic surgeon, Jay, and I'll tell you why. Remember that jumbo jet blown up by terrorists over Scotland? Nearly two hundred passengers blown to bits, about a third of them young American students. But you know what? When the pathologists came to identify the remains, they had to disregard the customary method of using dental records. Why? Because their teeth were *identical*. There was no way they could tell them apart. Now here's my point: what the dentists have done to our ivories the cosmetic surgeons are now doing to our bodies and faces. They, too, will soon be *identical*.'

In those days, Grist always communicated his literary needs to his researcher via a tape recording. This, in turn, was delivered to Jay's apartment by Greta Himmler, the writer's loyal housekeeper. That way meetings between them were kept to a minimum. He wouldn't even talk to Jay on the phone.

Marshall was never a fan of the human animal.

Off the page that is.

Jay can still remember that particular request. His employer was in a worse strop than usual. 'Dickheads around the world are buying into this crap, Jay. Why for Christ's sake? Aren't their cars, clothes, homes already homogenous? So why the fuck do they want to extend that state of uniformity to their own image? What the fuck's happening to the human species? Those poor kids on the plane couldn't be identified when they were *dead*. Soon we won't be able to identify our fellow beings when they're *alive*.'

The sound of rattling ice cubes intrudes.

Vodka was Marshall's fuel.

'I remember when we struggled to be different, to be individuals. Then along came the gods of consumerism, waved a wand and now we all look like we came off a conveyor belt. We're humans, not Model Ts. Jay, I want to know everything there is to know about this cosmetic surgery shit. Get me the lowdown on the world of human makeovers and the fuckers who practise it. These people are playing at being God. This book is going to be Old Testament stuff, Jay, an eye for an eye, a tooth for a tooth. Go forth, boy, and bring back the facts.'

And Jay did just that.

*

It so happened that Farrah Bangerter – a friend of Jay's married sister – had spent much of her family inheritance on every variety of body makeover.

Five years earlier, Farrah's parents had died in a particularly messy car crash. Their snappy little sports convertible was crushed by a freight train when the car stalled on a level crossing. Sadly, they'd collected it from the showroom only minutes before. Nobody knew why the car stalled, although the coroner suggested the driver – her elderly father – may have got cramp from sitting in the racing position required to drive it. He went on to warn other older folk against trying to appear youthful in fast cars when their reactive abilities and manual dexterity were inevitably reduced by age.

Nor can anyone explain *why* Farrah went on such a punishing schedule of cosmetic surgery. Was it a psychological reaction to seeing the mutilated bodies found in the crash? A way of repairing the shattered image of her begetters? Or was it her addiction to glossy fashion magazines, those evolutionary blueprints for reshaping the whole human species?

None of these theories interested Jay.

All he wanted was access to her reservoir of names and her impressions of the surgeons themselves.

But there was a problem.

Farrah's face had been heavily Botoxed. This, along with liposuction surgery, had severely restricted the pliability of her facial muscles. As a consequence, her voice seemed to come from any orifice other than her mouth. It was as if a ventriloquist was throwing her voice and *missing* the dummy. Only when Jay had settled into watching her throat for evidence of emerging words did the flow, fluency and speed of her delivery make its full impact. Unaware that her late father had spent his working life as a tobacco auctioneer in North Carolina, Jay was to be confounded when Farrah's story unfolded with the rapidity of an automatic weapon.

It was lethal stuff.

'You gotta understand this, JayBoy: within those cosmetic clinics the collected neuroses of the patients cling like poisonous vapours in a chemical plant; that's why the staff have faces that look like goddamn gas masks with eyes as dead as frozen meat; Jesus, being in any one of those clinics is like being in a deep freeze; another fact you gotta face, Jay, is that once they wheel you into that operating theatre, the centre of attention becomes *you* – all eyes are on *you*! *You* are the star. They ain't called *theatres* for nothing.'

Even when she laughs her lips don't move.

Farrah keeps firing words.

'JayBoy, you want to know what drives folk these days? *Dis*-satisfaction, insatiable *dis*-satisfaction, that's what's driving 'em and they're pressing on the gas pedal like never before; the whole human herd is now eternally on the move; mostly in the air; looking for new grazing grounds; folk want to be anywhere *except* where they are; and it's the same with their *bodies*; a lot of folk don't want to be in *there* either; these folk can fly around the planet all they like but their body goes with them wherever they go: it'll share the same seat with them, sleep on the same side of the bed, keep itself alive with the same food. They can never give their body the slip; the best they can do is change it *beyond* recognition. I speak as one of those folk, JayBoy.'

JayBoy notices Farrah take a breath.

'A *folie à deux*?'

'Right on *le nez*, JayBoy. Listen, I drew the genetic short straw; from the moment I popped out my mummy's womb I looked *exactly* like my *daddy*; whenever I went to a mirror there *he* was, my daddy, waiting for me along with my memories of his sticky baccy-stained fingers running all over my private parts; I tell you, JayBoy, I'm grateful to those clinics; they exorcised my *daddy* from me; I don't look like him no more and I'm mighty glad.'

JayBoy was feeling faint from the ferocity of Farrah's word power, grateful when she finally handed him her prepared list of the clinics and surgeons she'd used on her desperate journey of self-obliteration.

He casts his eyes down the names.

'Marty Graf? That name rings a bell.'

'It should! Years ago Marty's name was on every news channel worldwide; his wife brought an assault charge against him saying he'd drugged her before the implant operation and while she was under the anaesthetic he implanted a pair boobs the size...' Farrah hesitates. 'How'd she put it? Boobs the size of prize watermelons, her words exactly; she lost the case because he'd got her to sign off on the surgery, which she denied; then his personal assistant stepped up in court saying she'd acted as a witness to her signature and Marty got off; he married the assistant as soon as his wife divorced him; it turned out he'd been fucking her for years; most times on his operating tables, which figures, since his wife told the court Marty invariably wore surgical gloves when boffing her.'

Farrah pauses for breath, allowing JayBoy a nanosecond to squeeze in a question.

'On what part of you did Marty operate?'

'Eye bags; he was drunk and by the time he'd finished there were so many sutures they'd morphed into *string* bags; I had to find another surgeon to sort it out and threatened to sue; before you could say "Mack the Knife", a mean little shit comes knocking on my door saying he was a cosmetic surgeon, only he *didn't* bother with no anaesthetic; I dropped the case.'

Jay knew he'd found his man.

Marty Graf.

*

Marty Graf's company brand name – TransForm – has two dazzling white swans woven between the letters of its corporate logo. His Manhattan clinic, with its three operating theatres, occupies two spacious floors of an austere minimalist block designed by an ultra-cool Finnish architect. Its monastic interior, uninterrupted by the minutiae of everyday life such as windows, doors, switches, handles or knobs, immediately appeals to Graf. He intuits that his clientele will appreciate the purity of its sleek lines – desirous as they are to look as shiny and tough as the veneer of their limos.

Jay can hardly distinguish the clinic's receptionist from the décor in which she is set: the walls, floor, chairs, sofas, tables, everything is a *blinding* white and that includes her uniform and the counter behind which she resides.

Even her make-up is a white sheen.

When the glass doors silently part to allow him entry, her eyes remain cast down, even when he's standing in front of her. Jay can't resist glancing over the countertop to see *what* holds her attention, but he finds the space underneath *empty*: no screen, no book. She looks up, switches on a smile and her perfect teeth add the final touch to this bleached and bloodless space.

'How can I help you, sir?'

Jay notes the identity badge adhered to her tunic, revealing in white-on-white lettering that her name is *Saffron*.

'Yes, Saffron, I'm contemplating the removal of some surplus fat beginning to accumulate around my waist.'

Jay knew he was on safe ground here.

Unfortunately.

'Tummy tuck.'

Saffron's voice is as sexy as silk.

'Am I right in assuming, Saffron, that Dr Marty Graf is still the medical director?'

'No, sir. Dr Graf retired last year.'

Jay is about to leave there and then, but not before Saffron abruptly stands and moves away from the counter. He can now see how exquisitely her shape meets the necessary specifications for sexual arousal of alpha males weaned on pin-up girls. Including *him*. Saffron passes a hand over the back wall, thereby activating a hidden sliding panel and shelves piled with brochures and leaflets.

'Abdominoplasty.'

She lays a leaflet on the counter.

'You'll find all you need to know about this procedure in here.'

Her white lacquered nails drum the counter as she spins a second brochure to face him.

'And this has all there is to know about the TransForm clinic.'

'*All* there is to know?'

Jay smiles at her.

She doesn't smile back.

'Research reveals it's no longer just women who feel anxiety about looking good. A new study shows that men are more than happy to spend time and money improving their appearance. May I ask your name, sir?'

'Jay.'

'Well, Jay, it may interest you to know the average man now spends eighty-three minutes a day on personal grooming.'

'Eighty-*three* minutes.'

Jay tries to look suitably impressed before opening the brochure. A soft-focus image of a swan frames the brief introduction to the clinic by Dr Jesus Ruiz, the Medical Director of Aesthetic Surgery. Jay can't resist smiling as he reads on:

> *Zeus, the God of Gods, was constantly changing his appearance to conduct his numerous amorous encounters. As a Bull he violated Demeter; as a Cuckoo he took advantage of Hera. But his most dazzling transformation was effected to impress Leda who, when bathing in a pool, saw a Swan majestically floating towards her. It was Zeus.*

Jay can't help but read the next passage aloud:

> *Zeus is our inspiration. The White Swan our symbol. When you enter TransForm you are, dear friends, on the threshold of joining the Gods.*

'Gods indeed!'

Jay looks up to find Saffron's eyes on him.

She's come from behind the counter and now stands with her arms at her side, palms facing out and smiling blissfully, reminding him of an alabaster statue of the Virgin Mary. Then something extraordinary happens: this statue *winks* at him. Simultaneously her right hand vanishes into the whiteness of her tunic and returns with a business card.

She hands it to Jay.

On it is a printed phone number.

Astonished he retreats in confusion to consult the brochure in his hand.

'Eh... eh... there don't seem to be any prices in here?'

'It's simple. Two thousand dollars for a quickie; twenty thousand dollars for a night. Extra for deviancies.'

Jay still finds it hard to grasp what's happening.

Then it slowly dawns.

Saffron's job provides the perfect front for a hooker.

She's a high-class call girl.

And call her he will.

*

At first Marshall is reluctant to finance this fresh phase in their project. Jay has never before witnessed his employer show even the remotest interest in doing research himself and has to hard-talk him out of it. He suspects it's his casual remark about sexually transmitted diseases that finally deters him. Even so, Jay has to promise that if nothing comes from the time spent with Saffron he will repay his $2,000 investment.

All this is discussed over the *phone*.

That's how exercised Marshall is by the turn of events.

'Believe me, Marshall, Saffron's the best example of product placement I've ever come across.'

'Fuck that, Jay. It's Marty Graf I'm interested in. This Saffron said he'd retired, right? Bullshit! That creep's not the retiring sort. Find out *why* he got out and *where* he ended up. Remember this, Jay, Saffron can't give head and dish the dirt *simultaneously*. Right?'

With that he blows a *raspberry* down the line and hangs up.

An hour later the bell to Jay's apartment rings.

It's Marshall's housekeeper, Greta, with Saffron's fee. It comes in an envelope with a red wax seal impressed with Masonic symbols. As might be expected of a *paranoid* billionaire, Marshall is seriously into antique wax seals, collecting them in a major way.

Jay leaves Greta while he counts the bills in the bathroom.

Not a dollar over two thousand!

The housekeeper gives him a funny look when he returns to sign the receipt she's laid out on his desk. She's obviously aware of the money's final destination and *doesn't* approve. Greta is a devout Roman Catholic, attending Mass early every morning, taking communion and making her confession every week. Her life seems so pure, Jay finds it difficult to imagine what sins she could possibly reveal to her confessor. He wonders if she secretly lusts after priests: a not uncommon desire among devout Catholic women wanting to feel the hand of God upon them via his representatives on earth.

Flashback!

Jay had found Greta twelve years earlier, shortly after Marshall's widowed mother died. Greta's thick German accent and her family name, *Himmler,* hinted at an inherent propensity for the disciplinary, something sorely missing from Grist's life since the demise of the aforementioned parent. Jay's instincts had been right. Within days Greta had the writer's domestic world running as smoothly as a BMW, leaving limitless time for the ocean of words to flow from his head through to his fingers and onto the computer screen.

A chain of bestsellers followed.

Bookshop tables and shelves soon heaved with his thrillers.

It was never intended that Greta would actually *live* in Grist's apartment, but shortly after her initial engagement she had moved her worldly belongings into one of his numerous en-suite bedrooms.

Jay isn't certain if Marshall *ever* realised this.

Marshall rarely ventures beyond the blue haze of his computer screen while Greta drifts silently in and out of his consciousness like the ghost of his late mother. Although indulging Marshall's every whim, it's really Jay she dotes on, grateful for the comfort and security he's been instrumental in providing. She often treats him to softly sung *Lieder* and once even came bearing *Lederhosen* breeches, all of which irritates the hell out of him. Unfortunately, his childish irritation only reinforces the role Greta has chosen for him.

Jay's her *Little Fritz* and that's that.

This day things are no different.

Waving the receipt he's just signed, she scolds him.

'Dis money ist for research not for your weeny vinkle...!'

Jay, confused, interrupts.

'Vinkle?'

'Vinkle... vinkle...'

She angrily points at his testicles.

'Your little vinkle! It must stay in ze pants, not go cuckoo, cuckoo...'

Jay fumes even more when he remembers the infernal clock she'd installed on the wall of her room. He's about to insist, yet again, that it's removed, but she's already on her way out, delivering a final 'cuckoo' as she closes the door.

*

Jay is taken aback when a *man* answers the phone.

'You vant appointment wiz Paris?'

'Paris? I was hoping to speak with Saffron.'

Each word is mangled and mauled by an East European accent.

'Zat ze name zey give her at clinic. Arseholes! She ist Saffron by day, Paris by night. Vich night you after?'

'Tomorrow night?'

'You kidding? She booked all month. I look.'

Jay can hear him turning pages.

'How about thirteenth next month?'

'Listen, sir...!'

'No *sir*! Janek.'

'Janek, I'm only in town this week. All I want is a *quickie*.'

'You got three thousand dollars?'

'Saffron quoted two thousand.'

'Extra one thousand is for me to bump somebody out of bed.'

'Janek, I only want to *talk* to her.'

'Talk dirty? Price same.'

'OK, but no need to talk *all* night. Tell you what, Janek, I'll pay one thousand dollars for just ten minutes. Maybe tomorrow evening before her client checks in?'

Janek corrects him.

'No client – *patient*.'

Jay's sly eyes examine the phone's mouthpiece with the care of a dentist examining teeth before continuing.

'Ah? *Paris* is a sex therapist perhaps?'

Janek grunts.

'And *Saffron* a hooker?'

'You got there, baby.'

'Then it's *Paris* I want to consult.'

*

The apartment overlooks Central Park.

Its steel-studded front door swings open only to be replaced by the giant Janek. His crew cut brushes the top of the frame as he steps out to check the corridor before letting Jay enter. Watching the deadlocks being returned and the keys turned, Jay realises just how prized an asset Paris is. A milch cow requiring careful protection.

He follows Janek out of the spacious hall into an equally spacious sitting room with a breathtaking view of the park.

'Wait.'

Janek leaves him looking down on the tiny figures moving below. They could be ants, he thinks. Original thinking is not Jay's long suit. Anyway it's the cars plying the streets that really excite him. He has a sudden desperate urge to *play* with them. He blushes, realising Greta is sort of right. He is a little boy, a little *fat* boy.

Another unoriginal thought strikes him.

This is what it must be like *being* God.

Toying with his creation.

Such celestial musings are shattered with Janek's return.

The almighty giant towers over Jay as he points to the door he's just left open.

'Paris there. I stay here.'

He waves a finger the size of a cucumber.

'You behave!'

Jay goes to leave but Janek's huge right hand lands on his shoulder while the left one circles behind his head and hovers in front of his eyes. Its thumb and fingers rub together in a gesture recognised across our universe, and probably beyond, as a demand for money! Gelt! Shekels! Mazuma!

Flustered and red-faced, Jay takes from his inside pocket the same envelope Greta had delivered. It is, of course, lighter by $1,000, which pleases him. Rarely has he been he able to put one over on Marshall.

Janek studies the broken seal with puzzled eyes before counting the money. Satisfied it's the correct amount, he turns his attention back to the red wax.

'What shit this? Dry-ed blood?'

'No, no, wax. Wax. It's a seal. *Was* a seal.'

Distrust floods into Janek's eyes.

He reopens the envelope, takes out the dollar bills and counts them again. Jay nervously watches his whispering lips: the *outward* manifestation of the *inner* workings of the giant's sluggish brain. When they, the lips, eventually cease moving, Jay looks up to find Janek's eyes on him. They beam with concentrated suspicion, enough to make Jay deeply regret cheating on Marshall.

He whimpers.

'One thousand dollars, right? That's what we agreed, right?'

'You! Bad boy!'

Janek's hands suddenly shoot up to clamp Jay's head as if in a nutcracker.

'Why seal *not* seal? Eh? Eh? Where rest? I break you like seal!'

Jay's eyeballs look close to popping clean out of their sockets, unlike the words from his mouth. These emerge twisted and dented like discarded drink cans and are totally unrecognisable. With Janek lifting him painfully off the floor, Jay's arms flail about until they find the trouser pocket secreting the rest of Marshall's money. He manages to extract the bills and throw them in the air.

They cascade like confetti above a happy couple.

In a split second the wedding is off and Jay finds himself abandoned on the floor while Janek frantically scrambles to capture every fluttering note. So absorbed is he by avarice that he fails to notice Jay crawling at speed towards the open door into what turns out to be a bedroom.

It's deserted, although there are so many mirrors in which Jay is reflected that the room appears to be crowded, albeit with numerous versions of himself. His recent experience in the hands of Janek has left him shaken and breathless with his heart apparently attempting to escape through his chest. Perching momentarily on the enormous bed, he gives way to its sensual softness and lies on his back. Even here his reflection relentlessly pursues him and this time it's impaled in the mirrored ceiling. Only then does he hear the sound of somebody taking a bath, splashing and quietly singing.

It's a woman.

He sits up and calls out.

'Paris?'

As it's still early in the evening he wonders if the metamorphosis from receptionist to hooker has happened yet. Not taking any chances, he calls out again.

'Saffron?'

And the singing stops.

'Is this the guy who wants to talk dirty?'

'Yep.'

'Come on in. Come feast your eyes on me. No touchy-touchy though. Is your cock rising like a cobra in the kasbah to the music of my voice?'

Jay can't help but nod in agreement as he sidles towards the bathroom door. He finds Saffron/Paris immersed in an essence as white and steaming as warm milk. Her hands caress her breasts, playing lovingly with their nipples. The only blemish to this scene of sexual abandonment is the disconcerting Mask of Mud covering her face. But even that has its upside as the pack's rough brown texture brilliantly highlights the sky blue of her eyes.

They sparkle with amusement when she sees Jay.

'I remember you. Tummy tuck, right?'

'Right.'

'Jay, is it?'

'Right again.'

'Hey, your ears look all red. That fucker Janek given you a shakedown?'

'Yep. Janek has his very own version of a *face-lift*.'

'No aesthetic component?'

'That's one way of putting it.'

Her right leg breaks the surface of the water as she fondly runs her hands down it until they reach their destination. A light moan of pleasure escapes her lips before she speaks.

'The aesthetic component is important to me.'

'Is that so? Having a gorilla front of house can't help much. Which zoo did he come from?'

Jay looks nervously at the open door, hoping Janek is still happily counting his windfall and can't hear the escalating moans coming from the bathroom.

'Poor Janek, he loves me so. Some nights he gets a little jealous, that's all.'

'Customer *satisfaction* is obviously driving him crazy. I suggest you have him put down.'

Her eyes close in ecstasy as she parts her legs even wider, bending them so that her knees emerge, two dimpled brown islands in a calm white sea. Jay struggles to keep his own hands from joining the fun. Instead he concentrates his thoughts on having to return Marshall's money should he fail in his task.

'Saffron...'

'Paris!'

'Paris, I have to level with you. I'm not here to talk dirty but to talk about Marty Graf.'

'Is there a difference?'

She sits up sharply, torso glistening like white marble, eyes on fire. Alarmed, Jay takes a step back.

'Why the fuck do you want to talk about that creep?'

'I'm researching a book.' Quickly adding, 'Fiction, it's a work of fiction. The author just wants to know what goes on in the world of plastic surgery. The story *below* the cosmetic surface.'

'Let me get this straight: you want me to *dish* the dirt not *talk* it, right?'

'Right.'

Paris calms down.

Her eyes switch off while she thinks.

Then switch back on with a new intensity.

'You did pay Janek?'

Jay nods.

'How much?'

'One thousand. Two, if you include the *service* charge, which in his case is *not* optional.'

'Serbians adore capitalism.'

Paris stands, letting the water course around every sensuous curve of her body. She steps from the bath into a white towel bathrobe before sitting in front of a huge make-up mirror edged with shimmering light bulbs. Her suspicious eyes peer like two prisoners from behind the mud pack.

'So what do you want to know?'

'Can we start with the case brought by his ex-wife? Was she telling the truth?'

'Course she was. Marty got so aroused with Candy under the anaesthetic he tripled the usual amount of silicon. I'm not exaggerating. Candy Graf came out of that surgery so front-heavy she kept tipping over. But it was the bitch Marlene Joyboy who really screwed her.'

'Marlene Joyboy's the assistant who testified against her?'

'Correct. Marty had been fucking her for years. We all knew, but Candy was too busy being *sweet* to notice. Lying for him in court gave Marlene Joyboy the leverage she needed. After that Marty *had* to marry her. That cow's a gold-digger with a JCB. Since then Marty's scalpel never rests. The clinic may look white on the outside but inside it's very noir.'

'How come?'

'That gold-digger tunnelled so deep she finally reached the underworld.'

Jay felt his pulse quicken.

'Do you mean that literally?'

'Sure I do. Marlene and Marty became quick-change artists for drug dealers in Mexico and Colombia. They'd iron out their faces for their laundered money. That's how it started. Word soon reached the other ugly faces of big business. Embezzling corporate heads, fraudulent hedge-fund dealers, bent brokers, any high-flyer about to crash, they all came to the surgeries they set up in luxury hotels around the world. They provided offshore faces for offshore funds. Unfortunately when *word* gets out, it never stops where you want it to. Eventually it went on to reach the FBI.'

Her eyes swivel to the open door.

Jay turns as Janek fills it, his shoulder pads brushing the frame.

He consults a watch as big as his face.

'Time go. Next please.'

'Thank you, Janek,' snaps Paris. 'I'll be out in a minute.'

He's obviously been listening.

'You no dirty talk?'

'You heard what I said, Janek. Now fuck off.'

Janek fires a malevolent look at Jay before backing out.

Paris cracks the mud mask, fracturing it into a jigsaw of small pieces.

'When the FBI got wind of their operation it was their turn to disappear. Simple. They operated on each other, changing their appearances out of all recognition. That was two years ago. They waited six months before returning to the US with new identities.'

'Jesus Ruiz?'

'Correct.'

'The perfect name for a *resurrection*.'

'TransForm was still operative. They simply paid off the caretaker directors and started over. Smart move. The FBI will never think of looking for them there.'

She began to peel off the broken mask.

'That's it, Jay. Time to get your butt out of here.'

'One last question. Why do you stay working at the clinic?'

She pauses before replying, then continues to reveal her face piece by piece.

'The clinic's my Venus flytrap. I catch the flies *there* and digest them *here*. On top of which Marty is besotted with me. I've been fucking him for years. And Marlene Joyboy knows it but can't do anything about it.'

She laughs and the last chunk of mud falls away.

'I love driving that bitch crazy. It's such sweet revenge. You see, Candy Graf is my *sister*.'

*

Marty Graf, appropriately resurrected as Jesus Ruiz, remains blissfully unaware that the time has come for his crucifixion. That's until *Killer's Mask*, Marshall Grist's bestseller published a decade earlier, is delivered by Federal Express to TransForm. It waits, along with the rest of Ruiz's mail, in his office until the day's surgery is completed. Idly reading the blurb on the cover, he's immediately hooked.

The hero is a cosmetic surgeon.

Jesus devours the paperback *once* in the taxi to Grand Central Station and *three* times on the train home. When Jesus was Marty he'd trained to *speed read* before going to medical school. Whilst the technique certainly helped him come top of his class, it also induced a certain superficiality into his thinking which led, in turn, to an early switch in his surgical career to the cosmetic. Grist's paperback captures this superficiality perfectly. Its protagonist – alias Marty – is as narcissistic as his patients, as sharp and dangerous as his surgical instruments.

But it had not always been like this.

Marty had gone into medicine with the very best intentions: wanting to fight disease, cure the sick, bring solace to the dying. He'd even intended to volunteer for service in the Third World. As a young medical student, Marty travelled to the Greek island of Kos to see where Hippocrates had lived and practised. Sadly the inhabitants knew little about the father of modern medicine except for one significant fact.

He had *charged* for his services.

Apparently this was indisputable.

Hippocrates was in it for the money!

Or so Marty concluded.

His altruism and missionary zeal metaphorically disappeared down the toilet along with the hummus and feta cheese. And it's to the nearest *toilet* that Marty, now Jesus, runs when he finally reaches his mansion on Long Island.

The sound of violent retching soon filters upstairs to where Marlene sits engrossed, applying blood-red varnish to her fingernails. She quietly descends the sweeping marble staircase to the entrance hall and eases open the door to the powder room. There she finds Jesus doubled up on the floor, his body convulsed in spasms.

Moving inside she spies, floating in the pan, a lurid paperback covered in bile. A sordid sight. She gags and tries to speak. Marty tries to speak. She tries again. Neither achieves it. Only later does she learn the reason for her husband's parlous state. With each reading of *Killer's Mask* it had become clear to him that its author knew *every* squalid detail of their life together. When he finally finishes recapping Grist's grim narrative, both he and Marlene fall silent.

The truth is inescapable.

Somewhere in the wings waits a blackmailer.

*

Dr Jesus Ruiz sits behind the desk in his consultancy room. For the past week he's flinched every time his phone rang, panicked every time a patient entered, woken screaming every night from nightmares. Now his trembling hand reaches across the desktop to slide the next patient's file into place. He opens it, notes that the patient's name is new to him and that it's a consultation for a tummy tuck.

His hand presses the hidden button to green-light his secretary.

Minutes later the door opens.

Ruiz looks up and knows the *blackmailer* waits in the wings no longer. Fat Jay enters while the secretary quietly closes the door behind him.

'I sure do miss the *ex*-sister-in-law.'

'Ex-sister-in-law?'

'The exquisite Saffron? Wasn't she your sister-in-law?'

Ruiz ignores the question.

Instead he consults his file.

'Jay Carrion? That your name?' He looks up, cold and clear now the enemy is in his sights. 'And is it a tummy tuck that brings you here? I must say such surgery wouldn't go amiss.'

Fat Jay laughs, sits, rummages in his bag and bangs a copy of *Killer's Mask* on the desk.

'Snap!'

Ruiz picks it up and opens the title page.

'I rather hoped it would be a signed copy. Are you Grist?'

'No I'm not, Marty.'

'Marty?'

'Jesus, Marty, let's stop playing games.'

The surgeon closes the file as he leans back in his chair.

'So how much do you want?'

'No money, Marty. *Services.*'

Jay takes a folder out of his bag and lays out two large photographs. 'I want you to make this little old lady...' – he pats the face of Gloria Minette – '... look like this younger old lady.' The second is Greta Himmler.

Ruiz compares the images with great care.

Satisfied, he gives his verdict. 'No problem.'

'I knew you'd cooperate. My faith in human nature has now been restored.'

Fat Jay shuffles the photographs back into the folder.

'By the way, do I call you Marty or Jesus?'

Ruiz skips that one.

'So I do the job, then what?'

'Then *you* are off the hook. Marlene too. By then I, too, will be a criminal on the run. Just like you.'

As Jay makes for the door, Ruiz calls after him.

'Carrion, I'd be happy to throw in a tummy tuck and eye-bag removal as part of the deal.'

'Forget it, Jesus. If I ever arrive at those Pearly Gates I want God – *your* Father – to recognise me.'

Smiling, Jay blesses Ruiz with a Sign of the Cross as he closes the door.

EIGHT

Jay has to force open the door of his apartment, sweeping back the discarded pizza boxes, empty beer cans, tequila bottles and clothes accumulated in the entrance hall since Primo and Caesar checked in. The river of debris trails across the open-plan living area into the guest room where they lie, dead to the world, sprawled like murder victims across the bed with arms and legs spilling onto the floor.

Gunshots blasting from the television add to the sense of mayhem.

Jay delicately picks his way towards the TV and kills the sound. Two sets of nostrils, snoring like tugboats in fog, take over. Suddenly dizzy, Jay feels for the sofa. As he sinks into it, his weary eyes scan the chaos around him.

Until a week ago everything in Jay's life had been pristine, ordered, neat and tidy. Now, as if in a gesture of sympathy, the visuals on the muted television switch to scenes of carnage from some foreign war. Buildings and bodies are being blown apart. Not long ago they, too, were probably pristine, ordered, neat and tidy. Jay closes his eyes.

Primo twitches violently before rolling off the bed, grunting as he hits the floor. Even that doesn't disturb his druggy sleep. Jay holds his breath, hoping his tormentor won't surface. He waits, watching the two grotesques lying in the next room, helpless as babies, and weighs his chances of smothering them silently, one by one. His intestines stir ominously as he picks up a cushion from the sofa, stands and silently crosses to the bedroom.

Shaking all over, he hesitates.

Which to dispose of first?

He can hardly believe it when his lips involuntarily mouth, '*Eeny, meeny, miny moe, Catch a tiger by the toe, If he hollers…*' He doesn't get as far as '*let him go*', before the decision is made and not by him. Caesar, skimming the surface of some nightmare, suddenly screams and fends off an imaginary attacker

'Hey, man, no kill me! I no die! Shit, you got wrong man!'

Jay freezes. Close to fainting, his face drains of blood. Is Caesar having a premonition? *Et tu, Brute!* Then the little shit, still in the arms of Morpheus, abruptly drops his arms, smiles and whispers.

'You's cool, man.'

Not so Jay, who quickly backs from the room. His bowel, much irritated by this turn of events, has finally taken charge, forcing a rapid retreat to the bathroom. Once inside, he goes to secure the door only to find the lock's been dismantled. Holding his head in despair, he contemplates quitting his apartment and starting over in another city. Then he remembers Marshall laughing at him on the phone: '*That was a dirty, filthy gesture, Jay. Giving me the finger like that.*' That laugh still reverberates in his skull like it was an echo chamber.

Jay flattens his hand and contemplates the bulge of white bandage covering the throbbing stump of his pinky finger. It helps concentrate his mind. Like the target on a firing range, Marshall moves back into the frame. Only when that bastard hits the obituary pages will Primo and Caesar go top of his hit list. Like dog shit on your shoe, they're going to be tough to wipe off. So what? He'll find a way. Jay shakes his head, surprised at the murderous thoughts in his head.

Loud shouts jar him back into the present.

Almost simultaneously the television starts up at full volume.

His accomplices are awake.

The bathroom door bangs open, revealing Primo with his trousers already dropping as he makes for the can. He screeches when he sees Jay occupying it.

'Get the fuck off, fat mother! Or I dump on you.'

Jay jumps.

His white butt lifts off just as the brown one lands.

Touch and go, like in musical chairs.

Sadly the metaphor ends there. In no way is the disposal of human waste melodic. Jay retreats in disgust, closes the door behind him, and seeks refuge in his office. He'd managed to convince them that *this* space was not part of their playpen. His imagination had been sorely taxed to find a way that appealed to dudes permanently out of their minds. *Star Trek* happened to be on television at the time. That's how he found himself comparing his office to the control room of a spaceship, *their* spaceship, the one seeking Dollar Heaven for Primo and Caesar. They must stay out of there. If they fucked up the controls in his office, their ship would be sucked into a black hole.

'Black hole?' said Primo.

'Black hole?' repeated Caesar.

Jay nodded and watched their eyes momentarily go blank, then fill with funk. All those great minds, from Newton to Einstein, eternally pondering the Mechanics of the Universe, had finally come up with a term worthy of pulp fiction.

Black hole!

Primo and Caesar looked back at the television as if for confirmation. Chance would have it that the *Starship Enterprise* was in trouble, the crew in a panic.

That did it!

Jay knew he had leverage.

But it had to be used with care.

He retreats to his control room.

The biggest hurdle in his plan now loomed and he needed time to think. Getting Gloria and Marty on side was easy, not so Herby Strauss. Decades ago Marshall had shafted Herby big time. He'd not only double-crossed Herby but Jay himself. Not that this would make the task any easier.

Herby had the memory of an elephant.

Here's what had happened.

NINE

With the sweet smell of success wafting around him, and the big bucks starting to stack up, Marshall got Jay to trace a bent accountant. He needed someone to explain tax shelters, shell companies, every fake front and fraud the rich use to avoid paying taxes. No way was he sweating over a hot keyboard to help finance any of that socialist shit like welfare and Medicare. He sounded more unhinged than usual, breathing heavily and hissing, 'Leona Helmsley was right when she said only *little* people pay taxes!' Until this *volte-face* Marshall had always been a defender of the underdog, a fan of revolutionaries like Thomas Paine. It was the first time Jay had begun to question the sanity of his Master. As Grist rarely moved beyond the aura of his computer, Jay wondered if its luminous radiation had caused some form of mental meltdown.

Jay had no problem finding his man.

Now, a decade later, it would not be so easy.

Ensconced in his office, he got Herby's file out and flicked through the pages of notes and photographs. Who the hell is that? He found himself looking at a frowsy, middle-aged, dumpy woman.

Of course, it's Mrs Strauss, Herby's *mother*.

Herby, like Marshall, lived with his mother; he was that kind of guy. Jay smiled, muttering to himself, 'I bet he still does.' Even so it was going to be a tricky encounter. Marshall had not only used Herby to arrange his financial affairs, thereby giving two fingers to the IRS, but years later couldn't resist writing a novel with him as the protagonist.

Shifty was another blockbuster.

In it he used every detail of Herby *except* his name.

That would have been OK.

But for *one* detail too many!

*

Herby Strauss sticks a stubby finger into the socket and gouges out his glass eye, laying it on the table between them.

'Goddamn thing always itches in warm weather.'

Jay watches, mesmerised, while the empty crater closes tight as an anal sphincter. Herby plants the palm of his hand over it and starts rubbing. They're occupying a booth in a deli off Broadway. Herby's *working* eye fixes on Jay and doesn't waver.

'You shouldn't have dragged mother into this, Jay.'

'I didn't drag her in, Herby. She answered the phone.'

'It's fucking beyond me how you could speak that shit's name in her presence. She's a beautiful woman, Jay, and you polluted her mind with those two words.' Not prepared to say them aloud he mouths them, '*Marshall*' and '*Grist*'.

'I'm sorry but what else could I do? It's been seven years and I wasn't sure if—'

'If what? If I'd forgotten who you were? Jay, your name is tattooed on my cock right alongside that hack writer's. Waiting to fuck you both!'

'Your mother wasn't going to remember me, Herby. I thought if I mentioned Marshall it might—'

Herby angrily bangs the table, setting his glass eye rolling towards the edge. His hand shoots out and calmly catches it. 'How can you even whisper that fucker's name in *my* presence?'

'Because, Herby...' Jay shoots a nervous glance away from the *live* eye watching him suspiciously to the *dead* one peering out from Herby's closed fist. 'I know double-entry bookkeeping means fuck all to you, Herby, but I just thought now's the time to set the balance sheet straight. Marshall owes you.'

It was as if he'd stepped on a mine.

Herby explodes.

'Marshall owes me? YOU owe me! You introduced me to that emotionally stunted turd.'

Herby furiously rubs the suppurating cavity.

'Why the fuck are you stirring the shit again?'

'Revenge, Herby. *That* and all those billions of dollars you helped Marshall hide in tax havens around the globe, away from the sticky fingers of the IRS. Open sesame, Herby! I need you to be my Ali Baba.'

'A *Jewish* Ali-fucking-Baba? You're crazy.'

'No, I'm not. Some influential business colleagues...' – Jay can't help but smile when referring to Primo and Caesar as *business colleagues* – '... are arranging to occupy Marshall's apartment and, more significantly, his computer, long enough for us – or more precisely, *you* – to transfer his entire fortune into our very own Aladdin's cave.'

'Another fucking fairy tale, Jay? Listen, I'm not some lopsided Cyclops you can fuck with. My good eye may not be in the centre of my forehead but my memory sure is. Its readout reminds me it was *you* who introduced me to that two-timing dickhead. And the tale you spun me all those years ago was better than any by Walt Disney. You talked of this poor starving writer, after years in the literary wilderness suddenly being found, lionised, now about to hit the literary jackpot and desperately in need of somebody to protect him and his impending fortune.'

'Herby, Herby, that's the past.'

'No, Jay, it isn't. You're the spider that spun the web; worse, you watched while I got tangled in it. That fucker, Grist, wanted to milk me of all the tax dodges I knew, legal or illegal. Not content with that, after I'd put in place a tax scheme that was not quite kosher, he couldn't resist writing a novel with me in the lead. OK, so he changes my name and what does he call me? Shifty! Shifty Schumacher. Still, nobody need have known it was based on me except that he couldn't resist one extra little touch.'

Herby holds up his glass eye.

Its black pupil seems to pierce Jay's frontal lobe with a painful jolt. 'Shifty has a glass eye! You know how many accountants have a glass eye, Jay? It's a list of *one*! Me!'

Herby is close to tears.

'*Shifty* shot to the top of the bestseller list. Now word of mouth finishes me off. My clients, scared shitless, desert me, rats from a sinking ship. By the time the movie hit the multiplexes the IRS come smelling around. I had to take a runner, telling mother I'd taken a lucrative job abroad. I lived like a bum, starting off in the Cayman Islands, the very place where my clients had their mazuma syphoned away. Billions of dollars I dare not touch. Ten years spent in exile with only a tan to show for it! I looked like Sammy Davis Junior by the time I managed to tap dance past Homeland Security!'

Jay had to smile, he'd forgotten Sammy had a glass eye.

'It's not funny, Jay!'

'Believe me, Herby, I'm only here to make amends. A new life for you...' Herby wipes the tears away, '... *and* your mother. Think about it. It's not *me* you want to fuck over, it's Marshall. We're...' He stops, disconcerted as Herby idly rolls his glass eye from one hand to the other across the tabletop.

The spinning pupil seems to mesmerise him

'How the fuck you going to take over his penthouse? That apartment block's more secure than Guantanamo. And then there's *his* mother. Is she still patrolling the place?'

'Gracie died years ago. I got him a Kraut housekeeper, but we're going to kidnap her and put in our own.'

'What is this shit? A pitch for some crap movie, Jay?'

'Herby, this is for real! Marshall also stitched up this old movie star. She's so pissed off with him she's up for the role. So is the cosmetic surgeon he fucked over. He's going to make her look like the Kraut. Once installed, she'll clear a way past all the security codes and cameras.'

'You mean I just *walk* in? I don't get to zoom up to his observatory deck? No black leather jumpsuit, no mask, no cape?' Herby's bloodshot eye flashes red. 'Don't you dare fuck with me again, you fat turd.'

He bangs the table, causing the coffee cups to rattle in their saucers, but, more importantly, the glass eye to *jump*, then *bounce* over his waiting hand, *land* on the floor and *roll* towards the door of the deli, which simultaneously opens, revealing a pair of knee-length patent leather boots with a pink lead dangling beside them attached to a diamond-studded dog collar circling the neck of a fluffy white poodle. With a little bark of excitement, it spots the glass eye careering like a marble towards its dainty feet. Herby shoots from the booth whilst simultaneously planting a kick on the dog's snout before it gets to play catch-me-if-you-can.

The poodle's high-pitched yelps are matched by the screams of its owner. Her boots may be shiny and new, not so her face, which resembles an old pumpkin, a leftover from Halloween. Herby scoops up his eye, rubs it against his sleeve, opens the socket and squeezes it in. The woman, close to fainting, falls silent as she watches in horror while the flesh closes around it, leaving a white ball staring blankly at her.

'In the land of the blind, madam, the one-eyed man is king.' He ruffles the topknot on the poodle's head. 'Sorry little fella! But waiting for my eye to eventually pop out of your ass would have been too time-consuming.' He looks up at the pumpkin face. 'Madam, poodles used to be fine hunting dogs. Now they're just another goddamn woman's accessory!'

Sliding back into the booth, he smiles at Jay.

'Close call!'

'Herby, your eye! It's the wrong way round.'

'Inward-looking?'

'That's one way of putting it.'

'Shit!' He prises it out, pausing to thoughtfully contemplate the black pupil. 'If this crazy plan should work out, what's in it for Herby?'

'Besides me and my two business colleagues, there's a cast of five, so it should split—'

Herby interrupts. 'I'm not splitting the trawl eight ways if that's what you're thinking. Fifty per cent or I'm not in!'

Jay thinks it over.

Another murderous thought. Best leave Primo and Caesar to take care of Herby later, *after* he's worked his algorithmic magic.

'Fair enough. You're the wizard, Herby. Without your fingers dancing over the keyboard...'

'What about the voice? We'll need someone who *sounds* like Marshall.'

'That's the next piece in my jigsaw. It'll be in place before you get home to Mother.'

TEN

Grist's novel *Bad Mouth* was sourced from one Lou Gozzi, comedian and impersonator of national repute, a repute now somewhat tarnished. Given to freely using alcohol as lubricant for a vital part of his anatomy, his *voice box*, Lou's career has always been a turbulent one. When Jay accidentally came across him he immediately recognised his potential as a character for one of his Master's novels.

The circumstances under which he discovers Lou Gozzi bears repeating if only as a further insight, as yet only hinted at, into Marshall's parsimony. One of the ways his meanness manifests itself is the acceptance of all lucrative offers for personal appearances and have Jay attend instead. To this end, and one ideally suited to his intense paranoia, he's taken the precaution of having Jay's photograph, instead of his own, on all his websites. In a reversal of the usual agent's cut, each appearance fee is split 90 per cent to 10. Or as Marshall puts it, 'I take the lion's share, Jay, cos I'm the lion.'

So it is that Jay finds himself on a flight to Port-au-Prince, there to board the SS *Britannia* on its Christmas cruise. It had sailed from New York some days earlier, stopping at Fort Lauderdale where most of its passengers had boarded, then sailing on to Haiti. As the ship's purser, an Englishman in a starched white uniform, leads the way to his cabin, Jay casts his eyes over his fellow travellers. Not an original hair, tooth, hip, knee, lip or breast in sight. Many of them look close to death. It's like he is crossing the River Styx. Why the cruise had stopped at this poverty-stricken island puzzles him. He asks the purser, who smiles.

'We have approximately one hundred dollar millionaires on board and several billionaires. For them, seeing desperate poverty, enhances that feeling of...' – he hesitates – '... self-satisfaction? Complacency maybe?' He laughs out loud. 'Our casinos are their *natural* habitat. When they return from the company's tour of the island, having feasted their eyes on scenes worthy of William Hogarth, the sound of the roulette wheels soon wipes away any unwelcome images.'

He unlocks and flings open a cabin door.

'This is the Calypso Suite, Mr Grist. Notice the deluxe balcony with direct access to the ocean breeze: ideal for alfresco breakfasts or pre-dinner drinks. There's also butler service, magazine and newspaper selection, atlas and binoculars.'

He steps aside to let Jay enter.

Alongside the fruit, flowers and canapés on the cabin table stands a pristine white envelope leaning against a bottle of Bollinger Special Cuvée. Jay groans as he slides out the invitation for Marshall Grist to dine that night with the ship's captain, Winston McNaught, CBE.

The purser pauses at the door before closing it.

'You'll enjoy Captain McNaught. Been with the company thirty years. This, sadly, is his penultimate cruise.'

With the purser gone, Jay snaps open his suitcase to reveal a blue tuxedo, dress shirt and *ready-made* black bow tie, all seriously creased by closely packed books, sex magazines, medications and candy bars. These are the basic necessities for his impending *solitary confinement*. Cruise ships make Jay uneasy, paranoid; he keeps to his cabin as much as possible. If his deception is ever discovered at sea, there's no escape route aside from jumping overboard.

In this case from the *deluxe* balcony.

Understandably he keeps to his cabin as much as possible.

*

If Captain McNaught had *not* been dressed in an immaculate white dinner suit with four gold rings circling its sleeves and a line of glittering medals dangling below its lapel, he might easily have been mistaken for a pirate. His big frame, jade-black eyes and grey spade-beard seem more suited to a *cutlass* than the delicate silver-plated *cutlery* laid in front of him. His bow tie, obviously tied by his own stubby fingers, is slightly lopsided. Unhinged. With every guest finally seated he bangs a knife loudly against his glass of neat malt whiskey, closes his eyes and bows his head.

'Bless, O God, this food for thy use and make us ever mindful of the wants and needs of others. Amen.'

A few guests mumble *Amen* before McNaught turns his great god-like head slowly towards Jay sitting at his right hand.

'We're very much looking forward to your talk, Mr Grist. Myself I nay read any of your books but am assured they are excellent in their own *racy* genre.'

His Scots accent is as heavy as a claymore.

'Maybe you canna autograph one of your novels suitable for ma good lady wife? *She* reads.'

'My pleasure, Captain.'

Jay risks a furtive look into the man's black evangelical eyes. They drill into him as if seeking out his dark dirty soul and – having laid bare all his despicable sins – are now weighing up whether to have him *keel-hauled*.

McNaught nods towards an empty place at the table.

'One of our cruise entertainers was meant to have joined us but he's doona be answering his phone or steward's knocks.'

Opposite him sits a woman as heavily decorated as a Christmas tree who shakes her head and sounds like a wind chime.

'Maybe he's seasick?'

McNaught bellows with such insane laughter his guests watch with wide-eyed alarm.

'Seasick? Very unlikely, madam. With this ship's stabilisers it's like going to sea in a Las Vegas apartment block. We've even had passengers at the end of a cruise ask for a refund, convinced we dinna leave port.'

He slowly shakes his head. His sad, uncomprehending eyes blaze like a lighthouse on a stormy night. Captain McNaught's thirty years on cruise ships have patently taken their toll. A sallow little man sitting next to Jay gamely tries to keep the *small* talk *small* and points at the empty place.

'Tell me, Captain, who is the entertainer you were expecting?'

McNaught consults the list beside his plate.

'Lou Gozzi?'

At first the name is greeted with silence.

Then the Christmas tree shakes her head again and chimes in.

'Lou Gozzi? Is he still alive?'

*

Lou *is* still alive.

But only just.

He's sitting in his cabin, reading and rereading the invitation to the dinner now in progress, while drunkenly weeping and whispering to himself, '*Mr Lou Gozzi... Captain Winston McNaught, CBE requests the pleasure of your company...*' Tears splash onto the elegantly embossed card. '*Mr Lou Gozzi. Captain Winston... Winston... Winston...*' He pauses then breaks into a flawless impersonation of Winston Churchill.

'You men are going into a war zone.' He tries to stand but stumbles to the floor. 'And I – I am going with you.' Crawling across to the full-length mirror behind the cabin door, he peers at himself. 'Going with you as far as the – the *jetty*!' He finally claws his way up the door. 'To bid you *Bon Voyage*!' Attempting to emphasise the payoff, he bangs his head heavily against the woodwork, renders himself unconscious, slowly slides down the mirror with his lips acting as suction pads until he finally comes to rest by two empty bourbon bottles, making a perfectly composed still life.

Man and two bottles.

*

Lou's solo performance is sadly the culmination of his comeback cruise. Next morning sees the ship's entertainments officer use a pass key to gain entry into his cabin. In his report to the captain, he describes finding Gozzi on his bunk nursing a massive hangover, barking like a seal while starting on another bottle of bourbon.

Two days later the ship docks in Jamaica and – under cover of darkness – the disgraced impersonator is bundled by a security officer into the launch leaving for Kingston harbour. It so happens his undignified departure from the SS *Britannia* is witnessed by the *other* impersonator on board, also availing himself of the shuttle service.

Fat Jay is on his way back to New York.

That afternoon he had delivered his talk to a conference room full of ardent adoring eyes, each blazing with a fervour usually reserved for *messiahs*. As always, the experience filled him with a mixture of self-loathing and total bafflement.

Why, for fuck's sake, are *novelists* held in such awe?

What's so special about them?

If Marshall is anything to go by, they are most likely arrogant, self-obsessed, self-aggrandising, self-opinionated dickheads. Only when their latest masterpiece needs a puff of publicity do they deign to descend like Moses from the mountain to drivel platitudes over us lesser mortals. At least when Jay attends gigs posing as Marshall he *knows* he's a fraud. That thought rarely occurs to writers bloated with the complacency that comes with an overload of veneration.

*

A luxury hotel suite awaits Jay in Kingston. It's an overnight perch before his early-morning flight home. On his way to dinner he looks into the bar and finds Lou Gozzi, not unexpectedly, ordering a drink. A glut of empty glasses sits at his elbow.

Jay can't resist.

He takes out his mobile and snaps the incriminating image before priming his recording device and approaching.

'Mr Gozzi? Mr Lou Gozzi?'

Gozzi's heavy-framed black shades turn like the shield of a field gun, take aim at Jay and fire a brilliant Humphrey Bogart impersonation.

'Everyone needs to *believe* in something. And I *believe* I'll have another drink! Get lost, kid!'

'Lou, I'm a big fan.'

Gozzi swings back to the bar, still in Bogie mode.

'The problem with the world is that everyone else is *three* drinks behind.'

'So let me catch up, Lou. This one's on me.'

Next up is Robert Mitchum.

'In every movie I kept the *same* suit and the *same* dialogue. The studios just *changed* the title and the leading lady.'

'Sorry to intrude, Mr Gozzi, but I just love watching you work. Your John Wayne was always the best. They don't make 'em like that anymore. Or the likes of Lou Gozzi.'

'Too right. Nobody's *worth* impersonating any more. The new stars have voices like fairies, flat and boring. No grit. No hellraisers. No voices that have lived a life. Close your eyes and you recognise diddly-squat. You know why? Cos they're too fucking scared to smoke and drink whiskey. They just suck their thumbs. Hollywood Babylon has been downsized to a kiddie's playpen.'

'Right on, Lou. Same again?'

The barman brings two fresh glasses and pours out bourbons.

Jay salutes Gozzi and sinks it in one.

'Now I'm only *two* behind.'

Gozzi sinks his.

'Now you're *not*!'

'Did I hear you had a bit of a problem aboard the SS *Britannia*?'

It's Wayne that replies.

'Kid, you're short on ears and long on mouth.'

After Wayne comes Cary Grant, Jimmy Stewart, Gary Cooper, Kirk Douglas, Claude Raines and Edward G.

Lou Gozzi *always* gets lost in the shuffle.

Next up are the ladies. His mouth moves and out come the voices of Bacall, Davis, Hepburn, Dietrich, Crawford and finally Mae West.

'I used to be *Snow White* but I *drifted*.'

With that Lou lays his head on the bar and falls asleep.

Even his snores sound like *Sleepy*.

Jay slips away.

*

261

Back in New York, Jay traces Lou's agent to see if his client got back safely. The agent talks with a cigar in his mouth until Jay interrupts.

'Say that again?'

He does say it again.

'On the twelve-step programme for ten years! One night at sea and he takes step fucking *thirteen*. Unlucky for some.'

'What happens now?'

'It's back to step one I guess. If not, he'll sink without trace.'

Not so!

But then how would the agent, or Lou himself, know he'd soon be entering Marshall Grist's pantheon of human detritus? *Bad Mouth*, which soon hit top spot in the fiction bestseller lists, came with a prescient press release: 'Bad Mouth *is about a professional impersonator who captures not only his victims' voices but their lives. Onstage he spins laughter; offstage he spills blood.*'

*

Seven years pass, and Lou Gozzi still hasn't sunk without trace.

Not quite.

Jay traces him to a supper club on 47th.

The Sizzle.

He's billed as The Voice of a Thousand Movies – Mostly Black and White! His routine is slick, fast and funny. The customers even stop eating occasionally to applaud. Clear-eyed and rock-steady, he looks to be safely back on the wagon.

That's until he receives a copy of *Bad Mouth*.

Jay intends it as touchpaper to ignite a fever of revenge.

It works.

Unfortunately it also drives Lou to once again take that fatal step thirteen. When Jay gets wind of his relapse he visits him in his apartment. He politely explains his plan for releasing Marshall's funds to a select group of beneficiaries.

Including *him*.

The great Lou Gozzi.

That done he leaves him in the capable hands of Primo and Caesar.

In just three days the boys have him back on step one and within seven days back on step twelve. Once there, on step twelve, they ply him with Marshall's recorded instructions: instructions meticulously filed away by Jay over the years. They play them over and over until the impersonator masters every nuance of the writer's voice.

From now on Lou – primed and ready to go – keeps his mind not so much on the *spiritual* principles of the twelve-step programme as the bounty coming his way.

His just desserts!

It amuses him that revenge against Marshall Grist is being exacted for *identity* theft. Something he, Lou Gozzi, has perpetrated all his professional life.

ELEVEN

She lifts the veil of her pillbox hat, looks in the mirror and sees *not* wrinkled Gloria Minette but the much younger Greta Himmler. Her gasp is one of astonishment mixed with fear and excitement.

Marty Graf has performed a brilliant transformation.

'What do you think?'

Gloria's eyes dance over the image before finally coming to rest on her lips. 'Vas dis I tink?' She begins to softly sing. '*Wie gerne wollt ich mit dir geh'n? Mit dir Lili Marleen?*' In her element, she turns and leans seductively against the mirror. '*Who by the lantern will be coming then? With you, Lili Marleen?*' She kisses the image, leaving a faint imprint of her lips. For Gloria, the clock has been wound back decades to her days as a sex symbol. It's a strangely unsettling scene witnessed not only by Marty but by Jay, Primo, Caesar, Herby and Lou.

The whole gang has convened in Jay's apartment.

'I promised you one more great role, Gloria,' says Jay. 'Now you got it. That's Greta Himmler to a tee.'

'And in just three weeks. Always a quick learner. Each morning I shadow her to the shops. Greta is like clockwork, very precise. Her accent is so thick she has to repeat everything. That helped. One thing I did notice. Her memory muscle is *flabby*. She uses a notebook for the pin numbers to Marshall's apartment block.'

The significance of this information isn't lost on Primo and Caesar. They screech excitedly to each other, like firecrackers exploding. 'We go get Greta's notebook!' Knives, conjured into their palms, are flicked open. Sharp naked steel flares in the light. Gloria's hands clutch at her face to register horror while Herby's good eye swivels wildly. Even Marty Graf – familiar as he is to sharp instruments – looks like he's going to be sick. And Fat Jay's florid face now has the complexion of a suet dumpling. He dances away from the flashing blades, not wishing to yet again emulate the martyrdom of Saint Sebastian.

His mind is whirling.

Again the television – that *altar* on the wall, active since Primo and Caesar moved in – comes to Jay's rescue. The *Evening News* is playing and for some goddamn reason there's the Pope on a balcony in the Vatican giving his all to the vast crowd of believers massed below.

Jay grabs the remote and activates the sound.

Italian at full volume.

Primo claps his hand over Caesar's mouth to silence him.

'What he say?'

Jay, bowing reverently before the Pontiff on the screen, lifts his head and listens.

'He says, Primo, make sure you get the *go-ahead* from God before you act.'

'Why?'

'He didn't say.'

They all listen.

'What he say now?'

'He says treat *all* women like the Virgin Mary. With respect. Be gentle, he says.'

'I no hear him say Greta?'

'No. But I'm sure he means her to be included.'

Although Greta could be a pain in the butt, Jay has a soft spot for her. He's determined she be accorded the protection due to any innocent non-combatant.

Again they all listen to Il Papa.

Caesar gets twitchy.

'Black hole? He say black hole?'

'Several times. In Italian.'

'Why?'

Before Jay can answer, the news has moved on to a volcano erupting on some remote island. Smoke and molten lava fill the screen, bringing a suitably apocalyptic tone to the proceedings.

Caesar's edginess spreads to Primo.

'How we know when God give go-ahead?'

Out of the ensuing silence, Gloria rises slowly to her feet. Early in her career she'd once played off-Broadway in several Greek tragedies and is still able to render a measured *iambic trimeter*. This has a profound effect on all those present. 'He, the Almighty, has revealed He will speak only through me. Only through me will He give the go-go. Ahead!'

Jay kills the sound of the television and picks up where Gloria left off. 'Thank you, O Lord, for revealing yourself to us. And through a *woman*! We promise to treat Greta with gentleness and respect when you finally give us the nod to abduct her. Before that time is upon us, we will properly prepare a place for her to rest until such time as we have completed our Divine Retribution.'

'Amen,' say all.

Primo and Caesar look suitably chastised.

Safely back in their box.

They furtively ease the blades back into place.

The prayers and constant dropping of God's name, however, has a very different effect on Lou Gozzi. Still delusional and suffering severe withdrawal symptoms, he mistakenly thinks he's attending an AA meeting, jumps to his feet and solemnly addresses the assembled company.

'Hi! I'm Lou and I'm an alcoholic.'

'We are aware of that, Lou,' says Jay. 'Please sit down. We're here not to discuss human frailty but to examine the abduction plan in detail. Step-by-step.'

'Including getting the *go-ahead* from God.'

'Thank you, Gloria.'

Jay's patience is wearing thin.

'There must be no hiccups.'

Lou instantly obliges with one.

Jay ignores it.

He's anxious to move the party's attention to the cellar in which Primo and Caesar had initially incarcerated him. It is the obvious place to keep Greta hostage while they occupy Marshall's apartment. But, out of respect for her, it's in need of a makeover. This task he gives, somewhat reluctantly, to Primo and Caesar.

They, in turn, are reluctant to perform any domestic chore.

Especially for a woman.

Yet again God's name is taken in vain.

Gloria sees to that.

Like the Oracle at Delphi, she's now directing the game plan. 'The Lord says, "My Father's house has many rooms. And one of them is for Greta..."'

That did it.

Primo and Caesar set about refurbishing the cellar in their *own* image. Cushions and silk drapes in vivid primary colours are smuggled in along with plastic flowers and candles. Soon it takes on the appearance of a *bordello*. The ankle chains lying ominously across the mattress even suggest a space for more specialist deviant practices.

Everything is now ready for God to give the go-ahead.

TWELVE

Shadowing Greta took Gloria on a daily visit to St Patrick's Cathedral in midtown Manhattan, a short walk from Marshall's apartment. Here the housekeeper observed her inflexible timetable. Mass at 07.00 hours every morning, whatever the weather. On arrival, at 06.48, she would stop for two minutes to admire the decorated neo-Gothic spires rising above 5th Avenue. They never failed to bring back memories of the Fatherland and she would without fail momentarily hum *Deutschland über alles*. At 06.50 she would turn to face the Rockefeller Centre across the way. There the towering bronze statue of Atlas weighed down by the Celestial Spheres always affected her. Life was a cross we all have to bear, especially when your family name is Himmler and the cuckoo in a clock is your only friend. Saturdays entailed an extra trip. For the sacrament of confession.

Again Greta's routine was unwavering.

She always went in the evening at 17.30 hours and to the same confessor, one Father Dolan. His ornately carved wooden confessional was situated in a dark corner of the right side-aisle. Gloria noticed that her quarry always made sure she was the *last* to enter, waving any stragglers ahead of her. Once ensconced, there emerged a loud murmur as Father Dolan struggled to decipher Greta's endless list of venial sins. All this Gloria relays to the gang at their next meeting.

Jay has spent many hours pondering where best to abduct Greta without attracting attention. The choice of location was limited, as her perambulations were short and always in public places. Only when

Gloria talks of the cathedral, Father Dolan and the confessional does the *Eureka* moment occur. Jay leaps from his seat and yells like a fan at Yankee Stadium celebrating a home run.

'It's thumbs up from God! We'll kidnap Greta in St Pat's Cathedral!'

Primo looks at Caesar.

'Hear that? God give go-ahead.'

Caesar doesn't get it.

He goes to the window and peers at the sky.

'Where God give go-ahead?'

Gloria raises her arms evangelical-style.

'Caesar, how many times do I have to say it? My Father's house has many rooms. By leading me here to His room in New York City He has shown us the way – the way to nab Greta Himmler! O Lord, we thank you for your guidance.'

Aimee Semple McPherson could not have performed it better.

THIRTEEN

The following Saturday evening Marty Graf, wearing heavy dark shades, enters St Patrick's Cathedral. Closed-circuit cameras comb the entrance and he's anxious not to attract attention. Fully briefed by Gloria to appear as a devout believer, he dips his right hand into the holy water font inside the entrance and makes a sign of the cross. After genuflecting towards the altar, he makes his way along the right side-aisle until he reaches the row of dark wooden confessionals. There he seeks out the one with a sign indicating that *Father Dolan* is in situ.

Instead of taking a seat alongside the waiting penitents, he inspects the nearest *Station of the Cross*: fourteen of them line the cathedral walls. It's the tenth, appropriately subtitled *Jesus is Stripped of His Garments*. Marty notices Greta Himmler sitting patiently in an adjacent pew. Her coat and scarf are neatly folded next to her.

She is alone.

Just then Primo and Caesar materialise at the top of the aisle pushing a wheelchair with a figure slumped in it, face hidden under a wide-brimmed floppy hat. Moments later the confessional is vacated. Above the entrance a red light winks, inviting the next penitent to enter. Greta rents the silence with a deep sigh, stands, picks up her coat and scarf, walks purposefully to the confessional and disappears into its dark interior.

The dull drone of her sins being revealed, translated, interpreted, explained and expiated is well under way by the time the wheelchair arrives. Primo glances at Marty Graf, who takes a small syringe from his raincoat pocket. He removes the sheath and lets a little of the medication fly from the needle.

The murmurs emanating from the confessional suddenly cease. Father Dolan, sounding somewhat desperate, raises his voice to deliver a suitably light absolution. 'For your penance say *one* Hail Mary. No, *two*.'

Greta adds, 'I vill say *three* to be safe.'

As she emerges Primo and Caesar pounce, clap a hand over her mouth, effectively muffling her protests, pull her over to the wheelchair from which Gloria bounds, grabbing her hat and pulling it over Greta's head, while simultaneously Marty whacks the needle into her buttock and depresses the syringe. Greta ceases struggling and slumps on one arm like a rag doll. Her coat and scarf slip to the floor and Gloria, used to quick costume changes, is buttoned up and belted in a nanosecond.

The operation has the precision of a *pit stop* in a motor race.

Marty quickly melts into the dark vastness of the cathedral while the wheelchair, one wheel loudly squeaking from its lopsided cargo, proceeds towards the exit at a surprisingly measured pace, bearing in mind it has Primo driving it with Caesar riding shotgun.

Back at the crime scene, Gloria calmly retrieves Greta's shopping bag dropped in the scuffle. As she searches for and finds the crucial black notebook, Father Dolan, job done, comes out from the confessional, recognises Greta, appears to have something close to a cardiac arrest and quickly retreats back into his carved wooden box.

Gloria smiles.

God's representative on Earth has just confirmed she is now officially a doppelgänger.

*

It's some hours before Greta Himmler surfaces from her drugged sleep. She stares groggily at the grimy dungeon ceiling flickering in the candlelight. Alarmed, she tries to stand but finds herself constrained by ankle chains. Her mind whirls in confusion.

At first she's convinced she must be in Israel. If not there *already*, then certainly on her way. She curses Heinrich Luitpold Himmler

271

for giving her family such a bad name. Then she curses her father. Why hadn't the stupid man changed it like all the other Himmlers in Munich? Images of Simon Wiesenthal, the Nazi hunter, swim into her consciousness, only to be dismissed when she remembers he's dead. Whoever took over his job must have made an administrative error. Not everyone named Himmler had been a *Reichsführer-SS*. Yes, she *is* a devout Roman Catholic like Heinrich's mother, but that doesn't mean…

Her thoughts freeze when the rusty hinges of the cellar door grate as it opens. Caesar, wearing a balaclava, enters bearing sustenance.

Greta whimpers when she sees him.

'Vy? Vy? Vorld Vor Two long time over.'

Caesar is under strict instructions to remain silent. He places the offering within the prisoner's reach and leaves. The door grinds shut. Greta picks up the sandwich and examines it. Inside it's filled with salad, tomatoes, mayonnaise – and *bacon*.

Maybe Israel this is not?

Her temporary relief is shattered when she realises she's been stripped of her clothes.

An orange shell suit now encases her.

FOURTEEN

Brendan Branagan has been a doorman at the Brompton for exactly a quarter of a century. Only last week the residents had given him a trophy watch as a sign of their appreciation. A huge sparkling URWERK-110. Bernie Mandelson, chairman of the Residents' Association, in his speech at the presentation, revealed that the URWERK-110 was part of the brand's Moon-DNA collection and brings *the Magic of the Moon to your Wrist.*

A slight smile plays on Brendan's lips as he unwraps it. He, himself, has delivered so much bullshit in his life he's only too happy to take it from other people. He thanks the assembled residents while pondering how they'd decided to give a humble porter such a fancy present. Fastening its alligator strap, he smiles in the knowledge that Bernie's patients – Bernie is a dentist – include several mobsters. Shortly after treating every one of them Bernie, without fail, has some luxury line he's anxious to shift: fur coats, handbags, jewellery, and the one that now makes Brendan smile.

Trophy watches.

For Bernie Mandelson *time* is money.

That said, the one accessory you certainly didn't need when dealing with Greta Himmler is a *watch*. She operates with the accuracy of an atomic clock (i.e. at an uncertainty of one second every 30 million years). Even so, when Brendan sees her at the front entrance that Saturday evening, consulting her black notebook, about to punch in the code, he checks the time.

It's 18.33.

'What's dis, Greta?'

He taps his huge new chronometer as she enters.

'Tree minutes late.'

'Ja. Ze stop-light on Fifth vas slow, Brendan.'

Gloria takes a flyer on the *name*.

It was a name Greta often used when gossiping in the local deli.

'What penance did Father Dolan give you today?

'No your business!'

'Tis now, Greta. How many Hail Marys did he tell you to say? Not many, I'll bet. For the life of me I don't know what you can possibly be after confessing.'

'Ve all sinners, Brendan.'

'Is it dirty thoughts you'll be after having, or what?'

'You vikid boy, dirty Brendan!'

Gloria Minette is easing herself into her *new* skin, letting Greta Himmler inhabit her while keeping a canny eye on her audience. *Deception* is the actor's craft and so far it's working well with Brendan Branagan.

So much for the talk, now for the walk.

She clicks her heels, turns and, striding like a tin soldier, makes for the elevator. Branagan calls out as she punches the next code number into the security system.

'Is de *Scribe-in-de-Sky* still burning up dat computer keyboard of his? When can we expect de next masterpiece?'

Gloria is relieved when the elevator door slides open.

She escapes without having to reply before being lifted up to the eightieth floor.

*

The third and final digital combination listed in the black notebook lets Gloria pass into Marshall's penthouse apartment. Having memorised the floor plan provided by Jay, she confidently crosses the marble-floored hallway – lined on one side with Corinthian columns – to one of six doors. It opens onto a view of Manhattan that momentarily makes her dizzy.

The living area – the *Great Room,* so designated by a delusional realty agent – runs onto a vast AstroTurfed observatory deck stretching towards the skyline like the bow of an aircraft carrier. Two teak sunloungers lie side by side, two giant grasshoppers poised to jump. The setting sun burns red in the thousands of windows stacked in the panorama beyond. Darkness slowly filters between the skyscrapers and numerous little lights start to flicker into life, lending it the look of a toy town, while an eerie moan emanates from the wind curling around the building.

Gloria turns away, casting her eyes instead over the immaculately plumped-up sofas, the thick-pile carpets, the coffee tables with precisely placed coffee-table books, the bland *objets d'art* almost certainly chosen by some talentless interior decorator. In short, the usual empty trappings of the extremely rich.

It's a film set, not a home.

Engulfed with a sudden sense of despairing loneliness, she shakes her head as if to toss the melancholy away and quickly moves to another door. At the end of a short corridor is a bedroom, which she enters.

It's Greta's and it's seven o'clock *precisely.*

A loud winding sound startles Gloria until she locates the wall clock just as its little hand-carved Tyrolean door opens.

Cuckoo!
Cuckoo!
Cuckoo!

Gloria watches in horror as this painted piece of wood jerks its tiny beak open then shut. Its spiteful dead eyes follow her as she closes on it.

Cuckoo!
Cuckoo!
Cuckoo!
Cuckoo!

The beak suddenly vibrates angrily, seemingly pissed off that its seven seconds of fame is over. Finally the cuckoo itself shudders violently and, amid more grating mechanical noises, retreats inside, leaving the chalet door to close behind it. The clock now resumes its relentless reminder of time passing.

Tick-Tock!
Tick-Tock!
Tick-Tock!

Gloria snaps out of her reverie and curses herself. She whips off Greta's coat, opens a wardrobe to find a shelf full of neatly laundered pinafores, choses one, wraps it around herself and makes for the kitchen, which is back across the *Great Room*. There she stops when she hears a refrigerator door open, a bottle being removed, unscrewed and liquid rattling ice cubes in a glass. A cloud of cigarette smoke hangs in the doorway.

Gloria takes a deep breath and steps inside.

Marshall Grist has his back to her as he replaces the vodka bottle and slams the door shut. When he turns around to find her in the doorway, he jumps so violently he spills his drink.

'Shit! For fuck's sake, Gloria, don't creep up on me like that.'

Gloria hesitates, unsure how to address him.

'Sorry, Herr...'

'Herr? What's with the fucking *Herr*, Frau Himmler?'

'I vant us to be more formal. Zen you vont use bad verds.'

Marshall laughs before taking a deep draught of neat vodka, then a deeper drag on his cigarette, allowing Gloria the time to look him over. He's short and round: round like a tennis ball. And the similarity doesn't stop there: his skin, or what you can see of it, is *yellow*. The rest is hidden under an unruly black beard and tangled hair.

'Bad verds? Not *verds*, Greta, words! Words!'

Gloria lets her lips quiver with emotion before giving the word another mauling.

'Verds!'

Marshall bellows with laughter.

'That poor fucking priest. How the fucking hell does he manage your confession, Greta?'

'God knowz every-zing, every hair on our head.'

'Oh yeah? So how is He today? God? Pleased wiz his Vorld? His Creation, unless I'm misinformed, is in deep shit with wars breaking out all over, spreading like bush fires. Or is it like a computer game for Him? Are there any up-and-coming pandemics, earthquakes, floods, tsunamis, droughts, plagues of locusts we should know about? *Acts of God*, as the insurance companies conveniently call them.'

Marshall doesn't wait for a reply before shuffling off.

He stops and turns.

'You heard from that son-of-a-bitch Jay?'

Gloria thinks, then shakes her head.

'Not for veeks.'

'Weeks, Greta, not vecks. Weeks!'

'Veeks!'

'You know he tried to blackmail me, Greta.'

'You told me already.'

'I did? Vat did I tell you?'

'That Jay try blackmail you.'

'Yes, but how?'

'Zat you not tell me.'

Gloria risks it.

'Marshall.'

'Marshall? It's *Herr* Marshall from now on. I vant you to nurture the fascist pig in me.'

'Yes, Herr Marshall. You vont something eat?'

'I stay hungry, Greta. You know zat. Lean and mean. That's how you stay on ze top of ze dungheap.'

He leaves his office door open.

Inside Gloria can see a computer the size of a multiplex movie screen filling the room with green ectoplasm. Marshall is immediately enveloped in it, obsessively feeding the screen with words, paragraphs, chapters. It's an electronic succubus jerking off his brain, making his ideas swim like sperm. He lights another cigarette before screwing the previous one into a film can full of stubs.

Gloria watches, curious to observe the man who had stolen her life story and sold it like Judas for *thirty pieces of silver*. For that he will die.

'Zen I really *vill* have something to confess.'
Gloria smiles, satisfied with her first encounter with Marshall.
Now to deal with that damned cuckoo clock.
She hurries off.

FIFTEEN

They're waiting for rain.

Greta Himmler's notebook has yielded the security combinations for both the service doors and elevators at the back of the Brompton. They were on the last page and took some finding. When Gloria checks them out she notices CCTV cameras positioned inside and outside the rear entrance to the building.

This prompts Jay to reconnoitre the scene for himself.

A shower had forced him to take shelter in a doorway opposite. From there he was relieved to observe the domestic staff arriving with raised umbrellas that shielded their faces from the camera's scrutiny. Inside, by delaying the lowering of the umbrella, the same result could be achieved. Now he knew how it would be possible to smuggle his team into Marshall's apartment *without* their entry being recorded or arousing the security guards' suspicion.

That's *why* they're now waiting for the heavens to open.

Instead a heatwave arrives and the city is soon wilting under soaring temperatures. Every morning, after attending Mass, Gloria enquires of Marshall if she can do anything for him, but he only grunts and continues firing words into his computer. She empties the film cans stacked with crushed tabs and leaves, quietly shutting the door, not sure if he's even noticed her.

The hiatus is making her nervous; to calm herself she takes to circling the deserted apartment like a cyclist in a velodrome. Kitchen, Bedroom 1, Bath 2, Bedroom 2, Bath 3, Dining Room, the *Great Room*, Den,

Gym, Sauna, Bedroom 3, Powder Room, Laundry, Master Bedroom, Master Bathroom, then it's *back* to the Kitchen.

She tries to read but can't concentrate. She contemplates using the sunloungers on the deck but can see the air outside is sizzling. She finds the clipboard Greta uses to notate the *Domestic Duties* in the order they need to be completed. There's a column for each week of each month.

This week has a solid line of ticks.

Jobs done.

Everything's so perfect she doesn't know where to put herself and retreats to her room. She looks at the cuckoo clock and wonders if she should *replace* the batteries.

Activate it.

Just for company.

*

In the dank cellar, Greta Himmler is beginning to relish imprisonment. For the first time in her life she's been rendered indolent, forced into inactivity. Until now her lifetime's spreadsheet has been jammed full, every nanosecond accounted for. Since she was born, when her mother's milk was proffered on the hour every hour with the help of a stopwatch, the Regime of Relentless Precision has never let up. Not surprisingly, her enchantment with the freedom of captivity took her captors by surprise.

Her two brothers had both been eager Stasi agents, so maybe her ability to *locate* any form of surveillance, however minute, is genetic. Her hawk eyes quickly spotted the tiny camera installed by Jay. And once Greta honed in on it, she instinctively knew what to do.

She whispers to it like it was a priest hearing her confession.

'I zink I know who behind zis. You naughty fat boy, you knowz kidnapping ist a federal offence? I knowz zat, cos a German carpenter vent to ze electric chair for taking zat Lindbergh boy.'

When Jay hears this he nearly throws up.

Does she really know *he's* the naughty boy?

Or is she bluffing?

Greta continues.

'If you goot to me maybe ve can verk somzing out. For ze start

I no eat shitty food. Some *Sauerbraten* vood go down vell. Vis some *Brathering* as starter. For breakfast *Bratwurst*. Zen for lunch *Blutwurst* with *Pommes* on ze side. Dinner I zink about. Got zat?'

In his apartment Jay watches the monitor on which Greta points an accusing finger at *him* – and quakes. His chins and belly ripple with trepidation. Female intuition has always puzzled him. How the hell had she sussed that *he* was responsible for her incarceration?

And how the hell had she hit the bullseye so quickly?

Primo slyly watches Jay's thinking process as it slowly churns around his brain, along his nervous system, until it reaches his quivering body. He watches and waits, two gold teeth flashing a neon smile and his hand holding the ubiquitous knife.

He wiggles it so the blade glints in the light.

'Yes?'

'No!'

Jay is ashen white.

'She say *naughty fat boy*. That you.'

'Listen, Primo and listen good. No first-degree murder. Zat's vy ze fucking German carpenter vent to ze electric chair. He murdered Charles Lindbergh's child. It vos the trial of ze century. OK?'

Greta, unaware of what's happening in Jay's apartment, suddenly tunes in via the monitor. 'Hi zere, my little sausage, I remember asparagus ist in season. For dinner I vont *Spargel* wis Hollandaise sauce and potatoes.'

Feeling his bowels again shifting uneasily, Jay plunges his head into his hands. Revenge has blinded him. It's set him on a course of serious criminal activity with two highly volatile, violent characters, Primo and Caesar; an alcoholic impersonator, Lou Gozzi; an ancient ex-movie star who specialised in blow jobs, Gloria Minette; a rampantly rapacious cosmetic surgeon, Marty Graf; and a one-eyed fraudulent accountant, Herby Strauss.

This line-up is not the stuff of Hollywood.

He nurses the throbbing bandaged stump of his pinky finger, then impulsively sucks his thumb.

In desperation he looks to the gods for help.

And they abruptly reply with a flash of lightning!

SIXTEEN

Gloria, having circled the apartment for a second day, is now totally inert, her eyes locked despairingly on the simmering observatory deck. Contemplating it as a springboard into eternity is becoming increasingly enticing. Then, with biblical ferocity, the deluge arrives. Rain hits the AstroTurf with the power of a cluster bomb. The drops ricochet in some crazy drum solo. Simultaneously the pager provided by Jay alerts her to expect visitors.

*

Jay watches from a doorway at the rear of the Brompton. From here he watches Primo arrive, umbrella battered by the storm as he taps in the security code, enters, keeps the umbrella open until he's punched in the numbers to open the elevator before being whisked upwards. Minutes later Jay's pager tells him Primo is safely inside Marshall's apartment.

This routine is repeated until Caesar, Lou and Herby are all in place. The CCTV cameras have captured only the tops of four umbrellas. Jay – about to plunge himself into the maelstrom – is unexpectedly stricken by an image of Greta Himmler all alone with her personal security camera. Although he's arranged for a vast selection of *Sauerbraten, Brathering, Bratwurst, Schwarzwurst* with *Pommes* to be left within her reach, he still feels guilty, hoping it'll be enough for her to survive until Gloria goes on her next shopping trip, which will *include* a further incognito visit to the cellar.

He steps out into the torrent.
And feels born again.

*

As always, Marshall is clamped to his computer like a parasitic accretion. An *oyster fungus* or indeed any fungus. Absorbed in fiction, he's often unaware of fact. One fact is that his apartment is now an occupied zone. He keeps spewing words from his keyboard until *suddenly* – a word he often uses in his fiction – four tattooed arms drag him screaming from the dark green ectoplasm of his office into the daylight of his *Great Room*. He lies squirming on the floor, blinking at the quintet of captors towering over him.

Jay holds out his bandaged hand.

'I've come for my finger, Marshall. And the cheap ring that always gave you the creeps. Meet Primo: you stole his life for *Vicious Circle*. And Lou: you stole his for *Bad Mouth*. That's Herby. Show him your glass eye, Herby.' Gloria, peering from behind the men bearing down on Marshall, nearly passes out when she sees the eye glinting in Herby's hand.

Jay continues, 'You did a good job destroying his career with *Shifty*, remember? A genius at worming his way into offshore funds and trusts is Herby. Now his dubious talent – with your help – will worm its way back into your fortune and we'll finally get our just rewards. Herby is our Robin Hood. This time it's *your* life, Marshall, that's up for grabs.'

Grist whimpers and snivels when he sees Gloria.

'*Et tu*, Greta?'

'Not Greta Himmler! *Gloria Minette!* You stole my life story for *A Role to Kill For*, you unscrupulous cad. I look like Greta thanks to Marty Graf. He was the model for *Killer's Mask*.'

She pulls a scalpel from the pocket of her floral pinny.

'Marty gave me this to help us reshape *your* mask, bloodsucker.' The blade closes on his throat.

'You treated poor Greta Himmler like a skivvy, a drudge. I know cos that's how you treated *me*, her doppelgänger. The only company she had in this high-rise emotional deep freeze was a fucking cuckoo clock!'

Marshall Grist looks like someone destined for a straightjacket, muttering in confusion. 'Cuckoo clock? Doppelgänger? This is good shit. I must write it down before it escapes. Pin it like a butterfly.' His fingers are moving faster than Chopin's ever did. His bloodshot eyes are locked on the computer screen visible through the door of his office, absorbing him with one vast hypnotic eye. He scrambles to his feet as if in a trance and sets off for the nirvana of *writing*, the ultimate escape from reality.

This time it takes them all – Primo, Caesar, Lou, Herby and even Fat Jay flopping on him like a sumo wrestler – to overpower Marshall. As God in the Old Testament bestowed supernatural strength on Sampson, so the computer does on Marshall.

The struggle is Herculean.

Like a yellow hairy tennis ball, he bounces all over the place with no obvious protuberances to get hold of.

One eventually emerges: a tiny chin.

It *doesn't* take the jaw of an ass to bring him to heel. Only a left hook from Gloria. She'd starred in a boxing movie many years before and remembered the techniques of the ring.

Actors *have* to remember, remember.

Words.

Moves.

The others have to ask Fat Jay to raise himself from the struggling body before they could drag Marshall Grist screaming – albeit *silently* as his mouth is now sealed with gaffer tape – into his sauna. This is a space Marshall's little fat body has obviously never enjoyed. Like much of his luxury apartment – eighty floors above street life – it's a space rarely used. But then, for the rich, space is an essential *buffer* between them and the real world.

That's the rest of mankind.

Still – like the rest of mankind – the rich end up as ashes in a crematorium jar or buried whole in a grave the size of Grist's sauna. Primo, with roots deep in Roman Catholicism, is for turning the sauna into hell. He wants to activate it, turn the thermostat to *max* and throw water on its blistering stones.

'Melt the motherfucker!'

Jay, eternally the desperate mediator, explains to Primo and the equally agitated Caesar that they need Marshall to help unravel the labyrinthine places in which his fortune is secreted.

'Besides, he's a human being, not a candle. OK?'

*

Jay checks up on their captive every thirty minutes, making sure the chain and handcuffs are restraining but not harming him. Marshall shivers, shakes, froths and sweats for twenty-four hours. The withdrawal symptoms from his computer screen – as bad as any junkie's – take Jay by surprise. Never before had he realised *writing* is so addictive.

Then, abruptly, Marshall is calm.

Like a hermit crab finding a fresh shell to occupy, he slips gleefully into the role of *prisoner*. One of his early thrillers – *Ratty* – was about a man taken hostage by a gang of terrorists. Marshall knows all the angles on *Stockholm Syndrome*.

Bizarrely, he becomes a mirror image of their *other* prisoner.

Greta Himmler!

In an unconscious act of self-preservation, both Greta and Grist now *identify* with their captors. In Marshall's novel the trauma of being kidnapped that caused the onset of the Syndrome is later negated by *another* trauma. Waterboarding to obtain a password. Keeping this emotional *volte-face* from his captors, Marshall's protagonist lulls them into complacency, aborts their plan for a massive ransom and reaps bloody revenge. No wonder Marshall smiles as he's unshackled and led into the dining room.

There the whole cast sit at his long marble-topped table with Fat Jay sitting at its head.

'Marshall, we're glad you're over the...'

Marshall interrupts him.

'Forgive me Jay, but I need to contribute something here.' He pauses to look momentarily at each of them in turn – Primo, Caesar, Lou, Herby, Gloria and finally Jay. His eyes glisten like morning dew. 'I want to say *thank you* for breaking into this mausoleum of my own creation.

You have freed me. Until now I was a sorcerer living off the blood of my characters.' Again he slowly scans their faces. 'But who, I ask, was the sorcerer's *apprentice*? I won't point a finger, but you know *who* I'm talking about.'

All their eyes shift to Jay.

'Like Count Dracula in his tomb – unable to lift off during daylight, too scared to move – I, too, am frightened to leave this apartment, night *or* day in my case. But, like the Count, I continuously needed fresh blood, your blood, your lives. As the Count's family name happens to be *Dracula*, so mine happens to be *Grist*. Grist is the grain that's separated from the chaff in preparation for grinding to make bread. You *were* grist to my mill.'

Again he pauses to look into their eyes.

'Now you are chaff.'

Primo has had enough.

Talk of tombs and vampires has seriously disturbed him.

The knife in his hand is suddenly flitting about as crazily as a bat.

'Shut fuck up! You sick, sick.'

The blade caresses Marshall's cheek on the right side. He remains unfazed even as blood begins to percolate through his beard and drip onto his lap. Looking at Primo with limpid eyes, he speaks with the softness of a marshmallow.

'Why do you hate me so? After all was it not *me* who gave meaning to your life? Not only to you, but...'

He breaks off to look at Primo, puzzled.

'Forgive me, but is your name Primo? The Primo that I renamed Ray? I see you have a harelip and you dance around like a March hare, so you *must* be Primo. Jay brought me a profile of your fucked-up, clapped-out poisonous existence and I gave it life. I ask again why are you disfiguring me? When I am your *creator*?'

Primo's knife slashes again.

This time at Marshall's nose.

A deep incision slowly opens and blood spurts forth. Most would crumple into a whimpering heap, but *not* the great man of pulp literature, living eternally in a virtual violent world. His eyes follow the blood dripping onto his already blood-saturated trousers and smiles.

'But it's not only onto Primo's life that I bestowed meaning...' Again he scans his abductors. '... but on *all* your lives. Millions of readers around our planet have *met* each of you, come to *love* you, *hate* you, but most importantly, *learn* of your very existence. You should be grateful. You are *eternal*. And it was I who made you eternal. I who brought shape to your hopelessly messy lives.'

Primo screams.

'Look my fingernails!'

He waves his immaculate cuticles in front of Marshall.

'In movie you make dirty! You make me slob!'

'That's because you *are* a slob, Primo.'

Jay stays Primo's knife as it swings towards Marshall's throat.

'Cool it, Primo, we need to keep this shit *alive*. At least for a little while longer. Tell me, Marshall, what did you do with my pinkie finger? Did you feed it into the disposal unit? Grind it into grist along with *my* very existence. You didn't lift a finger to help me, to pay ransom money for my life. For you my life was worthless.'

'It *is* worthless, Jay,' Marshal retorts primly. 'I may write about criminals, but I *don't* associate with them.'

He casts a cool glance at Primo.

'Besides, your pitch over the phone was lousy. I didn't believe a word of it. Listen, buddy, I'll be in the *fiction* business for as long as our species continues to escalate its desperate need to escape reality.'

Marshall smiles and rattles his cuffs.

'Of course some of our species *can't* escape reality. Never. Ever. I glimpse them on television from time to time and they fascinate me. Those millions in refugee camps around this fucked-up planet. They have no choice but to face reality. Well, I *hate* reality! Give me fiction any day.'

He holds up his arms and shows them the cuffs.

'Do we have to keep these on?'

'Yes!' Was the unanimous reply.

Marshall laughs.

'Listen, you dickheads. Life is a game. A pointless pathetic game. Trouble is *once* you recognise this devastatingly obvious fact, the game is up. The fun is over. When you *can't* fool yourself any longer it's time to quit. Leave the party. That's where I am right now. Do me a favour, Jay. Eradicate me.'

Marshall scans his pristine *Great Room* gleaming like the pages of some glossy design magazine.

'This ridiculous apartment is the perfect metaphor for what most of us strive for. It represents the pinnacle of human endeavour. The bait that leads us to total insanity. Can there be anything more pathetic than a luxury penthouse? Empty. Cold. Without life. Well, there's nothing of me in here. This isn't what I dreamed of. I just ended up with it. My unrealised self lies in my novels. Unlike their creator, my novels are full of bitter compassion for those who *still* manage to fool themselves. That's you guys, right?'

His eyes shift to each of the faces staring at him.

'You are the innocents. You still think life is for real. Not a pointless game. Not an empty dream. That's *why* you inhabit my stories. No, that's why you *grace* my literature.'

Herby pops his glass eye out.

He holds it close to Marshall's face.

'This *graced* your shit literature all right. Once you put this on the page my professional life was dead. Look at it. It's not a marble, *not* something kids play with. But, Marshall, you *did* play with it.'

Marshall smiles.

'What you forget, Herby, is that I made you and your fucking glass eye immortal. *Shifty* will still be around when this planet finally sizzles into ash. It's had ten reprints already. And it'll never leave the shelves of libraries and bookshops and mail-order companies and even charity shops around the world. It'll always burn bright on e-books everywhere. You'll be discovered and rediscovered again and again long after you and I have died and been forgotten. You, Herby, will *always* be remembered.'

Again he pans across their faces.

'As will *all* of you.'

For a fleeting moment they try to digest Marshall's prediction of their eternal *fictional* life. The silence is broken when his phone purrs seductively. Until now, forty-eight hours into the apartment's occupation, Marshall's phone has remained silent.

That's not so surprising.

The recluse is a species rarely disturbed.

Being a solitary has its drawbacks.

Few care about you.

All eyes are on the phone as it grows more and more petulant.

Jay breaks the spell.

'Answer it, Lou.'

Lou Gozzi circles the receiver before taking a deep breath and snapping the handset to his ear.

'Grist!'

At first Gozzi listens.

Then the impersonator kicks in.

Pitch perfect.

Out of his mouth comes the voice of Marshall Grist.

'Why should I tell you that I've changed my tax adviser?'

He listens.

'Why? Cos you've been leeching off me ever since you took over my financial affairs, you goddamn parasite!'

Again he listens.

'Me? I'm your closest fucking friend? You were *never* my friend, Abe. Not once did *you* pick up the tab when we broke bread together. Without fail, when the bill came, you had short arms and long pockets. Pockets filled with *my* gelt, you mean, mealy-mouthed shit.'

Now Gozzi's eyes are blazing.

Lou is *in* character.

Gloria recognises the state of thespian euphoria and is envious. Lou has escaped from *himself*. Witnessing the unfolding narrative, Marshall can only smile at its audacity. His fingers begin to twitch; he yearns to be back at his computer.

Lou finally detonates.

'Go fuck yourself, Abe. By all means email that termination of services. I'll be happy to sign, scan and email it back to you. If blackmail is on your mind, Abe, don't forget we're like conjoined twins when it comes to the IRS. You squeal, I squeal *louder*. I'll make sure you spend the rest of your goddamn scheming, miserable fucking life contemplating double-entry bookkeeping. In the slammer!'

He bangs down the handset.

Silence.

Then applause ripples lightly across the *Great Room*. The great writer, whose *oeuvre* is renowned for being fast-paced and plot-driven, is beside himself with excitement. Sitting on the edge of his seat, he begins to rattle his handcuffs and shout.

'Bravo! Bravo! Author! Author!'

Lou bows in response.

His eyes drift longingly across to the booze bar set against the far wall.

Jay notices.

'Sorry, Lou. I had Gloria pour it all down the sink.'

He puts a comforting arm across his shoulders.

'Want a fruit juice?

SEVENTEEN

Greta Himmler has happily settled into her fourth day of incarceration. The day before she'd insisted via the monitor – now installed in Grist's apartment – on having both a laptop and a selection of films. Her doppelgänger, Gloria, giggles as Greta insists that 'ze fat boy' gets – for her *in-flight* entertainment – the following films: Wiene's *Cabinet of Dr Caligari*; Murnau's *Nosferatu*; Lang's *Metropolis*, and Pabst's *Pandora's Box*. Then as an afterthought she adds Riefenstahl's *Triumph of the Will* to the list.

'Ja! Zat's for ze start, Fat Boy.'

She smiles sweetly at the camera.

'I hope I haf ze time to get around to Fassbinder, Herzog, and ze other new boys. So you take all ze time you vant.'

Marshall chuckles.

He already spends much of his day watching Greta on the small screen as she voraciously tucks into her *Sauerbraten, Brathering, Bratwurst, Schwarzwurst* and *Pommes* on the side. Now he ponders on her choice of movies while muttering to himself, 'I was totally unaware Greta has such a *dark* side.'

Jay groans as he looks at the list.

Desperate to stay on Greta's *bright* side, he spends the next hour tracking down the DVDs, getting them couriered to Grist's apartment and then having Gloria take them to the cellar. Now, while murmuring murderous imprecations about Germans in general, Jay watches Greta load one into the laptop and lie back in her seraglio-stroke-cell.

She is content.

He is *not*.

He's uneasy.

Earlier he'd had to remove the cuffs from Marshall. So many signatures were needed for Herby to unpick the maze of trusts and shell companies, it was pointless keeping them on.

Primo, eyes permanently locked on Marshall, is twitchy.

His knife vibrates in his lap like a drumstick.

*

Every now and then Herby prises his glass eye out of its socket and uses the *good* one to study it. He passes a hand over its surface like it was a crystal ball about to reveal some new twist in the labyrinth of Marshall's financial affairs. Jay rarely leaves his side while he's at Marshall's computer, happy to watch Herby's fingers dance over the keyboard with the skill of concert pianist.

Chopin's *Etudes* are not what's on Herby's mind.

Only wormholes into Grist's vast fortune.

That and the satisfaction of revenge.

'This eye sees nothing, Jay. It's blind. Dead. Useless. Maybe having to concentrate with just *one* eye I see clearly what's going on? A flickering X-ray plate revealing a vast malignant tumour of corruption growing exponentially over our whole planet. Reaching into its every nook and crevice. Every day I'm forced to face that tumour I helped create and it makes me feel sick.'

Herby's live eye looks forlornly at its cold glass companion.

'I'm not religious, Jay. God forbid. But I now understand the meaning of *Purgatory*. Like those deluded Catholics, I ended up in a place where I was *made* to atone for my sins. Islands are prisons. After Marshall's betrayal I spent ten terrible years hopping from one fucking island to another. I'm not talking *happy* islands with locals limbo dancing, singing calypsos, fishing, tilling the soil. I'm talking tax havens. Bermuda, the Caymans, Turks and Caicos, the Virgins, the last tacky vestiges of the British Empire.

'Those islands are like sealed preserving jars full of a vile foetid pâté, a compote of capitalism and Mafia. Both equally ruthless. Both learning from the other. Mindless money machines. Jay, these were the *only* places I could get a job without any questions asked. Why? Because nobody dare ask questions in those shitholes. Bankers, lawyers, accountants have moved in. *Infested* them. They control everything.

'Their secrets must at all costs be kept from the prey. From the suckers. Us! On these islands trillions, quadrillions, quintillions of dollars slither and slide about like ballast in a ship that's bound to capsize and take us with it. But *not* them! They'll be on the shore waving as we go down and sink without trace. These smooth, smart-arse professionals, like their Mafiosi and Masonic doppelgängers, will destroy anybody who threatens to reveal their *secrets*.

'I witnessed reputations destroyed when anybody tried to blow the whistle. I saw people who stepped out of line driven from those islands. I heard rumours of others assassinated on the mainland. And all the time *knowing* that the local media, the only remaining outlet for truth, dare not speak out. Omertá is ultimately about *greed*. And islands are the perfect places to impose it.'

Herby sighs and returns to the task in hand.

Jay watches as he scans a release document before emailing it to a bank in Nassau, a document Marshall has happily signed. He seems weirdly relieved to be shedding all his worldly goods. The computer gives a satisfying *whoosh* sound to signal the document's departure.

'I know that bank, Jay. Only it's not really a bank. Six hundred brass plates on the *outside* and one part-time clerk on the *inside*. Sweethearts like General Pinochet and Kim Jong used it to hive off much of their country's finances. They reckon over one trillion dollars is syphoned off developing countries every year.'

He returns to the computer and starts punching the keyboard. A complex breakdown of a company's subsidiaries appears on the screen. The printer hums into life. While the pages spew out into the tray, Herby swings around to face Jay. Something's bothering him.

'Don't get me wrong, Jay, but do we *have* to kill him?'

Jay remains silent.

He looks at the freshly bandaged remains of his pinky finger; blood is again seeping through. Revenge may be satiated by cash for Herby, but for Jay *only* murder will suffice. Or will it? While he ponders on this, Gloria, loaded with pizzas, lets herself into the apartment.

Jay gets up and leaves.

Without answering Herby's question.

*

The pizzas are massacred in less than thirty minutes. Cardboard boxes, crumbs, ketchup-stained plates and cutlery cover the entire surface of Marshall's marble dining table. The man himself, while still free of his cuffs, is chained to a radiator. When all their jaws finally come to rest, silence falls. It's eventually broken by Herby, who speaks tentatively, almost in a whisper.

'You didn't answer my question, Jay.'

He shoots a nervous glance at Marshall who, having eaten more than his fair share, is struggling to keep his eyes open. He fails. His head slumps forward and a gentle snore follows. Jay stands, moves away from the table and stares out onto the observation deck. Rods of rain hit the AstroTurf and a sudden wind whips the edge of the closed awning. The only sound in the apartment is the light whistle coming from Marshall's mouth as he exhales.

When Gloria whispers, the rest of them can barely hear her.

'What was the question, Herby?'

Herby nods towards the sleeping man.

'Do we need to kill him? We got the money…'

Gloria interrupts.

'Good question, Herby. I think we should draw the line at *murder*.'

Raising her voice to emphasise her opinion carries it to the ears of their prisoner. Marshall's head ricochets into an upright position followed by a snort as loud as a stampeding horse.

With eyes blazing he lets rip at them.

'Draw the line at murder? You *have* to murder me! Never fuck with the punters! Cheat them and they'll turn into a lynch mob. They'll destroy you. They'll fuck you over with shit reviews on Amazon. Twitter and Facebook are now the murder weapons of choice. In cyberspace they can peck you to death quicker than any bird of prey. Deny them blood, they'll have yours. You stupid pricks, it's mob law in the marketplace now. The punters have been infantilised. They eat shit, read shit, watch shit. Why? Cos they're smart! Real smart! They realise they live in a world where you have to immunise yourself against *all* feelings, *all* emotions! Living is far too painful if you *feel*.'

Marshall rattles his chains angrily.

The company around the table watch in startled amazement.

Jay still stares at the rain now turning to sleet.

It's cold out there.

Marshall rattles his chains again,

'Look at the facts. Around the planet corporate man has traded in *his* feelings and emotions for a suit and company car. That's the deal! Dog eat dog. Exploit or be exploited. Our politicians love us when we're reduced to feeling *nothing*. *Numb. Brain dead.* Then they know they can safely screw the poor, the needy, the sick without a peep of protest. We've been digitalised – reduced to zeros and ones – so our every transaction, every reaction, every move can be monitored. Recorded with ease. This mindless process will relentlessly close in like a heat-seeking missile on our very *thoughts*. Even *before* we have them. Only when in that state of feeling *nothing* can we face the world we've created.'

Marshall slows to a halt.

No one speaks.

Jay slowly turns to face Gloria.

'We *created* this fucking monster, sweetheart. Now it's up to us to abort it.'

Marshall goes crazy.

'Jay, you fat fucker, *they* didn't create me. It was *me* who created *them*. These are characters I created from *your* clay, Jay. Old Testament wise I've programmed them in my *own* image. And like God in the Good Book, I'm a murderous son-of-a-bitch. My characters won't worry about little old me being butchered.'

He chortles insanely.

His lips move like he's having a conversation with somebody else.

Maybe several somebody-elses.

Marshall's bloodshot eyes pan across them all.

'I strip my characters bare. Down to the bone. What have I learnt? I've learnt that civilised man is just a savage in cling-foil.'

Jay crosses to the gibbering figure in chains.

'You needn't worry, Marshall.'

He takes his face gently in his hands and just as gently speaks.

'The executioner is on his way.'

EIGHTEEN

Chuck Ellington was the prototype for the main character in Grist's tenth novel, *Grip!* Back then Chuck had been only too pleased, even flattered, to collaborate with Jay in his research. But the euphoria that came with being the centre of the great writer's attention turned sour. The trouble started when the novel became a massive hit both as a book and movie. It earned the author millions of dollars worldwide and Chuck decided he wanted a share of the spoils.

Jay begged Marshall to show his appreciation by making out a modest cheque to Chuck. 'Tell him go fuck himself,' was Marshall's response. Chuck took the rejection badly and resentment had simmered until the day Jay rang and presented him with an opportunity for retribution.

He took it.

A brilliant engineer and inventor, Chuck could have taken his place in the higher echelons of the scientific world – but for one fatal flaw! A flaw as serious as metal fatigue in an aircraft or a disintegrating O-ring in a Space Shuttle.

Chuck simply couldn't fly straight.

He was sucked into the criminal underworld as if into a vortex. For him there was no adrenaline rush in being legitimate. His career in crime started with designing sophisticated equipment for cracking safes. When it became easier and safer to steal online, bank robberies became passé and he was forced to change direction. He shifted into designing containers with cleverly hidden spaces for drug and people smuggling.

Chuck is a sharp dresser, a handsome charmer, a narcissist.

The Mafiosi loved him.

For them he began by adapting a variety of weapons to meet their specific needs. Slowly they drew him into their inner circle. His deviant creativity – much like that of any parasite or virus – had found yet another host on which he could sustain his perverse take on life. Chuck nurtured *revenge* just as obsessively as his current sponsors. For Jay he agreed to create the most bizarre of all his numerous commissions.

Here we go.

*

Gloria lets him in.

Today Chuck has set aside his fancy clothes. Instead he's dressed in matching blue overalls and baseball cap, both inscribed with a breezy logo: *Save Me! Plumbing Services.* He's carrying two heavy bulging work bags. Jay immediately takes one of them.

'Let's get this over with.'

Following Jay into the apartment, Chuck glimpses Marshall through the open door of the sauna. He pauses to study him.

'You told me to go fuck myself, Mr Grist. That was a mistake, sir. A big mistake.'

Jay and he disappear into Marshall's office and close the door.

Primo and Caesar exchange smirks.

They alone know what's going on in there.

The others swap puzzled looks.

Gloria starts to shiver and twitch while they watch and wait until Jay emerges, leaving Chuck attaching a miniature device to the door lock.

'OK, so the trap is set,' says Jay. 'Now we're into an orderly retreat.'

'Hang on!' says Lou. 'What about the share-out?'

Jay smiles.

'Oh, ye of little faith. I was coming to that, Lou. Herby will show each of you how to access your account.'

'We each have our own password?'

'Right.'

'But if Herby knows them he could easily...'

Marshall, hearing the cacophony of voices, yells from the sauna.

'You're no better than me, you shit-faced paranoids. Don't you trust Herby? Herby's an honest man, he's just *stolen* my fortune!' He yelps with lunatic laughter so intense it would make even Francisco Goya recoil.

Herby waits for it to subside.

'Marshall's right. Just be grateful I've gone straight. Right now, each password is the *same*. You know how it reads? *Change Me*. All you have to do is *change* it to whatever password you like. Jesus, who'd believe we'd live in a world where we all need secret passwords? That used to be kids' stuff! Remember? Now it's for adults. Like Marshall said, we've been *infantilised*.'

Silence.

Gloria starts to quietly count on her fingers.

'Herby, Lou, Chuck, Marty, Primo, Caesar and me. Seven! *Seven Characters in Search Of An Author.* One more than Luigi Pirandello.'

They all look at her as if it's the onset of Alzheimer's.

Far from it.

'I played the *stepdaughter* on Broadway in nineteen...'

She decides against revealing the date. Instead she adopts a honeyed voice and sashays brazenly towards Jay. 'Believe me, sir, we are really six characters, and very interesting ones, even though we are lost.'

Norma Desmond in *Sunset Boulevard* comes to mind.

That's if you've seen *Sunset Boulevard.*

Gloria sways like a belly dancer towards Marshall, who looks like he's going to be sick as she wiggles her tush in front of him. 'The author who, once having created us, then no longer wishes, or is unable, to put us materially into a work of art. And this, sir, was a real crime. Because he who has the luck to be born a live character can even laugh at death. *He or she will never die.* The one who will die is the *writer*, the instrument of the creation. The creation never dies.'

Silence.

Gloria snaps out of it.

'With the exception of Jay and Marshall, each of us is both real and fictional, mortal and immortal, simultaneously.'

Marshall growls.

'Hear that? The one who will die is the writer. Let's get on with it.'

Jay almost whispers.

'You sure that's what you want, Marshall?'

'Sure I'm sure. You'll never know the number of times I've put a gun barrel in my mouth, poured sleeping pills into my fat hand, even looped a rope over that rafter up there. Unlike Hemingway, I never had the guts to do it. Just hope *you* do.'

'So be it,' says Jay.

*

Thirty minutes later, Jay and Lou emerge from Marshall's office. All eyes are on Lou as he beams an electronic remote at the door. There's a loud click as the key inside is activated, turned, and the lock secured.

A muted ripple of applause follows.

Outside, torrential rain is ferociously hitting the observation deck.

Inside is as sombre as a cemetery with everybody standing around like funereal statuary. All are clad in their dark outdoor gear: hats, scarves, bags, umbrellas.

The sauna is deserted.

The chain lies unoccupied on the floor.

In twos and threes, they exit the apartment at half-hour intervals.

In exactly the same manner as their arrival so they again deny the security cameras their identities before slipping away into the rain and the darkness.

NINETEEN

Later that same night Greta finds herself unceremoniously bundled by two men in balaclavas – Primo and Caesar – into the back of a limo. She's furious at being dragged away during Riefenstahl's *Triumph of the Will*, especially while a close-up of the Führer fills the screen, looking directly at her and seeming to watch events in the cellar.

They shut her mouth with gaffer tape.

She struggles desperately and, in an effort to calm her, Primo thrusts his immaculate fingernail, primed with cocaine, up her nose. Even so she manages to grab a handful of *Schnitzel* as they drag her away. With Caesar at the wheel, they careen into Harlem, ending up somewhere behind the Apollo Theatre. Greta, confused and terrified, mostly by Caesar's limited driving skills, refuses to get out of the car.

Primo's balaclava bulges and heaves as he struggles to speak.

'Get fuck out, bitch! Now!'

Greta is proving to be his match.

Maybe it's the effect of the cocaine, although most of it has served to highlight the downy moustache above her upper lip. At one point she manages to free her right arm, swings it and lands a punch on Primo's jaw.

Amend that to Primo's *glass* jaw.

Primo is out cold.

Greta rolls onto the sidewalk as Caesar roars off with the back door flapping like a great bird trying to lift off with only one wing.

On the back seat lies Primo.

Concussed.

Mentally in another place.

*

Primo finds *himself* looking at *himself* on a screen in a movie house. What's more, the Primo in the film – Ray – is looking directly back at Primo in the theatre. The Primo in the theatre, now back in the film, freaks and stumbles from his seat to the exit.

Into the daylight.

Blinded by the sun he mutters angrily at the cloudless sky.

'Hey, God!'

He points at the blue void.

'You got a moment?'

A passing seagull caws plaintively.

'You create me? Or I create YOU?'

He lowers his eyes to find the audience emptying from the movie house onto the sidewalk.

Among them is Primo.

Or is it Ray?

They look at each other.

Both move to the box office to check out the battered old peroxide blonde. Both prance up to the window and jig-a-jig a lewd tongue at her. Her pancake mask sits like a sphinx while her watery eyes scan both of them good.

As good as any security camera.

Primo and Ray speak in unison.

'Remember me, sugar?'

Her smeared, lipsticked lips quiver before she speaks.

'No way, shitface! I *never* see nobody. Go fuck yourselves.'

Both make for the bar next door roaring with laughter.

Their laughter commingles in an everlasting echo chamber, which in turn commingles into police sirens howling as their cars hurtle past the movie house. Inside one car Primo and Ray glimpse Greta Himmler, yet again the centre of attention, sitting on the back seat happily tucking into her *Schnitzel*.

Minutes later Primo regains consciousness, to find Caesar screaming at him to pull the car's back door into place. He does just that, shaking his head, not sure if what's happening is fact or fiction.

*

The Brompton is not used to any kind of plebeian invasion. A discreet haven for the rich and privileged doesn't expect its protectors to intrude in any way. Although occasionally the occupants – reluctantly – have to tolerate street life in their pampered environment.

This is just such an occasion.

The police cars screech to a halt outside. Cops with barbarian instincts naturally relish trampling through a foyer designed like a Greek temple, watched by sycophantic porters and doormen, while their boots scab the artificially marbled floors. Better still when they crowd into the elevators that will take them with the speed of a rocket into the outer stratosphere of the super-super-super rich.

The cops, hardened warriors of the streets, gasp when they enter Marshall Grist's penthouse. They find themselves in heaven. Mount Olympus. The Brompton's fake-Greek foyer should have alerted them that they were about to enter the capricious world of the gods. A world in which every human foible has already been explored and validated by time.

Plus ça change.

Greta Himmler cooly observes the law officers darting nervously, handguns drawn, from room to room, until they finally reach Marshall's office.

The door is locked.

Lieutenant Ryan Flanagan steps up and rattles it.

He bends to study the lock.

'The key's on the inside.'

'Somebody must be in there,' says his lickspittle sidekick.

Lieutenant Flanagan points his gun at the lock.

'There's only one way to find out.'

Muffled screams from inside the room cause him to hesitate.

'Did you hear that?'

303

'What? I don't hear nothing.'

Flanagan's finger tightens on the trigger until the firing pin strikes the primer, ignites the charge, sends the bullet hurtling along the gun's long barrel and into the lock.

It disintegrates.

The door slowly swings open.

And there is Marshall Grist.

One of the world's bestselling crime writers is firmly clamped in a guillotine elegantly adapted by Chuck Ellington from a substantial artist's easel, an archer's crossbow and a butcher's bacon slicer.

Marshall's mouth is taped shut.

White and tight.

The shape of a letterbox.

His nose above shimmers with running mucous.

His scared eyes spin like symbols in a fruit machine.

Flanagan gasps at the gruesome installation before cautiously entering the room, thereby breaking a laser beam, which in turn activates the slicer. A sudden flash of steel, sharp as a samurai's sword, and Marshall Grist's head is a millimetre above where it was a split second before.

The gap between skull and trunk widens.

Blood starts to spurt like a gusher.

Grist's severed head lands on the wooden floor, bounces and rolls until it finally comes to rest.

Dead eyes – still open – stare heavenwards.

Then the lids close as slowly as a cinema curtain.

The show is over for Marshall Grist.

*

Grist's apartment now seethes with homicide investigators, crime-scene photographers, forensic specialists. His decapitated body, still framed by the easel, has all the attributes of a Francis Bacon masterpiece. Here, in his office, a team of white-coated, masked medical examiners are at work. One holds out a plastic container while another picks Marshall's severed head from the floor, gingerly by the hair.

Blood drips into the pool below.

The medic holds it at arm's length.

'Crazy! Just think. His whole life happened in *here*. Everything was recorded and stored in this little baby. Then zap! Cut the power cable and it's all wiped.'

The head starts to slowly spin, driven by the air conditioning.

'Maybe life is just a trick of the *imagination*.'

The other medic shakes the container impatiently.

'Cut the crap and get on with it.'

No way.

His colleague is hypnotised by the spinning head.

'Get a life, they say! But what the fuck is a life? Movies, television, books, booze, drugs, clubs, football, golf, computer games – is *that* a life?'

He laughs.

'Then there's the *after*life. Get yourself an afterlife! OK, Mr Grist, what you got to say about that? You should know by now if there's an afterlife.'

With that he tears the tape from Marshall's mouth.

As it rips away the skin and beard, so Grist's eyes shoot open.

His mouth screams first.

Then bellows.

'SHIT!'

The medics are momentarily frozen with disbelief before being gripped by panic. Abandoning their clipboards and instruments, they make for the door, crashing into each other, slamming into walls, skidding in the lake of blood.

Marshall's head is among the items dropped.

It bounces across the floor, grunting and groaning, until it hits the skirting, rolls back and comes to rest by the patent leather half-boots of ashen-faced Lieutenant Ryan Flanagan.

Their eyes lock and Grist's blue lips form his very last word.

'Arsehole!'

*

That night Lieutenant Flanagan has difficulty getting to sleep. His mind obsesses with an endless horror-story loop in which a door opens and re-opens and re-re-opens to reveal and re-reveal and re-re-reveal Grist rigged and ready for the bacon slicer. He keeps asking himself why, why, why would anybody, however insane, plan such a crazy way to commit murder? So fucking elaborate.

Lieutenant Ryan Flanagan doesn't read much. And certainly not crime novels. Even if he did, it's unlikely he'd appreciate the prank behind Marshall Grist's demise. Unaware as he is of the conundrum beloved of crime writers since the beginnings of the genre in which a murder victim is found in a room with *no* windows and a door locked on the *inside*. How the fuck did it get there? Flanagan will go to his grave cogitating on the murderer's motivation. Humour is not Lieutenant Flanagan's strong suit. It would be hard for him to recognise the whole episode as a joke.

A black joke.

A very black joke.

Next morning Flanagan goes to his bathroom rubbing his red-rimmed eyes. He stops by the mirror, stunned, not believing what he sees. His abundant jet-black hair has overnight turned white.

Snow white.

*

Behind every great fortune lies a crime.

So wrote Honoré de Balzac.

And so it is with our cast of murderers.

Last seen slipping into the rain and darkness outside the Brompton, each went their own way. Gloria flies to Los Angeles and moves into a suite at the Beverly Hills Hotel. Every day at breakfast and lunch in the Polo Lounge, surrounded by movie executives, she has herself paged. Not one of the executives reacts. Then one day a very old man sitting at the next table smiles at her when the pageboy calls her name. 'I'm a great admirer of your work, madam.'

Much to his surprise, he's rewarded with a blow job executed in her suite. Gloria has to work hard and the effort causes her to have a massive myocardial infarction. She dies happy, doing what she does best.

Lou buys a chain of luxury residential rehab centres. One feature he introduces as part of the treatment is a daily performance of his brilliant impersonation of W. C. Fields. Each clinic is treated in turn to a re-enactment of the great man's films. Unfortunately, it drives the patients crazy not knowing if Gozzi is *impersonating* inebriation or is in fact drunk. Consequently the process of withdrawal goes into *reverse*, and the success rate of the chain falls sharply as most of the residents retreat into the fond embrace of Bacchus. Early one morning he's found naked and face down in one of the chain's Olympic-sized swimming pools. His clothes are neatly folded by the diving board along with a suicide note. No one, and that includes the cops, check the handwriting. But someone somewhere knows it is *not* his.

By far the most bizarre outcome is that of Herby.

Shortly after the events recorded in the previous pages, his mother, Dolly Strauss, dies. He blames her demise on Jay saying that – by just mentioning Marshall Grist's name – he'd undermined her health. After pining for over a month, he proposes marriage to her younger sister, Tammy. Tammy isn't, in fact, that much younger, but she is the spitting image of her sister. She accepts his offer with alacrity on the condition he wears a piratical black patch over his unoccupied eye socket. He agrees and his discarded glass eye now sits on top of the porcelain pot containing Dolly's ashes.

Not unsurprisingly Marty Graf stays as Jesus Ruiz. While Greta Himmler, also not unsurprisingly, changes her name by deed poll. At Marshall's funeral, and forever afterwards, she dresses totally in black. A black pillbox hat and veil provide that touch of mystery she's seeking. Later that year she returns to Munich, where she introduces herself to her remaining relatives as the grieving widow Greta Grist.

*

Jay Carrion spends a minor part of his fortune having his face radically transformed. He also has Jesus Ruiz surgically remove a vast amount of body fat. With his new face and streamlined torso, Jay buys himself a new identity.

Jim Joyboy.
Slim Jim.

These adjustments meant he didn't have to vacate New York.

One day he finds himself passing the movie house where this all began. He's surprised to see the same movie back, playing in a season of reruns. He's even more surprised to see Primo stumble from the bar next door. His one-time nemesis has changed not one bit.

The same harelip.

The same cheap clothes.

The sniffling nose.

The toothpick twitching in the mouth.

Jay, puzzled by this, was not to know that once the sextet had split and gone their separate ways, Primo nosedived into a mountain of cocaine. Surfacing a week later, he found his memory cells had suffered a severe meltdown. A loose synaptic neuron conjures up Herby showing him how to delete *Change Me* but *not* the password he changed it to. His key to *Dollar Heaven* lay as irretrievable as the reactors in Chernobyl.

Jay watches as Primo drunkenly runs a finger slowly along the credits at the bottom of the poster, mouthing the names, working backwards from the director, past the seven producers, before pausing at each of the ten scriptwriters. His long elegant scoop of a fingernail, not the dirty bitten-to-the-quick one in the movie, once again stops like a divining rod at the guy that wrote the novel. Primo knows this is the sorcerer, the vampire bat, the shitface soul-sucker. His lips meticulously chisel the name into a gravestone.

He smiles with satisfaction.

He knows the grave is now occupied.

Witnessing this unsettling ritual, Jay shivers, paranoid as ever, thinking Primo may be using some ancient spell learnt from his mother to wind the clock back and relive the whole grisly narrative. He needn't have worried. Primo, good Roman Catholic boy he once was, is simply revisiting the scene of the crime, much like he did so many times when following the Stations of the Cross.

All fourteen of them.

The Via Dolorosa.

Only this time it's not in sorrow or guilt but in *celebration*. So intent is Primo on relishing his revenge (while simultaneously trying to reactivate his memory loss) that he pays little attention to the movie's title. *For him that matters not at all.* But for you, dear reader, the irony will not go unnoticed.

Vicious Circle

Vicious Circle

Vicious Circle

Vicious Circle

For the Poor the Circle is one of Eternal Desperation.
For the Rich it's the Fruitless Pursuit of Happiness.

If your enemy is secure at all points, be prepared for him.
If he is in superior strength, evade him.
If your opponent is temperamental, seek to irritate him.
Pretend to be weak, that he may grow arrogant.
If he is taking his ease, give him no rest.
If his forces are united, separate them.
Attack him where he is unprepared, appear where you are
not expected.

Sun Tzu, *The Art of War*

A MONDAY IN SPRING

5.34 a.m.

The sun rises almost unnoticed.

A god no longer worshipped.

Its rays, dulled by low cloud, thread their way through the maze of London's streets, across parks and squares. Darkness is slowly diluted into weak shadows as the buildings are revealed.

Among them is the Croesus Palace Hotel.

This place is strictly for the rich.

Inside it's as quiet as a mausoleum. The turbo travellers are still asleep, their powerful minds idling, their *personal organisers* resting on bedside tables, standing by for another driven day. The only movement in the foyer comes from a mass of polishing hands and several humming machines skating across the palatial space. Before the elevators *ping* into action, gliding effortlessly up and down sixteen floors of luxury suites, the marble floor must be made to sparkle like crystal, every brass handle shimmer like gold. The kitchen phones, now silent, will soon need attention like petulant children demanding breakfasts in beds as big as council flats.

The trays are already being prepared.

Nobody must be kept waiting.

The rich are very impatient.

The night porter, known only as Boulder, or *Mr* Boulder, consults the wall clock behind his counter. A bulldozer of a man, swarthy and erect, he treads his earthly path thanks to a brief coupling between country colleen and passing tinker. Now, some seventy years later, rigid in a hotel porter's uniform laden with gold braid, campaign medals and epaulets, he struts towards the entrance. His pencil moustache and glazed boots represent the vestiges of an early life spent in the Irish Guards. The famous *Fighting Micks*. Then a sergeant major, now a tinpot dictator, he appears on the wide steps fanning down to the sidewalk.

Unmentioned until now is Boulder's magnificent aquiline nose. It scans the empty square just as the boot-black snout of a stretch limousine protrudes from an alley running alongside the hotel. It emerges slothfully. First the bonnet, then the driver's pod, followed by three mirrored windows, a rear door for the passengers, and finally a voluminous trunk. It momentarily straddles the street until the chauffeur, dimly visible behind the dark-tinted windscreen, swings the power-steering to straighten the vehicle. Manoeuvres more in keeping with an aircraft carrier bring it finally alongside the Croesus Palace, occupying over half its frontage.

Boulder swaps salutes with the chauffeur before returning to the foyer. Once inside, he surreptitiously produces a hip flask, unscrews the lid and takes a swig. He gasps as the whisky bites his throat. In a much-practised routine, the flask vanishes like a conjuror's prop.

*

Slump, the aforementioned chauffeur, has been driving stars of stage and screen for decades. As did his father, Slump Sr., before him. Obsequience runs in the family's blood the way oil runs in engines. Many a Rolls-Royce, Daimler and Bentley have felt Slump's capable hands as he steered celebrities to work, to premiers, casinos, nightspots. These vehicles, shorter and more modest, allowed for intimacy between the occupants. The driver could see, hear and *over*hear everything. Each journey ended with Slump's head full of gossip bursting to be shared with lesser mortals. These crumbs of showbiz tittle-tattle gave him status, respect. Sadly, those halcyon days are now over. As our galaxy is said to be continually expanding, so it is with our celebrities' salaries, status, egos – *and* limos!

Alone in his driver's pod, connected only by intercom, Slump is remote, anonymous, severed from the action and the dark matter of rumour and schmooze. The once-enjoyed intimacy has been downsized to the indignity of sifting debris in the passenger compartment: damp patches of champagne on carpets, traces of cocaine, used condoms, ripped panties, pages angrily torn from scripts (some with 'SHIT!' scrawled over them.)

In the old days he was proud to be observed in his limo waiting outside restaurants and discos, often for hours, filing his fingernails, kipping, or reading a newspaper. If the weather was fine, he'd even get out and pass a feather duster over the windscreen and bonnet. Now, holed up inside a giant phallus, all dignity in work has wilted. Beyond the dark windows he sees people, often crowds, ridiculing him, shaking their heads and miming *wanker* with curled thumb and first finger driving piston-like from between their legs. He feels a pariah, a laughing stock.

Worse is to come: the boss is acquiring another model.

One fitted with a *Jacuzzi*.

Slump shudders at the thought.

*

Arriving back at the porter's counter, Boulder answers the phone and listens. 'He's not picking up, is he? Lazy bugger. Thanks for that. I'll be on the case.' He dials a room number, muttering curses to himself. Just then the foyer lights, including the chandeliers, flicker violently. Boulder waits impatiently until they settle. He hangs up and punches in another number.

It's answered.

'Did I wake you, Eamon? Those halfwit electricians are still at it? The place is twinkling like a Christmas tree. I thought they were meant to be out of here Friday.'

Boulder listens then explodes.

'Today *isn't* Friday, Eamon, today's Monday. You sound pissed! Been on the juice all de weekend, have you?' He holds the headset away from his ear, recoiling with disgust at the sobs coming down the line.

'So God help me she dumped you, so what?' More snivelling follows. 'Give over, Eamon! You knew dat girl's the hotel bicycle. By now some other idiot will be after slinging his leg over her. Just get down here and start kicking up shit with those electricians.'

He cuts the call dead and redials the room number.

It's engaged.

*

On a first-floor windowless corridor, pools of light thrown from above each door give it the appearance of an aquarium. A pageboy, footsteps silenced by thick carpet, rounds the corner, selecting newspapers from his satchel and dropping them outside each suite. Traditionally uniformed, even down to the pillbox hat, cheeky young Trinder abruptly stops in his tracks.

Outside the Abraham Lincoln Suite sits a man on a gilt chair. Clad in a black outfit of suit, socks, shoes and tie, and with a black holdall on the floor beside him, his head lolls on his chest. A gentle snore can be heard. Trinder, well accustomed to paranoid guests with private bodyguards posted outside their doors, carries on as before, if more cautiously. Instead of *dropping* the newspaper, he bends to place it quietly on the floor.

The man doesn't stir.

The boy takes a closer look at him.

His bottom jaw is slack, thereby elongating the tiny crucifix tattooed on his right cheek, while his top lip rests on a toothpick jammed between two upper incisors. Trinder's nose quivers at the lingering scent of incense. About to move on, he notices the earplugs crammed into both auditory canals. This prompts him to clap his hands, quietly at first then loudly.

The man remains comatose.

'Security? My arse.'

Shaking his head in disbelief, Trinder moves on, letting the newspapers hit the carpet with a muffled thump before turning the far corner. As he vanishes, so the lighting along the corridor flickers briefly then plunges into total darkness. It immediately springs back to life, only to vibrate more violently than before. While in no way comparable to the electric charge needed to galvanise Victor Frankenstein's monster into life, it curiously has the same effect on the dormant man outside the Abraham Lincoln Suite. He wakes with a start, seemingly uncertain of his whereabouts, staggers stiffly to his feet before his rigid limbs attempt some faltering steps. His arms, now dangling, are as long as that of an ape. Very slowly he registers the vibrating lights and fixes them with a stare.

The flickering stops immediately.

He nods with satisfaction.

More now on this man in the gilt chair.

He goes under many names.

The current one is Rattle, simply Rattle.

As with Boulder, he has no use for a first name.

It's like that with some people.

Rattle painfully exercises his neck and eases out both earplugs. Suddenly uncertain, he unbuttons his jacket, takes a handgun (a Smith & Wesson .38 to be precise) from its shoulder holster, breaks it open and examines the cylinder. Satisfied, he smacks it back into place, primes the safety catch and returns it from whence it came. He settles, takes a deep breath, places his hands in his lap, palms up and closes his eyes.

*

'*Going up*,' says the simulated human voice as Boulder enters the elevator. The brief ride to the first floor allows him just enough time to consult the mirror, time to straighten his braided cap and lovingly stroke his moustache. Ping!

'*First floor*,' chimes the voice before the door slides open and Boulder steps out. Like a general about to inspect his troops, he strides briskly along the corridor until he reaches the Abraham Lincoln Suite. Casting a disapproving eye over Rattle in his gilt chair (one he recognises as taken from the hotel's conference room), he presses the doorbell and waits.

And waits.

And waits.

Cursing, he knocks impatiently on the door and waits.

And waits.

The night porter removes his cap and wipes his brow, pondering on a course of action. As he turns to march away, there's a quiet knock from within the suite. He stops as a brown envelope slides under the door. Before he can react, Rattle springs from his seat and snaps it up.

Rattle is a man not just of many *names* but also many *roles*: moments ago, a slumbering gunslinger, now a mischievous leprechaun. With a wicked glance at Boulder, he opens the envelope and takes out a glossy portrait photograph.

It shows a US Army recruit.

On the back he finds a scribbled message.

The mighty Boulder, whose ever-expanding bulk, alcoholic intake and age have seriously affected the sensory links between brain and limbs, slowly unfolds a white gloved hand until it is flat, ready to receive the package.

He and Rattle remain motionless, eyes stubbornly locked.

Rattle smiles and returns the photo to its envelope.

His whisper barely breaks the silence of the sleeping corridor.

'It's a security matter. Everything that passes in and out of that suite is *my* concern. *Our* concern. Those are my orders from head office. I need it for *identification* purposes.'

The synapses in Boulder's brain smoulder momentarily then laboriously fire up before he, too, whispers.

'*Identification* purposes?'

Puzzlement fills his face.

'Are you, by chance, a creature from *another* planet?'

'Do I look like one?'

'I wouldn't know. Otherwise I would not have asked.'

'Of course, you'd know.'

After decades of nights spent alone, pacing the cold marbled spaces of the Croesus Palace, Boulder has allowed many weird thoughts to occupy his imagination, one of which is about to surface for the delectation of Rattle.

'What if you've been taken over by an alien spirit *without* realising it? While you slept? And your external shell did not change when this monstrous ectoplasm infiltrated your soul?' He adds forcibly, 'Via your *ears*.'

'Impossible.'

'*Impossible*, de man says.'

'I wear earplugs.'

He holds them up for inspection.

Initially taken aback, Boulder doggedly persists.

'It tranquillised you, then *removed* your ear plugs, slipped inside and replaced your soul with an automatic guidance system. You're no longer capable of making decisions. You're on course all right, but one *selected* by powerful malignant forces.'

The man in the gilt chair slowly, very slowly, raises his right arm and twiddles his fingers. Much pleased with himself, he studies the action closely before finally lowering it.

'It seems I still have my free will.'

'Free will?'

Boulder grunts in disgust.

'A dodgy one is dat free will. An idea as artificial as a wooden leg.'

Rattle stretches out his leg.

It's patently not *artificial*; he bends it as if to underline the fact.

Boulder watches, transfixed, confused. Deciding against extending this exchange any further, he changes the subject.

'Will your boy be coming out today?'

Rattle slides the photo from the envelope enough to read the message on its back.

'No.'

'Right then, I'd better be off to inform our Mr Zigzager.'

Ever the old soldier, Boulder executes a smart about-turn and quicksteps silently along the carpet, disappearing around the corner. Rattle reacts to the distant disembodied voice. '*Going down.*' He takes from his holdall a tiny toothbrush and equally tiny tube of paste, *airline freebees*. Meticulously he applies them both to his upper and lower pearly white teeth. That done, he jerks at his black tie until the Velcro at the back splits with a loud, disquieting rip. He plucks from his bag another pre-tied version, a London-clubby-looking number, and slips it into place under his collar. All this is executed with the expertise of a quick-change artist.

For Rattle a new day has dawned.

With a deep breath, he adopts a meditative position and closes his eyes.

And that's *exactly* how Boulder finds him when he returns from the foyer some fifteen minutes later.

Well, in truth, not *exactly*.

Rattle's meditative position has melted into slumbering mode with his head resting heavily on his chest. The porter listens attentively to his whistling snores. While constantly alert to any change in volume, he tiptoes around him towards the holdall. His index finger is about to part it when Rattle's snoring ceases and he wakes with a start.

He pins Boulder with his eyes.

The night porter rarely blushes but this moment is an exception. His face pulses red with embarrassment. Again, the murmured exchange could be that of two conspirators.

'Thought I'd better be after zipping it up. Just in case, you know. You never know if...'

Rattle lifts the holdall to his lap and meticulously begins to itemise its contents. Boulder is bluff and bluster, albeit muted, squirming before Rattle's searing look.

'Nothing missing, I hope?'

Rattle slowly closes the holdall; its zipper's teeth grind ominously. He lowers the bag softly to the floor while his black eyes follow Boulder as he crosses back to the door. Only then does he speak.

'Tell me about this Mr Zigzager?'

'Like a bar of soap in the bath. Always keeps his cell phone switched off so this one slippery fella can never be traced. His assistant says he must be on his way to the studios. Meanwhile I'm to stand by, waiting to see if there's any action.'

A moan as low as a Tibetan horn emanates from Rattle.

'*Action*. All they want is action. Action, action, action.'

The night porter nods in uncertain agreement before painfully bending to pick up the newspaper by the door. Ignoring the front-page report of a terrorist atrocity in some foreign land, he turns instead to the business section. Here, in these pages, atrocities of a different calibre are reported. Frauds. Financial killings. Company coups. Boardroom assassinations. Boulder scans the photos on every page. Over the years he's become skilful at identifying the flaccid faces of these corporate warriors as they cross his foyer.

Rattle stretches out an arm, his left one this time, and has his fingers dance in the air.

'I still think I enjoy free will.'

'Impossible,' hisses Boulder. 'There's your bloody genes for a start. They put the straps on you from the off. Just think about it...' He hesitates, distracted. In the share price index, he notices an improvement in the value of a particularly relevant stock.

'It seems supplying *security* is something of a growth industry these days.'

'Perceptive,' mumbles the weary Rattle.

'One directly linked to the escalating growth in people's *in*-security.'

'Succinct.'

'And the more consumer goods we possess, the more protection we'll be after needing.'

'Visionary.'

'So if consumerism continues apace, we'll all be ending up *behind* bars. Locked in with secret codes, passwords, electronic alarms, high-security fences.'

'Mobile dog patrols,' adds Rattle, yawning.

'We'll be in *prison*.' Boulder stifles his laughter. 'Which is more than you can say for most burglars. A comic reversal of roles I must say. Am I right?' Rattle, barely awake, nods in agreement as Boulder continues, 'And you're doing very nicely, thank you?'

'Thank you.'

'I ask as one always seeking an alternative career on my retirement.'

Rattle, irritated, sighs. 'Why not concentrate on your *current* one? Shouldn't you be back in the foyer?'

'Don't worry about yours truly, sir. No need for that. I already handed over to my relief. I'm here because I was *asked* to be here. In case there's to be any action.'

He turns the page and continues reading.

Rattle nods off as a peaceful silence descends on the corridor. The only sound is the gentle hum of the overhead lighting.

'Here's *another* growth industry.'

Rattle jumps awake when Boulder speaks.

'What is?'

'*Health*.'

'You seem obsessed by growth industries?'

'I am indeed. Not with gardening centres though.' He meticulously folds the newspaper back to its original form before continuing in low confidential tones, 'Twin-top propagators, cordless grass shears, fertiliser dispensers, impregnated slug tapes hold no interest for me. The wife, though, is a very different kettle of fish.'

Rattle, struggling to keep awake, moans in desperation.

'Don't tell me she's into aquatic centres? Trout farms?'

Boulder is startled.

'How'd you know that?'

'I'm telepathic.'

Now the night porter is really fired up.

'So's Bernadette. Do you get premonitions? Warnings from the other side? I think her brain must be cellular like mobile phones.'

Without warning Rattle rolls slowly off his chair, landing on the floor, exhausted. He quickly picks himself up and sits. Boulder looks on, a master of fake concern.

'You poor man. Been here all weekend, have you? It's Monday morning and still nobody to replace you. Would you like me to phone your head office?'

Rattle spears him with steely eyes. 'No!'

Boulder's nose twitches with nosiness.

'Tell me then, *why* haven't they sent a relief?'

'That's classified information.'

'Classified? And why may that be?'

'That's classified, too.'

The bodyguard returns to his yogic position.

Boulder watches him, wary about probing any further, then risks it.

'Will you be carrying a gun?'

Rattle's eyes snap open. 'No!'

Backing away, Boulder whispers, 'If you've no gun, how can you possibly protect…?'

'I have my ways,' snaps Rattle.

He rises in slow motion, shapeshifting into a lethal exponent of karate, swinging a stream of well-executed chops. 'As master of many different forms of unarmed combat, I *have* my ways.' His choreography finally brings him elegantly back to his gilt seat where he rests as relaxed as a samurai warrior.

Not schooled in karate styles, Boulder is unaware he's just witnessed one known as *Tudi Sakukawa*. He's also unaware that one of Rattle's expert strikes has stopped millimetres from a pressure point in his neck. If the strike had been completed he'd be dead. Unnerved, Boulder briefly contemplates making an orderly retreat but decides against it. Time spent in the *Fighting Micks* dictates otherwise. Instead he faces Rattle, not as a slavering bulldog, more as a weasel. With words to match.

'No offence was meant, sir. You know that? My reference to a creature from *outer space*.'

Rattle is not to be schmoozed.

'*Planet*. You asked if I was from another *planet*.'

'Another planet,' says Boulder meekly.

'There is a difference.'

'I was merely...'

'Merely?' yelps Rattle. It's not a word he likes.

'Just! I was *just* pointing out that behind this door we have a star from another galaxy. *The silver screen*. A movie star. Right behind this door.' He passes his hand lovingly across the gold lettering, *Abraham Lincoln Suite*, before continuing to confer in a low conspiratorial voice. 'Whilst at my station in the foyer, I overhear famous filim producers, major distributors, international directors, first, second and even *third* assistant directors talk of your client as *mega*. The biggest. Not out loud, mind you, but in hushed, reverent voices.'

The night porter is surprisingly delicate on his feet for a big man.

He tiptoes away from the door, closing on Rattle so he can whisper directly into his ear.

'Since he's been here, my foyer's become like the anteroom to a royal bedchamber. Bellboys fight to deliver the large packages that arrive full of contracts worth millions, perhaps billions, of dollars to this very room.' Tiptoeing back to the door, he points at the bell. 'To press this very bell. Merely – whoops – *just* to catch a glimpse of his face.'

He finally presses the bell and doesn't take his finger off.

Nobody answers.

Rattle sits, composed, eyes closed, registering nothing.

Boulder moves, almost *en pointe,* backwards to face him.

'Women cross each other in the foyer, back and forth like worker ants, *en route* to his suite. Some are simple creatures with flowing hair and dressed in tattered denims. Others are sophisticated, sleek, with styled hairdos and silver-fox furs, and wearing only black stockings and silk lingerie beneath.' Dropping his voice even lower, he confides, 'Sometimes he has five or more women in there at *one* time.'

The night porter studies Rattle's stony face for a reaction. It stays stony. He tentatively takes out his hip flask, looks at it longingly, hesitates, then returns it to his pocket.

'Chambermaids turn to jelly waiting right here with their cleaning trolleys. Inside, so they tell me, are hundreds of *unopened* film scripts. The dreams of writers lie there, broken among the cartons of decaying junk food. Do you not find that *ironic?*'

Moments pass before Rattle, inscrutable as a sphinx, finally speaks.

'Do I find that ironic?'

One eye opens to peer long and hard at Boulder before answering the riddle.

'No!'

'That does surprise me,' whispers Boulder. 'Boxes of chicken legs (legs they hardly got to stand on) torn apart with voracious excitement while the works of great men remain undigested. And you don't find that ironic? A sad metaphor for a decaying civilisation?'

Rattle is getting impatient again.

'Come to the point, will you?'

'Point? What point?'

'How I could *possibly* be a creature from outer space?'

'Another planet. There is a difference.'

'Not in my book there isn't.'

His eye flashes angrily, deflates Boulder's complacency, then shuts.

'But only a moment ago you said...'

Rattle emits a fearsome, albeit almost silent *samurai* grunt.

Boulder, disconcerted, tries another tack.

'The point is that…'

Another grunt causes him to hesitate before continuing.

'The fact is that your client's face, often unshaven, has graced the covers of *every* periodical on *every* newsstand around the world.' His Adam's apple wobbles alarmingly. 'So why, in God's name, do you need his photograph for identification purposes?'

Boulder can no longer contain his agitation.

The hip flask appears in his hand.

Keeping wary eyes on Rattle, he takes a gulp.

Only then does he press home his hypothesis.

'I mean if everybody on this planet *knows* what your client looks like, and *you* don't, one might be justified in assuming *you* are a creature from—'

Rattle interrupts with another angry grunt.

He does *not* like the drift of the night porter's reasoning.

But Boulder is determined to pursue it.

'The point is—'

A further grunt fails to deter him.

'The fact is that the autographed photograph that came under that door is almost certainly for my *niece*.'

Rattle's eyes shoot open.

He rummages in his holdall and brings out the photograph.

'Is her name *Stanley*?'

'Niece,' barks Boulder. 'I said *niece*.'

Adding quickly, too quickly, '*My* name's Stanley.'

He shoots a sly glance as Rattle again consults the photograph.

'This is for a *Trevor*!'

Boulder, now slightly the worse for drink, goes ballistic. He hits the bell to the suite with his fist and keeps alternating his blows between it and the door itself.

Rattle watches calmly.

'Why persist in pestering my client when you know he has no intention of answering?'

'I'll tell you why.'

Boulder hiccups.

'A limo awaits the little shit to take him to the studios. He's late!'

Banging the bell again, he goes dangerously puce in the face. An irate guest further along the corridor appears in a fluffy white bathrobe like a well-fed ghost. Myopic and without his glasses, he sees a blurred Boulder move away from the door while saluting him reassuringly. Noting the night porter's pencil moustache, gold braid and dancing medals, he assumes some South American dictator's in town and retreats grumpily into his suite.

Undeterred, Boulder returns to low confidential mode.

'Meanwhile one hundred men and women (highly paid technicians and actors) have finished their bacon butties and digested the tawdry pickings of the popular press while passing vast quantities of rich excrement (all that's left of the lavish quantities of gourmet food provided by Mr Zigzager) into a mobile shithouse inappropriately called a *honey wagon*. That done, they're now ready and waiting to devote themselves to the task of immortalising your client, thereby making it possible to export his image around the planet.'

Rattle holds up his hands in capitulation, hoping to hold back the verbal tsunami.

Fat chance.

Boulder's on another roll.

'To Brazil, Malta, Raipur during the monsoons, Karduna (what used to be called de *white man's* graveyard), Hiroshima (presumably now rebuilt) and Brindisi, where you can take a ferry to Greece. And your boy hasn't even shaken his poxy leg yet! Meanwhile, the overextended limo, as specified in one of the numerous sub-clauses of his sodding contract, is causing traffic jams at *both* corners of the block *simultaneously*.'

The storm of words finally abates.

In the blessed silence Rattle pulls a much-used Bible from his holdall. He kisses it before waving it at the door, seemingly in an act of exorcism. '"*And it came to pass that he rose up against his brother and slew him. For sin lieth at this door. And unto thee...*"'

He dries, stopping abruptly.

'Et cetera,' adds Boulder, anxious to keep the ambience sweet.

Boulder, always impressed by biblical quotes, is at first touched then inspired to try a different tack with this obstinate fellow. One based on a parable quoted by many an army padre: '*Well done, thou good and faithful servant.'* Surprising himself by remembering the source, Matthew 25:21, he immediately plunges into snivelling mode, a mode much loved by padres and hotel porters alike.

'Please, sir, understand the delicacy of my position. I guaranteed Mr Zigzager that your client will leave *on* time. *Every* morning. And in the *stipulated* vehicle.'

Rattle looks puzzled, even peeved.

'And what about my client's complexion?'

'His *complexion?*' queries Boulder, equally puzzled and peeved.

'Has your Mr Zigzager no concern for my client's complexion?'

'As far as I'm aware it's not on his list of priorities. No. His only concern (as stated to me) is the *meter.* The financial one that's relentlessly ticking and turning from the moment those hordes of technicians clock in at the studio.'

'That was his *only* concern? The meter?'

'His *only* concern.'

Boulder starts to strut like a rooster as he expands on the very nature of his sponsor, Zigzager. In the excitement of delivering, albeit *sotto voce*, further evidence of his exceedingly fertile imagination, he even takes swigs from his hip flask.

'There's genuine fear about Mr Zigzager when he talks of the meter. His tan fades, his razor-cut hair turns limp and greasy, his dazzling teeth dim. Blood bursts into his eyes and beneath them heavy bags swell up like toads.'

'A metamorphosis occurs?' asks Rattle.

Boulder gives a boozy nod of agreement.

'Exactly.'

'In which he comes to look like *the rest of us?*'

'*Some* of us, yes,' says Boulder, furtively returning the flask to its secret pocket.

Rattle smiles at the night porter's embarrassment.

'And this metamorphosis occurs *only* when he's pressed financially? Broke? Skint? Like *the rest of us?*'

Boulder bristles.

'You could say that. I speak as one who, for many years, has moved among the rich and famous and witnessed their desperate fear of the fiscal *pinch.* Seeing as they have more to lose than the *rest of us.*'

'Tell me, *Stanley*,' says Rattle. 'Do you look at yourself in the mirror when you get up each day?'

'I do,' replies Boulder, sensing a trap. 'But only to see if my cap and tie are straight and there are no hairs or dandruff on my jacket.'

'So you *only* look at your hat, tie and jacket.'

'Correct.'

'And *never* your face?'

'Never.'

'So if I was to say your nose is *brown*, dark brown, you wouldn't know if I'm telling you the truth, would you?' He conjures up the photograph from his holdall. 'Unlike *yours*, Stanley, my client's image is everywhere.' Hiding his face behind the star's glossy image. 'As you so eloquently put it, in *"Raipur during the monsoon rains"* and *"Brindisi where the ferry sails for Greece"*. His name will without doubt be *scratched* on columns of the *Acropolis*.' Playing *peekaboo*, he now leers over the shimmering smiling movie still. 'Now *that's* what I call ironic. A metaphor for a decaying *civilisation*.'

Boulder's lips suggest words about to emerge only to be brutally cut off by Rattle. 'Let me finish! With this in mind, is it so surprising my client, after completing his beauty sleep, next turns his attention to his *complexion*?' He looks at the photo lovingly. 'In a mirror, a magnifying one with a light, he examines every pore of his luminous skin. For the camera *loves* him. Almost as much as he loves *himself*.' Jumping to his feet, Rattle silently spins like a ballet dancer with the glossy studio still as his partner.

Suddenly freezing, he fixes Boulder with his black hawk eyes.

'But does he? Does he *love* himself?'

His head swivels like a bird of prey when a door along the corridor opens. A tall blonde woman steps out, wobbling precariously on vertiginous high heels as she cautiously closes the door with a quiet *click*. Stuffing a wad of cash into her gold lamé handbag, she nervously lets her extra-long legs hurry her past the *tableau vivant* poised outside the Abraham Lincoln Suite. Their collective eyes follow her until she disappears around the corner.

'Continuing with my examination of the psychopathology of my client, *Stanley*, I wonder if he really does love himself? Or is his metaphorical penetration of the hearts, minds and *quims* of fantasising female fans worldwide merely a manifestation of self-loathing? Of vengeance against women? Stardom as a form of *revenge?*'

Boulder's numerous chins shake as he looks at Rattle, nonplussed.

'I'll not be qualified to answer that.' His right hand dives into his tunic to bring forth a fob watch. 'But I would like you to concentrate your attention on...'

Rattle halts him with an upheld hand.

'I've no objection should you wish to contact my client by *phone.*'

The night porter simmers with fury.

'Your client's phone is off de hook. That's why I'm here. At *his* door. Ringing *his* bell. Occasionally.'

'Each morning,' whispers Rattle, holding a finger to his lips, 'my client steams his translucent skin with special herbs and oils, thereby removing all traces of acne, pimples before they peak, and blackheads, however miniscule. When embarking on such cosmetic journeys he can't risk being *interrupted*, now can he?'

'Quite,' agrees Boulder. 'Now, how about picking up—'

Rattle nips in quickly, 'Picking up where we left off?'

'At the *meter?*'

'No, Stanley. At *growth* industries. You didn't expand on *health.* Can I assume your interest in that industry follows directly from your job?'

'Correct. The rich and famous are obsessed by health.'

'*Their* health.'

'Always *numero uno.*'

'*After* money.'

'Right again,' says Boulder. 'My days are spent listening to the rattle of vitamin pills as their luggage crosses de foyer. Every evening when I come on duty I watch them jog and torment their bodies in our leisure centre with machines that might have been designed by medieval torturers.'

Such vivid imagery sparks Rattle to raise his Bible. '"*It is harder for a rich man to enter the Kingdom of Heaven than...*"' His lips tremble with hesitation.

'Et cetera,' adds Boulder, wanting to continue his spiel on the rich.

331

'And, of course, they have to be permanently...' – he hesitates, reluctant to let the word leave his lips – '... *brown*.' Then muttering inaudibly, 'All over.'

'All over.' Rattle points an accusing finger. 'Not just their noses! Ah, *brown*, that mysterious colour of good health.'

'They continually baste themselves in oil,' continues Boulder, without enthusiasm. 'Every muscle kneaded by masseurs. Every scalp weeded of dandruff. Every organ X-rayed. Samples taken. Tests made. Pressures read. And then it's time for eternal colonic irrigations.' He allows a moment for this unsettling image to sink in before going on. 'Whole lives spent cultivating *perfect* health.'

Rattle nods and sighs sadly.

'And for what purpose, I ask myself.'

'To be fit.'

'Fit for *what*?'

'To be seen at the races. Award ceremonies. Balls. Hunt balls.'

'And then?'

'They die. Cut off like overpriced orchids.'

Another sad sigh from Rattle.

'Ah, the wretchedness of being *rich*.'

'And this wretchedness is spreading,' adds Boulder.

'Trickling *down*.'

'Right. But not in the way we were told. Those spoilt, dissatisfied faces used to appear *only* here in this hotel. Then the *trickling down* started. Now you see them *everywhere*. The working class has been exterminated.'

'Consumerism equals genocide,' sighs Rattle.

'Worse, we are left with no one to look down on,' laments Boulder.

Rattle stands, stretches, ready to explore the germ of an idea.

'I, too, sometimes wonder what *my* true purpose is.' He looks up, apparently consulting some deity manifested in a small stain on the ceiling. 'Forgive me for even voicing such a thought, but it's the truth. Why am I here at all?'

He lays hands on the suite door, stroking it.

'What *exactly* am I guarding here? If, behind this portal, there was a statue of great cultural value whose perfection and truth humankind was moved to emulate, I would understand. Or a masterpiece by a great French Impressionist, now worth more than even his rampant imagination could have envisaged.' Adding for good measure, 'Even when pissed on absinthe.' Agitated, he's on his feet again, pacing the corridor, confiding quietly to Boulder, 'Sadly it's *not* a statue or a painting in there but a human being: an unfathomable, unpredictable animal. So what principles are involved here? Am I prepared to lay down my life for a mere *icon?*'

'An icon not a *brand?*' posits Boulder.

'A *contemporary* icon,' expands Rattle.

'An icon for being on magazine covers?'

'For his contribution to culture.'

'As a role model?'

'That's my problem, you see. Should I be prepared to lay down my life for a narcissistic, attention-seeking, infantilised tosser?'

Both fall silent, allowing time for each adjective to sink in.

'I still don't understand *why*,' adds Boulder.

'Why?' Rattle turns squally. 'Why *what?*'

'Why are you here?'

'Why am I here?'

'Yes. Why are you here at all?'

'You don't know *why* I am here? At all?'

'No.'

Rattle steps up to study the porter's spinning eyes.

'You really don't know, do you? I – *we* are here to do God's will, to suffer in this world and be happy with Him in the next.'

'Yes, but front desk doesn't know that. Nor does room service.'

Rattle's right arm whips to Boulder's ear, latches onto it, pulling it close to his mouth. 'Repeat one word of what I'm about to impart or an *Angel of the Lord* will rip out your windpipe.' His lips brush the night porter's lobes as he imparts his dreadful secret. Boulder stops yelping, startled by the information being fed into his brain. His eyes rake the ceiling like searchlights looking for enemy planes.

'But *who'd* want to do that?' he bleats.

'If I knew that I wouldn't be here. Now would I?'

'I suppose not.'

'*Suppose* not? Did you fully digest what I said?'

'Somebody has threatened to assass... sass...'

Boulder dries, gurgles, then appears to swallow his tongue before falling silent. Rattle, looking pleased, lets go of his ear.

'So where were you trained?'

'Trained?'

'At withstanding interrogation. One of our Secret Services? MI5? MI6? Or the Catering Corps? *Counter*-intelligence?'

Rattle's laughter is like being clubbed.

'How do you know if it's true? What you just divulged?' grumbles Boulder.

Any possible answer is overtaken by a naked figure suddenly bursting from the same door as the blonde. Shiny, bald, fat, bespectacled, and hiding his testicles with a luxury handcrafted leather briefcase, the man staggers drunkenly while looking wildly both ways along the corridor. Crazed, he searches endlessly inside the case without success, angrily stamping his feet. 'Bitch! Bitch! Bitch!' With a whimper, he lurches back into the suite and slams the door shut.

Boulder, now no longer attending the hotel's *bonding* sessions, still remains very much a *company* man, blind to any suggestion of impropriety taking place on the premises. Unfazed, he removes his cap to study the gold braid edging its peak.

'What if this suggestion of yours is just a publicity stunt?'

Rattle reacts like a man possessed.

'"*Thou shall not raise a false report: put not thine hand...*"'

His pulsating Bible freezes in mid-air as Boulder interrupts impatiently.

'Et cetera.'

Without pausing, he pursues another random thought that may explain the actor's reluctance to emerge. 'Maybe your boy is *paranoid*? Could be his role in the movie is affecting him? *Adversely*.' He nervously continues, 'Even now the cameras should be capturing it on celluloid. Would you mind if I gave his bell one more go?'

'I would.'

Rattle, much agitated, starts pacing about.

'Are you saying my boy, my client, may not be *himself*?'

334

'Well, yes. But that's his job. To be somebody else.'

'And *not* himself?'

'Don't you see?' Boulder is in the ascendant. 'He *has* to be somebody else. But not so much like somebody else that the fans don't know it's him, *himself*, that they've paid to see playing *himself* as if he were somebody else altogether.'

Rattle stops pacing. His countenance is a weather map of worry and alarm as Boulder goes on. 'Some stars are not as good as others at becoming somebody else. So they stay the *same*. In *every* film. Apparently they get paid the same, which seems unfair. But that's the *biz* for you. I gather your boy is from the *other* school.'

The night porter selects his words with care.

'I'm told your boy favours becoming *totally* somebody else. Now that can cause problems.' He shrugs in despair. 'We could, sir, conceivably have an *identity* crisis happening behind this door.'

Rattle, clearly disturbed by these revelations, studies the door before raising his Bible to exorcise the devils possessing those who choose to become *celebrities*, including his client. '"*Thou shalt not make unto thee any graven image. For I, the Lord thy God, am a jealous God...*"'

Both are now distracted by a distorted sound coming from the suite. It soon identifies itself as a muted bass drumbeat, slow, rhythmic, hypnotic. A snare drum chips in, sharp and dangerous. It's as if they've been transported to a *kabuki* theatre.

Rattle seems cast in its spell.

All colour drains from him as he whispers from behind his white mask.

'Voodoo?'

Boulder laughs in his face.

'Voodoo, my eye. *Management* paid for the little bugger to have silencer pads fitted to that drum kit. Just to keep him happy. He promised to practise only between midday and midnight.'

Out comes the fob watch.

'Six a.m. precisely.'

Rattle is unconvinced.

'Sounds like voodoo to me.'

Then, smitten by a lightning thought, he moans.

'My God, that explains all those *chicken* legs.'

His words fall like barren seeds.

Boulder's head is elsewhere.

'I hope the bastard's not going to be throwing bog rolls out the window onto the street again.'

The drumbeat uncannily picks up on the confusion reigning in the corridor outside. It intensifies. This subterfuge allows for its security spyglass to be prized from the door and fall silently onto the carpet, unnoticed by Boulder and Rattle, still locked into ecclesiastical niceties.

'If he's into voodoo, why, in God's name, did he ask head office for a Mormon?'

Boulder looks at him in surprise.

'Are *you* a Mormon?'

'I'm *affiliated*.'

'Really. How many wives do you have?'

'I've never taken a wife.' His eyelids drop. 'For reasons of hygiene.'

'So you're not a practising member?'

'I told you I'm an affiliate.'

'A *celibate* affiliate?'

'So to speak.'

'Not much point in being a Mormon if you don't have multiple spouses. Tell me, would you be knowing if voodoo is a *religion*?'

'Voodoo is a *cult*. Christianity is a *religion*.'

'So religions and cults are not the same thing?'

'Religions are official. Cults *aren't*. Cults offer up sacrifices.'

Boulder, preparing himself for intellectual combat, finally speaks.

'Didn't the Jews offer sacrificial—'

'Lambs, only lambs.'

'*And* Jesus Christ. Every day your Christians eat his flesh and drink his blood,' retorts Boulder, much pleased with himself. 'You take my point?'

Intent on such theological intricacies, both fail to notice the trickle of red liquid oozing from the now empty spyhole. The door appears to be bleeding like a stigmatic.

'Nothing quite like a good chinwag about religion,' says Boulder. '*And* cults. Tell me, does head office employ Hindus?'

'No way. Any belief in *reincarnation* could prove fatal in this job.'

'Buddhists?'

'Out of the question. Those seeking *Nirvana* will never find it with our dodgy clientele.'

The drumbeat stops, drawing Rattle's attention to the door. His jaw drops, his eyes rotate, his chest pumps like a church organ when he sees the red fluid slowly coursing down the white frame.

'Moslems?' says Boulder, unaware of what's happening behind him.

Rattle mouths, a goldfish in a bowl, but no words emerge. He can only point at the red puddle now forming on the floor. On seeing it, the night porter staggers, an avalanche on the brink of collapsing.

'Is it blood?'

Rattle ignores him.

'I *knew* he was into voodoo.'

As if to confirm his worst suspicions the drum starts again. This time the beat, still muted, becomes frenzied. Coincidentally the corridor lights choose to flicker, slowly, then frenetically.

The effect is apocalyptic.

For Rattle it certainly is.

He rises magnificently to the occasion, waving his Bible at that small stain on the ceiling like some crazed fundamentalist preacher. '"*For the trumpet shall sound and the dead shall be raised. For they have shed the blood of saints and prophets and thou hast given them blood to drink...*"'

'Stop the nonsense, will you? It's only the emergency generator being replaced. That's all. It's not *Armageddon* yet.'

Lights slowly settle.

As does the drum.

In the eerie silence, Boulder bends to inspect the growing puddle.

Rattle peers over his shoulder, pointing with a quaking finger.

'Looks like blood to me. Taste it.'

'Taste it yourself.'

'I'm vegetarian.'

'Thought you might be.'

Boulder straightens up.

'I've had enough of this malarkey. What the hell is keeping Zigzager?'

He hurries off along the corridor.

As he recedes, so the drumbeat returns, quietly at first but steadily growing with intensity. Rattle riffles through the pages of his Bible until he finds the appropriate passage. He faces the red puddle, genuflecting before blessing it with a reading from the sacred book: '*Take this, all of you, and drink. For this is my blood...*'

With the delicacy of a priest celebrating Mass, he pauses to genteelly dip his finger and taste it. His tongue's receptor cells prepare to inform the gustatory areas in his brain *if* the liquid is, indeed, blood.

This they do.

It *isn't*.

Instead they tell him it is, without doubt, tomato ketchup. Probably of the *Heinz* variety. Once his brain finally assimilates all this, the rest of him, even the furthest outposts of his physical form, go crazy. He bangs on the door like it's the walls of *Jericho*, even drowning out the muffled drum, which is trying to give as good as it's getting. Rattle resorts to mouthing muted screams through the unoccupied spyhole.

'You tricked me! You took me for a sucker! You phoney!'

He turns and flings the Bible, a lifelong companion, up the corridor. Coincidentally the drummer resorts to cymbals for the first time. A provocatively flashy solo seems to mock Rattle. With lips thinned by anger, he whispers ominously into the empty spyhole.

'So that's how you want to play it, buddy boy. Game on!'

At this the invisible drummer stops, but *not* Rattle. He pulls a black balaclava from his holdall and over his head. He unsheathes the handgun, cracks open the cylinder, smacks it back in place and returns it to its holster. That done, he settles like a bird of prey on his gilt chair. But not for long. The eyes, peering from the woollen holes, soon slip into a meditative state, a state so deep Rattle remains unaware of the elevator's return. With it comes a woman, rangy in stature but owl-like in round black spectacles.

It's Welty.

Welty is Zigzager's assistant. Dressed in her work clothes (long winter coat with fur collar, jeans tucked into fur boots, and topped by a significant flaming-*red* beret), she looks bravely incongruous striding between the suites harbouring the pampered guests. Approaching the

Abraham Lincoln Suite, she keeps her cell phone just far enough from her ear to know when Zigzager's *verbals* finally cease. When they do, *fate*, tricky as ever, steps in. The drum rumbles into life, as it has in many a Hollywood *Western*, with a *war dance*. Composed to scare the bejesus out of the characters on the screen, it did the same to audiences around the world. Even Welty experiences a shiver of apprehension before whispering into her mobile.

'*Yes*, he is playing his drum kit. And *yes*, it is before twelve. And *yes*, the meter is running. And *yes*, he did throw his script out the window onto the street.'

She bends to examine the red puddle at the foot of the door.

'And *yes*, it does look like blood.'

Zigzager whinnies inaudibly before Welty, exasperated, interrupts.

'If he's cut his wrists it's unlikely he'd *still* be playing the drums.'

More from the boss.

Again Welty cuts him short.

'OK, so you saw this movie when a severed hand got to play the piano. This *isn't* a movie, you berk!'

Welty addresses Rattle for the first time.

'You must be hotel security?'

A samurai grunt is his answer, prompting her to step back, swing away, whispering nervously into the phone.

'I think our security guard...'

Zigzager's voice rises as a distorted squawk.

Welty's face slowly freezes like a jelly setting.

'Nobody asked for a security guard? Well, somebody *must* have.'

She looks over her shoulder to reassure herself. Yep, there's Rattle all right, eyes flashing angrily through black holes in a balaclava. He's real enough.

'This guy sure looks the part. From his wardrobe I'd say he's seen all your movies.' She eases the phone away from her ear, allowing a dull whine to escape. 'Stop fucking whinging! It's tough at the top. You feel *faint* because the air's thinner up there. Get your fat arse over here, OK? It's only on the *first* floor so you won't need oxygen.'

But the whine returns, relentlessly. Zigzager's masochism needs feeding as carefully as a carnivorous plant. Welty hits her stride with relish.

'Face facts, douchebag, that narcissistic dickhead you cast in your shit movie has got your number. He's a fucking sadistic prankster and you're his whipping boy! Wise up, for Christ's sake. Fuck making movies. Use your suffering to start a new religion. There's big money in religion.'

She examines the spyhole in the door.

'And here's your very first miracle. A *bleeding* door! What's more you have a superstar on course to be Hollywood's *Padre Pio*. His fans will love it. Tell you what, let's take the door off its hinges and set it up in some desert. New Mexico, maybe. And organise pilgrimages. *The Unhinged Door of Perception*. Just think of the merchandising.'

She snaps the mobile shut and whisks off the red beret, letting her long hair cascade around her shoulders. Taking a brush from her coat pocket, she runs it through the tresses while watching Rattle's eyes flicker with interest. Welty locks straight onto them. 'I knitted a balaclava for my son. He's shy.' Rattle, evading her eyes, plunges a hand into the holdall, bringing out another well-worn book.

The *Tao Te Ching*.

Welty bends to read the title.

'*A Guide to Leadership, Influence, and Excellence.* So you're shy as well.'

Rattle riffles though the pages and settles for a specific chapter.

Welty peers over his shoulder.

'Chapter Fifty-One: The Way of Moderation.'

She giggles.

'Moderation? Are you sure you're outside the *right* door?'

Rattle breaks his silence.

'"*Those who know do not speak. Those who speak do not know*".'

With this Rattle smacks the book shut, dumps it back in his holdall, takes a meditative position before letting go a mantra.

'Ommmmmmmmmm...'

*

Boulder's snozzle, a feature in its own right, leads his exit from the elevator. It rounds the corner and comes upon a Bible tossed carelessly in the corridor. He picks it up and marches on until halting in front of Rattle.

'Ommmmmmmmmmm...'

'Excuse me, is this yours?'

'Ommmmmmmmmmm...'

Rattle opens an eye. It alights on his Bible.

'I've gone off it.'

The eye closes.

'Ommmmmmmmmmm...'

Boulder reels as if in the initial stages of cardiopulmonary arrest.

'Gone off the Bible? I'll have you know I was brought up on the *Good Book*.'

Rattle snatches it from the night porter's hands, waves it angrily in his face, then *freezes.* A loaded breakfast trolley, pushed by a waitress, emerges from the service lift at the other end of the corridor. He waits until it turns away and disappears. With biblical fervour deflated, he swings his wild eyes from Boulder to Welty and back again. Whispering, he strokes the Bible as he would a fetish.

'In here you can find the authority to do *whatever* you want. You can use it to justify war or peace, greed or charity, capitalism or socialism. You can use it to persecute fornicators and queers or justify going to bed with them.' He hands it back to Boulder. 'The trickster's manual. A good book. A great read. Sadly it's fallen into the wrong hands. I've moved *eastwards*.'

Boulder, reddening as intensely as lava flowing from a volcano, watches while Rattle perches on the gilt chair, settles, then slips into a state of mind enlightened to the illusory nature of self, thereby transcending all suffering and attaining peace.

'Ommmmmmmmmmm...'

Boulder teeters on the brink of an eruption that includes stuffing the Bible down Rattle's throat. When his fevered imagination extends to suite doors flying open, guests clad in their nightwear pouring out, rubbing sleep from their eyes, and clamouring for his immediate dismissal, only then does his anger abate. '*Softly, softly, catchy monkey*' is a saying attributed to Lord Baden-Powell, creator of the Boy Scout movement. It pops unannounced into the night porter's mind and leads to a sly change of tactic.

'Only a moment ago you were a cringing Christian begging a firm of electrical engineers to save you from eternal damnation.'

He appeals to Welty as a reluctant witness.

'What's he now? A Buddhist?'

'Why not? Pilots *change* airlines.'

'And uniforms.'

Boulder tentatively risks flicking the balaclava.

'What you dressed like that for?'

Rattle ignores him.

'Ummmmmmmmmm.'

Boulder leans close to his ear.

'I suppose you think dat's smart, sitting there, charging your battery.'

'Ummmmmmmmmm.'

The night porter sidles slyly away, nodding for Welty to join him in a confidential *tête-à-tête*.

'This man is *sick*. Luckily I'm very experienced in medical matters.'

'Good,' says Welty. Her owl-like eyes widen ever wider. 'So what's that bulge under his left arm? A hernia?'

'We're talking mental. He's *mentally* sick.'

'Ummmmmmmmmm.'

Both turn to Rattle, humming happily away like a beehive.

'His habit of adopting different religions must tell us something. I'm wondering if he hears *voices*.'

Voices?

An invisible guillotine drops, cutting off all sound. Even Rattle stays his breath. He opens an eye. Hearing *voices*? His one eye looks into Welty's two. The idea of having strangers banging around in one's head unsettles them all. Especially if they're psychotic.

The distant clunk of the service elevator arriving breaks the spell. Out steps Trinder. His arms embrace bunches of roses wrapped in cellophane. Whistling happily, he arrives at the Abraham Lincoln Suite, smiles at the assembled cast and goes to press the bell.

Boulder grabs his white-gloved hand.

'I wouldn't do that if I were you, son. We have a dangerous stand-off in progress. Touch that bell and it could aggravate matters.'

A fancy gift card peeks enticingly from the red blossoms.

Boulder can't resist.

'So what have we here?'

He delicately plucks the card out and squints at the message: '*Hope to see you back at the studio soon. We love you. We need you. Best wishes from the crew. P.S. And all their dependents.*'

His eyes water with false emotion.

'Isn't that lovely?'

'Is *dependents* underlined?' rasps Welty.

Boulder again squints at the card.

'Yes.'

'So is *love*?'

'Yes.'

'And *need*?'

'Yes.'

'They're from Zigzager.'

Zigzager! That name acts like a clap of thunder. Trinder takes cover.

'Don't say I told you, madam.'

Welty calms him with a smile.

'Where is he now? In the men's room? That's where he usually hides.'

'He's not well, madam.'

'A bowel disturbance?' chips in Boulder, concerned.

'He's got what you usually call the *shits*, Mr Boulder.'

Trinder can't disguise his delight at the night porter's discomfort. He places the roses beside the door. Since his arrival he's been taking crafty looks at Rattle in his balaclava. Now he openly gawps.

'Ummmmmmmm.'

'There's more roses, Mr Boulder. *And* a wreath.'

Boulder twitches with irritation.

'So bring them up, boy.'

The page can't shift his attention from Rattle.

'Don't just stand there. You've seen security men before.'

'Not dressed like that I haven't. Is he going to blow the door open and bring him out alive?'

'No, he is not.'

'He looks like he is,' Trinder points at the red puddle. 'And what's that? Tomato ketchup?'

Boulder cannot but smirk.

'Taste it and see.'

Trinder doesn't hesitate. He sticks his index finger into the liquid, withdraws it red, red as his dad's commie flag on the wall at home, guides it to his mouth, sucks the liquid away and returns it clean for all to see. As with Rattle, his receptor cells inform his gustatory areas that the liquid is, indeed, tomato ketchup.

'Probably *Heinz*. Bet you thought it was blood, Mr Boulder.'

'Watch it, boy.'

Welty takes a five-pound note from her wallet.

'Needless to say, Mr Zigzager didn't tip you?'

'Needless to say, madam.'

'Go tell him we request the pleasure of his company.'

She hands him the fiver and plucks a rose from the bunch.

'Give him *this* and tell him, if he doesn't come right away, I'll stick one of these into his every orifice. Tell him that by the time I've finished he'll look like a war memorial on Armistice Day. Got that?'

'Got it, madam.'

Trinder takes both rose and fiver before running off.

Boulder can't hide his appreciation of the roses.

'Generous gesture by Mr Zigzager nonetheless. Touching.'

Welty pulls another from the bunch, holding it out for him.

'They're from our property department. This afternoon we're scheduled to shoot a funeral.' She smiles. 'It could be Zigzager's if *boy wonder* doesn't come out.'

Boulder plunges his magnificent nose into the rose's petals, expecting to savour a delicate scent. Instead he withdraws it sharply.

'Mr Zigzager disappoints me. Does he really hope to impress with *plastic* roses?'

'Sure he does. Plastic roses never die. They're *eternal*. For egomaniacs eternity is a dream to be nurtured. If Zigzager could be filled with silicone like his mother's tits, he would be.'

Rattle's mantra had ceased, unnoticed, some time before. Attention shifts back to him when he begins to snore. His body slumps, the photo slips to the floor and Welty picks it up. Boulder sidles up to her, tongue flicking like a lizard's.

'He autographed it for my nephew, *Trevor*.'

The photograph is, indeed, autographed, as Welty can see.

'This is for *Sabrina*.'

Boulder shoots a venomous glance at Rattle.

'Sabrina? Ah yes, *she's* my niece.'

Welty reads the dedication scrawled across the star's moody unshaven face: '"*Hi Sabrina, Thanks for your tweet. You're right, baby, making movies is hard work. Up every morning before dawn and into make-up. With fans like you it's worth it.*"'

Boulder, touchstone for every false emotion, nods happily.

'Such a sweet little girl.'

Welty reads on, '"*Thanks for your selfie. Wow! What a body?*" Sabrina can't be that *little*. Or that *sweet*.'

'She's a good girl really.'

Welty turns the photo to the writing on the back.

'And Sabrina's right out of luck. So is Trevor. It's for Zigzager.'

She reads, '"*Hi Zigy, sorry buddy but I can't get a handle on this role. Looking for the truth ain't easy. Need time to rework it. A week at least. You always say you're a perfectionist so I know you won't mind.*"'

Muffled drumbeats again percolate insidiously from the suite. This time it's clumsy, inept, somebody fooling around on the kit. Boulder and Welty put their ears to the door. High-pitched giggles are part of the sound mix.

Boulder steps back in shock.

'*Girls?* He's still got women in there.'

'How many?' asks Welty.

'I saw *two* crossing the foyer last night. And there may be *one* left over from lunch yesterday.'

'Only *three*? Relax, he'll be out by breakfast.'

She turns to find Trinder back from the foyer but hidden behind a thicket of cellophane-wrapped plastic roses and a funeral wreath weaved into a red, white and blue simulacrum of the Stars and Stripes. He places them in front of the door.

'Did you find him?' asks Welty.

'No, madam. He'd gone. Gary in the men's room said Mr Zigzager shot out without washing his hands or leaving…'

'A tip,' interrupts Welty.

'Do you want mine back, madam?'

'Invest it.'

Trinder rubs his tummy and smiles.

'Straight into the *piggy bank*, madam.'

He tap dances away, *away*, *away*, towards the service elevator, his life eternally spent before imaginary footlights, giving auditions that one day will lead to a role other than the one he's currently playing.

Boulder's ears twitch.

They're picking up supple sounds heard only by hotel night porters. In movie parlance the *sound design* emitting from the suite is changing: the drumbeat slips slowly into delicious silence then into sighs of sensual pleasure, grunts, groans, gasps, slops, slides, slithers, *there*, *there*, *yes*, *yes*, *yes*, *yes*...

The night porter's excited voice is even more hushed than before.

'My God, an orgy.'

'So?' says Welty. 'Orgies in Hollywood go way back. Film stars are so full of themselves they can't stop ejaculating.'

Boulder winces.

'Don't look like that. You're not so lily-white. Who gets Zigzager his hookers?'

'Hookers?' Boulder nearly bellows before applying a vocal brake just in time, '*Escorts*! A pretty woman on his arm for film premieres. First nights at the theatre. Award ceremonies.'

'He doesn't call them *escorts* when he's bragging to his friends.'

The night porter's protestations, gathering across his face like storm clouds, are blown away when the corridor lights without warning start to strobe. The effect is to momentarily jerk Boulder, Welty and the comatose Rattle into the flickering of a *silent movie*. Boulder, cursing and arm-waving, gives the production a definite Biblical flavour before all are cast into total darkness when the lights fail altogether. Many moments later, out of the silent blackness, comes a whine like a car's fan belt slipping.

'Good morning.'

Welty gasps, recovers, then snaps back.

'Good morning, he *lied*.'

All blink, white-faced and disoriented, when power is abruptly restored. And there he is, Zigzager in person. A small man dressed entirely in brown. His suit, tie, shoes, socks are all in different shades of human excreta. As is his ill-fitting toupee.

Welty's eyes narrow to slits.

'Your entrances always make me think of *Count Dracula*.'

She points at the red puddle.

'You're just in time for breakfast.'

The American shudders.

'Is it *real* blood? I can't tell the difference any more.'

'Maybe your predatory instincts are on the wane?'

'Stop that, will you. Why are you so aggressive towards me?'

'Come on, you love being tongue-whipped.'

'I do?' Puzzled. 'What was it you called me just now on the mobile?'

'Berk!'

'Berk?'

'Short for *Berkeley Hunt*.'

'I don't get it.'

'Rhyming slang, right? I thought you Americans loved it.'

'What rhymes with *Berkeley*...?'

His mouth works away, trying various permutations until...

'That's horrible. Christ, why can't you be gentler, more feminine?'

'Because femininity and survival are *not* compatible.'

'Mother manages it.'

'Only if you equate femininity with being a *cow*.'

'There it is again – the aggression. At your job interview you were very feminine. Dressed in silk – a blouse and stockings. You had great legs I remember. So what happened?'

'I got the job.'

'What about the other producers you worked for? Were you aggressive with them?'

'That depended on *their* needs.'

'*Needs*? What needs?'

'Each was warped in different ways.'

'*Warped*? Milton isn't warped.'

'Are you kidding? Milton can't get it up women who have pubic hair.'

347

Zigzager is delighted.

'Why? Is he scared his cock's going to be *ambushed*.'

Silence while the consequences of this revelation sinks in.

'But it was *Milton* who recommended you?'

'I wasn't into sexual topiary so he wanted rid of me. Then you rang.'

'That bastard!' Suddenly suspicious. 'What did he tell you about *my* needs?'

'That you were into humiliation. With a penchant for dominatrixes.'

The producer's hands fly to his face in horror.

'He said *what*?'

'That you were *possibly* a faggot but *definitely* a masochist.'

Welty passes him the photo.

'Talking of masochism, *this* is guaranteed to give you an erection.'

Zigzager looks at the image of his leading man.

'What do I want this for? I hate the little shit.'

'Read what's on the back.'

He does and immediately his mouth gasps for air.

'*Perfection*? Fuck perfection!' Sobbing like a baby. 'Doesn't this mother understand fucking economics?'

Welty turns to Boulder.

'Note the link between *mother*, *fucking* and *economics*. Is that Oedipal or am I a monkey? Now prepare for lift-off.'

At first Zigzager rumbles internally, then splutters outwardly and finally explodes like a firecracker.

'I'll kill the little prick! I'll make sure that cocksucking, dickhead, shitfaced fucker never ever gets to make another movie.' To Welty: 'What time is it over *there*?'

'Heaven or Hollywood?'

'Don't fuck with me.'

Seeing her stiffen like a snake about to strike, he simpers.

'Pleeeeeease.'

Dialling on her mobile, she simultaneously confides to Boulder, 'After lift-off his pull on reality dwindles. Male security drops away. He's now fuelled by *paranoia...*'

She points at Zigzager, head in his hands, as he rocks and wails to himself, 'What have I done to deserve this? All I wanted to do was make a simple war film and look what happened.'

Welty chimes in on cue, '… after paranoia comes *hypochondria*.' Zigzager immediately staggers, stunned by pain, and clings to her. It's a scene she's familiar with. On autopilot she snaps her fingers at Boulder. 'Standby with the *kiss of life*.'

The night porter, paralysed by anxiety, watches as a useful source of income appears to be drying up. He perks up, much relieved, when the producer seems to partially recover, gasping, 'Doesn't that goddamn little cocksucker know the *meter* is running?'

Welty, patiently waiting on the phone for a connection, again snaps her fingers at Boulder. 'Stand down! It's the *other* ticker. The fiscal not the physical. See how easily he gets the two confused?' The choreography and precision of this *pas de deux* might just earn a standing ovation.

Her eyes switch to the cell phone.

'Hi! I have Mr Zigzager on the line for Mr Solomon.'

With her hand covering the phone, she whispers to Zigzager.

'I think *Mrs* Solomon picked up.' Turning to Boulder: 'Solomon cuts everything in *half*. Scripts, budgets, films, salaries, people. The only thing that escapes his obsession is *cigars*. Those he just *circumcises*.'

Sugar-sweet, she purrs into the phone, 'Putting you through, Mr Solomon.' Holding the phone out to Zigzager: 'He doesn't sound too enthusiastic.' Muttering an aside to Boulder: 'Which isn't surprising. It's *his* money we're spending.'

Zigzager takes a deep breath. His face, clouded in desperation, switches into a smile of untold happiness as he takes the phone.

'Hi Sam! How are things in *Tinsel Town*? Is the weather—'

Rudely interrupted, he pales chalk-white; close to fainting, he steadies himself on Welty.

'Eh, Sam… Sam… Sam…'

The instrument, seemingly glued to his ear, vibrates ferociously. His hand shakes along with it until he mewls feebly into a dead line, 'Sam, may all your dreams have happy endings.'

He tosses the phone like a hot potato to Welty.

'Don't ever, *ever*, let me do that again. He goes to bed one hour after the box offices close.'

He starts to hyperventilate, crazy with angst. Again Welty recognises the symptoms and knows the corrective. It starts with a strict reprimand. 'Now stop that! At once!'

Out of her coat pocket comes a brown paper bag. She places it over his nose and mouth, gently resting his head against her chest. Zigzager, like a baby breastfeeding, begins regulating his breathing.

'Good boy. You handled Sam very well. Firm but polite. He'll respect you for that.'

Zigzager's grateful eyes never stop watching her mouth. His breaths, recycled inside the paper bag, slowly allay the panic attack. Welty pats the top of his head.

'Better now?'

The producer nods his head and she eases the bag away from his face.

'You know your problem?'

Zigzager shakes his head.

'It's called *arrested* development. And you're not alone. It's very prevalent in the movie industry. Now, just go knock on that door and ask the little fella inside to come out and play with you.' She eases him away. 'But keep things cool, OK?'

Zigzager creeps to the door, putting his ear to the panelling.

Silence.

'Can you hear me? Zigy here. I realise what a bitch it must be finding this role. Believe you me, I know just how elusive the *truth* can be.'

He drops penitentially to his knees.

'Christ, you must be wondering whether to approach the character from the outside *in*, or the inside *out*.' He looks to Welty, who gives him a one-thumb up. His confidence rises. 'I want you to know that I feel for you, inside there, all alone, giving...' – he hesitates then blurts – '... *birth*!' Drawn irresistibly to look at the red puddle, he nearly gags. 'Honestly I do.' Another thumb-up from Welty and he careers on. 'Trouble is, that with all the money involved here, we may have to perform a...' – he swallows hard then lets the word fly – '... *caesarean*!'

He looks nervously from Welty to Boulder.

They all wait for a response.

It comes.

A drumbeat, slow, hypnotic.

Zigzager grits his teeth but keeps smiling.

'Glad you're enjoying the drum kit. We've tried to give you *everything* you need. A drum kit *wasn't* in your contract. I personally signed off on that. You know that, don't you?'

Clash, a cymbal replies.

Zigzager begins to sweat.

'Is it the funeral scene that's fucking you up?'

Clash. Clash.

'Hey buddy, I've been round the block a few times. Death is *never* a problem on film. We'll change the funeral to a *wake*, a celebration of life. Relax. Let's have fun. It's all just make-believe. You guys, the greats, the immortals – shit, you get shot, knifed, blown up, garrotted and seconds later get up and walk off to your Winnebago. Come play with us. Correction, let us come play with *you*.'

The players outside the Abraham Lincoln Suite, frozen like figures in a waxworks, wait in silence. All have forgotten about Rattle, collapsed like a beanbag, occasionally murmuring and whispering to himself but remaining remarkably immobile.

Inside, cymbals and sticks are abandoned.

Two hands now take to the drum.

The beat digs deep, primal, way, way back into the human psyche.

Zigzager freaks.

'Stop that! We don't use *drums* any more. We phone, fax, telex, tweet, Skype. And I'll use them all, buddy boy, to make sure you never *ever* work again. I'll contact every studio executive on the coast. Lawyers, ruthless as Rottweilers, will take to the air, baby.'

Drum stops.

Silence.

Girls giggle.

Zigzager jumps like he's been touched by an electric cattle prod.

'Jesus fucking Christ, he's got women in there. He's fucking while the *meter's running*.'

He loses it. His total disintegration starts with his hairpiece. The verdant clip-on forehead double quiff slips over his right eye. Such visual impairment doesn't stop him banging on the door and screaming, 'How many whores you got in there?'

Sound of such fury violently rips Rattle from his place of peace. He stands, shakily focusing on the crazed film producer.

'Come out, you little shithead!'

Rattle pulls the handgun from its shoulder holster, waving it about like a magician's wand. He finally focuses, steadying it expertly on his left wrist.

'Get away from that door! Freeze! This is a warning! Get away from that door!'

Zigzager turns in amazement. His face is as fractured as crazed paving. With a life dedicated to manufacturing *fiction* he finds it difficult recognising *fact*. As with the pool of blood, so it is with the Smith & Wesson .38.

'Don't pull that crap on me. I know the *real* thing when I see it.'

He was always a lousy poker player.

Rattle's finger instantly depresses the trigger.

The handgun shivers and a wisp of smoke escapes from the barrel.

The detonation arrives a nanosecond later.

Many images on *how* best to die burst like shrapnel in Zigzager's brain. We *all*, at some point in our lives, try to imagine our own deaths. Zigzager's no exception. He chooses Robert Capa's iconic image, *Falling Soldier*, from the Spanish Civil War and throws his arms wide as if crucified. That done, he hits the floor. Like a jaded stuntman he groans as he rolls into the red puddle and back out again. Eyes wide open in shock, he lies still. His chest a suppurating wound.

Welty stifles a scream.

Boulder checks the corridor in both directions. None of the doors fly open. No guests pour into the corridor. Most are probably still asleep. Those awake will almost certainly have television's morning news *rolling* into their suites. The sound of one more bullet can easily go unheeded among the cacophony of destruction and mayhem beaming in from around our planet.

The night porter sighs with relief.

Any impending scandal can *still* be averted.

He sees Rattle fleeing towards the service elevator, black holdall thrown over his shoulder.

And is pleased.

Best he's out of the way.

Outside, on the streets and in the squares, the trickle of pedestrians and vehicles is turning into a steady stream. The stretch limo still lies alongside the Croesus Palace. Slump is asleep. The driver's pod situated in the cap (or *glans penis*, to use the medical term) of his phallus-on-wheels is filled with music from his favourite *Nice 'N' Easy* box set. A gentle bump wakes him with a start. Consulting his rear and wing mirrors, he sees a Nissan compact squeezing into the available space behind.

Across the Nissan's bonnet is an impressive logo for Mobile Medics. It's a red cross encasing the smiling face of a white-coated doctor with the inevitable stethoscope around his neck. The driver's door flies open and an Indian clutching a medical bag runs up the steps. At the top waits Boulder, looking agitated.

Slump ejects himself from his seat onto the sidewalk, taking the steps two at a time, crazy to know what's happening. He's too late. Convinced Boulder has turned a blind eye to his shouts and waves, Slump's perennial paranoia is only compounded when he sees a parking officer, having pounced during his brief absence, about to give him a ticket. Unfortunately for him, this particular officer is particularly well qualified for the job. First, he is African and huge. Indeed when Slump confronts him he appears to be addressing the man's belly button. Second, he speaks no English and is therefore immune to reasoning and verbal abuse. Expletives and racial insults wash over him like shower gel. Third, back in Ghana he'd flirted with Pan-Africanism, so to now find himself being *paid* to subvert the psyche of his ex-colonial masters gives him much pleasure. After all they had *parked* on his homeland for over a hundred years.

Before he can complete the ticket, however, Slump has reinserted himself into his monstrous machine, where Dean Martin is currently singing 'Everybody Loves Somebody'. He screams, '*Fuck you, Dean!*' as he tries to ease into the line of traffic. Frustrated by the continuous stream of feisty, sperm-sized cars refusing to let him in, he doesn't notice the black hand, big as a shovel, use his windscreen wiper as a clip for the penalty notice. Once on the move he realises the chances of finding *three* consecutive unoccupied meters necessary to accommodate him are zilch.

Like the *Flying Dutchman*, the ghost ship destined never to make port, Slump is destined to circle the hotel endlessly. Desperate, he dons his cell phone headset *with adjustable headband and boom-cancelling microphone* and gets through to the hotel.

He asks for the Abraham Lincoln Suite.

'*Engaged,*' says the telephonist.

He asks for Boulder but is cut off.

*

Boulder is feeling well pleased with himself. The impending public-relations disaster, whilst not as damaging as a careless oil-well blowout, has been successfully capped. It was conducted with military precision. When the aftershock of the shooting evaporated, he immediately ordered Trinder to bring a bedding trolley to the first floor. With Welty's help they loaded Zigzager's prone body, suppurating chest facing upwards, and whisked it unobserved to a vacant suite on the same floor. Once there he summoned a chambermaid to attend to the red mess outside the suite's door. With the immobilised spyglass safely in his pocket, and with the disenchanted Welty holding Zigzager's ketchup-splattered toupee, all incriminating evidence had been removed. It's as if nothing untoward had occurred outside the Abraham Lincoln Suite.

7.14 a.m.

The Mezzanine, a floor situated between the ground and first, houses the hotel's grand conference centre. Picture windows stretch the length of the hotel's frontage, overlooking the square. Early-morning light fills the room and shimmers over the multitude of gilt chairs stacked almost to the ceiling. Rattle sits on one of them, his black holdall at his feet, watching and listening to the scene below. There's no sign of any law-enforcement activity, no police cars screeching to a halt outside, blue lights flashing, sirens wailing.

He's seen the doctor arrive and leave.

His visit had taken barely fifteen minutes.

Assuming it safe to return to his designated place of duty, he picks up his holdall and, using the back stairs parallel to the shaft of the service elevator, reaches the Abraham Lincoln Suite.

The drumbeat is relentless, albeit muted and funereal.

Extra bunches of flowers, real ones with greeting cards evident, rest alongside the plastic roses each side of the door while the wreath is now laid where the red puddle had been. It's a sombre sight like the entrance to a mausoleum.

Rattle sees that his gilt chair has been removed, drops his holdall, and retraces his steps to the back stairwell. As he vanishes, the service elevator arrives and Trinder steps out, burdened with yet more flowers left by fans in the foyer. He lays them carefully by the others before casually selecting various greetings cards and reading them. His condescending smile freezes when he recognises the black holdall sitting where Rattle has dropped it. Tossing away the card in his hands, he scampers like a frightened rabbit back to the elevator. As its door slides shut, so Rattle comes through the swing doors to the stairs, a gilt chair in his hands. Both men have appeared, disappeared, and reappeared like mechanical figures in a medieval clock. Rattle places the chair exactly in the position it occupied originally and sits. Agitated, he takes the Smith & Wesson from its holster, smacks the cylinder open and empties the bullets one by one into his waiting palm. Using both hands he now shakes them like dice, before selecting *one*. He spins the cylinder, waits for it to stop, then inserts it into the chamber while chanting, 'He loves me.'

Spin, stop, load.

'He loves me *not*.'

Rattle could be blowing on a dandelion's parachute ball instead of a lethal game of chance.

Spin, stop, load.

'He loves me.'

Spin, stop, load.

'He loves me *not*.'

With the final bullet inserted, Rattle smacks the cylinder into place and returns the handgun to its home under his arm. Relaxed, he smiles and puts his crazy mind into neutral.

But not for long.

The service elevator clunks to a stop and the door slides open revealing Boulder, Trinder and Welty, now clutching a bulky file of documents. They approach with caution. Welty goes to speak but Rattle stops her with a raised hand.

'Sorry about that. My finger slipped.'

A pronounced twitch in his right eyelid betrays his discomfort.

'I thought he'd understand.'

'Well, he *didn't*,' says Welty, firmly.

'A man in his position should know the difference by now. *Blanks* are used all the time in films.'

Trinder is overjoyed when he hears this.

'I said it was a blank, Mr Boulder, didn't I? If they used *live* ammo in movies, the acting would be a lot better.'

Boulder reacts angrily.

'You! Back to de foyer.'

The pageboy mooches off, grumbling.

'Sod that! It was me who found him.'

Reaching the elevator, he pulls imaginary six-shooters from imaginary holsters and fires imaginary shots with sound effects added.

Boulder and Welty don't take their eyes of Rattle, who looks contrite.

'When he came round he heard angels singing,' says Boulder with a sigh.

'Only it wasn't angels. It was sparrows in the lift shaft,' says Welty, also sighing. 'You frightened the life out of him.'

'Only *temporarily*,' retorts Rattle, peeved.

Boulder remains stony-faced.

'The doctor's still with him.'

'Funny, that,' says Rattle. 'I saw him leave half an hour ago.'

'That was de *first* doctor. We got a second opinion.'

'His mother's flying in,' adds Welty.

'Lawyers are on their way.'

Welty pats the bulging file in her arm.

'The fatter the file, the meaner the lawyer.'

Pulling out a hefty document, she waves it in Rattle's face.

'Your client is well and truly stitched up. More love and care went into this contract than into the script. *This* is the real art form. A legal string quartet.'

Rattle squirms at first, then rallies.

'Isn't he a bit *old* to have his mother flying...'

Welty cuts him short.

'Don't underestimate Ruby. She's everything he *isn't*. Which is probably why he *isn't* everything he should be.'

She eyes Boulder, who responds, leading a two-pronged attack.

'Your boy's in deep shit.'

'Up to his neck.'

'And still rising.'

'And so are you. You're lucky the police weren't called.'

'Cops only lower the tone of the place.'

'The hotel doesn't want any trouble.'

'Nor does Mr Zigzager.'

Boulder lets all this sink in before paying off the patter.

'We'd prefer you to leave *voluntarily*.'

'Under your own steam,' says Welty, sweetly.

Rattle seems to physically sink out of sight like a landmine waiting to be stepped on, muttering to himself, absorbing their proposition. He straightens suddenly, moving as fast as a ramrod, pulling out his Smith & Wesson. Welty and Boulder shoot backwards, half-turning, nano-thinking their odds of escape, then reluctantly accepting fate. Boulder resorts to the limited armoury of a night porter facing the rich and powerful.

He grovels.

'In your *own* time, of course, sir. Whenever is convenient for you.'

Rattle is seemingly unaware of the apparent threat he just posed. Innocently opening the gun's cylinder, he spills out a bullet and observes it with the same intensity as Yorick's skull.

'I had hoped Mr Zigzager would see my gesture as a symbolic act.' He holds up the bullet. 'I had hoped he'd see *this* as a symbol of the only reality left to us. Look at it! Even its very shape is telling us something.'

Welty and Boulder study it respectfully.

'Don't you see? It's a suppository.'

'A suppository?' says Boulder, looking nervously at Welty.

'A *truth* suppository.'

'A truth suppository?'

'Once inside you, all is revealed. The question that's haunted man since the beginning of time is finally answered. Is there life after death?'

All three ruminate until Boulder breaks the silence.

'I don't think Mr Zigzager got that.'

'For him suppositories mean only one thing,' chips in Welty cheerily. 'Haemorrhoids.'

Rattle shakes his head in despair at her.

'Mr Zigzager is a big disappointment to me.'

'He is to most people.'

Returning the bullet to its cradle, Rattle idly spins the cylinder.

'So it seems we're dealing with a philistine. Well, that's OK by me.' He whacks the cylinder shut and stands, twirling the gun on his forefinger. 'While accepting the omnipotence of Almighty God, who is said to be everywhere, no skills whatsoever are now needed for us mortals to pull off the same trick. To have your image wrapped instantly around the planet you simply have to shoot either a *multiple* of people or *one* famous one.' He chuckles at the thought. 'And it's not just the act itself that occupies the media, it's the endless post-mortems on *why* it happened.'

Boulder and Welty don't even blink when he pins them with his eyes. 'But *why* the why when the killer is *always* found to be a loner. A loner on a mission from God. A loner who hears *voices*.' His laugh makes the night porter squirm. 'A split personality. A sexually repressed paranoiac. A highly volatile substance likely to go off at any moment.'

He closes on Boulder.

'How would *you* describe *me* to the media?'

'Friendly,' snivels Boulder, looking wildly about. 'Outgoing. Someone who enjoys a joke. One of the lads.'

'*Not* highly volatile and given to uncontrollable rages?'

'Not volatile, no. You're… you're… empathetic!'

'Empathetic?'

'Empathetic.'

Rattle's eyes are suddenly as cold and sharp as stalactites.

'So what's wrong with being a highly volatile substance liable to go off at any moment?'

'Nothing,' says Boulder, his chins vibrating with terror.

The squall passes and Rattle turns warm.

'Exactly. What everybody forgets is that on the very day the killer struck, the media itself was *volatile*, liable to go crazy at any moment. As were our politicians, our stock exchanges, our commodity markets, company board rooms, air traffic controls, sports stadiums, all prone...' He stops when he hears the service elevator arrive and quickly returns the Smith & Wesson to its holster.

'When the frying pan gets too hot the fat will fly.'

Trinder exits the elevator carrying a bound and battered document.

'He threw his script out the window again. Landed on the front awning. Bloody near broke my neck getting it.'

'Watch your language, son.'

'Language? You should read that fucking script, Mr Boulder.'

Rattle holds out an expectant hand.

'My client's property, I believe.'

The boy looks to Boulder before passing it over.

Rattle riffles repeatedly through the pages.

'This is where training shows. No hidden drugs, nail files, or razor blades. All we want in here is *sharp* dialogue.' He starts to read random pages. The others exchange shifty looks while waiting for his verdict. It's soon apparent and it's not positive. 'Oh dear, oh dear. No wonder he threw it out the window.' He smacks it shut in disgust. 'Depraved images waiting to be seared into people's minds. Violence ready to ooze down television aerials into our homes.'

He looks at Trinder with fresh paternal eyes, pats his head and puts an arm around his shoulder.

'Has it ever occurred to you, *Stanley*, that our children look longer into television screens, iPads, smartphones, than into their mother's eyes?'

'Yes,' says Boulder confidently.

Rattle moves up close, nose to nose, until the night porter capitulates.

'No.'

He wilts even further under the penetrating stare.

'I'm not qualified to answer that.'

Rattle, triumphant, waves the script in each of their faces.

'This film will not ooze into any child's mind until I have given it my fullest consideration.'

He walks smartly off towards the stairs, then remembers his holdall. Welty is waiting by it with a smile.

'Are you *leaving* us?'

'For good?' Boulder's voice palpitates with faint hope.

Rattle ignores them, shoulders his holdall and departs.

The group don't move, not daring to speak, until Rattle disappears into the stairwell. Once out of sight, Welty dumps her file on the gilt chair and takes out her mobile phone. Boulder urgently rounds on Trinder.

'Quick, follow him.'

The pageboy is horrified.

'Follow him?'

'I want to know where he goes.'

'What if he's a paedophile?'

Boulder angrily claps his hands.

'Chop! Chop! After him, *now*!'

Welty's phone is answered.

'Mr Zigzager's suite, please. Suite 13.'

Trinder is still reluctant to give chase.

'The gun could be loaded.'

'With *blanks*?' Boulder relishes the score being settled.

Welty waits, watching Trinder sloping off, muttering curses to himself. The hotel telephonist is soon back on the line. Suite 13 is not answering.

'Keep trying, please. He may be sedated.'

Boulder is standing by.

'He'll be pleased to hear I got that weird fella off his back. That *special* look of mine soon sent him packing. It always works.'

Welty's eyebrows lift off at this before returning to the phone.

'He may be in the restaurant. Try there, please.' She faces Boulder with a wicked smile. 'Ruby would have told him to have breakfast. Ruby believes in breakfast.' Into the phone. 'Do you have Mr Zigzager there? Suite 13.' Boulder remains wallowing in his own complacency. 'I insisted we didn't need the police and I was right.' Welty's eyebrows are too weary to react, so she retreats into irony. 'You handled him brilliantly.' Boulder puffs up. 'Thank you.'

Welty, like Aesop's scorpion, can't help but sting.

'Now go change your underpants. I won't tell.'

Boulder is *not* amused.

'Of course, I had to *humour* him.'

'Well, you certainly succeeded with me.' Into the phone. 'Are you sure he's not there? You can easily miss him. He's devoid of any special features. Dressed all in brown. He could easily be mistaken for a plate of muesli.' Listens, then replies, 'You think he's just left?' Listens again. 'No, I'm sure he's not gone to the pool. He can't swim.'

Welty *is* patient.

'OK, if you say so.'

Boulder is *not* patient.

'Leave it to me. I'll find him.'

He slips away, into his past, furtively, as if tracking a potential usurper in occupied territory. Welty shrugs and waits for the hotel leisure centre to answer. It does, eventually.

'Could you page a Mr Zigzager for me?' She listens. 'No, he's *not* one of your regulars. He'll be in a brown one-piece and could be mistaken for a lilo.' She listens. 'I am being serious.' Another long wait. 'He's in the sauna and can't be disturbed? Just watch!' Stomping off towards the elevator, she mutters to herself. 'First thing Ruby does is *weigh* him.'

Lights tremble briefly along the deserted corridor.

Drumbeat returns softly.

Ominously.

Three suites away a swarthy middle-aged woman steps out and waits. She straightens her extra-soft leather jacket and skirt, then lowers her massive black shades like a knight's visor. A man joins her and carefully closes the door, checking it's secure, *twice*. He, too, is clad totally in brown leather, the texture of which happens to complement *both* their faces. Together they move towards the elevator, creaking like Chesterfield sofas. Following them, a chambermaid appears, pushing a heavy trolley loaded with fresh bed linen, towels, soaps, shampoos, sprays and detergents of such potency as to remove all human odours, all traces of our very existence. Behind this slow-moving mound of whiteness lurks Zigzager. Crouched like a hunter tracking his prey, he waits until the trolley draws alongside the Abraham Lincoln Suite before peeling off.

He sidles up to the door, listens, takes a deep breath, and knocks.

'It's me, Zigy,' he whispers. 'How about a pow-wow? Just you and me.'

The beat changes.

Now it's a tom-tom signalling war.

Invisible squaws giggle.

Puffs of cigarette smoke, imitating smoke signals, billow through the empty spyhole.

Zigzager moans as he struggles to contain his frayed nerves.

'This is going to end in tears, buddy boy. I know you have a very original sense of humour, but this has gone beyond a joke. There's already been one attempt on my life, right? Which I'm prepared to forget. But now I'm going to have to kick ass if you don't...'

Drumbeat stops abruptly.

He hears the service elevator coming to rest. Keeping close to the wall and scampering flat out, he just makes it to the stairwell as Trinder steps out, whistling happily to himself, carrying more flowers, fresh white *calla lilies*. Their phallic pistils, a symbol of lust and sexuality, need no message from the fan. Just a name and contact number. Beside the door they add another fine funereal touch. About to leave, Trinder notices Welty's file on the gilt chair. He wriggles his white-gloved hands like a magician, before gently lifting the cover. On top is the contract, a fat document, stapled at one corner. This he slips out and spins through the pages until he reaches the only heading that interests him.

Compensation.

His eyes stretch wide in astonishment as he runs a finger along the dizzying row of *zeros*. 'Fuck me! Fifty million dollars!' He looks to the door with increased admiration, lays his head close to the keyhole, and whispers in awe.

'A salary that's truly galactic. Way out there *beyond* obscenity.'

Cymbals break into an exuberant solo.

Exuberance is not the expression on Welty's face as she rounds the corner and sees Trinder moving to the wild rhythm. Her footsteps are lost in the thick carpet as she comes upon him from behind and gently prises the contract out of his hand.

The pageboy misses not a beat.

'I want to work in the movies.'

'I wonder why?' says Welty, returning the contract to the file. 'Did you follow him?'

'Right into the men's toilet. He's still there, reading the script.'

'In the toilet. How appropriate. Any reaction so far?'

'A lot of groaning. Like he's constipated.'

'So he really *is* reading it.'

For a moment Trinder ponders on her reaction.

'If it's *that* bad, why's it being made?'

'Everybody liked the poster.'

'Are you being serious?'

'The first thing you learn about the movie business is that few people in it actually read. And those who do are limited to numerals and dollar signs. So for them we do a big colourful drawing depicting action, excitement, guns, big breasts, pouting lips, a slice of arse and some leg.'

She peers over her owl glasses at him and smiles.

'An *hors d'oeuvre* of women's body parts.'

Trinder relishes this lesson on the intricacies of movie marketing.

'But that's not for *every* film?'

'For gangster and war movies we do a poster *flambé* with explosions, towering infernos, charred bodies. More of a *mixed grill* look.'

'And that's it?'

'Not quite. The poster is then sent to every territory in the world. If the distributors think it'll get bums on seats they buy the film sight unseen. Like pork bellies or soya beans.'

'And if it *bombs*?'

'Simple. The distributors lose all their money. As compensation they have a *poster* to hang on their office wall, in front of which they spend many hours trying to work out *why* it didn't work. Hours ruminating on which human pleasure cells it didn't tickle.'

'Don't they bollock the producer who sold it to them?'

'Yes, but the producer blames the director for not making a movie as good as the poster.'

'And who does the director blame?'

'The audience. He says the movie's ahead of its time.'

Trinder spends a moment digesting this.

'I *still* want to work in movies.'

'Forget it. It's not a job for grown-ups.'

Welty shoots him another smile but Trinder's not to be deterred.

'I want to be *somebody*.'

'You already are somebody.'

'Somebody *else*, then. When I'm watching movies I become somebody else.' His voice takes on a fresh urgency. 'I'm crazy for them.'

'So was I. Until I worked on them.'

'You used to go to a lot of movies?'

'Three, four times a week.' She removes her glasses and massages her nose. 'We called them *flicks* when I was your age. In those days the screens were hidden behind heavy curtains, which made it all very mysterious and magical. As they slowly parted your heart would miss a beat. Then, when the projector burst into life, it cut through the darkness and filled your life with colour and music.'

Welty shrugs, hooking her glasses over her ears.

The owl again.

'Now, when the lights go down, the darkness remains. And I see only greed, hear only hype, feel only a sense of loss.'

She puts her arms on his shoulders, looking him in the eyes.

'Is that what you want?'

Trinder scratches his neck, puzzled.

'So why don't you do some other job?'

'I need the money. I've a son at boarding school.'

'And a husband in jail. He's a stuntman, isn't he?'

Welty drops her arms, taken aback.

'Who told you that?'

'I heard someone talking in the bar. He wasn't being nice about you.'

'You bet,' she grins. 'It pays to be a bitch. That way you get treated with care.'

They fall silent when they hear the service elevator door open. Boulder strides purposefully towards them.

'So where did he go, boy?'

'The men's room.'

'Oh Mary, Mother of God! I just saw Zigzager slip in there. He'll be having a heart attack if he sees him. Off you go, boy. Try to warn him.'

Trinder protests before slouching off.

'I could get arrested, hanging around men's toilets all the time.'

Drumbeat, slow and mournful, draws their attention back to the door.

'Did you talk to Zigzager?' asks Welty.

'Didn't have a chance. He was too fast for me.'

'Like a rat up a drainpipe.'

Boulder's nose, resting on the empty spyhole, quivers.

'You have to hand it to him. He *is* elusive.'

The corridor lights twitch convulsively.

The night porter curses.

'Incompetent cretins! Call themselves *electricians*, will they not be leaving us alone with their shenanigans? You can bet that Eamon's still on the bottle while...'

His words falter along with the lights. Darkness snaps itself around them, bringing with it total silence. Boulder and Welty could be incarcerated in a tomb. There's a rustling sound, then a baleful caw.

'What was that?' whispers Welty.

'What was what?' retorts Boulder, the imperturbable.

Another caw, closer, more distinct.

'That!' says Welty.

'It's a crow,' says Boulder, confidently.

'A crow?' says Welty, less than confident.

Another caw, still closer. Boulder holds his ground.

'A crow. Definitely a crow.'

Another caw. Boulder wavers.

'Definitely. Or a rook?'

Silence. Then out of the blackness comes an alien whisper.

'Or a raven?'

'Who was that?' Boulder's voice quivers. 'Security, is... is... that you?'

'Security?' repeats Welty, alarmed.

A bass drum roll crashes like thunder, in turn triggering the lights into a display of sheet lightning. When they finally hold firm, Boulder's proboscis swings around wildly until it settles on Rattle perched on his gilt chair, the script in his lap, eyes closed, tranquil as a Buddha.

'So now you're a sodding bird impersonator?'

'Ommmmmmmmmm.'

'Don't start that racket again. Show us how you did it, the crow call. Go on.'

Rattle shapes his mouth like a sink plunger but only a *hiss* emerges.

'Very good. Now try a raven.'

'Ommmmmmmmmm.'

'What you doing back here anyway? You are *persona non grata.*'

Rattle raises the script high above his head. 'My client will not be appearing in this...' – he lets it drop, hitting the carpet with the dull thud of a cowpat – '... shit!'

Boulder acts shocked.

'*Shit*,' he says, 'and in front of a lady.'

'Crap!' says Rattle, winking at Welty.

'That's it!' Boulder storms off. 'I'll have the front desk call the police. Even if it does lower the tone of de place.'

Welty watches him go before taking out her mobile phone and punching in a number. It's answered.

'Have Mr Zigzager paged in your men's room, will you?' She listens, irritated. 'I wouldn't ask if it wasn't urgent.'

Rattle, ears alert, eyes shut, composed and complacent.

Welty moves closer to him, keeping the mobile to her ear.

'It's not the police you want to worry about, sunny-boy. It's Ruby. Ruby goes through people like a chainsaw.' Into the mobile. 'I know he's in there. Would you try again for me? He's anally fixated and may not have heard your pageboy. Thanks.' Back to Rattle's inscrutable face. 'You won't keep that smug smile on your kisser when Ruby hits town.'

Rattle dives into his shoulder bag and brings out a rattle. Its handle is wrapped with feathers and the gourd crudely decorated with bison drawn in primary colours. He shakes it in Welty's face, which laughs back at him. 'You think that'll help? Ruby's louder than a police siren.' Speaking into the mobile. 'No luck? He's sure it *was* Mr Zigzager's car? Find out if he was definitely in it.'

366

She watches anxiously as Rattle moves towards the suite door.

So menacing is his shuffling dance and the clacking of his rattle, it makes her think of an Inca priest worshipping at some ancient sacrificial altar. Somewhere like the Altar of the Condor at Machu Picchu, which she'd visited only a year ago. Welty shivers at the thought and quickly wraps things up on the mobile.

'Thanks. If you should ever locate him, tell him his PA needs to speak to him urgently.'

Boulder returns, looking shaken.

'I found this.'

He produces a black feather.

'It was in the elevator.'

Bewildered, both turn to Rattle, who now has his head resting against the suite door and is murmuring an incomprehensible incantation. From inside, the drumbeat returns, low, slow, menacing.

Boulder takes Welty aside.

'We were wrong. It wasn't him.'

'It has to be,' whispers Welty. 'A crow couldn't get up here. He put it in the elevator to fool us.'

Rattle's incantation abruptly stops.

'I wouldn't stop that praying if I were you,' warns Boulder.

'You'll need all the prayers you can get when Ruby claps eyes on you,' adds Welty. 'Even as we speak Zigzager's limo is speeding back from the airport.'

Rattle, seemingly in a trance, moans.

'Mrs Zigzager has been grounded.'

'Grounded? How do you know that?' growls Boulder.

The rattle rattles and the feathers flutter.

'My talisman prevents any person, animal, boat or cart from moving.'

'What about broomsticks?' snaps Welty.

Rattle fixes her with his eyes.

'Treat me as a fool if you wish, but tread carefully.' He slowly begins to circle around her, ominously punctuating his words with sharp handclaps. 'Fools are not to be laughed at. Shakespeare took fools seriously. *"The fool doth think he is wise, but the wise man knows himself to be a fool."'*

Welty follows him with her eyes until he again faces her.

'Don't fool with me. I'm warning you.'

Continuing to circle her, Rattle wraps her in angst.

'We must *all* be fools in our search for the soul. And stay fools to complete it. It's a dangerous journey. A delicate operation performed *by* oneself *on* oneself. Only wise *fools* know how to turn their pain into laughter, their sickness into a cure.'

'Stop this! Now!' hisses Welty.

But Rattle doesn't stop.

'For the sickness, once uncovered, can spread like fire and destroy you. Only *fools* know how to devour and disperse it. Fools stay alive. Heroes die.' He bows deeply and reverently towards the door.

'The fool is like the actor who plays many roles using the *same* ingredients, pulling them from within, devouring and dispersing them again and again and again. The greater the actor, the more dangerous the game.' He comes full circle again. 'So it is with the *medicine man*.'

Boulder's magnificent nose twitches testily as he contemplates Rattle now comfortably returned to the gilt chair.

'During our brief acquaintance you've been a born-again Christian, a Buddhist—'

'A trickster, a fool,' chips in Welty.

'Are you now telling us you're a *medicine man*?'

'Thou sayest it.'

'What kind of answer is that?'

'The one Christ gave to the Pharisees.' Rattle concludes with a flourish from his rattle. 'Just before they crucified Him.'

Boulder is outraged.

'Jesus Christ? Are you now comparing yourself to *Him*?'

'That's what He asked us to do.'

'That's blasphemy!'

'Then blasphemy is a compliment to God.'

Drumbeat changes its rhythm.

Welty cups an ear.

'So *medicine man*, what do the drums speak of now?'

Rattle looks to the ceiling before answering.

'Power struggle.'

The corridor lights flicker intensely before failing to hold fast.

Drumbeat falters and stops.

Welty giggles nervously.

'What if they speak with forked tongues? Like the fools installing that poxy generator.'

'Don't worry,' reassures Boulder. 'They're probably just executing their final tests. Each corridor is on a separate circuit. Everything's under control.'

'That's why we're in the dark,' says Rattle.

Lights snap boldly back to life.

'God said, "*Let there be light.*" And there was light,' sneers Boulder. 'Power struggle, indeed? Once again the evil forces of darkness have been repelled.'

His attention is taken by three gentle knocks from inside the suite, heralding the arrival of another brown envelope, slid under the door. Rattle retains his yogic pose while Boulder bends to grab it.

'You don't want it?' Boulder winks at Welty. 'Not for *identification* purposes?'

Rattle opens one cold eye, which settles on Boulder.

'The face is but a mask.'

'Yours maybe, but certainly not *mine*.'

The eye stays locked on Boulder. 'In our brief acquaintance I've seen *you* shuffle through more faces than a deck of cards.' Then it switches, unblinking, to Welty. 'But *you*, you only wear one face. The face pack of disillusion. The face of someone drained of all beliefs.'

'Unlike you, who believes *everything*,' bats Welty.

'Who *entertains* everything,' says Rattle. 'You, who loves watching movies, images flickering in the darkness, entranced by the illusion, believing all you see and hear.' His rattle rattles. 'Just like the Aborigine contemplating the *Sacred Soak*. Or the Plains Indian sitting in the *Earth Lodge*.' Another punctuation from the rattle. 'Your movies even defy death itself, inhabited as they are by ghosts. Gods you can actually *see*. Instead of Gorgon you have Garbo and Gable. Instead of Vishnu you have Valentino. You have more gods than the Hindus. So what's wrong with your gods that you've ended up in such a spiritual wilderness? Is it because you offer up *money* instead of prayers?'

'Even gods can't live on bread alone,' blusters Boulder. 'How can anyone live without money?'

'Answer that, *medicine man*. Bring down rain on our spiritual desert.'

With a magician's sleight of hand, Rattle plucks a flower from a bunch by the door. 'Just look at a simple flower.' He contemplates then brings it to his nose. 'Smell its sweet fragrance. Ponder the beauty of its petals and stamen.'

Boulder gets bolshie.

'That simple flower cost some fan an arm and a leg.'

Rattle ignores him.

'Go to a park...'

'My taxes pay for that park.'

'Go to a forest. Forests speak to deeper centres than do city streets.'

'We'll need a car to get there,' Welty joins in the baiting.

'And who'll pay for the petrol?'

Welty holds out her hand and scans the ceiling.

'I feel no rain. I see no clouds. The sky is pure *silver*.'

'The horizon is solid *gold*,' adds Boulder.

Rattle closes his eyes, immediately withdrawing.

'Ommmmmmmmmm.'

'Stop that,' commands the night porter.

And he does!

The silence is soon broken by a drumstick beating the door with the regularity of a metronome. The metrical ticks seem to hypnotise them all.

'Waiting for Zigzager,' sighs Welty.

'*And* his mother,' intones Boulder.

Rattle remains undefeated.

'*My* talisman is very powerful.'

'Ruby's is more so,' retorts Welty.

'*Money*!' Boulder leans on the word, as does Welty.

'*Money* breaks through the walls of space and the barriers of time. *Money* breaks into the vaults of the human psyche unreachable by those who *don't* have it.'

'And Ruby *does*.'

'Ruby even beat cancer.'

Rattle listens mournfully.

'With *her* talisman?'

'The days of your medicine men, tricksters, old-style shamans are gone forever.' Welty stays in attack mode. 'Now we pay fees to specialists. Proctologists, gynaecologists, opthalmologists, sexologists, dermatologists, dental mechanics.'

'Arbitrageurs, brokers, junk bondsman, hedge funders,' adds Boulder, anxious to contribute.

'Legitimate medical and fiscal specialists.'

Lights tremble momentarily.

Boulder looks up at them and growls.

'Bloody cowboys! The world's run by *cowboys*.'

'Instead of *Indians*,' says Rattle with a pathetic shake of the gourd. He tries his breath exercise but coughs instead. *Ping*! Out of sight, around the corner, the elevator has returned.

Boulder waits anxiously.

'What does Ruby look like?'

'Even God wouldn't recognise her.'

'She's had a facelift?'

'Lifts!'

'A nose job?'

'Now it's a button mushroom.'

'Hair transplants?'

'The Forestry Commission was called in.'

'Implanted silicone tits?'

'Twin peaks.'

'Does she wear lifts?'

'Even in bed.'

Zigzager appears from the back stairwell. Silent as a snake, he stops behind them while they remain glued to the distant corner.

'False fingernails?'

'Like an eagle's.'

'And ended up looking like a transvestite?'

'That's Ruby.'

Welty laughs as the elevator's occupant rounds the corner.

'And that's *not* Ruby.'

A man in dazzling white robes has appeared. Better he had slid from the saddle of a camel than emerge from a hotel elevator in London. Certainly more romantic. A long way from Saudi Arabia, he passes silently as if walking on sand. Their eyes follow him only to come upon the distinctly *un*romantic Zigzager lurking behind them.

'You don't like Mother, do you?'

Welty's tongue moves for the kill.

'I admire Ruby. She's the one person I know who survives without a vital organ. The *heart*.'

Boulder, confused at a seeing Zigzager, remembers the envelope in his hands.

'This came for you, Mr Zigzager. Another message perhaps. I kept it safe until I saw you.'

Zigzager regards it with horror, hesitates, reluctantly takes it, slides out another photograph and reads the scrawl on the back. Rattle, refreshed, jerks into life. He sweeps up the script and stands, ready to go places, bubbling with *new* ambitions. His *old* ones having been so severely mauled.

'Right, Mr Zigzager, we must talk. This script is—'

Zigzager snaps like an alligator, 'Not now.' His face drains of all colour as he absorbs the message from his star. 'This is complete—'

'Shit!' Rattle is not to be interrupted. His opinion of the script happens to match what Zigzager is reading.

'Can you believe it? He wants to relocate the story to *Brazil*. The fucking guy is nuts. A World War Two movie set in Brazil?'

Rattle paces about excitedly.

'I can help you there, Mr Zigzager. We'll reset it in the jungle. Compress some scenes, dispose of others, clean up the dialogue.'

'I don't want the dialogue cleaned up.' Zigzager grabs the script from Rattle. '*This* is excellent box-office material. Sustenance for those poor people waiting out there in the dark. They're not battery hens, you know. They can get up and walk out.' He strokes the script lovingly. 'Jesus, the time is just right for a war movie. You can feel it out there. On the freeways, in the football stadiums and shopping malls. Everywhere. Just look at the number of chic people wearing *khaki*. Christ, are they ready for this movie.'

Grabbed by some flashy stick work coming from the suite, he drops to his knees by the door, whispering.

'Hi, buddy boy, you're getting better all the time.' An impudent cymbal doesn't deter the producer. 'What say you come out and we *parlez*? Talk about Brazil.' The beat switches to a burst of samba. 'Right on.' He looks to Welty who gives him a thumb-up. 'Let's give it another shot. We owe it to the ten, twelve, fifteen – who cares how many – writers who gave their all to this script. They didn't just take the money and run. Their names are enshrined right here.' He strokes the script lovingly. 'So let's you and I go over the top together. Cannon fodder for the critics, maybe, but who cares when you're making *art*?'

Drumbeat stops dead.

Welty winces.

Zigzager stands expectantly; but the door remains stubbornly shut. His confidence evaporates as he frantically seeks another tack.

'Maybe *art* is the wrong word. It's an entertainment. A pleasant way to spend your allotted time on planet Earth. Of its genre, it's very good, with a clear narrative line. It's available to all. Even a moron could follow this one.'

'That's true,' groans Welty.

Rattle, tired of being sidelined, suddenly executes a dramatic nasal breath exercise. In yoga circles it's known as *Bellows Breath*. Loud, rapid and rasping, it can cause considerable anxiety for the uninitiated. Zigzager is one such. He looks to Boulder, who shoots him a warning sign to back off, which he does.

'As perfection is what we're after, some *small* changes could be made without hurting its textural quality.'

'A wise move, Mr Zigzager.' Boulder nods his approval. 'If the script isn't changed, I think he'll not be letting his client star in it.'

Zigzager looks desperately at Rattle.

'On what grounds?'

'He said it was *shit*,' says Boulder, tentatively.

'OK, but did he talk about story structure? The dramatic arc?'

'No, he just said it was *shit*.'

'So he ignored the twelve steps of the hero's journey? Not even mentioning step seven: *the approach to the innermost cave*? Or step eight: *the supreme ordeal*? What about steps eleven and twelve: *the hero's resurrection and return of the elixir*?' Zigzager shakes his head with an incredulity bordering on sadness. 'Hell, why am I wasting my time here? For a few thousand bucks anybody can learn about screenwriting on a weekend course.'

Another burst of *Bellows Breath* brings Zigzager back into line.

'So his objection must be *moral*?'

'You hit the nail on the cross, Mr Zigzager.' Boulder nods in agreement.

'Then there's absolutely no problem. It's *already* a very moral movie.'

Sadly, even with this adjustment to the morality of the script, Rattle increases the velocity of his breathing. Zigzager, now extra-sensitive to the security man's changeable nature, adopts a conciliatory attitude.

'But I *am* prepared to make it *more* moral. And for that I'm prepared to pay a reasonable script fee. Do you think he'd be interested?'

'Yes!' Rattle leaps to his feet.

Welty is disgusted. 'So you – once so full of moralistic crap – are you selling out?'

'On *your* recommendation.' He turns to Zigzager. 'A warning, Mr Zigzager. *Morality* is a rare commodity. Difficult to find and extract from the dark twisted minds of men.'

'And expensive?'

'Very, Mr Zigzager. Once exposed to reality it loses its intensity. That's *why* it's rare.'

Welty and Boulder swap glances at this neat *volte-face*.

'I must say I'm disappointed in you.'

'Why, *Mr* Boulder? I'll be a man of means. I'll buy a fur coat, be a bear of a man. I'll pass through your foyer, comment on your *brown* nose, even tip you.' He gives his rattle a last shake and casually drops it into his holdall. 'No need for that any more. Enough of that ancient, sacred, mythological, anthropological nonsense. Ignore the past, look only *forward*. To the rewrite, Mr Zigzager.' He smiles. 'May I call you *Zigy*?'

Zigzager ignores the offer of intimacy. 'I don't want a rewrite. Only your cooperation. Help with your client. Your *ex*-client.'

'But, *Zigy*, the subject of your movie concerns us all.' Another nasty smile from Rattle. 'War!'

'I know. I know. Actually, my movie's *anti*-war.'

'But it could be seen by some as *glorifying* it. Especially by those morons you spoke of.'

Boulder immediately looks troubled.

'I have two sons, Brendan and Fergus.'

'Two young men created from the loins of Mr Boulder here,' intones Rattle. 'Both eligible for any future conflagration. You see the dilemma we're facing, *Zigy*?'

'I'm *not* facing it,' whimpers Zigzager. 'We've spent millions of dollars on arms, ammo, uniforms, badges, sandbags. Now we've *got* to use them.' He turns beseechingly to Boulder. 'It's only *conventional* warfare, for Christ's sake.'

'Ah, *conventional* warfare,' Boulder is relieved. 'Trenches, camaraderie, football with the enemy on Christmas Day.'

Rattle waves his arm like a referee spotting a foul.

'Not so fast, my friend. We could be playing with fire here. What if this movie's successful?'

'Why don't I finish it so we can find out?' pleads Zigzager.

'Hold it there, *Zigy*.' Rattle is like a terrier. 'What if some president or prime minister or dictator gets to see it and admires the movie's *production* values? We could end up with a succession of *copycat* wars. And for the same reason. As a diversion from reality at home.'

Zigzager is outraged.

'Hey, whose side are you on?' He points at the door. 'Our first objective lies in *there*.'

Rattle ignores him. Instead he closes his eyes, pirouettes like a spinning knife and stops, opens his eyes and looks straight at Welty's coat pocket. From inside comes the muffled sound of her mobile calling for attention. Simultaneously the drumbeat tunes in slowly, ominously.

Welty reluctantly answers.

'Yes?' A murmur, morose and monotonous, curls into her ear as she listens in shock. 'Are you quite sure? I see I see. I'll tell him. Thank you.'

She closes the phone.

'I got bad news, Zigy. Ruby's dead.'

The film producer staggers like a felled tree.

'Dead? Mother's dead?'

'Her plane hit a mountain soon after takeoff. There are no survivors.'

'It can't be true,' sobs Zigzager. 'She just beat cancer. A clean bill of health only yesterday. Now she's dead?'

Welty, albeit reluctantly, puts her arms around his convulsing frame, straightens his wayward toupee, and lets his tears flow onto her all-weather coat. Boulder, embarrassed by this display of emotion, takes Rattle aside to consult him.

'What happened to your talisman? How come she took off? You said it would stop all movement of any person, animal—'

Rattle interrupts angrily.

'And what about *her* talisman? Money.'

Boulder, in solemn contemplative mood, reaches a conclusion. '*Money* isn't everything.'

'That's rich, coming from you,' Rattle is smarting.

'You can't be taking it with you.' Clichés are irresistible to Boulder. 'Not even as *excess* baggage.'

Distracted when Zigzager blows his nose loudly, having wiped away his tears, they turn to face him. He's back in the cockpit, ready to take off in a fresh direction.

'The show must go on. Mother would have had it no other way. I'll *dedicate* the movie to her.' He snaps his fingers at Welty. 'Where are we on dedications?'

Welty flicks the pages of her notebook until she finds the answer.

'So far it's dedicated to *Those who gave their lives in the past, and will give their lives in the future, defending civilisation, globalisation and the free market economy. For they have seen the unseen, the enemy without and the enemy within, and have known the great unknown.*' She smacks the notebook closed. 'That seems to cover Ruby.'

This dedication instantly moves Zigzager to engage with that mysterious lump of emotion lodged in his throat by raising his arms to the hotel ceiling and beyond.

'What's it like out there, Ma? In the *Great Unknown*?' Then adding an afterthought. 'Where the buffalo roam?' He immediately cheers up. 'Hey, that's a great title.' He's still in finger-snapping mode. This time it's directed at Rattle. 'Right, buddy boy, let's get this show back on the road.'

Again Rattle stares at Welty's mobile and again it calls out, plaintively. Welty nearly drops it in fright. The others freeze, only their eyes move, nervously dancing from one to another and back again.

Welty groans to herself.

'God help us, Ruby's going to be the *only* survivor.'

The mobile persists.

She steels herself before answering.

'Mr Zigzager's assistant.'

She listens and immediately brightens up.

'Well, hello. You want to speak with *Big Boss*?' Nodding towards the door, she whispers to Zigzager, 'It's *him*.' Into the phone: 'No problem, he's right here.' The great international film producer is close to collapsing as he hears Welty say, 'I know he'd like to speak to you.' Welty listens. 'Sure, we *still* love you. Of course we do.'

A distinctly human whine comes down the line.

'That's not true. We really *love* you. Here he is.'

She has to stop Zigzager from running off.

'Sweetheart, it's true. We *love* you, *love* you, *love*, *love* you.' Now listening. 'Pardon me?' Now incredulous. 'I'll check with him.'

Again she whispers to Zigzager.

'He says he won't speak to you unless he can *die* at the end of the movie.'

'Did you say *die*? That's two deaths in as many minutes.' Zigzager beseeches the ceiling gods. 'And I'm known for happy endings.'

Welty interrupts his pleadings.

'And he wants the *dog* to die with him.'

'*Dog*? What dog?' screeches Zigzager. 'There's no dog in this movie.'

Welty smiles with delight.

'There is *now*. Shall I tell him to go fuck himself?'

'No! No!' yelps Zigzager. 'Don't do that.'

An awful truth dawns.

'My God, I'll have to change the *poster*. There's no dog in it. They'll all have to be recalled. The whole of Hollywood will know. I'll be a laughing stock. It's the end of my career.'

He turns his tear-smeared eyes to Welty.

'What am I going to do?'

'Capitulate!'

Then it's back to the mobile.

'*Big Boss* thinks it's a great idea. The bow-wow will add insight to your character. War movies shouldn't be too happy, blah, blah, blah. Here he is to tell you himself.'

One last coo wraps things up. 'I *love* you, too.'

Big Boss takes the mobile in his quivering hand while trying to shake off the rictus gripping his mouth.

'We all *love* you. What a great idea? The *dog*? You… you… you've done it again, buddy boy. That's why you get the big bucks, you son of a…'

Before he gets to say *gun,* a distant explosion rocks the hotel. Plaster falls from the ceiling. His rictus now widens in horror as the corridor lights flicker violently. Dust fills the air, softening the blinding flash that follows, before leaving them coughing, spluttering, and in total darkness.

Zigzager is the first to speak.

'Holy shit, what was that?'

Boulder stumbles over one of the numerous flower vases, curses, while feeling his way noisily towards the back stairwell.

'I'll be off to find out, Mr Zigzager.'

Another painful thump and another expletive follows before he meets the swing doors and is away.

Nobody moves.

Nobody speaks.

Black is the blanket that embraces them.

The far-off rumble dies away to a ghostly silence.

Zigzager suddenly whinnies, startled.

'Who goes there?'

'Me,' says Rattle in a hoarse whisper.

'Is that a gun you have there?'

'It is indeed, *Zigy.* We don't want anything unfortunate to happen to you. Is my client still on the line? I need to know he's safe and sound.'

'Are you still there?' cries Zigzager out of the darkness, close to tears. 'Great! What a crazy idea about the dog. Who'd think of having a dog feature in a war movie? Except *you*! Are you thinking of a German shepherd or a Rottweiler?'

He listens and nearly chokes.

'Don't you think a *poodle* is rather effeminate for this movie?'

The answer is brief.

'You're right, poodles *are* intelligent. Anything that'll add depth is OK by me.'

Zigzager's breathing is punctuated with stifled gasps.

'So the poodle belongs to a hooker who follows you back to the front line from the brothel? Brilliant! Then...'

He's forced to pause.

'Why am I *repeating* everything you say? I'll tell you why. Cos I have a fresh writer out here, raring to go. He's hanging on your every word. You'll love *his* work. He loves *your* work. Hold on a minute, will you?'

He whispers to Rattle, 'Excuse me, but why are you holding that gun to my head?'

'We haven't negotiated the size of my screen credit,' whispers Rattle.

The film producer explodes, 'Are you crazy?'

'A hundred per cent of the main title. And I'll need a stretch limo.'

'A stretch limo? What the fuck for?'

'To *write* in.'

'I don't believe this is happening to me.'

In the darkness he hears the gun's safety catch released.

'Agreed!'

'Good. Now tell that to my client.'

'Are you still there, buddy boy? This writer's just great on character *motivation*.'

'And snappy dialogue,' adds Rattle.

More murmuring comes down the line.

'So by day the hooker is a *sniper*,' Zigzager cries out in pain. 'She picks off our boys as they go about their *humanitarian* duties? No, let me guess. She's the one who kills you at the end? Accidentally, of course.' Forced to listen again. 'She meant to blow away the poodle? Because it has *rabies*? Well, dude, what can I say?'

Zigzager, already teetering on the edge of a total nervous breakdown, can only laugh insanely when the subject switches to *casting*.

'For the part of the hooker? Sure I'll audition her. *Them*? But if you've been rehearsing all night you don't need me...' He resorts to pleading. 'But I understand nothing about your craft, you know that. *Acting* is a complete mystery to me. True! True! We can't make movies without actors.' He's interrupted again. 'Why did I come into the movie industry? Why, why, why? I came into our great dream factory for...' He squeals, outraged. 'Big bucks and blow jobs! Shit, never! Sure we can talk about it. Any time you like.' His voice shoots up an octave. '*Now?*' He tries to summon up his John Wayne impersonation, but it comes out castrated.

'Just open up those *Pearly Gates*.'

The suite door slowly opens to reveal a powerful flashlight. Its beam plays on Zigzager's terrified face, white as a lily. Welty sidles up beside him, takes back her mobile and listens. Zigzager turns to her in a panic and whispers.

'What do you think?'

'Ruby would have expected nothing less.'

'That's not the point. He sounds fucking demented.'

'So what's new?'

'Maybe I should take some flowers?'

'And look like a bridesmaid? Christ, you're the fucking producer.'

'You're right.'

Drumbeat now seeps into the corridor as the flashlight retreats further back into the suite, luring him to follow. Slowly, tentatively, Zigzager enters. As soon as he passes the open door there's a flurry of female arms. Two pairs grab his arms while a third quickly undoes his belt and zipper.

'Hey, what the fuck are you doing?'

Zigzager struggles and tries to run back but, with his pants now about his ankles, he falls helplessly to the floor. At that moment the flashlight is extinguished and the drum stops. Out of the darkness come girlish giggles and the seductive flapping of flesh. Zigzager calls out like a trapped animal.

'My God, you're *not*...? Oh my God, you *are*...'

He groans and moans in quick succession. 'No! No! No!'

Then changes his plea. 'Yes! Yes! Yes! Don't stop! Yeeeeeeessss!' A final gasp escapes him. 'Oh my God! And with Mother lying on a mountain peak.'

He roars, 'You bastard!'

He sobs.

'You evil bastard.'

Muffled laughter melds with Zigzager's whimpering. Simultaneously the corridor lights start to violently strobe as the engineers in the basement struggle to revive the generator. Welty's startled face, Rattle wildly swinging his gun about, and Zigzager stumbling out from the suite all flicker like images in a penny arcade machine. With his pants still around his ankles, he's forced to his knees as the door slams shut behind him.

Welty speaks into her mobile. 'Hi! Hi! Is anybody there?'

It seems not.

She switches it off.

Strobing begins to slow before the lights cut out altogether.

Zigzager, struggling to pull up his pants, mewls like a baby.

Manic laughter filters from the suite.

In a bizarre but fortuitous twist of fate, flickering candles emerge from the back stairs. Eerie shadows fall on the corridor walls as Boulder approaches, holding before him a dazzling silver candelabra.

'It's the best I could do, Mr Zigzager. Found it in the conference centre. Those berks not only blew the emergency mains but the *main* mains, which then made contact with the gas supply…'

He hesitates when he sees his benefactor, the great movie producer, still on his knees, dishevelled and snivelling. Zigzager, robbed of his hairpiece, runs a hand over his bald pate.

'My rug! My rug! Where's my rug?'

Boulder looks down on this miserable creature.

'What happened to him?'

'Something ambiguous,' says Rattle.

'At first he didn't say *yes*,' says Welty.

'Then he couldn't say *no*,' intones Rattle.

'It was degrading.'

'He'll never be the same man again.'

'Hopefully,' adds Welty.

Drum erupts with a crisp marching beat. The candles cast a quivering light on the door as it slowly begins to open. Welty peers into the darkness of the suite.

'He's coming out.'

She and Boulder back off, leaving Zigzager grovelling on his knees. The cringing wreck of a man squawks in terror, 'He's crazy! Don't let him near me.'

'Don't you worry, Mr Zigzager,' proclaims Rattle, brandishing his Smith & Wesson .38. 'I'm right here beside you. After all, you're my key to fame and fortune. I'll do whatever you ask.'

Boulder moves closer to the open door, throwing more flickering light onto the interior. Our Neanderthal ancestors must have done much the same when surveying caves for suitable accommodation. No wonder Boulder jumps out of his skin when Zigzager's toupee flies out of the darkness like a bat.

'Oh Lord above, it's like something from a horror film.'

'But I'm *not* making a horror film,' bleats Zigzager.

A figure is moving inside.

Boulder takes a step back, gagging.

'He's inhuman.'

'And in character,' mutters Welty, the woman with one face.

Rattle shows the handgun to the movie producer. 'Shall I frighten him to death, Mr Zigzager? Like I did with you?'

Zigzager, dazed and demented, responds with maniacal laughter, 'Yes! Yes! Scare the shit out of him.'

Rattle cracks the gun open and spins its cylinder for Zigzager to see.

'What if it's a *live* bullet this time?'

'Even better,' jabbers Zigzager.

A near-naked figure slowly emerges in the sputtering light, revealing a torso greased brown, a blood-soaked bandanna wrapped about the head, half of which appears to have been blown away, leaving a suppurating wound. Around his neck hangs a drum.

Zigzager reacts in fury.

'Jesus wept, he's had my make-up artists in there all night. I don't pay those bitches to *jerk*...'

That *word* reduces him to a sobbing heap of quivering flesh.

Rattle aims the gun as the drummer emerges like a zombie, closer and closer, from the suite.

'Shall I do it now, Zigy?'

The movie producer hesitates.

'You have to call *action*!'

'Action,' says Zigzager, faintly.

'Louder,' shouts Rattle. 'Remember it's an order. Everybody has to hear it.'

'ACTION!' yells Zigzager.

Rattle's finger tightens on the trigger. The drumbeat falters, then stops altogether. Puncturing the ensuing silence is a deafening explosion. Smoke hangs in the air as the drummer sinks to his knees, grunts and keels over. Again, silence falls on the scene.

Blood oozes from the body.

It's the *only* part of it that's moving.

Zigzager is elated. He jumps to his feet, pulling up his pants and laughing like a hyena. 'CUT! CUT! Print that one.' Strutting about like von Stroheim.

'Set up to go again!'

Boulder kneels to examine the motionless body, feeling its pulse. He straightens up, erect, very much the sergeant-major he once was. Looking at each of them in turn, he finally delivers his solemn announcement. 'He's a goner.'

'Bullshit,' screams Zigzager. 'It's another of that bastard's crazy tricks.'

'Not this time, it isn't.'

Stunned at first, Zigzager quickly recovers. Film moguls are biologically hardwired to accept *disaster*. Then, following in the steps of his fellow producers, he tiptoes ever forward towards certifiable psychosis.

'An actor assassinated outside the Abraham Lincoln Suite? I just don't believe it.' His right hand flicks across his chest, making a sign of the cross. 'Jesus, that's way over the top.' He shoots a sly look at the assassin, Rattle, motionless, with the handgun dangling by his side. Placing an arm across Welty's shoulder, he takes her aside for a quiet consultation.

'Best get on to the insurers.'

'Are you serious?'

She studies his face and realises he *is*.

Incredulous, she finds the number and punches it in while Zigzager takes a closer look at the corpse.

'Who in their right mind could commit such a barbaric act?'

He fires another fleeting glance at Rattle.

'One of the brightest stars in the cinema's galaxy, *gone*.'

Still muttering, he slinks back to Welty.

'Gone! A box-office dinosaur. Irreplaceable!'

'I have Mr Zigzager on the line. Here, Judas.' Welty hands him the mobile. Unable to face her, Zigzager turns away, hoping to be out of earshot.

'Marty, we've had a little bit of an accident here.'

Boulder gives Rattle a stern look and summons a voice of immense portentousness. 'This time it *will* be the police, you know that?'

'I know.' Looking forlornly at the corpse: 'He's smaller than I imagined.'

'They always are. In *real* life.'

Rattle spreads his arms wide. 'But up there on movie screens around the world he'll always be big. Just like Almighty God.' He hacks out a dry laugh. 'Do you think we'll ever be *big* enough to live without such nonsensical illusions?'

Boulder looks blank.

'Face it, Mr Boulder, our lives are so rooted in fantasies that—'

He doesn't get to finish before Zigzager explodes into the mobile.

'My responsibility? Are you going deaf, Marty? It was his own fucking bodyguard who shot him.' A nasty look at Rattle, fast as a poisoned arrow. 'That has to be a first!' Mumbling rolls from the earpiece, causing Zigzager into another bout of apoplexy. 'No, I'm not going to turn the experience into a goddamn movie. I make fiction, arsehole. Strictly *fiction*, that's me.'

Boulder nods his great head in agreement.

'Everything about him is *fiction*. He gave that order to shoot. I heard him with my own ears.'

Rattle replies softly.

'Action. All they want is *action*.'

Zigzager, noticing all eyes are on him, lowers his voice. 'Marty, at least be sympathetic. *Two* deaths I've had to face already and I haven't even had breakfast.' He desperately tries to be patient. 'Marty, being shot by your own security man cannot be called death from *natural* causes. Not even nowadays!' Now on his knees, pleading. 'On my life, Marty, this is *not* a publicity stunt.'

Boulder slowly lifts the candelabra above his head, making the shadows from the assembled company grow longer and longer, fainter and fainter, weaker and weaker.

Welty finally speaks. 'So where do we go from here? A chase sequence?'

'Too late for that,' says Rattle, bringing the handgun to his open mouth. 'No, it's time for the *truth* suppository.'

Welty and Boulder freeze.

The freeze breaks apart as Boulder steps out of the frame and asserts his authority. Here is a man who faced the horrors of many wars, survived them all, only to face the horrors of a world facing galloping infantilisation. He looks at Rattle, who seems to be sucking the barrel of his gun.

'Wait!'

Rattle lowers the gun.

'Why wait? Mine was a cameo role. I'm just a bit-player. They're the ones who get blown away cos they don't cost much. Dispensable. Disposable. That's the way the world is.'

Boulder, past his best at disarming an enemy, lunges heavily at Rattle, who easily sidesteps and turns the gun on him. The night porter, forced to back off, pleads with him.

'Not yet! Please!' Desperately clutching at a straw. 'If you top yourself, what will I be telling the media?'

'Tell them what you said when we first met.'

Boulder struggles to remember until Rattle prompts him. 'Alien spirit? Ectoplasm? Soul?'

'Ah yes. That you'd been taken over by an alien spirit *without* you realising it. While you slept. And your external shell didn't change when this monstrous ectoplasm infiltrated your soul. Via your ears.'

'Correct.'

'And you said it was impossible because of your earplugs?'

'Well, I've changed my mind. You were right. That monstrous

ectoplasm *did* remove them without me noticing. Tell that to the media. They'll love it. It'll make the news headlines for weeks.'

Boulder is pleased to be vindicated. 'Let me get this straight. You want me to say that you *were* infiltrated? That an alien spirit *did* tranquillise you? That it stopped you thinking for yourself? Then replaced your soul with an automatic guidance system?'

'Not just me. *Everybody*. Say it's the *Spirit of the Age*.'

Welty, listening with increasing incredulity, interrupts.

'Bullshit! Do you really think the media will take that crap seriously?'

'One trip to a shopping mall should convince them,' says Rattle before returning the gun barrel to his mouth.

Zigzager suddenly shouts into the mobile, 'Leave God out of this, Marty. How can he say *Cut!* when, in his terms, the action goes on forever? Don't be an arsehole!'

It's as if Zigzager has pressed a button triggering the *Apocalypse*. A volcanic rumbling in the bowels of the hotel precedes a massive if muffled explosion. The swing doors to the stairwell fly open as a wind with the velocity of a tsunami barrels up the corridor. It reaches the *tableau vivant* assembled outside the Abraham Lincoln Suite. Boulder's cap, Zigzager's toupee, Welty's file whips open and papers all shoot away horizontally into the darkness. The flames on the candelabra flatten, splutter momentarily, then give up the ghost.

7.47 a.m.

Slump has never read Dante's *Divine Comedy*. He knows nothing of the *Nine Circles of Hell* as he circumnavigates the Croesus Palace Hotel in his obscene vehicle, waiting obediently for a signal from Boulder to come alongside. Having unwittingly passed around six hellish circles, *Limbo*, *Lust*, *Gluttony*, *Greed*, *Anger*, *Heresy*, he approaches his seventh, *Violence,* when he witnesses a devastating explosion at the side of the hotel. What shakes him most is the realisation that he'd passed that very spot only two hours earlier. In fact, the large generator he saw being unloaded lies in the roadway, simmering in smoke and horribly twisted. Slump rarely prays these days but this morning he offers up a barely remembered *Lord's Prayer* in thanksgiving for his lucky escape.

7.50 a.m.

Silence reigns outside the Abraham Lincoln Suite. The wind is stilled as abruptly as it was stirred. In deep darkness the world is becalmed, only to be shattered by a gunshot and a sliver of red flame.

Zigzager's voice quivers like a tuning fork. 'What's happened?'

Boulder is slow to reply. 'Security has left us.'

'No *security*? What are we going to do now?'

Welty laughs. 'Be *in*-secure.'

'That's not funny,' snivels her boss.

'What about being *secure* in our own *insecurity*?'

Boulder rarely lets a moment of gravitas pass without buttering it in pomposity.

'Even as I speak he's probably looking into the face of Almighty God.'

There's a brief moment of solemnity before a small cough and Rattle's apologetic voice intrudes.

'It was a *blank*! Sorry about that.'

With that there's the crack of the gun's cylinder opening, spinning, settling, slamming shut and firing. The slump of Rattle's body hitting the carpet is followed by silence. Like the candles on the candelabra, it seems that he, too, has given up the ghost. But not quite.

7.52 a.m.

Seconds later the corridor lights spring back to life. Not so Rattle. Night porter, movie producer and assistant, ghostly white in masonry dust, peer up though the murk to see a hole in the ceiling. Then peer down to see no sign of a brain or blood-splattered corpse. The bullet was *live* but Rattle is *dead*. He apparently changed his mind, took the gun from his mouth and let the ceiling have it instead.

An autopsy later that week revealed that the violence of the gunshot had caused cardiac *arrest*. Rattle *hadn't* waited around for the police. No wonder his corpse is smiling. What the autopsy couldn't reveal is that the explosion had pierced a time capsule in his brain, a tumour maybe, thereby releasing a record of the last two hours and eighteen minutes.

Out of the darkness came a rush of cawing rooks rising in alarm, elevator *pings* pinging, computer voices in a loop of inanity, insanity, *door closing*, *door opening*, *first floor*, rattles rattling, drums beating, all mixed in a loud cacophony which slowly faded to eternal silence. It was, all in all, a suitable departure for a medicine man, shaman, trickster, bird impersonator – and *fool*.

TUESDAY

7.43 a.m.

Next morning, Slump waits patiently at the entrance to a riverside complex of luxury apartments. Another day, another *celebrity*. Ensconced in his driver's pod, he pores over the morning's newspapers. For Slump, reading the lurid details of what happened inside the Croesus Palace Hotel while he was navigating the *Circles of Hell* may not be as spiritually rewarding as the *Divine Comedy*, but it's definitely funnier. Even he, humourless as he is, has to smile at this headline.

Evil Ectoplasm Removes Star Killer's Ear Plugs!

Welty was wrong.
The media bought the bullshit.
They usually do.

U Unbound
Liberating ideas

Unbound is the world's first crowdfunding publisher, established in 2011.

We believe that wonderful things can happen when you clear a path for people who share a passion. That's why we've built a platform that brings together readers and authors to crowdfund books they believe in – and give fresh ideas that don't fit the traditional mould the chance they deserve.

This book is in your hands because readers made it possible. Everyone who pledged their support is listed below. Join them by visiting unbound.com and supporting a book today.

Geoff Andrew
Chloe Aridjis
Robert Armstrong
Miles Baker
Valerie Baker
Jason Ballinger
Dennis Bartok
Vicki Berger
Charlie Best
Mark Bould
Roy Boulter
Bruce Bowie
Peter Boyle
Celia Britton
Tim Britton
Ed Bruce
Jon Bunker
Maddie Burdett-Coutts
Marcus Butcher

Rose & Jamie Campbell
Alistair Canlin
Sheelagh Capstick-Dale
Glen Carroll
Eva Chadwick
Michael and Susan Chaplin
Robert Chilton
Keith Javier Claxton
Selina Cohen
GMark Cole
John Crawford
Helder Crespo
Krisztina Csortea
Will Darmody
Sara Davies
Roger James Elsgood
Steve Fawcus
Dane Flannery
Martin Fletcher

Dick Fontaine
Adam Fransella
Anthony Frewin
Charlie Galloway
Susan Godfrey
Kate Hardie
Alan Hardy
Evangeline Harrison
Paul Harrison
Anthony Heath
Deborah Herron
Fred Hogge
Stephen Hoppe
Paul Howard
George Stanley Irving
Maxim Jakubowski
Alison Jeffery
Nicholas Jones
Andres Kabel
Mike Kaplan
Dan Kieran
Charlotte Madelon Koolhaas
Sylvia Libedinsky
Judith Liddell-King
Richard Loncraine
Anthony Maplesden
Celine Marchbank
Russell Mardell
Kez Margrie
Alexandria Matthews
Sean McCloy
Martin McKeand
Jonathan Meades
Lucy Mellor
John Mitchinson
Massimo Moretti

Mark Morley
Laura Mulvey
Antoinette Myers
Carlo Navato
Michael Nesbitt
Kim Newman
David Nicholls
Alexis Nolent
G Oommen
Scott Pack
Justin Pollard
Dan Reed
Joe Roman
Kevin Sampson
Justin Sayer
David Scott
Ivan Sharrock
Alastair Siddons
Hazel Slavin
MTA Smith
Chris Springhall
Mike Sumner
Richard Todd
Nick Triplow
Un Known
David Usborne
Jonathan Wakeham
Steve Walker
Errollyn Wallen
David Walliams
Mike White
Tony Williams
Malcolm Williamson
Paul Woodgate
Brendan Woods